BOOKS BY A. B. YEHOSHUA

Mr. Mani

Five Seasons

A Late Divorce

Between Right and Right

The Lover

Early in the Summer of 1970

Three Days and a Child

M R . M A N I

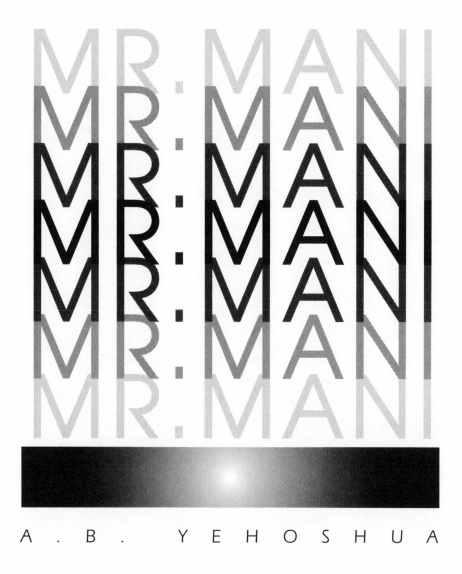

A . B .   Y E H O S H U A

Translated from the Hebrew by Hillel Halkin

DOUBLEDAY
NEW YORK LONDON TORONTO SYDNEY AUCKLAND

PUBLISHED BY DOUBLEDAY

a division of Bantam Doubleday Dell Publishing Group, Inc.,

666 Fifth Avenue, New York, New York 10103

DOUBLEDAY and the portrayal of an anchor with a dolphin are trademarks of Doubleday,

a division of Bantam Doubleday Dell Publishing Group, Inc.

A segment of this book, in slightly different form, originally appeared in *The New Yorker* magazine.

Library of Congress Cataloging-in-Publication Data

Yehoshua, Abraham B.

[Mar Mani. English]

Mr. Mani / by A. B. Yehoshua; translated from the Hebrew by Hillel Halkin.—1st ed.

p.   cm.

Translation of: Mar Mani.

I. Title.   II. Title: Mister Mani.

PJ5054.Y42M3413   1992

892.4′36—dc20   91-24908

CIP

ISBN 0-385-26792-4

BOOK DESIGN BY CAROL MALCOLM-RUSSO

PRINTED IN THE UNITED STATES OF AMERICA

MARCH 1992

1   3   5   7   9   10   8   6   4   2

FIRST EDITION

To my father,

a man of Jerusalem and a

lover of its past

THE ORDER OF THE CONVERSATIONS

T H E

Conversation

P A R T N E R S

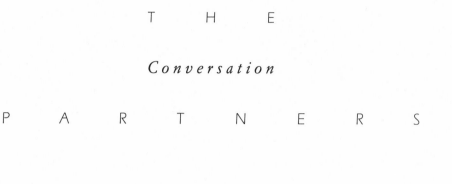 HAGAR SHILOH, *Student (1962–)*

YA'EL SHILOH, *(NÉE KRAMER), Agricultural Worker (1936–)*

EGON BRUNER, *Feldwebel (1922–)*

ANDREA SAUCHON, *(NÉE KURTMAIER), Former Nurse (1870–1944)*

IVOR STEPHEN HOROWITZ, *Lieutenant (1897–1973)*

MICHAEL WOODHOUSE, *Colonel (1877–1941)*

EFRAYIM SHAPIRO, *Physician (1870–1944)*

SHOLOM SHAPIRO, *Estate Owner (1848–1918)*

AVRAHAM MANI, *Merchant (1799–1861)*

FLORA HADDAYA, *(Née Molkho) Housewife (1800–1863)*

SHABBETAI HANANIAHA HADDAYA, *Rabbi (1766?–1848)*

MR. MANI

FIRST CONVERSATION

Mash'abei Sadeh

7 P.M. Friday, December 31, 1982

T H E

Conversation

P A R T N E R S

≈ *HAGAR SHILOH* Born in 1962 in Mash'abei Sadeh, a kibbutz thirty kilometers south of Beersheba that was founded in 1949. Her parents, Roni and Ya'el Shiloh, first arrived there in 1956 in the course of their army service. Hagar's father Roni was killed on the last day of the Six Day War as a reservist on the Golan Heights. As Hagar was five at the time, her claim to have clear memories of her father may well have been correct.

Hagar attended a regional high school in the nearby kibbutz of Revivim and finished her last year there without taking two of her matriculation exams, English and history. She began her army service in August 1980 and served as a noncommissioned counseling officer with a paratroop unit stationed in central Israel. Because her base was far from her kibbutz, she spent many of her short leaves in Tel Aviv, where she stayed with her paternal grandmother Naomi. She was very attached to this grandmother, from whom she liked to coax stories of her father's childhood. The old woman, who enjoyed her granddaughter's lively presence, sought repeatedly to persuade her to register at the University of Tel Aviv after the army. And indeed, upon finishing her military service, the last months of which were highly eventful because of the outbreak of the war in Lebanon in 1982, Hagar flouted the wishes of her mother, who wanted her to return home for at least a year before beginning her higher education, and persuaded a general meeting of the kibbutz to allow her to continue her studies. This decision was facilitated by the fact that, as the daughter of a fallen soldier, Hagar stood to have her tuition fully paid for by the ministry of defense.

Hagar hoped to study film at Tel Aviv University. However, lacking a high school diploma, she was not accepted as a fully matriculated student and was first required to register for a year-long course to prepare her for the exams she had missed. She was also asked to take courses in Hebrew and mathematics to upgrade her academic record.

In early December of that year, at the urging of her son Ben-Zion Shiloh, Hagar's uncle and the Israeli consul in Marseilles, Naomi decided to take a trip to France. In effect this was in place of her son's intended visit to Israel the previous summer, which was canceled when the consulate was forced to work overtime to present Israel's case in the Lebanese war. Although loathe to leave her beloved granddaughter for so long, she could not refuse her only son, a forty-year-old bachelor whose single state worried her greatly. Indeed, she was so determined to help find him a suitable match that she stayed longer than she had planned in order to attend the various New Year's receptions given by the consulate.

Hagar, a short, graceful young woman with the dark red hair of her late father, looked forward greatly to having her grandmother's large, attractive apartment to herself. At first she thought of asking her friend Irees, whom she had met at the university, to stay with her. Irees's father had also been killed in battle, in the Yom Kippur War, and she had an amazing knowledge of the various benefits and special offers that the Ministry of Defense made available to young people like themselves. In the end, though, she was unable to accept the invitation, which was just as well for Hagar, since at the beginning of that month she had struck up a relationship with an M.A. student named Efrayim Mani that could now be pursued in her grandmother's apartment. Her new boyfriend taught Hebrew in the preparatory course, and their romance got off to an intense start before he was called up on December 9 for reserve duty in the western zone of Israeli-occupied Lebanon, a far from tranquil area despite the newly signed "peace treaty" between Jerusalem and the government in Beirut.

YA'EL SHILOH, NÉE KRAMER Born in a suburb of Haifa in 1936, Ya'el was highly active in a socialist youth movement and left high school in 1952 for a year of training in a kibbutz as a youth counselor, as a result of which she never graduated. In 1954 she began her army duty, serving with a group from her movement in the kibbutz of Rosh-Hanikrah near the Lebanese border. It was there that she met her future husband Roni Shiloh, a movement member from Tel Aviv. Trained as a paratrooper like the other boys in the group, he saw action in a number of border raids and in the 1956 Sinai Campaign. In their final months in the army Ya'el and Roni were stationed in Mash'abei Sadeh, a young kibbutz in the Negev desert. They liked it well enough to stay on and become members after their discharge, and in 1958 they were married. Both of them were employed in farm work, Roni in the grain fields and Ya'el in the fruit orchards. In 1962, after returning from a tour of Greece sponsored by the Israel Geographical Society, they had their first child, a daughter to whom they gave the biblical name of Hagar, as seemed fitting for a girl born in the desert. Four years later, in 1966, they had a second baby, a boy, who died several weeks later from acute hepatitis caused by his parents' incompatible blood types, which the hospital in Beersheba had neglected to test them for. With proper precautions, the doctors assured them, all would go well the next time. However, there was to be no next time, because Roni was killed in the Six Day War along the Kuneitra-Damascus road.

Despite the pleas of her own, and especially, of Roni's parents that she leave the kibbutz for Tel Aviv, Ya'el remained with her five-year-old daughter in the desert, which she more and more felt was her home. She knew of course that in a place so small and remote her chances of remarrying grew poorer from year to year, but she liked her work and was eventually put in charge of a special project to develop new methods of avocado growing. During the Yom Kippur War, when the general secretary of the kibbutz was mobilized for a long period, Ya'el was chosen to fill in for him. Although some of the members found her overly rigid ideologically, she stayed in the position for several years to the satisfaction of nearly everyone. Her relations with her daughter Hagar were intense but far from easy. Now and then, encouraged to get away by her friends, she attended kibbutz-movement workshops in education and psychology. Sometimes she even traveled to Beersheba for special guest lectures in the psychology and education departments of the university. In 1980, although by now a woman of forty-four, she let herself be persuaded to sign up for a singles encounter group, at the end of which she swore never again to do such a thing.

Ya'el feared that the close ties developed by her daughter with her grandmother, a widow since the mid-1970s, would entice her to leave the kibbutz, which was why she opposed Hagar's studying at the university immediately after finishing the army. Indeed, when Hagar applied to the kibbutz for a leave of absence, Ya'el secretly lobbied against her. In the end, however, Hagar was granted her wish in accordance with the liberal policy then prevalent in most kibbutzim of giving young members just out of the army ample time to "find themselves" before pressuring them to return. The stipend offered her by the defense ministry was also a factor in mustering a majority in her favor. After settling in Tel Aviv, she kept in close touch with her mother via her grandmother's telephone. The two made a point of talking twice a week even though the members of Kibbutz Mash'abei Sadeh did not yet have private phones in their rooms in 1982.

Ya'el's half of the conversation is missing.

—But even if I disappeared, Mother, I didn't disappear for very long. You needn't have worried . . .

—But I did phone you, Mother. I most certainly did, on Wednesday evening from Jerusalem.

—Of course. I was still in Jerusalem Wednesday evening. Yesterday too.

—Yesterday too, Mother. And this morning too. But I left you a message.

—How could you not have gotten it?

—Oh, God, Mother, don't tell me that another message of mine got lost!

—How should I know . . . whoever picked up the phone . . .

—Some volunteer from Germany.

—But what could I have done, Mother? It's not my fault that no one in his right mind on the whole kibbutz will pick up the telephone in the dining hall after supper, because no one wants to have to go out in the cold and run around looking for whoever it's for. Why don't *you* try getting the kibbutz some winter night, to say nothing of talking in English to a foreign volunteer who's too spaced out to hold a pencil. If you did, you'd understand what a mistake you made when you led a crusade against private telephones as if the future of socialism depended on it. Lots of other kibbutzim have had private phones for years. They take them for granted as a necessity of life . . .

—I've yet to see the kibbutz that went bankrupt from its phone bills, Mother. That's just your fantasy.

—But I didn't disappear, Mother. I simply left Tel Aviv for three days.

—With him? Fat chance of that! He's still with the army in Lebanon. But it was because of him that I went to Jerusalem to see his father, and I was stranded there until this morning.

—I stranded myself.

—But that's the whole point, Mother. That's the whole point of the story . . .

—No. It started snowing there Wednesday afternoon, but by yesterday it had all melted.

—No. That old coat was given me by his father. Mr. Mani.

—That's how I think of him. *Mr. Mani.* Don't ask me why.

—But that's the whole point of my story. That's the only reason I came home today, because it's crazy to be sitting here with you when I should be in Tel Aviv studying for an exam . . .

—I told you. I have an English exam on Monday, and the last thing I want is to flunk again.

—No. I left all my books and notebooks in Grandmother's apartment in Tel Aviv. I didn't take a thing with me to Jerusalem on Tuesday, certainly not any books. I thought I was only going for a few hours, to do Efi this favor. But once I was there I felt I couldn't leave, and so I stayed for three whole days . . .

—No. I didn't come via Tel Aviv. I came straight from Jerusalem.

It was a last-minute decision. I was waiting in the bus station for the Tel Aviv bus when all of a sudden I saw this middle-aged redhead standing on the next platform. He was someone I recognized from around here, I think from Revivim, and it made me so homesick that I just couldn't wait to get back to our own darling little boondocks and tell you everything, Mother. I couldn't hold it in any longer. I was always like that. Don't you remember what you've told me about myself? I could be in the nursery, or at school, and if some child fell and hurt himself, or if the drawing I was working on tore, I had to tell you so badly that I would run outside to look for you and shout the minute I found you, "Hey, Ma, listen to this!" . . .

—Right. I always got away with it, because I had this knack for latching onto . . . how did you used to put it?

—Yes. Right. That's it . . .

—Yes, that's it. To some surrogate father who would do anything I asked, maybe—it's a pet theory of mine you're sure to like—because he felt guilty that it was my father and not him who was killed. And so everyone took me in tow and passed me on, from the dining hall to the laundry, from the chicken coops to the cowshed, from the stables to the fodder fields, and on to the orchards and to you, Mother, who I threw myself on and told everything. Which is just how it was in Jerusalem today, standing in line in that station among all those wintry, depressive Jerusalemites when suddenly the bus for Beersheba began pulling out and I saw that redhead looking out the window at me—maybe he was trying to guess who I was too —and suddenly I couldn't stand it any longer, I missed you so badly that I jumped over the railing and was on the steps and inside the bus before I knew it. But the first thing tomorrow morning, Mother, I have to get back to Tel Aviv and to my books, or else it's another F for sure. You'll have to find me someone who is driving there, and if you can't think of anyone, think again . . .

—All right.

—No, wait a minute. Take it easy. I didn't mean this second . . .

—But what's the rush? I feel so cold inside. Let me warm up a little first.

—It will take more than just hot water.

—Don't be annoyed at me, Mother, but for my part I can skip the Sabbath meal in the dining hall.

—I'm not at all hungry. Whatever you have in the fridge will be fine.

—That's okay. Whatever you have. I'm really not hungry.

—If you're so starving that you must go, then go. I'm staying here. I'm sorry, Mother, but I'm just not up to sitting in the dining hall and smiling at everyone all evening. Followed by that New Year's Eve party with all its phony revelry . . . I absolutely will not take any chances and dance . . .

—All right, all right. Go. What can I say? Go. What more can I say?

—Go . . .

—Go. I'm already sorry I came here instead of going straight home . . . I mean to Tel Aviv . . .

—Because I didn't think of it as coming to the kibbutz tonight, Mother. I thought of it as coming home. To you. To tell you about what happened in Jerusalem . . .

—I'm not being mysterious. Stop being so critical . . .

—All right, fine, so I am a little mysterious . . . maybe mysterious is even the best word for it . . . but so what? What's wrong with a mystery? Suppose you open the door of a strange house and are so horrified by what you see there that your soul, yes, your soul, Mother, is sucked right out of you . . . but the mystery, you see, isn't the horrifying part, because anything really horrifying has to be obvious and isn't mysterious at all. The mystery is in the *encounter,* even if it just seems like a coincidence. And that's what happened to me, that's what I went through in Jerusalem, even if you're not going to believe it . . .

—Because you're not, Mother. You've been educated all your life not to believe in mysteries, and you're certainly not going to believe in mine. In the end I know you'll tell me that I just imagined it all . . .

—But there isn't any quick version. There's no quick way to tell it, Mother.

—Because if I did, it really *would* sound like a figment of my imagination . . .

—You know something, it doesn't matter. Let's forget it, it's not important. Go have dinner, and I'll take a shower. The whole thing really doesn't matter, Mother. I was wrong and now let's forget it

. . . Just do me a favor and ask around in the dining hall if anyone is driving to Tel Aviv in the morning and has room for me . . .

—No, I'm just not in the mood anymore to tell you about it. Maybe you're even right and I did imagine it all . . .

—I know. You may not have said it yet, but it's not my fault that I always know what you're going to say.

—I'm sorry.

—All right. I'm sorry, Mother.

—I said I'm sorry.

—No, I really thought you didn't feel like hearing about it now . . .

—Are you sure?

—But maybe you shouldn't miss the Sabbath meal in the dining hall. It's a ritual you're so attached to . . .

—Are you sure?

—Well, then, Mother, if you think you can skip it, how about doing it properly, so that we can sit here in peace and quiet? Let's draw the curtains to keep the light in, and let me lock the door for once . . . Where's the key?

—Please, just this once. I beg you, Mother, let's shut out the world to keep it from knowing we're here, so that no one comes and bothers us. We'll put some water up to boil . . . and turn the heater on . . . but where's that key?

—Later. I said I'd take one later . . . I'm bursting too much to tell you my story to take time to shower now . . . Why must you always make such a fuss about showering?

—So my dress is a little sweaty . . . it's no tragedy . . .

—Fine.

—No, Mother, it's the same.

—Maybe a little nausea now and then.

—No, it's the same.

—Is that what you're still hoping?

—But why? I've already told you, Mother, I knew right away it was real. I'm absolutely certain. I can feel it encoded inside me . . .

—This thing . . . the embryo, the baby . . . whatever you want to call it . . .

—You can do the arithmetic yourself. My last time was on the nineteenth of November. I'm exactly two weeks overdue . . . there's nothing else it can be . . .

—But what do I need some doctor poking around inside me for? What more can he tell me? And anyway, I already saw a doctor in Jerusalem . . .

—An internist.

—I'll get to that.

—Soon, Mother. Why can't you be more patient?

—He did . . . just a minute . . .

—No. Just a quick checkup.

—Just a minute . . .

—Don't kid yourself. It's not psychological. It's absolutely real . . . and I *am* pregnant. You've been so brainwashed by all those courses you've taken that you think everything is psychological . . .

—Right now I'm not doing anything. I already told you that. There's plenty of time to decide.

—First of all, for Efi to come back from the army.

—In ten days. It's not just his decision, though.

—There's time . . . there's time . . .

—It's not up to me whether he wants to be a father or not, Mother . . . as far as I'm concerned, I can have the child without him, if that's what I feel like doing . . .

—Because the defense ministry, I already told you, helps out in such cases, even if there's no legal father. You'll be surprised to hear that they're very liberal . . .

—Well, they are about this kind of thing. Maybe they also have guilt feelings . . . who knows . . .

—Irees told me. Irees knows. She checked it all out.

—She knows everything, Mother. She's become an expert on our legal rights. She keeps going back to talk to more officials, and each time she comes up with some new right. There are all kinds of rights for war orphans that you and I never even heard about . . .

—I know it annoys you terribly, but what can I do about it? It wasn't me who raised the subject.

—Revolting? That's going a bit far. What's so revolting about it?

—But so far I haven't asked anyone for anything and I haven't gotten anything. What are you so worked up about?

—But I've already told you. It's all in my story. You simply aren't letting me tell it.

—No. Yes. It's as if you were afraid of it and didn't want to hear it. That's why you've kept putting me off since I phoned that morning a month ago to tell you that I'd gone to bed with him . . . that I'd gone to bed with somebody . . . I mean that I'd finally done it. It's as if something had snapped in your trust in me. You seem, oh, I don't know, confused like, up in the air, as if you'd finally lost the reins to your pet colt . . .

—Yes, the reins. You always held me by these subtle reins . . .

—Subtle. Invisible.

—It doesn't matter.

—Of course.

—Don't get angry again. I really didn't come here to anger you.

—Fine. Let's suppose that what alarmed you, Mother, was not what happened but the hurry I was in to tell you about it the next morning. What was wrong with that? What was even so wrong about paging you from the orchards to break the news? Ever since then, Mother, it just kills me to see how threatened you are by all kinds of things that you used to like hearing about. I've even begun wondering if it's fair to burden you with them and to tell you everything I've been thinking and doing without keeping anything back, as if we still had to obey that lady, that ridiculous psychologist sent by the army when father was killed, who said that you had to get me to talk, that you had to make me get it all out. How did she put it? *To keep the pus of repressed thoughts from festering,* ha ha. Ever since then, Mother, I swear, I have this fear of pus in my brain. That's why I keep blabbing away and you have to hear it all . . . because if you don't, who will . . .

—Efi? We'll have to wait and see . . . who knows? What really do I know about him . . . and now, after this trip to Jerusalem, I seem to know even less . . .

—But I did mention him to you. Didn't I mention him to you?

—How could I not have told you that two weeks after the semester began two of his classes were suddenly canceled? And I certainly mentioned him at the beginning of the semester when you asked me about my teachers and I told you how I liked him the minute he stepped into the classroom. He stood there looking hardly any older than we were, all flustered and curly-haired, and it was almost touching how hard he worked to convince us that we really needed his course in Hebrew expression, because some of the students were up in arms and even insulted at having to take it, as if we were some kind of disadvantaged children . . . so that when they told us that two of his classes had been canceled, I decided to go to the office and see if he was sick, because I thought that if he was I might visit him, and they told me that his grandmother had died in Jerusalem and that he had gone there to be with his father for the week of mourning. That's when . . . but how could I not have told you . . .

—Well, to make a long story short, I wrote down his father's address and went that same day to Jerusalem to pay a condolence call or whatever you call it in the name of our class, although "our class" is not exactly a feeling you have at the university. You can imagine how startled he was to open the door and see this four-week-old student of his whose name he hardly remembered coming all the way from Tel Aviv to express her sympathy for his grandmother. Once he got over his bewilderment, though, he got the point right away, which was that my condolence call wasn't exactly a condolence call but a little signal I was putting out. And since he wasn't used to being pampered with signals from women . . .

—Because he's not especially good-looking or anything . . . just a plain-looking guy who's nice inside . . . and he was so thrilled by the rope I had thrown him that he decided—after I had sat for a while, feeling like a fool, next to his father, who really did look pretty mournful, not like all those middle-aged people who become so much lighter and livelier the minute their parents die—to return with me that evening to Tel Aviv. As soon as we were on the bus we began to talk, and after he had asked me all about myself and my plans and the kibbutz and the Negev and seen how open I was, he began to open up too and tell me about himself. At first he told me about his dead grandmother, whom he really had loved, and then about being worried about his father. It seemed nice to me that he was, because his father had been very attached to his mother, I mean to Efi's grandmother. He had lived with her since he was a child and had been saved by her during the war . . .

—Just imagine, they lived in Greece then. On that island, you know, Crete . . .

—Really?

—Of course I know about that trip you took with Father . . . it was before I was born . . .

—No, Efi's parents were separated long ago, after his bar-mitzvah. He and his mother moved to Tel Aviv and she married again. He has a younger stepsister, but they've all been living in London for the past few years and it looks like they're on their way to settling there for good. He lives by himself . . . he told me all this on the bus ride, although mostly he talked about having to serve soon in Lebanon. I could feel how frightened that made him, and how angry he was at the university for not helping to get him a deferral . . .

—No, he's just a plain reservist, a corporal at most. He's a medic . . . And that, Mother, is how we began getting close on that bus ride from Jerusalem to Tel Aviv. I found myself liking him more and more, and I could feel myself falling in love again, but this time so much more sensibly. By the time we reached Tel Aviv I knew that if I didn't find some way of hanging onto him then and there all the effort I had put into going to Jerusalem that day would be wasted, because we would lose touch the whole month he was in the army, after which the semester had just one more month, and it was only a one-semester course, and he didn't have any more grandmothers left to die for another condolence call. And so, although it wasn't that late at night, I asked him to see me home, I mean to Grandmother's apartment. Maybe it was the difference between the two grandmothers—one who had just died at the age of sixty-eight and one who had just flown off to France at the age of seventy-four like a young lady—that made him curious to come upstairs. At most I thought we might neck a little, but suddenly we grabbed hold of each other, and he was so gentle and yielding, even if he did undress in this awful hurry, and it was all so natural and hardly hurt a bit that I asked myself, Mother, what was I waiting for all this time? What was I so afraid of? Unless maybe there was just something special about him, although to tell you the truth, you'll see what I mean if you ever meet him, he's not at all handsome or anything, just this slim, curly-headed type with glasses and nothing spectacular about him. But anyway, that's why in the morning, as soon as he left, I ran to the telephone to tell you . . .

—Why?

—I just wanted to make you feel good, Mother. What did you think?

—Yes, Mother, it was just to make you feel good. Even if I knew you would have to walk two kilometers from the orchard to the phone and back, I thought it was worth it, because I could feel how anxious you were beginning to get about my staying a virgin . . .

—I thought . . .

—But what do you mean, you never knew? Don't act so innocent, Mother!

—You would have known the minute it happened. Haven't I told you that I always tell you everything?

—Yes, *everything*. So far.

—No. There were four more times before he went to Lebanon. Five altogether.

—He didn't take any precautions. He must have thought that I was taking them. And I already told you that I got the dates confused, and besides, I thought that if you douched right away with hot water . . .

—Naturally. Don't you always know exactly what's going on in my subconscious?

—Yes, in Grandmother's apartment. It was the most obvious place, and if you must know everything, it was even in her room, that is, hold on tight, in her big double bed . . .

—But what's wrong with that?

—Deceitful? Toward who?

—Not at all . . . I'm sure Grandmother would be thrilled . . .

—Something drew us there . . . right into her bed . . .

—No, not especially. I just thought it might interest you.

—Oh, I don't know . . . maybe psychologically . . . you must have some interpretation of it . . .

—But if I don't mind telling you everything, why should you mind hearing it?

—Are you out of your mind? Who else could I tell? Only you, Mother, there's no one else. You're the only person in the whole world . . .

—But in what way . . .

—What doesn't matter?

—I want you to tell me. What doesn't matter?

—Coffee for me. But what doesn't matter? Tell me!

—No. I don't think I was making a fool of myself.

—No.

—No.

—Are you back to that again? Why must you keep rushing me off to the shower? I'll take one later. It's as if you kept trying to head me off . . .

—From telling you my story.

—But what are you afraid of? I didn't do anything bad in Jerusalem, Mother. I only did good.

—Because that's where my story begins. The rest is ancient history by now. Efi left for Lebanon two weeks ago, and I didn't hear from him again until the beginning of this week . . .

—No. I couldn't have told him before he left.

—Because I wasn't sure myself yet.

—Of course. But late Sunday night he suddenly called from some mobile phone unit they had brought to this checkpost he's manning near Beirut, and before I could make up my mind if and how to tell him, he asked me to get in touch with his father, because he couldn't get through to Jerusalem to tell him he wasn't coming to the unveiling, which the army wouldn't give him leave for. Of course, I promised him to do it, and I even felt good that he was asking me so casually, as if I were the person he was closest to. But when I started dialing Jerusalem, it was the strangest thing, one minute there was no answer and the next the phone rang busy, although I kept trying all evening. The next day, which was Monday, I had a full schedule at the university and could only try dialing three or four times, and then Monday night Efi called again to ask if I had gotten hold of his father and how was he. I told him the phone seemed out of order, and then, Mother, he started up in this imploring tone, but really anxious like, begging me not to give up until I contacted his father, because he was very worried about him . . .

—No, I didn't tell him anything. How could I? I could see how tense he was about his father, and there he was in Lebanon, standing out in the wind and the rain without even his glasses, because he told me he had broken them and wasn't able to read . . . which is why I thought, why hassle him even more, what kind of a time is this to scare him with the news that he's about to become a father himself? For the time being I owed him that much quiet . . . and so that same night, which was Monday, I began dialing Jerusalem again, but really thoroughly, nonstop. I kept it up until midnight, only so did Jerusalem. Either it was busy or else there was no answer, and the same thing happened the next morning, which was Tuesday, when I got out of bed especially early and started in on the phone immediately. In the end I called the telephone company to ask if the line was out of order, and they told me that no one had reported it and that to the best of their knowledge it was not, but they suggested I try information to see if the number had been changed, because sometimes, it seems, numbers get changed without notice. Well, I called information, and the number hadn't been changed. And then, Mother, don't ask me why, I felt that I just had to get through to that father, whom I actually remembered quite well from my brief visit the month before, unshaven and in his socks on the living room couch, this stocky, pleasant, Mediterranean-type man sitting next to two little old Sephardic ladies who had come to pay their respects and looked straight out of some Greek or Italian movie, and I went on dialing him from the university between classes, I even left my last morning class in the middle and dialed and dialed, because like I say, by now it was a matter of principle . . .

—No, Efi didn't leave me a clue where else to look for him. I knew vaguely that he worked in the court system as a judge or a prosecutor, but I had no idea where or for what court, and when on a whim I tried calling the Supreme Court, the switchboard operator had never heard of him. All morning long I went on dialing like an uncontrollable madwoman—it was as if Efi's sperm inside me was transmitting its anxiety around the clock. I couldn't stop thinking of that apartment in Jerusalem with its three rooms connected by a long hallway like an old railroad flat. I kept imagining the telephone ringing away there, drilling down the hallway from room to room, and by two o'clock I was so beside myself that I decided to cut English and go to Jerusalem to see what was happening. After all, what is it to Jerusalem from the coast these days, barely an hour in each direction. And so I went home to return my books and change clothes, and it was a lucky thing that I took this heavy sweater with me at the last minute, because even in Tel Aviv I could feel a cold wave coming on. And Mother, I really did mean to call and tell you I was going, so that you wouldn't worry if I got back late at night, but I knew the kibbutz office was closed and that no one but the cats would be by the dining-hall telephone at that time of the afternoon, and so I didn't bother trying. I was halfway out the door when something told me to take my toothbrush and a spare pair of panties, and so I put them in my bag and started out for Jerusalem . . .

—I don't know . . . I just did . . . I mean . . .

—Yes, yes, I know you've been taught that no one "just" does anything. Don't get carried away, though. I've kept a spare pair of panties in my bag for the last two weeks just in case I got my period, although that still doesn't explain the toothbrush. What did *that* mean? Well, I'll leave that to you, you've learned all about psychological symbols in those courses of yours. Just don't tell me that subconsciously I meant to stay in Jerusalem, because in that case I should have taken along some pajamas too, and I didn't . . . unless my subconscious is dumber than I think . . . or maybe it has a subconscious of its own and that's what made it screw up . . .

—Don't take me so seriously.

—No, but it's starting to annoy me, because you're turning it into a religion.

—All right, all right, never mind . . . it's not important. The point is, Mother, that I upped and went to Jerusalem that Tuesday, and that while I left Tel Aviv in broad daylight, it was pitch black when I arrived. It was foggy and raining with this thin, sleety sort of rain, and I was so confused by the darkness that I got off the bus a stop too soon and ended up in this neighborhood called Talbiah. Not that I regretted it, because it was like being in some city in Europe. I was in this big plaza surrounded by beautiful stone houses that looked absolutely splendid and magical in the light of the street lamps with their arcades and columned porticoes and courtyards full of cypress trees . . . it was just fantastic . . .

—Yes, exactly, how did you know? But it's not just the President, Mother. It's the Prime Minister and Foreign Minister too, they all live near that big, beautiful plaza, although I could have walked

right by it without knowing if not for this policeman sitting in a little
hut who I asked for directions. I also asked him what he was guarding, and he showed me the President's house and even let me peek
past the gate, and I had this most wonderful feeling, Mother, of
having entered the true heart of the city . . .

—No, you're wrong. I was never there. As far back as I can
remember, I was always brought to Jerusalem in groups of school-
children or soldiers, always for some ceremony or field trip that took
place in some museum or archaeological site, or else on the walls of
the Old City, which we had to run around on in this sweltering heat
after some nuisance of a tour guide. And if we spent the night there,
it was always in some youth hostel on the outskirts of town, either
next to the military cemetery on Mount Herzl or in that frightening
forest near the Holocaust Museum, never in the city itself, in the
true inner heart of it. And so with the help of that policeman who
was guarding the President, I didn't have to get back on the bus but
took a shortcut to this neighborhood called Ghost Valley through
an empty field and a little woods that led me straight to Efi's father's
street, which I entered contrariwise . . .

—I mean from the wrong end.

—You don't know it. It's called The Twenty-ninth of November
Street. You have to walk down a hill behind the old leper hospital.
It's a long, narrow street you've never been on.

—The German Colony?

—I don't think that's its name, Mother. On the map it clearly said
Ghost Valley. When I first looked up the address I had been given
at the university, I thought that only a Jerusalemite could live in a
place with such a scary name, because no Tel-Avivian would ever
stand for it—and now this fog was drifting all around and it took me
forever to find the building because I was coming from the wrong
end of the street, and when I did I was so wet and cold from the
rain, and my shoes were so full of mud, that I just stood there in a
corner of the entrance, pulling myself together. And then, Mother,
right there in that dark stairwell, it suddenly began, do you hear me?
Do you?

—This strange feeling, which I kept having all the time I was in
Jerusalem . . . as if, Mother, I wasn't there just by myself but . . .

how can I put it . . . as if someone had put me on the opening page of a book . . .

—A book. Some novel or story, or even a movie, for that matter. Mostly it was the feeling of eyes being on me all the time, even my own eyes, which kept watching me from the side as though tracking me. I don't mean in reality, but in a book . . . as if I were being written about on the first page of some story, where it said . . . something like . . . something like . . . an old book that began like this: "One winter afternoon a fatherless student left her grand-mother's apartment in the coastal metropolis on an errand for her boyfriend, who had asked her to find out what had happened to his father in the inland capital, all contact with whom had been lost . . ." Something simple- and innocent-sounding that was about to become very complicated. Next you see her step into the entrance of a plain but respectable apartment house on a cold winter evening —where, after a few seconds, the light goes out, so that the camera shooting her from outside has to grope its way in after her and finds her standing before a greenish door on which is the single word: *Mani.* That's how it starts, this story or movie or whatever you call it, Mother, with a light knock and a quick ring, and then a second ring and a third. But the man inside doesn't want to open up, even though our heroine, the young lady from the metropolis, will make him do it in the end, and by forcing her way into his apartment, Mother, will save his life . . .

—Just a minute . . . listen . . .

—Just a minute . . .

—One minute.

—One minute. No, there was no answer. And maybe, Mother, it was that feeling I had on the stairs that I was in a story and not in real life that kept me from giving up, because I was sure that he was hiding there inside the apartment and not coming to the door for the same reason he hadn't answered the telephone. In the end, after ringing and knocking in every possible way for a good ten minutes, I pretended to leave by walking back down the stairs, and then I tiptoed up again as quietly as I could and stood pressed against the door in the darkness, almost hugging it while holding my breath, just like in one of those thrillers, until I heard faint steps and real-ized that he was coming to the door, that he was standing right on the other side of it. And then, in this soft, friendly voice that wouldn't scare him, I said, "It's me, Mr. Mani, I've brought you an important message from your son Efi"—at which point he had to open up . . .

—Just a minute. Listen . . .

—Will you wait one minute!

—Not at all, Mother. He's only your age, maybe even a little younger, somewhere in his middle forties. He could look pretty good if he wanted to. But when he opened the door that evening he was scary-looking, like some kind of depressed animal coming out from deep in its burrow, with this month-old mourner's beard and a raggedy old bathrobe, all red-eyed and wild-haired. He was in his socks, and the apartment behind him was dark but heated like a furnace, and he seemed so surprised and upset by my having gotten him to open the door that all he could do was stand there blocking it and looking hostile. I could see there was no point in reminding him who I was, or in telling him I had been in his apartment a month ago on a condolence call, because he was so into himself that a month might have seemed to him like a hundred years or more. And so I just mentioned Efi again and gave him the message as quickly as I could before the door was shut in my face, and he stood there listening without a word, just shaking his head absentmindedly while beginning to close the door. But as luck would have it, Mother, just then the telephone rang—you would have thought that part of myself had stayed behind in Tel Aviv to keep on dialing. He looked around as if pretending not to notice it, or at least hoping I would go away so he could answer, but when he saw I had no intention of doing that and that the telephone wasn't stopping, he went to pick it up in the living room—and then, Mother, perhaps because of the book I was in now, or because I knew I'd be protected by the photographer and the director and the whole camera team that was following my every movement, I decided not to take that head shake of his for an answer and I slipped inside uninvited, because I knew I had to find out what was going on in there . . .

—Because there must have been something if he was that determined to keep me out when I had come all the way from Tel Aviv with a message from his son and was standing there on the landing, soaking wet and half-frozen . . .

—You don't say! I was waiting for that, Mother.

—I was waiting for it. I was wondering when you'd get around to that, so why don't you just spill it all now . . . I've been expecting it for the last quarter of an hour, so if you must say it, this is the time . . .

—Yes, yes, why don't you say it, go right ahead. *There goes our Hagar looking for a father figure again . . . as usual, she's latched onto some older man* . . . I know that routine by heart . . . every time I would tell you when I was in the army about some officer a little older than me whom I happened to like, you'd get that pitying smile of yours right away . . .

—Yes, I know you didn't, but it's what you wanted to say, why not admit it, goddamn it? It follows logically from all those trite, pathetically shallow clichés you've been taught about the psychology of orphans . . .

—You mean there's no special field of Orphan Psychology?

—How come?

—Well, you can be sure they'll invent it soon . . .

—No, I already know all that . . .

—Just a minute. Listen . . .

—But that's what you want to say, I know you do, so say it . . .

—Say it . . . what's stopping you?

—I'm not angry.

—Because the truth may be very different. So why don't you try, Mother, for once in your life, to think differently too. Did it ever occur to you, say, that what I'm looking for is not a father for me but a husband for you?

—Yes, a man for you . . . an honest-to-goodness man who could rescue you from this sterile life you've chosen to live, which is drying you up without your knowing it, so that even your best friends, as kind and sweet to you as they are . . . yes, they too . . . for all they admire you . . . are a little . . . what's the word . . . tired of you, and worried about your growing old on them here in the desert—where, as long as you insist on working out in the fields, there's not the ghost of a chance of meeting anyone, *anyone,* with some life in him whom you might feel close to and love . . . be-cause one day I won't be here anymore, either . . . so that maybe

2   4

it's not just for my sake that I sometimes, let's say, suppose we just say, latch onto older men, if that's really what I do, but also for . . .

—Yes. I'm finished.

—Exactly. To marry you off . . .

—You find that funny? I'll bet you do! What's wrong with it? It's time you stopped being so stubborn and . . .

—What's the same thing?

—How is it the same?

—Maybe . . .

—It's possible . . .

—It's possible . . . but so what? It may end up having the same result, but it's not the same thing . . .

—No, don't turn on any more lights. There's enough light.

—Maybe, but so what? And this time in Jerusalem I didn't thrust myself on anyone, Mother, because I had a perfect right to barge in . . .

—The right of the formula inside me, Mother, even if you don't take it seriously . . . of the little tadpole that's swimming inside me and nibbling away at my cells to create someone new . . . of this teensy little bloodball, which, say what you will, is going to burst out of me screaming at all of you next summer whether Efi owns up to being its father or not. And that, Mother, is why it was not only my right to enter that apartment without permission, it was my duty to the future Mr. Mani, who was curious to meet his ancestors on their own turf, because for the time being, until he's old enough to represent himself, I'm his only representative, do you hear me?

—As a matter of fact, I understood in a flash what drew me to that apartment—and don't tell me it was my imagination, because I know better, Mother, and it was not. It was absolutely, definitely not my imagination! I'm telling you right now that I don't agree with a word you're going to say, because I saw at a glance, Mother, the true horror of what was lurking there, which fully explained his strange behavior, and Efi's anxiety, and the errand he had sent me on, and all my determined telephone calls, and there not being any answer, and most of all, the unfriendly way he blocked the door and tried forcing me back out into the foggy cold even though I had come on a mission of good will, because I, Mother, listen carefully, I literally stopped that man, Efi's father, this Mr. Mani, from taking his own life . . .

—No, I'm not imagining it.

—Yes, I mean it. Listen to me, because it's the truth, and it can happen in life too and not only in books, and by the simple act of going to Jerusalem on Tuesday, and not budging from the door, I kept that man from killing himself . . . yes, killing himself . . . because that's exactly what he was going to do, it was clear to me then and it's clear to me now. It all adds up . . . and if I hadn't come along just then . . . when I think of it . . . and . . . and . . .

—No . . .

—No.

—I'm all right.

—I'm all right . . .

—No. I'm crying and trembling because I'm thinking of what happened then, because I know you can't believe me . . .

—Because you don't want to . . . you simply don't want to . . . you've been educated not to . . .

—Here, give it to me.

—No . . .

—All right . . . that's enough . . . I'm through . . .

—All right.

—All right . . .

—Because while he was standing there in the living room, wishing he didn't have to talk to whoever was on the telephone, I breezed right in on a blast of all that hot air, and instead of stopping politely in the living room, I kept heading down the hallway until I came to an open door through which I saw, in that dead grandmother's bedroom, which was pitch black except for a bit of light shining through the window from the night outside, something so awful that . . . I can hardly talk about it even now . . .

—There was this hangman's scaffold there . . .

—Yes. A scaffold.

—Just what I said. I mean, at first all I saw was that the room was in this absolutely frenzied state. The bed was a mess, but really crazy, as if someone had gone berserk in it: the pillows were thrown everywhere, the sheets were ripped, there were books all over the floor, and the desk was littered with crumpled papers . . . but the worst thing, Mother, was the blinds on the big window, which were shut so tight there wasn't a crack in them. The blinds box above them was open, so that you could see the bare concrete and the unpainted wood, and in it, Mother, the belt was dangling from its rod—it was like the one in this room but wider and stronger-looking, yellow with two thin, red stripes down its sides—it was off the pulley and hanging free, with this big noose knotted at one end of it . . . You're laughing at me . . .

—No, that is *not* all. Beneath it was standing a little stool, just waiting to be kicked away . . . everything was ready, I didn't have the slightest doubt . . . it couldn't have been more obvious . . . and if any more proof was needed, it was his own behavior, because the minute he saw me follow him inside and head past him for that room, he went absolutely wild. He threw down the phone in the middle of a sentence and ran to stop me, to get me out of there, or at least to shut the door and keep me from seeing. I could tell by how frantic he was, all panicky and confused and I guess embarrassed too, that he realized I had understood everything, *everything* . . . are you listening, Mother?

—No. Yes. I was already inside that dark room. I was too stunned by that scaffold to move, and he grabbed me from behind and tried wrestling me out of there . . .

—Nothing. He didn't say anything . . . that's the whole point. If we had spoken to each other it might have been different. And by now I was good and scared too, not only because of this terrible rage he was in, but because I could feel he was naked underneath his bathrobe, although at the same time I knew that if I wanted to save him, I had to resist. And so, Mother, I wrestled with him and even tried grabbing the blinds belt and tearing it down, but he started dragging me out of there, pulling me toward the front door, and I knew that if I didn't dig in my heels by finding something to sit or lie down on, I would be outside in a minute, out of the apartment and out of the picture . . . And so all at once I made believe, it was just a trick, I pretended to pass out in his arms, and he was so scared that he let go of me for a second, and I threw myself into this little armchair that was standing by the living room door. We still hadn't said a word to each other, because we were too dazed and surprised to, but when he saw me all scrunched up there like some kind of frog, he simply gave up and left me, he went back to the bedroom and shut the door behind him . . .

—That was all.

—How should I know? I guess he was waiting for me to go away.

—I just sat in that chair, Mother, and I didn't move.

—I sat there.

—I didn't look at the clock.

—Several hours.

—Yes. Several hours.

—It wasn't ridiculous at all, Mother.

—I know what you're thinking . . .

—Say it, I'm listening . . .

—Yes.

—Yes.

—Yes.

—Of course. Every word.

—Yes, I understand . . .

—That's your explanation, Mother, but it isn't mine.

—I already told you . . .

—Because I knew that my being there was enough to keep him from doing such an awful thing, even though theoretically he could have killed himself behind the locked door without my being able to do anything about it, I might even have been suspected afterward of murder . . .

—Just a minute . . . I know you don't believe me . . . but there's more . . .

—I'll get to that . . . it wasn't my imagination . . .

—I sat there without moving, soaked in that overheated apartment, which felt like it hadn't had any fresh air for days and staring at the receiver of the telephone, which was still lying on the table next to a figurine of a horse and a row of little pottery urns. That was, I realized, why it had rung busy for two days—that is, what it was busy with was lying off the hook by that horse, which actually looked more like a mule . . .

—I sat there.

—No, Mother, there, in that chair. I didn't move.

—I don't know. I felt like a fossil, as if all the life had gone out of me . . . as if the author writing me, or the director photographing me, had put down their pen or camera and gone out for dinner, or maybe just for a breath of fresh air while waiting for some inspiration what to do with me . . .

—But what should I have done?

—You must be joking!

—You're not serious . . .

—No. I simply waited.

—I suppose for him to come out of the room. The one thing I knew for sure was that I musn't leave him . . . it would have been absolutely immoral to get up and walk out . . .

—Yes. Immoral.

—Exactly, Mother. That was all. I just sat there . . . I didn't touch anything . . . I didn't even put back the receiver. At first it buzzed a little, and then it stopped. The front door was slightly open, and now and then I heard voices outside. People went up and down the stairs and the stairway light kept going on and off until in the end it got so quiet that I could hear the neighbors talking in their apartments or listening to their radios and TVs. Mostly, though, I heard the wind, which was howling like crazy outside.

—No. I just sat there without touching anything . . . as if something inside me, Mother, were keeping me from moving, because that was the condition for staying in this house I had barged into. I even forced myself to sit with my hands clasped, because I didn't want to leave any fingerprints, anything that might incriminate me if he went and hanged himself in the end . . .

—Incriminate.

—I don't know, Mother. I thought someone might blame me . . . for encouraging him, or not stopping him . . .

—I don't know, I do not do not do not! Why must you keep cross-examining my insides, Mother? All I know is that I kept sitting in that armchair in the corner of the living room. I didn't even get up when I began feeling hungry and thirsty, because I hadn't eaten or drunk since lunchtime. There was a little basket with some sucking candies there, and I didn't take a single one of them. I didn't take my sweater off either, although I was roasting from the heat. I just sat staring at the black screen of the television across from me, or reading the same lines over and over in an open book that was

lying diagonally in front of me and that I didn't even dare straighten
out, some book about old neighborhoods in Jerusalem. The more
time went by, the quieter the building became and the more I felt
that I was being embalmed like a mummy by some invisible hand. I
began dozing off in that chair, in which I seemed fated to spend the
rest of my life, a fossil waiting for my author or director to return,
resigned even to the possibility that my Mr. Mani might already be
dangling at the end of the belt, when at last—it must have been
about midnight and I was in a total fog—I saw him come out of the
room, a new man. He had taken off that raggedy bathrobe and was
wearing a sweater and pants, and his hair was combed too, so that
instead of some wild, morbid animal preparing to die, he looked like
a man who had just woken up and gotten a new lease on life. He
didn't even look surprised or angry to find me there. He just looked
at me with this slightly embarrassed smile, closed the front door,
replaced the telephone receiver, and very politely asked me what my
name was and what exactly I wanted from him . . .
    —I don't suppose he really heard me the first time.
    —No, Mother. Just wait. It was *not* my imagination . . .
    —Wait, Mother, wait . . . hold on . . .
    —Not *every* detail, but still . . . the details are important . . .
    —But for God's sake, why can't you be patient . . .
    —No. I'll make the other days shorter.
    —No. No, there wasn't a word about our little wrestling match.
You would have thought we'd never touched each other . . . Anyway, I gave him Efi's message and this time it got through to him,
although he didn't seem particularly disappointed to hear that his
son couldn't make the unveiling. He began asking me all kinds of
things about Efi, as if it were obvious that I knew more about him
than he did, and so I told him about his breaking his glasses, and he
was so concerned that he wanted to look for another pair. And so
perfectly naturally, as if nothing at all had happened, he invited me
back into the same bedroom he had thrown me out of before, only
now the room was neatly arranged and looked more or less normal.
The bed was made, the sheets were folded, the papers were in a neat
pile, and most of all, the blinds were opened and raised, so that I
could see the trees tossing in the wind outside. The blinds box was
closed and the belt with its noose was back inside it. He began

rummaging through the drawers of his desk until he found a few pairs of glasses and asked me if I thought they were Efi's, because he didn't know whose they were. In the end he put them all in a little cloth bag and said, "Here, send these to him in Lebanon, maybe he can get by with them until he comes home." By now he didn't seem in such a hurry to get rid of me anymore. He gave me a long look and asked, "But where do I know you from? Where can I possibly remember you from?"—and when I told him with a little smile that I had been in his apartment a month ago to pay him a condolence call, he didn't seem satisfied with the answer. I don't think he even remembered it, because he kept trying to discover where else we might have met. He was all full of this sudden curiosity and wanted to know if I had ever lived in Jerusalem, and all about my family, and about you, Mother, and about father, and about who your parents were, and about where they came from, and if there weren't some Jerusalemites among them. It was so strange, Mother, this family interrogation that he suddenly began with great patience in the middle of the night, as if there were no clocks in the world and time itself didn't exist. And since I really don't know much about our family history, and I was very tired, in the end—but only in the end, Mother—I blurted out that . . . I mean . . . I did it again . . . I just couldn't help myself . . .

—Right. Yes. That I lost my father in a war . . .

—I knew you'd say that. But this time I didn't mean to do it. I'd sworn to myself to stop mentioning it all the time.

—That's easy to say. It's very easy.

—Naturally. You always know everything.

—No . . .

—No, no, but it's beginning to get on my nerves how you're always so sure that you know just what I'm going to say and just what I'm going to do. Well, hang on, because you've got a surprise in store for you tonight . . .

—Hang on. Have a little patience.

—Yes. A surprise.

—Then? Naturally, Mother, it wasn't my fault. He started gushing with compassion like they all do . . .

—That's what you think. I might have liked it once, but I don't anymore. It aggravates me the way everyone feels they have to be so protective, him too. Not that he wasn't tactful about it, but you could see how worried he was about my going back to Tel Aviv in such weather, especially since he was sure it was going to snow. It was *his* idea that I spend the night there and let him take me to the train or bus station in the morning—and though I knew it made sense, I took my time answering because I wanted to be sure he really thought so himself and wasn't just trying to be nice . . . only before I could make up my mind, he was already making the grandmother's bed for me and primping the room in whose doorway we had wrestled like two savages, as if trying to prove to me that that scaffold had never existed . . .

—No. Efi doesn't have his own room there. It was that dead grandmother's. You could tell the minute you walked into it.

—By everything, you name it. By the furniture. By the pictures on the walls. By this weird old doll of a Turkish dancer with shiny pants and a fez on her head. By the dresses and slips still hanging in the closet. Even by the sheets he made the bed with, which were yellowed from so many laundries. He took a nightgown from a drawer and handed it to me, this heavy old flannel antique covered with hand-embroidered red flowers no two of which were alike, and for a minute, Mother, it gave me the creeps, not so much because it was that grandmother's as because I felt sure that seeing me in it was what made him so glad to have me stay for the night . . .

—You've got to be kidding!

—What an idea, Mother. He only came back into the room once to lower the blinds when I was already under the blankets and to ask me if the nightgown fit, and I could see how happy I made him. He was actually glowing, and with one easy yank he lowered the open blinds, no doubt to prove that there had never been any scaffold but just some blinds that needed fixing . . .

—It was not a figment of my imagination.

—Because I saw it.

—I know exactly what I saw . . .

—But just wait a minute. Why can't you have a little patience?

—So what? We have all night.

—But you agreed to skip the New Year's Eve party.

—Then what are you so tense about?

—*That?*

—Suppose I did? So what?

—Yes, that's right, Mother. It didn't bother me in the least . . . why should it have? If Efi didn't mind getting into my grandmother's bed, why should I have minded getting into his grandmother's bed?

—Suppose she did? What of it? That was a month ago . . . you don't think something was still left of it, do you? Death isn't something slimy and catching like life. It's not like you, Mother, to suddenly start believing in ghosts!

—Never. It was perfectly natural. You know I always had a thing about grown-up's beds, maybe because of that disgusting children's dorm I had to sleep in on the kibbutz . . . and in fact I climbed right into it and fell asleep at once, without any problems, even though he was still fussing about in the apartment and the wind was blowing harder outside. But after an hour or two, Mother, I woke up, not just totally disorientated, but starving, as if *he* were beginning to eat out my insides down there. I had to get up and look for something to eat, and so I groped my way up the hallway of that dark railroad flat, tiptoeing past Efi's father's closed door and into the kitchen, where I didn't turn on the light or even open the fridge but just found a loaf of bread and cut a few slices and poured a little oil on them and sprinkled them with salt and some spices lying there and wolfed down half the loaf before I was full. As I was heading back down the hallway I saw his door open slightly, as if he had been waiting for me. And so I stopped for a second, Mother, and I heard him drowsily calling my name in this low voice, as if I were already a member of the family. He wanted to know if it was snowing already—and all of a sudden, don't ask me why, I had this terrible fear of him . . .

—I don't know. Maybe that he was going to start wrestling again. I couldn't say a word, and so I slipped back to bed and tossed and turned until I finally fell asleep again. In the morning, when he came in to wake me at seven-thirty, he was in a hurry. He was very nattily dressed, in this black suit and black tie, because he really is a judge, a justice of the peace. I even saw him presiding . . .

—In a minute. I'll get to that too. Just let me tell it in my own sweet time . . .

—Don't rush me, Mother. He woke me by letting some light into the room and tapping me lightly on the shoulder, and the first thing he said was, "Forgive me. It's my fault you were hungry last night. I forgot to give you supper . . ."

—I hadn't breathed a word of it, Mother. Heavens, no, not a word yet . . .

—Because I didn't want him to suspect me or to think, who knows, that maybe I didn't come to Jerusalem to bring him Efi's message but with some secret plan to extort . . .

—Oh, I don't know . . . some promise having to do with the baby . . . or maybe money . . .

—How should I know what he might have thought? For a doctor maybe . . . or an abortion . . . that's why I was so careful not to say anything. Even though he was very quiet and in control of himself, standing there and spreading a slice of whole-wheat bread with goat cheese for me while looking out the window to see if the rain had turned to snow yet, I kept reminding myself not to forget for a minute that this was the same man who had tried ending his life the night before like some kind of stricken animal . . .

—No, just a subtle hint, to keep him on his toes . . . I only said, real innocently, "I see you managed to fix the blinds and unknot that belt," because I wanted to make sure that he knew that not only had I seen it all, I had understood everything I saw . . .

—No. He didn't react. He just nodded and kind of smiled to himself, and then he began prodding me to leave—and suddenly, Mother, I felt sure that all his being so nice and polite was just a ruse to get me out of Jerusalem and make sure I didn't stick around to keep an eye on him, which must have been why he invented some important business he had to see to not far from the bus station, so that he could drop me off there. For a minute I thought that that was good-bye and that I had better get back to Tel Aviv. I had already missed enough classes because of the whole crazy adventure. But in the car on the way, which was crawling through the rain in this terrible traffic, I began studying his profile in the silence that had come over us, and what I saw was this depressed Sephardic gentleman with breath that smelled like old wine who seemed all alone in the world—and suddenly I thought, Mother, why, this is the only grandfather that the little formula swimming in my fluids will ever have, shouldn't I get to know him a little better? And so I began asking him about himself. I even mentioned that book on old neighborhoods in Jerusalem next to the figurine of the horse that I diagonally read a page of, and he brightened up right away and started telling me about it, and about how he enjoyed reading it, and about this neighborhood he was on his way to now, which was called Abraham's Vineyard, where he rented out an old house that he had inherited from his great-grandfather, a famous gynecologist who ran a maternity clinic ninety years ago in which all the women of Jerusalem, Jews and Arabs, came to give birth. Well, no sooner had he told me that, Mother, than something seemed to burst inside me. I was actually red with emotion, because despite the traffic jam and all that annoying gray rain dripping down the windows, there was such a marvelous fatedness about having met him and about driving with him now to this place where women gave birth a century ago that it seemed the most natural thing to want to go with him and see it for myself. He was a little taken aback by that. There was nothing to see there, he said. It was just a house with a few small apartments whose tenants' leases he had to renew, because that was the money that paid for Efi's studies. I didn't back down, though, I almost begged him: if I didn't go with him to the house, couldn't I at least take a look at the neighborhood? He kept trying to convince me that it wasn't worth it, that it was just another neighborhood of super-religious Jews in black coats. But I stuck to my guns, Mother. Suddenly it mattered terribly to me, and in the end he had no choice, he couldn't just throw me out of the car—and so he didn't stop at the bus station but drove straight to this crowded neighborhood, which really was full of Jews in black clothes. It seemed very colorful, though, and we parked in a street by an old stone house that didn't look small at all, it had two stories and a red tile roof. But he must have felt very embarrassed, because he said, "This is the house, you can see there's nothing to see"—and he politely asked me to wait outside while he went in, because the tenants were very religious and wouldn't approve of me or my being there . . . Well, Mother, that made me laugh, as if they had any idea who I was, but I agreed to wait outside, and he said, "It may take a while. If you get tired of waiting you can take a bus to the central station." He began warning me about the snow again, how it would cut the road to Tel Aviv if it started falling, and then he shook hands and apologized for all the trouble he had caused me by leaving the telephone off the hook and disappeared through this big iron door. I went for a stroll around the neighborhood, trying to imagine what it had been like a hundred years ago. It must have had nothing but empty space all around it, just like the kibbutz does today. After a while I began to think about the baby, because once it was born that house would belong to it too, and through it to me, a whole big house with a red roof when here on the kibbutz we don't even have a shack we can call our own. All around me religious men were walking in stiff, straight lines with these transparent plastic covers on their hats and these black umbrellas that they carried like rifles, and the raindrops were becoming long and sticky, all smeary-like, although I knew they weren't snow yet, even though I had never seen snow in my life, and so I went back and stepped into the house, which had these mailboxes without lids and these dark, narrow stairs with lots of baby carriages tied to the banister. I climbed them to the second floor, where there was a corridor that you could see had once been the veranda of the original building, part of which had been torn down and redone in a whole hodgepodge. There were doors there that might have belonged to apartments or maybe just to some sort of storerooms, and for a second I had the strange thought that perhaps this Mr. Mani of mine had gone off into one of those little rooms to finish killing himself quietly, but I kept walking along the hallway to a back stairway that led down to a little courtyard paved with stones and surrounded by more small rooms and apartments, at one end of which was a patch of earth where some dear soul was trying to get something to grow—it was touching, Mother, to see how these city people had planted pepper bushes and tomato vines in some big old basins and potties. By now I felt lots of eyes on me. Windows were opening and heads were sticking out of them, and finally a pregnant young woman stepped into the courtyard and tried tactfully finding out what I was doing there. She seemed very worried when I said that I was waiting for the landlord. She must have thought I wanted to rent something, and so right away she began explaining that I must be mistaken and that there was nothing for rent. It was obvious, Mother, that the idea of someone like me wanting to live there was too much for her, which made me so mad that I said, "But maybe something will become available," and she

said, "Oh no, there's a long waiting list and no one ever moves out"
—and all at once, Mother, I realized how uncomfortable I made her
feel. She couldn't stand the thought of my even looking for an apartment there. I saw her signal some neighbors to come help persuade
me that it was hopeless, and so I told them angrily, "I'm waiting for
Mr. Mani, I came with him," and they said, "But the judge has
already left," and so I hurried back out to the street and saw that his
car was really gone. Well, I thought, at least he hasn't killed himself,
he's just run away—and at that point, Mother, I don't know what
got into me, but I decided I was going to go after him . . .

—To the Russian Compound, where the courts are.

—There you go again . . .

—I hear you . . . I just wish you'd say something original for a
change . . .

—Fine, suppose you're right, Mother, and that I'm always looking for a father, which is the psychological, the trivial, the *technical*
way you've been taught to think of everything, always looking for
some simple, superficial, dumb little subconscious motive to get
your hands on and criticize. So what? What made me choose him,
of all people? Why this Mr. Mani and not someone else? I swear I
could find myself a thousand fathers a day, there are middle-aged
men just waiting from morning to night—not all of them even want
to go to bed with a girl, Mother, some of them aren't even capable
of it, all they want is a few hugs and kisses in return for being warm
and protective. Why go all the way to Jerusalem to end up with a
depressive Mani? What does he have that anyone else doesn't? I'm
sorry, Mother, but you'll have to do better than that . . .

—Incredible! You're bringing that up now? And all this time
you've been saying it was just my imagination . . .

—But what does that have to do with Father? Now I really don't
get it . . .

—I don't get it . . .

—I still don't get it.

—Now you're frightening me . . .

—Fine, but later, later . . . I'm begging you, give me time before you start bombarding me with all your interpretations . . .

—Okay.

—Okay.

—Okay. Later we can talk about everything—all evening, all night, as much as you want, but first let me finish my story, all of it, to the end. That comes first. Because I'm still back there, Mother, in that place called Abraham's Vineyard . . .

—Right.

—Yes, down the hill from that army base, Camp Schneller. Do you know what it once was?

—No, before that.

—No. A German orphanage.

—Exactly, off to your left—which is from where, instead of taking a bus to the station and from there back to Tel Aviv and the university, I set out in the opposite direction, contrariwise . . .

—Contrary to what I should have done, which is gone back to Tel Aviv and studied for my exams instead of taking a bus back into town to the Russian Compound and walking through the cold and the rain past all those old court buildings with their long, dark corridors full of people in black robes—who were actually very kind and helpful when it came to giving directions—until I found him, our Mr. Mani, sitting in the courtroom of the justice of the peace, which was such a tiny room that I had to laugh at first, because I never knew that courtrooms were so small. It wasn't any bigger than this room, Mother, with three or four benches facing a big black platform, and there he was on it, sitting in his black robe with his back to a big arched window sunk into the stone wall and judging away. He was so flabbergasted when he saw me come in, slipping into the room with my head down and moving some wet coats to clear a place for myself on the last bench, behind the defendant and his lawyer, that he blushed, took off his little reading glasses, and looked around to see if anyone else had noticed me. Right away, though, he recovered, and for the rest of the morning he ignored me completely and went on presiding with this kind of stern humor that I hadn't realized he had. Mostly, he teased and scolded the lawyers. When the defendants took the stand he was much more patient, shutting his eyes and playing with that little mourner's beard of his, which he still didn't seem to be quite used to . . .

—Yes. I sat there for a couple of hours, until noontime.

—It can be very interesting, Mother. It's very dramatic when the defendant stands up to be identified, and the prosecutor reads the charge against him, and he has to plead guilty or not guilty, but there's also a lot of haggling with the lawyers about all kinds of petty little details that didn't mean a thing to me, and all this coming and going to the judge's bench with documents until he'd lose his temper and call a halt to the proceedings and go off with the lawyers to his office, which was right off the courtroom, leaving me, Mother, all alone with this Arab defendant accused of stealing a Jewish ID card, who suddenly turned around and began talking to me . . .

—I don't know what kept me there . . . But this time too, Mother, I had this sinking, frozen feeling that wouldn't let me move. And of course, the weather outside was awful, you could see the rain getting worse all the time through the window and the sky getting grayer and lower. And nobody seemed to mind me, because nobody knew I was there to keep an eye on the judge, who seemed very lively and energetic and so far from suicide that I began to think what you're thinking right now, that everything that happened the night before was just a fantasy of mine . . .

—Wait . . . just wait . . .

—No, he never acknowledged my existence, not even with a glance. You might have thought he didn't know me. I went on sitting there until noon, feeling like a stone. Finally, he disappeared with the lawyers into his office for such a long time that the last remaining defendant got tired of waiting and walked out too, leaving me all by myself in that little room, looking out at the rain, which had turned into these icy pellets of hail bouncing off the window, and I thought, damn it, Hagar, what on earth are you doing here when you could be back at the university, on a campus full of life? But just then, Mother, the bells began ringing in the Russian church, pealing away in the courtroom . . . it was so solemn and primitive . . . and once again, Mother, I had the same strange sensation I had had the night before, on the stairs to his apartment, like I told you . . .

—Yes. Exactly. That someone was standing off to the side and writing or filming me . . .

—Right. It was the weirdest feeling.

—What's so funny?

—What kind of delusions of grandeur? As a matter of fact, it wasn't that at all. This wasn't my own *personal* story. It was other people's too. I wasn't being asked to go off to some corner with my own little self but on the contrary, to have patience for everyone—for Efi, and for the baby, and for everyone—so that they could all make some sense of it . . .

—Wait . . . just wait . . . why are you in such a hurry to-night . . .

—You needn't worry, nothing bad happened to me. Anyway, when I finally got up and peeked into his office to see what was doing there, all I found was a neat, quiet room. His coat and brief-case were gone, which meant that he had given me the slip again, this Mr. Mani of mine. But I didn't give up this time either, Mother. I hurried back out into those dark corridors and began looking for him, asking all the black-robed people if they had seen him, until finally I found him standing in a large entranceway, bundled up in his heavy coat with his robe folded over one arm while having a friendly chat with a young prosecutor who had argued a case before him. He must have been waiting for it to stop hailing, and at first I didn't know if I should approach him, but as soon as he saw me he turned to me warmly and even took my hand and said, "Well, Ha-gar, how was I?" He wanted to know what I thought and if I liked it, he even introduced me to the young lawyer standing next to him as his son Efrayim's girlfriend—and I, Mother, don't ask me what came over me, I actually had tears in my eyes. Maybe it was his calling me Hagar and maybe just his being such a darling, but I wanted so badly to cling to him and snuggle up against that big, hairy coat of his that if there actually was a minute, Mother . . . I mean a moment when maybe . . . *maybe* the thought crossed my mind . . . yes, I admit it . . . that he could have . . . just for a second . . . maybe . . .

—I mean . . . that he could have soothed that deep sense of loss that maybe I really do go around with all the time . . .

—Yes, like a kind of father . . . but it was only for a minute, no more than that, believe me . . .

—But he didn't. That was the confusing part, Mother. Because all this time I had the feeling that he too was sending these hidden distress signals, as though he were whispering to me, *Yes, you're right, what you saw last night was no mistake but something that almost happened, don't leave me,* while at the same time I had the feeling that he wanted to get rid of me. Anyway, he offered to drive me to the bus station again—it was as if he wanted to make sure that this time I really left Jerusalem. He walked me under his umbrella to his car and opened the door for me like a gentleman to make up for jilting me and even stopped in some little street in the marketplace and took me to a tiny joint where he ordered this special Jerusalem hummus for me with a hard-boiled egg diced into it and behaved really sweetly, even if he did fade out from time to time as though the lights had gone out inside him and there was a power failure there. But each time they came on again and he asked some new question, whose answer didn't really interest him, about Efi, who he seemed to think I knew more about than he did. There was a point in all that noise and winter weather when I had an urge to tell him what was in store for him in this little stomach of mine that he was stuffing with hummus, but I controlled myself and didn't. And when we left the restaurant, he not only drove me to the station, he went out of his way to buy me a ticket and bring me to the platform and stand me in line as if I were a retarded child—and even then he didn't say good-bye but waited patiently until I got on the bus and it began to pull out, which was actually very nice—I mean, all that being taken care of and being chaperoned, especially since I really did want to get home and out of the cold and the rain, even if it was also a little humiliating to see how he was manipulating me back to Tel Aviv, as though I were a mental case that had walked into his life instead of a perfectly innocent messenger on a mission of good will . . .

—Wait.

—No, just a minute, Mother, wait . . .

—Yes, it was two days ago, on Wednesday afternoon. I actually did leave Jerusalem . . .

—I really did leave it. It was storming outside, and everyone in the bus kept talking about how it was going to snow . . . about how it just *had* to snow . . . and I thought, well, that's it, it's over with, what do I care, maybe I really did just imagine it, and anyway, I have to go home, I can't spend the rest of my life chasing after him. The bus was already speeding down the mountains toward the coast, there was nothing but fog all around, and right outside the city we drove into such a thick cloud of it that you couldn't see a

thing . . . at which point, the bus suddenly turned off the highway
into a side road. Mr. Mani, it seemed, had been so eager to get rid of
me that he had put me on the local instead of the express! We
started winding through the fog, in and out of all kinds of villages.
Everything was dripping wet outside, it was all so green and damp,
and every now and then some hillside popped out of the fog into the
window. It was sleeting too, and I thought, if it's like this halfway to
the coast, there must be snow in Jerusalem—the same snow Mr.
Mani warned me about but was also looking forward to, maybe
because then he could lock himself up in that railroad flat, and
switch off all the lights, and turn up the heat, and take off his
clothes, and open the blinds box in Grandmother's room, and take
the belt off the pulley, and knot one end of it, and kick away the
stool, and bye-bye Mr. Mani . . .

—Yes, Mother. I couldn't stop thinking about it. The more we
drove in and out on those roads outside of Jerusalem, the more it
haunted me, so that when the bus finally rejoined the main highway
and picked up speed again on the soft curves of those woodsy hills
near the bottom of the mountains, and I knew that in another minute we would be flying over the coastal plain, something rebelled
inside me, Mother, and I stood up in my seat . . .

—Yes. What rebelled was my desperation at having been made to
leave Jerusalem against my will. I stood up all at once, and something propelled me to the front of the bus, and I said to the driver,
"I'm very sorry, sir, but I'll have to ask you to stop and let me out,
because I'm pregnant and all this speed is bad for me and the
baby . . ."

—Yes, the baby too. Don't ask me what made me say it . . .

—I'm telling you, I did. What's wrong with it?

—But what did I say?

—No, he was very nice about it. He slowed down a little and
suggested that I move to the front of the bus, because it's not as
bouncy there, but when he saw that I was determined to get off, he
didn't argue. He stopped right at the bottom of the mountains, near
that gas station there, and opened the door and said "Watch your
step" and drove off into all that rain and fog. There was this total
silence all around, and without thinking twice about it, Mother, or
knowing what made me do it, I crossed to the other, the *contrary*

side of the road, and headed for that old ruined building there, you know, the one where the road starts climbing back into the mountains . . .

—Yes. Someone once told me it was an old Arab khan where travelers to Jerusalem stopped to rest their horses. Anyway, there they were, waiting for me in the stillness . . . I mean that author or that director with his big black camera. Apparently, I had forgotten that we had arranged to meet there, and they were sitting on a stone terrace next to some dripping-wet trees, their heads in their hands just like yours is—don't look at me that way, Mother, I promise you I'm not going crazy . . . Shhh . . . shhh . . . someone is knocking . . . don't move . . .

—No. *Don't move.* Who can it be?

—It doesn't matter. Never mind. So you won't answer for once in your life . . . so what?

—No, don't get up . . .

—Would you rather I stopped?

—But what's the matter?

—No . . . no . . . don't be so worried . . . it's just that I keep trying to explain this new feeling to you that I've never had before, which is that I'm not so alone anymore but part of a much bigger story that I don't know anything about yet because it's only beginning, although if I'm patient, I'll find out. It was simply a way of calming myself, Mother, and I was even beginning to enjoy that old ruin, which everyone sees from the highway but no one ever bothers to explore. There was a sound of running water all around me, and I began to imagine all the travelers who must have stopped there on their way from Jaffa to Jerusalem, because a hundred years ago it was the place in which they all spent the night—and all at once, Mother, I had this feeling of great peace inside me . . .

—Yes. Of a lull in all the running around and studying for exams and other headaches. I could have gone on sitting there, hidden in that old ruin while watching the cars fly by in both directions and looking out over the valley, where the sun was fighting for its life with a black sky, only just then I thought to myself, even if you only imagined it, why don't you put your mind to rest by making absolutely sure, this Mr. Mani-Depressive can be a grandfather soon if he doesn't do anything rash, and so I left the khan and tried hitching a

ride back into the mountains, and half an hour later I was in Jerusalem again, the streets of which were whitened by real snow . . .

—Yes, honest-to-goodness snow. That was Wednesday afternoon. Wasn't there anything about it on the radio?

—It was wonderful.

—I know you haven't. That's why I was so determined not to
miss it, so that for once I could be one-up on you, Mother . . .

—It was real but just beginning, you couldn't tell if it was going
to stick. And yet there was already something grand, something
noble, in all those long feathers fluttering quietly about. It made me
feel that I was in Europe—and what made that lovely European
feeling even stronger was the fact that I soon found myself back in
that circle near the President's house, walking down streets whose
houses were familiar and watching the snow settle over them. I went
to have a look at the Prime Minister's house too: next to it was this
little tent with posters against the war in Lebanon and two demon-
strators wrapped in a big bright blanket taking shelter inside from
the cold, while across from them was an abandoned table with a
torn sign that must have belonged to a counter-demonstration. I
kept on walking, looking for drifts of snow I could step in and
praying they would not melt overnight while working up the courage to go back to his apartment, because how could I explain it
without making a fool of myself—and I absolutely did not want to
make a fool of myself and give him an excuse to ditch me again,
even if he did it like a Sephardic gentleman. And so I followed my
legs past the Jerusalem Theater, which was completely dark, crossed
the empty parking lot below it, and cut across the field behind the
old leper hospital, where I was thrilled to see that the snow, which
had melted on the streets and sidewalks, was sticking and piling up
among the rocks. There was even enough of it to make a big snow-
ball that I threw at some whooping children who had thrown one at
me. I kept walking until I reached his long street, but I didn't go
into his building. I passed it and stepped into the next house to get
out of the snow and warm up, because I was chilled to the bone and
my sweater was soaking wet, and suddenly I felt afraid that all the
games I was playing might freeze that teeny thing inside me and
spoil its formula, which would have made it a criminal act not to
have gone somewhere to warm myself . . .

—I knew you'd say that . . .

—Fine. Fine. So it was just a rationalization . . .

—Fine. I admit it. That didn't make me any less of a fool. Of course, I wasn't thinking of myself right then but only of what was inside me, but still . . .

—All right, all right. It doesn't make any difference. In the end I went up there like a fool and rang the bell. There was no answer, and I said to myself, this time I am not making an issue of it, I don't care if it's my imagination or not, I've had enough. When I went back down to look for a bus stop, I saw his car parked in the street. I could tell it was his by the robe in the back—but still, Mother, I told myself: it isn't your business, if he wants to kill himself you can't stop him, you can't come running to the rescue every night from Tel Aviv. And so I started to walk and turned into this little shopping center, where there was a café I went into to warm up and eat something. I sat there thinking about you and wondering if you were worrying—that's when I called the kibbutz and left that message that the German volunteer never gave you. I sat by the window and had something to eat and drink while watching the snow to see if it would stick, because all those cars and people were very hard on it. I had begun to care about it as much as Mr. Mani—not that I knew why he cared about it either . . . By then it was nine o'clock. The evening news was on the television in the café, and there were shots of the snow in Jerusalem, and everyone sat there staring at it as if they knew that even if it melted, it would still exist on television. It wasn't too late yet, Mother, to take a bus back to Tel Aviv, and I went to pay the bill with every intention of doing that. Before I did, though, I decided to make one last little telephone call, just to see if he had made up his mind to hang himself yet, and it was the same story now too—there wasn't any answer—and I said to myself, he can't possibly be playing these revolting little games again unless he's already dead, and I sniffed and thought, well, there goes Grandpa number two, this little Mani of mine will have nothing but women around when he's born . . .

—Efi won't be there either.

—He just won't . . .

—Because I have no illusions about him.

—I don't . . . it's just a feeling that I have . . .

—It's nothing specific, but I have no illusions . . .

—I've already told you. There was no chance to tell him. I'm sure he won't like it, though—I mean having a baby and all . . .

—Because I think he has other plans. He wants to study abroad, and the last thing he needs is a baby. Besides, who knows if we're really in love or if it isn't just one of those things . . .

—No, for goodness' sake, Mother, not now . . . there's time . . . I'll get to that . . . if you'll only wait . . . because now I left the café and went back to the street and into the building just to see if I would again get that solemn feeling of not being alone and of following someone's instructions, but nothing happened. No one was waiting for me there—no author or director or photographer. It was as if I had run out of sponsors and was back on my own again— and that, Mother, was when I began to feel a little desperate, to say nothing of exhausted from my first time in the snow, which can be very fatiguing if you're not used to it, and so I said to myself, I've had it, it's time to say good-bye to this Mr. Mani once and for all. I climbed the stairs to his apartment, but I didn't knock or ring. I just sat there quietly by the door to warm up a little before leaving. I must have been feeling kind of angry for letting everyone abandon me there in the dark . . .

—Everyone . . . everyone . . .

—Everyone . . . all of you . . . everyone who wants to ditch me . . .

—Never mind. Forget it. Later . . .

—Wait . . . wait . . .

—Forget it . . . I didn't mean it. Anyway, Mother, just then the stairway light went on, and I saw this middle-aged woman coming up the stairs, this plump, nice-looking woman who turned out to be the next-door neighbor. And when she saw me sitting like an out- cast by the door, she asked me, perfectly matter-of-factly, as if she knew who I was and that I belonged there, "Well, what's the matter: did you lose your key again?"

—Yes. She must have confused me with someone else, or else seen me coming out of there that morning. And so I quietly said "Yes" in this passive kind of voice, which was enough to make her go get the extra key she had in case Efi forgot his—which put me,

Mother, in this awkward situation, with the key to the apartment in my hand . . .

—No. Yes. I thought I'd stall for time and slip away the minute she went back inside, but she just planted herself in her doorway and waited for me to open the door. She gave me no choice, Mother. I even turned the key quietly and gave the door a little push and said thank you with a smile in the hope that she would be satisfied and go away, but she just went on standing there as if it were all too fascinating for words, so what could I do but go inside and shut the door behind me . . .

—No. I didn't mean to go any farther.

—Of course, Mother. How could you even think it? I thought I'd stand quietly by the door for a minute and step back out again without being noticed—assuming, that is, that there was anyone in there to notice me. But the apartment was so exactly like the night before, just as dark and overheated and quiet, that I began to wonder: what is going on here? Is it happening all over again or am I traveling backward in time? I was getting to be too contrary for my own good, because this time I was sure that he had really gone and done it—and I had to give him credit, Mother, for being civilized enough to turn off the lights and do it in the dark . . .

—Good God, no, Mother, why would I want to frighten you? What for? I'm just telling you my thoughts. I hadn't seen anything yet, and though I knew the apartment by now, my eyes were still getting used to the dark and I was just beginning to make out familiar objects, like the telephone in the living room next to the figurine of the horse, or the row of little Greek urns. I could see as far as the closed door of the grandmother's room, and I remember thinking, Mother, all right, Hagar, this is the time if you feel like it to let out one of those screams, you know, those blood-curdling screams that people go to the movies to hear, except that this isn't a movie, it's not even a book, and no one will hear it or share it with you, you'll be screaming purely for your own pleasure, purely for your own terror, so what's the point? As long as you're here anyway, and there are witnesses who have seen you, which means that you're sure to be investigated, you may as well know what to answer, so why don't you go see what's happened . . . And so I began inching my way down the hallway, still in the dark, Mother, because I didn't want to see the full horror, just its shadow, although plenty of people are more frightened of shadows than of what casts them, and as soon as I opened the door I saw that the room, which I had left neat and orderly in the morning, was . . .

—No, listen! Listen. You have to . . .

—No, you have to. You can't just keep saying I imagined it all and leave me with this story that's overwhelming me so I can't breathe, Mother, because the room looked as if it had been hit by a hurricane, as if some madman had run amuck there, attacking the bed and ripping the sheets and throwing around old clothes and old papers and pictures. And this time too, Mother, like in one of those recurring nightmares, the little scaffold was set up again: the blinds were shut tight, the blinds box was open with the belt hanging from the rod and knotted in a noose at one end, and even the stool was back in place. It was a repeat performance. Maybe, I thought, he put it on every night to rehearse his own death until it became so obvious and convincing that he could stop fighting it . . . and then, Mother, for the first time I felt so sorry for him that I really wanted to help, so that instead of walking away from that scene, which— you're perfectly right—was much too private and intimate for me to have any business being there, I wanted to work my way deeper into it, to keep moving in that contrary direction that was pulling me like a magnet, and so I walked down the hallway to the back of the apartment, to this little bathroom off the kitchen, because I thought that if everything was happening again, he was probably in there washing himself as part of his suicide exercises . . .

—I'm glad I finally got a laugh out of you.

—Yes, Mother, it was definitely funny, my walking around that dark apartment like some kind of sleepwalker so as to find him and talk him out of this suicidal frenzy he was in. I would have broken down the bathroom door too, but it already was open, as was a door behind it that led to this little rear terrace that I hadn't noticed before—and there, on the terrace, which was cluttered with all kinds of brooms and buckets and what-not, was my suicidal Mr. Mani in his big, heavy overcoat looking more like a ball or a closet than a man, peacefully smoking a cigarette in the fresh air beneath this sky that had suddenly cleared and even had stars in it, so absorbed in himself that he didn't even notice me come in. I was still wondering how to let him know I was there when suddenly he turned around—and all at once, Mother, he went into the most terrible shock. The cigarette fell from his mouth and he let out this strange, painful cry as if he too were in some movie or book and the director had asked him to give it his all. Right away, though, he realized who I was and pulled himself together. He even laughed and tried making a joke of it and said, "Good God Almighty, don't tell me it's you again! You're really something! I've never seen anyone so stubborn. Just tell me this, though: how in hell did you get into this apartment? Did you steal the key this morning when you left?"

—Yes, but not in anger, Mother. He was perfectly good-natured, as though he were secretly happy that I had come to save him again. I began to mumble something about the neighbor who all but made me enter his apartment, and right away he said, "Yes, that Mrs. Shapiro, she's always worrying . . ." There was this vague resentment in his voice, as if Mrs. Shapiro took so many liberties he wasn't even sure what they were, and then calmly—he was still standing on the terrace—he began talking about the snow, as though trying to convince the two of us that that was what had brought me back to Jerusalem, that I wanted to see it while it still was there, because the weather was clearing, and cold as it was, it wasn't cold enough to keep the snow from melting. Well, Mother, when I saw him all squirming and embarrassed like that I felt so weak myself that instead of confronting him with the horrible truth of what I had seen and understood, I began to murmur something about the snow too, to which I added that I really had come back for Efi's sake, because I wanted to go to the unveiling in his place . . .

—Yes, that's just what I said. I didn't want him to guess that I had been following him around to keep him from killing himself. At first he looked very surprised, as if he had forgotten all about the unveiling . . . and in fact, if he had really meant to die that night he couldn't have been planning on going to it, since the dead don't attend ceremonies for the dead. Gradually, though, the idea seemed to please him. Maybe he really wanted to believe that that was the reason I had crashed his apartment again. Anyway, he bowed his head with this sort of doleful acknowledgment and only said with a strange smile that it was a shame I wasn't a man, because he needed ten men for the cemetery, without them he couldn't say the mourner's prayer . . .

—It would seem so.

—Yes, it's very odd . . . you would think it was this intimate thing that you said whenever you felt like it, but that isn't the case at all. He even tried explaining it to me . . . but suddenly—he was talking about it and I was looking out at that field by the old leper hospital, which was covered with these white splotches of snow— suddenly he said something, Mother, I don't remember what, that affected me so that I got this big lump in my throat and burst into tears, don't ask me why, right there on that little terrace between the brooms and the laundry rack . . .

—Yes, real tears. They came from deep down and kept coming. I couldn't stop them even though I knew they were making me look ridiculous. He didn't say a word, though. He just stood there listening to me cry and calmly smoking another cigarette, as if I were getting what I deserved for hounding him and intruding on him . . .

—No, Mother. He was not right.

—No, he was not, and neither are you. Because what you think of as presumption, or even total irresponsibility, was simply my duty, Mother, a duty that was being spun out of me like the thin web of a spider . . .

—The spider inside me right now.

—The one made by the formula.

—That's what we learned in school about the development of the embryo . . .

—I'm telling you we did . . . I remember . . . there was even a chart with all these pictures . . .

—You must have forgotten. Or else you never studied it.

—Don't worry.

—There is nothing the matter with me.

—I'm imagining that too? You're certainly making life easy for yourself tonight!

—Why hunt for what doesn't exist?

—There's nothing beneath the surface but what you put there.

—Maybe beneath the avocado trees in your orchard, but not beneath the surface of my story . . .

—I didn't mean to hurt your feelings . . . Good God, Mother . . .

—I'm sorry . . . I'm sorry . . .

—I know perfectly well what I said.

—I don't care. That's not what I meant.

—What?

—What did you say?

—No, what an idea! You're too much . . .

—Of course not. How could you even think it?

—So that's what's been bothering you . . .

—Then why didn't you say so?

—You can calm down then . . . not in my wildest dreams . . .

—Incredible!

—Although I must say in parenthesis—and only in parenthesis—that Mr. Mani's charms are considerably greater than his son's . . .

—I can't easily explain it. You'll see what I mean when you meet them . . .

—No. Just in passing. As we were walking back up the hallway past the grandmother's room, I said, "I see that the blinds belt is broken again, it looks like a hangman's rope." He let out a big laugh and reddened and said, "So it does, and the room's a mess too, because I've been looking there for something I can't find. You'll sleep in the living room. The couch folds out into a bed . . . that's where Efi always sleeps when he visits." And without another word we passed that self-destructing room and went to the living room, where he pulled out the bed and brought me that old, embroidered nightgown again and all those half-torn sheets—I couldn't tell if I or someone else had last slept on them—and quietly and not at all angrily went about setting me up for another night's stay . . .

—No. We hardly spoke. We didn't even bother to wrestle, because we had arrived at what seemed like a temporary alliance, or maybe it was more of a truce. He pulled out the telephone plug and left me in the room with the warning that we had to rise very early, and I told him not to worry. "I'm a kibbutznik from the Negev," I said, "and we're the world champions at early rising." Well, he just smiled at that and shut the door and left me all by myself in what was beginning to seem by then like home. I turned out the lights and opened the window to let in some air, and I could see that it

was getting clearer and calmer outside. I moved the pillow to the
other end of the bed and tried reading something, but I was too
tired, and so I switched on the television without the volume until
the news was over, and then I turned it up a bit to watch the movie,
I don't know if you saw it, it starts out nicely and then gets worse
and worse . . .

—You did? I thought it started out nicely.

—No. I didn't want to bother him with another request, and I
didn't know if there was hot water or if I would have to wait for it to
heat. I knew I'd be on my way back to Tel Aviv early in the morning, straight from the cemetery, and I thought I'd take a big bath
and wash my hair when I got there, because I was getting tired of
living like a nomad . . .

—Soon . . . in a minute . . . I'll wash up soon . . .

—If the water's so hot, why don't you turn off the boiler?

—Soon . . . in a minute . . . there's plenty of time. And so,
Mother, I slept over there another night, and at 5 A.M. I looked up to
see him standing over my bed all in black. He had this black suit
and this black tie and this black beard—only his eyes were red from
not sleeping. I had no idea why he was in such a hurry to get to the
cemetery—you might have thought he didn't want to keep his dead
mother waiting. Breakfast was already on the table, a loaf of bread
and some olives and these different goat and sheep cheeses, but he
was looking awfully worried, and suddenly he said to me, but really
serious, as if he were sounding some kind of a warning, "If anyone
asks who you are, tell them the truth, I mean that you're Efi's girlfriend, and that you were supposed to come with him, and that at
the last minute he couldn't get away from the army . . ."

—Yes. It was such a weird thing to say, "Tell the truth"—as if
otherwise I might tell some lie that would get him into trouble . . .

—How should I know? Maybe that I was his new mistress and
that he wanted to do it with me in the graveyard . . .

—No, I didn't say anything. I didn't know what he was talking
about. I was too taken aback to do anything but nod. I was sleepy
too, and I was having this new kind of cramps, which went from my
stomach down into my knees . . .

—No. Yes. Cramps like when you have your period, only worse.
We left the house at about six. It was very cold out, but dry and

clear, with just a little snow left on some of the cars and fences. And then I realized what the rush was about, because two big taxis were already waiting in the street to drive behind us and pick up all the others . . .

—No. I asked him about them afterward. They weren't relatives at all.

—Yes. He belongs to an old Jerusalem family that moved to Crete and back again, but he doesn't have much family in Jerusalem. Mostly he stopped for a lot of old women, all these widows who were friends of the grandmother and didn't want to miss the ceremony, weather permitting, which it was. They looked like something out of a Greek movie, all these quiet little early birds all bundled up and dressed in black, waiting like lonely crows on the corners for Mr. Mani to pick them up and usher them tenderly, respectfully, into one of his taxis. A few of them were accompanied by old men wrapped in scarves, who made Mr. Mani so happy that he hugged them for joining his prayer group. Everyone kept saying how lucky it was that the snow had stopped, and after an hour of cruising the streets, which were just beginning to wake up, Mr. Mani had filled his taxis with old women and put the rabbi and the tombstone carver in his own car, plus the young lawyer who had argued the case before him in court. He was very worried, though, because he was still short three men. No matter how much the rabbi and the stone carver promised him he would find them in the cemetery, he couldn't relax. "You're forgetting," he kept saying, "that it's such an old cemetery that it's hardly seen a funeral for forty years . . ."

—It seemed strange to me too. You would have thought he'd have had some friends he could bring instead of depending on taxi drivers and stone carvers. I wasn't sure if he was really such a loner, or if he just didn't want his friends to have to get up so early and travel all the way to the east end of Jerusalem, beyond the walls of the Old City . . .

—No, it wasn't on the Mount of Olives, it was beneath it. To get there, Mother, you don't go by way of Mount Scopus. You have to travel through the Arab part of the city and start out on the road to Jericho, which dips down to a bridge over a wadi in this lovely valley with olive trees, after which you turn into a big, beautiful church that has this bright relief over its entrance . . .

—He told me its name, but I've forgotten . . . It's a church with another church above it, farther up the hillside, full of turrets and little golden domes that look like flowers or onions. You have to drive down this narrow, awfully steep lane with stone walls on either side that's hardly any wider than the paths between houses on the kibbutz, only—I swear, Mother—it's, like, tilted in midair, I've never seen such a street. You could feel the cars go tense with fear but also pick up speed, honking warnings to each other until suddenly we'd squeezed through and were in this old, old cemetery . . .

—No, I just told you, it's not on the Mount of Olives, it's below it. It's much farther down, a huge expanse of old graves on this bare, pinkish hill. There's a fantastic view from there. You can see the whole Old City with its big mosques in their huge squares, and the church spires, and David's City, and the white towers of Jewish Jerusalem in the background. It was such a clear, clear day, Mother, and we had the sun at our backs. It's this terribly old cemetery, without paths, without flowers, without a single tree, perfectly bare and full of broken tombstones. It's a really captivating place . . .

—No, you were never there.

—You couldn't have been. You're wrong. I can't believe you ever were there . . .

—No. It's not a place tourists get to. There's something unworldly about it. I'll take you there some day and you'll realize you've never been there. It's awfully captivating . . .

—Captivating . . . you'll understand when you see it. Even that young lawyer, who was born in Jerusalem and knows the whole city, was so excited to be there that he couldn't thank Mr. Mani enough for drafting him into his prayer group. We began moving forward in this slow little line with the stone carver leading the way, because there are no signs there or anything. The rabbi ran up the hill to look for some more men, and the lawyer and Mr. Mani and me lent the old ladies a hand and helped them past the broken tombstones, some of which still had a little snow on them, because we didn't want them to slip and break their necks . . .

—It was an experience, Mother. If only those cramps in the pit of my stomach hadn't kept getting worse . . .

—Just a minute, wait . . . that's part of the story . . .

—No . . . yes, like the cramps when you have your period, but not exactly. Listen, though. In the end we came to this new tombstone, and the old women stood around it all agog to read the inscription, one of them even started sobbing a little to herself, and we waited for the rabbi to find two more men while the stone carver tidied up around this grave where there were bits of cement and gravel—not Efi's grandmother's grave but the one next to it, an old headstone half-buried in the ground that Mr. Mani had asked him to uncover. He even cleaned it and made a mound of dirt to prop it up on and started explaining something to Mr. Mani and the lawyer, who bent down to get a better look. I went over to look too, but I could hardly read what was written there. I couldn't even figure out the dates. All I could make out was the name *Yosef Mani* in big letters. Meanwhile, Mr. Mani was explaining to the lawyer, who was so fascinated that he was practically face-down on the headstone, how he had found it and intended to restore it, and so I asked him if the grave was his father's. He gave this startled laugh and said, "Good lord! Can't you see how old it is? Look carefully, it's from the nineteenth century. It may even be my grandfather's grandfather's . . ." When he said that, I actually felt for a moment that that stone *was* his grandfather's grandfather, who had turned into a pink slab that was rounded at one end . . .

—No. I don't remember any other graves there belonging to his family. He would have showed them to me if there were any, so that must have been the only one. Still, Mother, standing there off to one side, because I didn't feel like mingling, I had this feeling of taking part in a ceremony like you see in one of those family graveyards in the movies. These little old ladies in black were all around, and Mr. Mani started reading from some book in his natty black suit and hat, and I thought, I must be crazy to have imagined he wanted to kill himself, why, just look at all these people who are here in his honor! You could see they thought a great deal of him, even the two workers I first mistook for Arabs that the rabbi had come back with, who already had skullcaps on their heads and were holding these little prayerbooks he had given them and rocking back and forth in prayer. And even if I was keeping my distance, by now I felt like one of the family, although it wasn't exactly a family yet but only a formula for one . . . at which exact moment, Mother, without turning around, I knew that *they* were back, that author or director or cameraman or whoever. I had thought they had left me for good, but they had been following me from a distance, or from high up, and now they took charge of me again. The rabbi sang the prayer for the dead real rhapsodically, in this oriental scale, and Mr. Mani finally got to say his mourner's prayer, his voice catching and then breaking without warning into these sobs that made all the old ladies burst into tears too. One of them began calling out some name —it must have been the grandmother's—and screaming something. But she seemed more moved by duty than by grief, as if she were only trying to get us into the spirit of things, and meanwhile the rabbi was crooning away again—and I, Mother, I stood there entranced by it all, intrigued by all those ancient Sephardim, although it was really that little thing inside me that felt that way, because by now I was dizzy and had a headache, and I felt that not only was I getting my period but that something more serious was going on. Something down there was squirming to get out, I was sure of it now. All the exertion of running after Mr. Mani to keep him from killing himself was making Mani Junior flop around like a fish on dry land—and, Mother, I was so afraid that I was going to lose him right there and then in front of everyone that I sat myself down on a grave to hold him in or at least to keep everyone from seeing . . .

—No, just a minute . . . please . . . please . . .

—No, listen . . . please . . .

—Later . . . later . . .

—No, it wasn't blood. It wasn't that sticky feeling. It wasn't a liquid feeling at all. It was more like these light little legs running up and down, over my crotch and my thighs . . .

—Yes, like someone's legs. I called it a spider before, which made you wince, but that's what I was thinking of. Is it really so disgusting or upsetting to you, Mother, if I call it a spider? But who can I tell my feelings to if not you?

—All right . . . never mind . . .

—No, not at all. It wasn't strange or disgusting. It was this feeling of being about to lose something oh-so-lovely that I was attached to, of . . . oh, I don't know . . .

—A fantasy . . . maybe . . . but how can you know if you never miscarried yourself?

—I was scared to death, Mother. I just froze and decided not to move . . . And so when the ceremony was over, and everyone got ready to go, and they all put these little stones on the grave, and Mr. Mani remembered me and came over, all contented-looking and full of his mourner's prayer, I told him that I wanted to stay and look at the view. It was such a beautiful day, I said, and I would find my way back to the bus station by myself. He seemed to have no idea how frightened I was, and he wasn't afraid to leave me there because the stone carver was staying behind to do some things too, and so he said good-bye in this casual manner, as if it were the most natural thing, maybe because he felt sure that in any case I'd come bouncing back to him like a yo-yo, and started to lead his little band of old ladies back to the taxis . . .

—Wait . . . wait . . .

—Yes, all by myself . . . But it was the middle of the morning, and everything seemed so quiet and safe there, and up on top of the hill, in the cemetery on Mount Zion, right below that big hotel, there were lots of Jews and tourists—and anyway, I had to wait for the contractions to stop, I had to do what I could to save a life . . .

—Of course I'm not in control of all that happens down there, but I had to do what I could, Mother . . . and after half an hour or so it really did let up and I was just left with this terrible heaviness in my arms and legs. I looked around and saw I was alone, because the stone carver had taken off somewhere down the hill, and so I decided to take the contrary route again, and rather than head back down toward that crazily steep, narrow lane by the walls of the church, I started up toward the hotel and all those people . . . and anyway, going up was better and less bouncy for *him* . . .

—Right, right, exactly, the Intercontinental, the one with all those nice arches. It looked so close from below with the sun shining down on these slabs of white graves, much closer than it really was. It was only after I had started up the path from the old Sephardic cemetery to the Ashkenazic one above it, past all those tombstones whose inscriptions kept getting jumbled in my head, that I realized that it was a steeper, longer climb than I had thought, especially since I had to keep stopping, because the cramps kept coming back. There were still little patches of snow here and there, and I felt I might start bleeding any minute—this whole miscarriage was beginning to seem more dangerous to me than to *him*. I was getting good and frightened, Mother, and so I walked faster, using every ounce of strength to reach the road in front of the hotel where there were all these German tourists standing around a camel and a little horse decked out in bells and bright saddlebags and some children selling souvenirs. I can't tell you how exhausted I was. I must have looked a wreck too to judge from how people were looking at me, because before I had even reached his taxi, a driver jumped up to open the door for me. He stepped on the gas while I was still getting into my seat, so that by the time I saw he was an Arab we were already driving off and it would have been awkward to stop him and get out . . .

—No. I thought it might have to do with my being alone, but I only had to say one word to him, which was "hospital" in English, for him to nod right away, as if that were the very word he had been waiting for, and start saying "Okay, okay" to calm me down, although he drove like such a madman that I thought I would miscarry right there in the back seat of his taxi. It was just a two-minute drive, though, and before I knew it he was pulling into this inner courtyard of a church, that big, massive building the other way from Mount Scopus, I had never known it was—

—Yes, exactly, Augusta Victoria, how did you know? I can see you know your way around there . . . but it's not a church like everyone thinks it is, it's a hospital . . .

—Right, right. The lower tower, the squat one, with those dark walls, not the tall, thin one . . .

—Yes, that's it. Did you know it wasn't a church but a hospital?

—Yes, a hospital. You enter this huge inner courtyard with trees and stone benches and gardens and fountains and the wings of the building all around them, just like in those TV series about the British Empire in India or Egypt, with these immense, silent corridors and these big rooms with high ceilings. Every movement that you make has this somber echo, and the taxi driver, who was falling all over himself to help, kept saying "Hospital, hospital" to prove that he had brought me to the right place despite the ride's being so short. He even helped me out of the taxi and began walking me carefully to the emergency room . . .

—What should I have told him? "Leave me alone, get me out of here, I don't want your Arab hospital"?

—No, tell me! What should I have told him? You want me to have told him right to his face, "Take your dirty hands off me"?

—Then what are you trying to say?

—No, I know that's not what you said, but it's what it's beginning to sound like. You always give me the feeling that if I tell you anything the least bit strange about myself, you right away think there's something wrong with me . . .

—Wait . . . wait . . .

—Yes, Mother, I was admitted as a patient . . .

—Wait . . . just a minute . . .

—No. Just until the evening.

—I wasn't out of my mind at all. I still had these cramps, I felt weak, and something down there was still moving and walking around. I was afraid I might start to bleed any minute. You have no idea how exhausted I was, I had gotten up exhausted that morning, and so the minute I saw some beds in this room the man brought me to, which wasn't the emergency room at all but just an empty room belonging to some ward that he took me to by mistake, all I wanted to do was to flop down on them. It was so quiet under those high ceilings and those big, arched stone windows that I felt not only back in my story, in that movie or book that went wherever I did, but that the story had ended and I was now being shown or read, which fit perfectly with all that had happened since the minute I arrived in Jerusalem. And so I took off my shoes and lay down on a bed, and the taxi driver, who was wearing this bright cap and seemed to like taking care of me, put a pillow beneath me and covered me with a blanket and went to look for a nurse . . .

—What's the matter?

—What was crazy about it? It was actually rather nice to be lying there quietly under that warm blanket, facing this huge stone window that looked out on the Wilderness of Judea. It was like being outside the world. The driver took a while to find a nurse, who realized as soon as she came that I was an Israeli and not just some tourist and gave me this disapproving look. I began to stammer something in English, but that taxi driver was driving me crazy, he wouldn't leave and just went on standing there—I tell you, it was

like out of some comedy, the way he listened without the least embarrassment . . . and the worst part was that after all those years of
studying English I couldn't get out the simplest word like "pregnant" or "miscarriage" or "bleeding," so that soon the driver began
butting in and explaining things in Arabic, which made the nurse
even madder at him for bringing me uninvited instead of taking me
to Hadassah . . .

—Yes, exactly. I could see that she didn't even want to examine
me. She wanted me out of that bed and back into that taxi and out
of that hospital. But since her English was no better than mine she
had to use sign language, saying "Hadassah" over and over while
pointing to the driver, who began making these big, desperate ges-
tures himself, because by now he was frightened of what he had
done and kept urging me in this excited voice, "Hadassah, Jewish
hospital." Except that, suddenly, Mother, I had this need to stay put
and absolutely not to move, because not only was I exhausted by
that whole adventure in the cemetery, I felt that I might start bleeding any minute and musn't get up if I wanted to keep my baby. And
so I just shook my head and curled up like a fetus myself beneath
that blanket, holding onto it for dear life . . .

—Yes, they would have had to tear me away from it, why not?
And besides, my feelings were hurt too. Why not? If I had landed
up in their hospital, the least they could do was examine me and see
what was wrong. What were they so afraid of? That they might have
to take care of a Jew for once in return for all the Arabs we take care
of in our hospitals . . . ?

—But what kind of complications, Mother?

—But how? That's ridiculous . . .

—That isn't so. There was nothing disturbed-looking about me.
Don't try defending them, they just didn't want to . . . Anyway,
when that nurse saw I wasn't budging, she stalked out of the room
with the driver, who had this hangdog look. She must have gone to
get someone else, but in the meantime an hour went by and there
still was no bleeding. I felt cold and fell into this really delicious
sleep, opening half an eye now and then to look out the window at
the desert, off which this dry eastern light was glinting, while thinking that the worst was over with. I even decided to go to the bathroom to see what had happened down there, maybe there was some

sign, and out in the corridor I saw the driver looking depressed. God knows what he was waiting for, maybe to take me to Hadassah or for his fare—and so I went back to the room and brought him some money to cheer him up, after all, it wasn't his fault, "It's not your fault," I said to him with a friendly pat on that bright cap, and he understood what I said and even gave a wave of his hand. From there I went to the bathroom, which was very old and big and full of light. It was incredibly spic-and-span, with these gleaming copper faucets and giant sinks, and I went into a toilet to check my under-pants, and there wasn't any blood but there was this scary stain, Mother—it was black with something smeary in it, maybe some part of *him,* and I felt so desperate that I began to cry inside of me. I wrapped the underpants in an old newspaper that I found there, and then I put the dress back on and returned to the room. The driver was gone. There was just the echo of his footsteps down the corridor, and so I got back into bed and lay there in despair, dozing on and off, until the nurse shook me a little to wake me. She had a dark young doctor with her who spoke a little Hebrew, and he began asking me questions in this dry manner, and I answered ev-erything and took out the newspaper and showed him the stained underpants, and he glanced at them without a word and took them to the window to get a better look while I went on telling what I felt. All the time he didn't touch me or write anything down, he just interrupted me once or twice to ask—I couldn't tell if he was angry or laughing—"But what makes you so sure you're pregnant? Who told you?" No matter how much I explained it to him, the dates, and missing my period, and everything, he wouldn't believe me. Not that he was an extremist like you, Mother. He never said it was only my imagination. But he kept aloof and didn't even take my pulse, although I would have been happy for him to examine me, I knew he was thinking, these Israelis, they only come to our hospitals to make trouble, even if he wasn't sure yet what kind of trouble I was making. Whatever it was, he was going to avoid it like the plague—and so when I asked him again about the stain and did he think it was dangerous, I saw he wasn't taking it seriously, "It's nothing," he said, "it's just—" and I knew he wanted to say "dirt," but he didn't, he caught himself and said "mud," he was so pleased he could say it in Hebrew that he said it over and over . . .

—Yes, that was all. He wrapped the underpants back up in the newspaper to take them for a lab test and pointed to the west and snapped rudely, "Why don't you go back there? Go back to your mother, go back to your father, go back to your health fund, you people have *health funds,*" he pronounced the word, Mother, with this really weird hatred, you would have thought that the whole trouble with us was our health funds, and not even them but the word for them. Afterward, though, he became a little kinder. He said I could stay and rest a while if I wanted, and then he said something to the nurse in Arabic and they left, and a while later she came back with some lunch . . .

—I don't know. I wasn't in any rush. I wanted to rest some more, and I had already warmed up the bed so nicely, and outside that arched window was the desert with this lovely blue patch of the Dead Sea, and I knew that I'd never again in my life have such a private view of it . . .

—Yes, Mother, the desert, of all places . . . the good old desert . . . I've always loved it and I always will, take my word for it. And now it had this fabulous patch of blue right in the middle of it . . .

—But I was under a blanket, Mother, taking in a desert just like the one we have here, with this extra scoop of blue that we always used to dream about, and all of a sudden it had this flock of black goats in it too, a huge flock of them on a hilltop flowing on and on, you couldn't see the goatherd for the goats, they kept moving toward my window and disappearing beneath it as if they were entering the hospital . . .

—Around five or six. It was already getting dark. Some patients began drifting in, these elderly Arab women, and I hurried to put on my shoes and get out of there. I walked to the street, which was dimly lit by a street lamp, and there on that fading horizon, Mother, were the blurred, jagged skylines of the two cities, the Arab and the Jewish, all jumbled up with each other, and men were selling vegetables and groceries from stands, and I saw them all look at me and point to someone who was calling to me from an ambulance that was taking some hospital staff home, and it was the same nurse who had taken care of me, she had just come off her shift and was in her street clothes, wearing makeup and all spiffed up. She must have felt guilty for not wanting me in her hospital because now she offered me a ride, or maybe she was worried that one of those men might start up with me. But anyway, she said she would be happy to take me "to Jerusalem"—as if we weren't in Jerusalem already but somewhere else, on our way there, and there were no other place in the world I could hope to get to. And really, right then and there on that hill, looking out on those two cities stewing in the same twilight, Tel Aviv, Mother, seemed as far away as could be, it seemed unreal, and so I started back down into Jerusalem from the opposite direction, and it was the most wonderful ride, Mother, through all these places you've never been in, all these Arab neighborhoods and villages inside the city. We kept crossing these empty wadis that still had bits of snow in them and coming out in these dark streets full of potholes and puddles that suddenly opened up into these lively little village centers full of people and children and shopping baskets and donkeys. It all looked so nice and cozy, Mother, as if they really had themselves a good life, and had maybe even gotten used to us, and the driver, who was driving as slowly as he could up and down these narrow streets, kept sticking his head out the window to talk and joke with all the people. He brought all the passengers home to their front door, making this big circle until he dropped the last nurse off by Jaffa Gate. I thought I would get off with her, but he said he would take me to the Jewish part of the city, he even asked the address to show me he knew his way around there, only I didn't want him to have to look for it, so I said, "It doesn't matter, just drop me off by the Jerusalem Theater," and for the first time in three days I felt that I wasn't going against the current anymore but flowing right along with it. We drove through the same streets that had been so empty early that morning, and now they were full of life. And even though there wasn't a snowflake left in them, Mother, you could see that the memory of the snow was making everyone happy, it was as if they had survived some great ordeal of nature. And so I was back at the Jerusalem Theater again, and at the exact same time of day too, because it was exactly six-thirty. But this time the theater was all lit up and people were waiting outside it, and without thinking twice about it, Mother, as if it were something I did every evening, I cut across the field behind the parking lot by the old leper hospital like an ordinary person going home. The day had made a real Jerusalemite out of me, an old-time Sephardi with a touch of Arab! I wasn't even thinking of his suicide anymore. I only wanted to say good-bye and make sure he hadn't been hurt by my leaving him so abruptly that morning. As soon as I turned into his street, though, I saw there was a power failure there. Everything was blacked out, the houses, the streetlights, everything—and so I climbed the stairs in the darkness and knocked on the old door, and as usual, Mother, there was no answer, but I thought, he's just forgotten how to open it, and so I took out the neighbor's key that I still had and opened the door, and this time the apartment wasn't hot, it wasn't dark either, because these little candles were burning everywhere, and I saw him come out of the bathroom, all pale and frightened in his pajamas. He was holding a big razor blade and his face, Mother, was shaven. The beard was gone from it, but it was all cut up too, and he was bleeding from the throat . . .

—Yes, bleeding . . .

—The hell it was! It was not my imagination . . . absolutely not . . . and as soon as he saw it was only me he smiled like a naughty boy with this sheepish sort of smile, although maybe it was also a little mocking—I don't think it was, but it wouldn't have mattered if there was a bit of mockery in it—and he said, "Honestly, young lady, I was beginning to worry what was taking you so long . . ." And, Mother, I was so thrilled by that new tone of his, which was so much freer and easier, and especially by that darling "young lady," that I walked down that hallway in a trance and grabbed his hand and said quietly but firmly, "Please, don't do it again." Well, Mother, this shocked look came over him. He was completely taken by surprise. He ran his hand over his face and throat and was alarmed by all the blood on it—and all at once, Mother, I stopped being angry with him, the truth had finally dawned on me, which was that he couldn't control this impulse he had to do away with himself every evening, because he had no reason for doing it, Mother, he only thought that he did, and even that thought wasn't his own but came from someone or somewhere else . . .

—Maybe that grandmother had left something behind in her room that was haunting him without his knowing it . . .

—No, listen, Mother, please. Don't just laugh off everything I say. Listen to me . . .

—Yes, from someone or somewhere else . . . shhh . . . shhh . . . don't move . . .

—No, wait . . . don't move . . .

—No, don't open the door . . . not now . . .

—You can always say we were sleeping . . . you've a right to . . .

—You don't have to lie . . . but you can't just open that door automatically for this whole kibbutz as if it were the door of a bus . . .

—Shhh . . . shhh . . .

—What's not nice about it?

—There, thank God, they're gone . . . Who could it have been?

—Then I'm turning out the light . . . Are you listening?

—Yes, a real mystery, that's what I felt. Except that instead of getting all uptight, which is what you would have done, I did just the opposite and began to feel this great calm . . .

—Impossible. His mourner's beard, Mother, was just an excuse . . .

—To go on cutting himself . . .

—I do know . . . I do know . . .

—I saw it . . . and I know . . .

—You don't believe me, Mother, because you don't want to believe. You have this great mass of collective wisdom behind you, and maybe here in the desert you need it to bolster you, but you're so pitifully spooked by the least hint of mystery, which is why you have to root it out so ruthlessly with the iron logic of broad daylight . . . But it doesn't spook *me*, Mother, any more than Mr. Mani and all his real or imaginary suicides. I found some towel to staunch the blood with, and we sat in the kitchen while waiting for it to stop, and I lit some more little candles and we drank some milk, because we couldn't boil water on account of the power being off, and we had a real face-to-face talk at last, and suddenly I realized, Mother, that over the past three days we had made a secret pact, it wasn't anything written or clear, but it was enough to make me tell him what had happened to me in the cemetery, and how I got to Augusta Victoria, and he sat there hanging on each word. I could see that the idea of someone's seed inside me didn't bother him in the least, not even if it was his own son's, which was why he didn't rush to turn everything into a hallucination like you do, because psychology is just a parable for him and not reality itself. He simply sat there daubing the blood on his throat and looking at it now and then on the towel, and we began to be friends. He told me all about Augusta Victoria, and the German Kaiser's visit to Jerusalem, and how and why the place was built—and when I told him about my ride in the ambulance and all those neighborhoods I never knew about, he said how sorry he was that I was going back to Tel Aviv without seeing the real Jerusalem, by which he meant the Jerusalem of his ancestors, and he mentioned how he goes every Friday to the marketplace in the Old City, because the courts aren't in session then . . . and I was so touched, Mother, by his faith in my ability to extricate myself from Jerusalem in the end and get back to the coast or the desert without compulsively walking in on him every night that I said to him on the spot, "As a matter of fact, I'd love to see the Old City with you tomorrow morning, because not only don't the courts sit on Fridays, the university has no classes either . . ."

—Nothing special. We waited for the lights to come back on, but they didn't until eleven, and meanwhile there was no television and no radio and no hot water to drink or wash with. We just sat and shivered in the dark, wrapped in blankets like in some tent city, reading the newspapers by candlelight. From time to time I tried getting him to talk about his childhood in Crete, and he showed me some photographs of his family, and of Efi as a little boy, and in the end he put me to sleep in that grandmother's bed, the same one I slept in the first night . . .

—No, the room was perfectly normal. Maybe now that he was into razor blades, he didn't need scaffolds anymore . . .

—I'm not laughing, Mother . . . I didn't laugh once in the course of those three days, and I'm perfectly serious now too. It's all I can do to keep myself from running to the dining hall this minute and phoning to see if he's dead or alive . . . shhh . . . shhh . . . I swear, there's someone outside the window . . . it's unbelievable . . . maybe it's me they're looking for, not you . . .

—A couple of people saw me get off the bus.

—Oh. Yes, of course. Anyway, it must have been toward midnight, I had been tossing and turning, because I couldn't fall asleep after spending most of the day in bed. I kept thinking of that wonderful view of the desert with the blue scoop of the Dead Sea and that flock of black goats trooping into my window. In the middle of the night the phone rang, and this time Mr. Mani was good enough to answer it, and I realized at once, just from hearing his end of it, that it was my poor darling Efi, who'd had a visit from the mobile telephone unit at that checkpoint he's stuck in outside Beirut. I listened to his father tell him about the unveiling, but he didn't say a word about me, not one single word about my having telephoned or come to Jerusalem or stayed over or gone to the cemetery. It was as if he were afraid to admit that I was there on the other side of the wall, afraid of being suspected of trying to be his own son—and I was devastated, Mother, not by him but by myself, by what this terrible need for a father has done to me . . .

—Yes . . . yes . . .

—It's true . . . I admit it . . .

—Yes, yes . . .

—Maybe you're right, maybe it was just some fantasy of mine . . . there, are you happy? Does that make you feel better?

—For me? For *me?* Do you really have doubts about my sanity?

—Yes, you do . . . why don't you admit it . . .

—No, I'm not crying. I'm really not . . .

—It's nothing . . .

—Dearest Mother . . . Mother . . .

—The next morning? Nothing. I couldn't go back on my promise to let him take me to the marketplace, and it was a bore. He put on these old clothes, not even a tie, just a sweater and an old jacket, which made him lose all his presence and his charm, and we went with these baskets to buy all sorts of things for a few shekels less in the alleys of the Old City. After that he took me to the Wailing Wall, as if I hadn't already been there, and then he wanted to visit some Arabs he knew in Silwan. The more he talked about them, the less I knew what he was saying about them, whether they hated us or loved us or wanted to get rid of us or were attached to us or were peaceful or were up to no good. I couldn't tell what he needed them for, and by then Jerusalem was getting me down. You could already smell that awful Sabbath of theirs coming on, and I was afraid that the bus station might shut down early and leave me stranded there again, so I tried tactfully telling him not to get too carried away with all those back alleys of his. "Don't forget my bus," I said, "I have to get home," and he finally got the hint and brought me to the station and put me in line for the bus to Tel Aviv, and I jumped the railing at the last second and caught the bus to Beersheba, because I wanted to be with you, my one and only mother, and to say, *Hey, Ma, it's me, listen to this,* even though I knew you'd say, *There goes Hagar, looking for a father again,* and you're right, you're always right, Mother, what can I say, I know you are, but I also know there's something deeper than your psychology, maybe even something astounding, why is it that you never remarried all these years, what made you stay faithful to that man over there whose photograph glows in the dark, more peaceful than the bookcase that it's standing on, never moving, never changing, our impossible, our dead hero, who exists more than any of us in a single photograph, which follows us everywhere like some ultimate test, staring out with me into the darkness like a ghost, and that's not my imagination, maybe he's inside me right now, straddling, how do I know, the thin line between life and death . . .

B I O G R A P H I C A L

Supplements

HAGAR SHILOH Hagar returned to Tel Aviv the next morning but could not concentrate on studying for her English exam because that Saturday evening she got her period, which was accompanied by strong cramps and heavy bleeding. She preferred to think of it as an "early miscarriage" rather than as a "late period," and her mood improved when Efrayim Mani returned from the army and their relationship resumed. Since Efrayim, who was fresh from the harsh experience of serving in Lebanon and bitter over a new stint of reserve duty already scheduled for him, did not seem eager to hear about Hagar's visit to Jerusalem, she told him only briefly about it. Not wanting to scare him off, she did not mention her "pregnancy" either. A few weeks later, however, she became pregnant for real, although less enthusiastically than the first time and more as if in fulfillment of an obligation to Efi's father.

When he found out that Hagar was pregnant, Efrayim was both alarmed and furious. At first he broke off with her completely. Eventually, however, on the advice of his father, who thought that Hagar was a bit strange, he agreed to acknowledge paternity.

The child, a healthy baby boy, was born in the autumn of 1983 and, despite Hagar's mother's objections, named Roni after her father. Although by then Hagar had successfully finished her preparatory course at the university, she did not begin her studies in the film department because her grandmother Naomi, young in spirit though she was, could not cope with a baby in the house; Hagar was a heavy sleeper, and when the child cried at night Naomi had to take care of him, which soon brought her to the verge of collapse. And so Hagar was forced to move back to the kibbutz, especially since the rehabilitation department of the defense ministry was not liberal to the point of supporting a child born out of wedlock. The best Hagar could do, after knocking on many doors, was to obtain an increase in her monthly stipend.

Efrayim Mani not unjustly felt deceived and refused to marry Hagar. He was willing to take formal (but not, as he put it, "emotional") responsibility for the infant, and he agreed to allot a third of his salary to its support. Gavriel Mani, on the other hand, or *Mr. Mani,* as Hagar continued to think of him, became attached to his fatherless grandson and sometimes traveled to the Negev to see and play with him. These visits, which became more frequent when Efrayim went abroad to study in London, deepened the tie that had already developed between the child's grandfather and grandmother.

Once her son was six, Hagar, who had felt isolated and neglected during her first years on the kibbutz, found it possible to resume her studies. In 1988 she registered for a joint major in the Jewish history and education departments of the University of Beersheba, where she was accepted without a high school diploma on the strength of her preparatory year in Tel Aviv in 1982. Today, at the age of twenty-eight, she is still not married. Despite pressure from her mother and her friends, she refuses to go for therapy or even for psychological counseling.

❱ YA'EL SHILOH   Although she sought to conceal her pleasure over the telephone, Ya'el was greatly relieved when, twenty-four hours after their conversation, she learned that Hagar was not pregnant. But Hagar, who went on seeing Efrayim Mani, was less candid with her mother when she really did become pregnant several weeks later, and by the time she broke the news to Ya'el it was too late to take medical measures.

Ya'el felt deeply hostile toward Hagar's pregnancy, which seemed to her completely uncalled for and a source of future aggravation. She also felt sure that Hagar's becoming pregnant was a provocative act aimed at herself. Moreover, although her progressive views compelled her to admit that it was his right, Efrayim Mani's refusal to marry Hagar seemed a slap in the face to her. In the earlier stages of Hagar's pregnancy she still hoped for a spontaneous abortion, but this did not materialize. When the child was born in October 1983, Ya'el was secretly pleased that Hagar did not return to the kibbutz with it and sought to continue her studies in Tel Aviv. Within a few weeks, however, once it became clear that Hagar's seventy-five-year-old grandmother could not manage with an infant in her apartment, Hagar was forced to come back to Mash'abei Sadeh. The moment Ya'el saw her and her baby get out of the truck that had brought them from Tel Aviv after delivering avocados there, she underwent a change of heart. It was as if all at once she understood that there might be a deeper reason for the child's existence, and from then on she did all she could to care for it and help Hagar.

Although the young father, Efrayim Mani, traveled to the Negev now and then to see his son, he was so aloof toward him and Hagar that his infrequent visits were a burden. Once, in the early spring of 1984, when Efrayim was again doing reserve duty in Lebanon, his place was taken by his father, Justice of the Peace Gavriel Mani, who wished to have a look at the grandson he had not seen since the circumcision.

Indeed, it proved to be an unusual and memorable visit, not only because of the lovely presents that the grandfather brought, but even more so, because of the warmth he displayed toward Hagar and her mother and the interest he took in their surroundings. Upon hearing, for example, that the grave of Ben-Gurion was in the kibbutz of Sdeh Boker some twenty kilometers away, he insisted on seeing it and was accompanied by Ya'el.

Their trip there and back took longer than expected, and when they returned to the kibbutz that evening Hagar noticed a new glow in her mother's face. As soon as Mr. Mani drove off, she demanded to know what had happened. Although taken aback, Ya'el was forced to admit that she found Roni's grandfather quite attractive, even if he did come from an unfamiliar world.

Two weeks later Mr. Mani arrived again, dressed in black as was

his custom with a thin red tie. This time he asked Ya'el to take a trip
to Mitzpeh Ramon, because he wished to see the famous canyon
there.

Their excursion, which was even longer than the previous one,
brought them closer together. On their way back indeed, although
she tried making light of it, Ya'el mustered the courage to ask the
judge whether there had been any thought of suicide in his mind at
the time of Hagar's visit to Jerusalem in December 1982. While he
did not seem surprised by the question, which he in fact appeared to
have anticipated, Mr. Mani answered it vaguely, almost as if it concerned someone else. In practically the same breath he mentioned
that Hagar's behavior during those three days had seemed rather
odd to him, although perhaps it had to do with her being in Jerusalem by herself for the first time. Once back in the kibbutz, he hurried to set out for Jerusalem and would not even stay for a cup of
coffee.

Nevertheless, Mr. Mani maintained his ties with the Shilohs, and
after his son Efrayim went to London for his doctorate, he regularly
began coming in his place. Once every few weeks he would appear,
a genteel man always dressed in dark clothes. After taking his grandson for a walk on the bare, tawny hills around the kibbutz, he would
sit with the two women on their front lawn and tell them about his
family or some court case while the toddler ran in and out among
them. These conversations never touched on politics or social issues,
about which he either had no clear opinions or preferred to keep
the ones he had to himself, even though he was always curious to
hear those of others. And yet as friendly and "judicially attentive" as
he was, Ya'el soon realized that she must be patient and not expect
any quick "romantic" developments. Fortunately, he did not mind
the arid landscape. On the contrary, he often went hiking in it with
her and seemed to relish the desert views.

When Hagar and her mother found out that Mr. Mani was driving to the kibbutz via the West Bank, along the road from Jerusalem
to Hebron, they sought to talk him out of it. Mr. Mani, however,
insisted that there was no need to take the long way to Beersheba,
since the route through Hebron was perfectly safe and the villagers
along it were peaceful. Once, at some gas station, he related, they
had even tried selling him a horse.

Nevertheless, in the early autumn of 1987, a large rock was thrown at the judge's car as he drove through Dir-el-Mana, a village some twenty kilometers south of Hebron. That evening he confessed to Ya'el that it would be wiser to stop coming via Hebron, even though he felt drawn to that route.

SECOND CONVERSATION

Heraklion, Crete

4 to 7 P.M. Tuesday, August 1, 1944

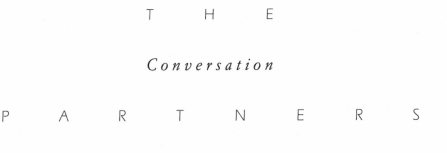

T H E

Conversation

P A R T N E R S

EGON BRUNER Twenty-two years old. Born in 1922 on
an estate near Flansburg, in the north German district of Schleswig-
Holstein, to Werner Sauchon and Mariette Bruner.

Admiral Werner Sauchon (b. 1861) was one of the most highly
lauded German officers in the First World War, in which he served
with special distinction in the great Baltic Sea battles of 1914. In
1916 he and his wife Andrea lost their only son Egon on the Western Front, in the trenches of Verdun. At first they considered adopt-
ing an infant born to a family relation of theirs, but to their great
disappointment, the child died soon after birth. Despairing of any
other solution, they decided jointly, after much debate, that an or-
phaned young servant girl named Mariette Bruner, whose parents
had worked on the Sauchon estate for many years, should secretly
bear the admiral a child. It was agreed that the offspring would
maintain ties with its mother and bear her name as her child out-of-
wedlock, but that it would be raised by the Sauchons as a "candi-
date for adoption"—which, should it "prove worthy," would be
recognized as their heir at the age of twenty-one.

When Egon was a year old, his mother Mariette left the estate and
moved to Hamburg, where she eventually married Werner Raiman,
the director of a proletarian theater, by whom she had a second

child. Egon grew up on his father's estate and was encouraged to call his father and his father's wife "Grandfather" and "Grandmother," or more affectionately, "Opapa" and "Oma." He studied both with private tutors who were brought to the house and at a nearby village school. For the most part, his schooling was supervised by his "grandmother" Andrea, who devoted herself to making it as close as possible to the excellent education received by her beloved son killed in World War I. Egon was a slim, rather nearsighted, blond boy of average height who showed a clear preference for the liberal arts. When he was young, he was sent to Hamburg during school vacations to stay with his mother and stepfather, but after the death of Admiral Sauchon in 1935, when Werner Raiman ran afoul of the Nazi police in Hamburg and the Raimans moved to a village in Bavaria, Egon's contact with his mother was greatly reduced.

In 1940, at the age of eighteen, Egon was called up by the Wehrmacht and inducted into the navy at the request of his grandmother, who wished him to carry on the family tradition. Because of his poor eyesight, he was sent to a medic's course at a naval base in Hamburg. After completing the course in early 1941, however, he was not posted to a naval vessel, because starting in March of that year, plans for the impending invasion of Russia led to a redeployment of forces in which many sailors and naval officers, who had been relatively inactive, were transferred to the infantry. In April 1941, once again on his grandmother's intervention, Egon was posted as a medic with the 7th Alpine Division based near Nürnberg, and in May he was attached to the 3rd Brigade, then being augmented in preparation for action in the Balkans. On May 16 he flew with the brigade to Athens, from where he was parachuted into Crete with the special task force of General Student in the second wave of the German airborne invasion that took place on Tuesday afternoon, the twentieth of May. Although Egon's unit suffered extremely high casualties and was evacuated to Germany several weeks after Crete's conquest, Egon remained behind on the island with its occupation garrison. In the laconic postcards he wrote to his grandmother, he promised to explain the circumstances of this development when he came home on leave, but his first furlough, which was scheduled for April 1942, was postponed because he ceded his place to a comrade who wished to get married in Germany. A second leave, in January 1943, was canceled in the wake of the disaster in Stalingrad, and Egon did not set out for home until April 1944, when he flew in a military transport plane to Salonika and joined a northbound convoy there. After the latter was attacked by Greek partisans and forced to return to its base, however, he decided to forego the journey to Germany and returned to Crete on a Greek ship. His infrequent letters did not reach his grandmother either, because, from 1942 on, Crete was lumped by the military censors together with the Eastern front and much mail from there was never delivered. Egon himself, on the other hand, received all his grandmother's letters and even an occasional letter from his mother. He was also sent the copies of Homer's *Iliad* and *Odyssey* that he requested, as well as a history of ancient Greece, which arrived via navy general staff headquarters. In late July 1944 he was informed that his grandmother Andrea was planning to visit him—and indeed, she arrived on the first of August in a light aircraft that flew directly from Athens and landed at Heraklion Airport early that afternoon.

ANDREA SAUCHON Born in 1870 in Lübeck, the daughter of a Protestant minister named Kurtmaier. She graduated nursing school in Hamburg in 1894 and went to work in a military hospital, where she met the naval officer Werner Sauchon, who dropped by frequently to visit some sailors of his who had been wounded in a naval exercise. They were married in 1896 and took up residence in the officers' barracks of the imperial navy, and toward the end of that year their only son Egon was born. Once Werner had risen through the ranks, the Sauchons moved to the family estate in Holstein, where Egon was raised. With the outbreak of the world war, Egon was called to the colors and sent to the Western Front after a short period of basic training. He was only twenty when he was killed. His death affected Andrea more severely than it did her husband, who was involved in fighting the war, in which he served with great merit and won the highest decorations. However, when Werner Sauchon retired from active service after the German defeat and the Versailles Peace Treaty, he too began to feel the enormity of his loss. Before long the bereaved parents started looking for a surrogate son, which they found in Egon

Bruner, who was conceived in 1921 in mutual agreement and trust. To spare his beloved wife the slightest embarrassment, the admiral insisted that the boy bear his mother's name until the age of twenty-one. Although Andrea was over fifty when the second Egon was born, she devoted herself to him like a young mother while making sure he kept in touch with Mariette, who left the estate amicably a year after her son's birth. Andrea herself was quite content to be called "Grandmother" by the boy.

The Sauchons regarded the Nazi rise to power with a mixture of curiosity and mild sympathy, believing that the situation in Germany could not fail to improve if law and order were imposed. After her husband's death in 1935, Egon's upbringing became Andrea's sole responsibility. She kept in close contact with his unit when he was inducted into the navy in 1940 and received regular reports on his progress from the base commander. When she heard that sailors were being transferred to the infantry in advance of the planned invasion of Russia, she used her influence to arrange for Egon's posting to a crack paratroop unit. As a result, however, Andrea, whose connections in the infantry were not as good as those in the navy, lost contact with her grandson for a long period. And yet as distressed as she was by this, she was thrilled to hear that Egon had taken part in the daring conquest of Crete in May 1941. His participation in this battle, she felt, in some way made up for the first Egon's death at Verdun and she could hardly wait for her adopted hero to come home. But Egon did not return to Germany with the 7th Paratrooper Division and remained with the occupation force in Crete, from where his postcards, starting with the winter of 1942, were almost secretively brief. And yet although this made her long to see him even more, she was forced to conclude, after vainly waiting for him three times, that he looked forward to their meeting less than she did. Nevertheless, she wrote to him more than ever and sent him the Greek history and the Homer that he had asked for. It seemed most odd to her that he had stayed in Crete with a rear-line unit instead of moving on with his old brigade, which was now fighting in the East. In the summer of 1944, after numerous German setbacks and the Allied invasion of Normandy had stricken her with the fear that she might never see him again, she used all her connections in the high command to have him recalled to Germany for the coming last stand on its soil. However, although she succeeded in having a transfer request issued by a ranking commander in the Berlin theater, the order vanished in bureaucratic channels on its way to Crete. Now too, though, Andrea Sauchon refused to give up. Taking the initiative again, she organized a group of war widows and wives of high naval officers who had fought with her husband and petitioned the general staff to allow them to visit Athens and its historical sites before these were "returned to the enemy." Her stubbornness, her resourcefulness, and above all, the renown of the name Sauchon, crowned her efforts with success and the elderly women set out across Europe for Greece, where they successfully toured Athens and its environs. A photograph of them standing among the columns of the Acropolis even appeared on the front page of the *Frankfurter Zeitung*. Andrea's real destination, however, was not Athens but Crete, where she intended to deliver Egon's transfer order personally. And so, when her traveling companions returned to Germany, she remained in the Greek capital and persuaded its military governor to fly her to Heraklion in a light craft. Twenty-four hours before her take-off, a wireless message arrived on the island announcing the distinguished old lady's arrival. Naturally, she was greatly excited by the prospect of seeing her "grandson" again after their three years' separation. He, for his part, knew nothing about the signed order in her pocket.

Her half of the conversation is missing.

—And even though I know you're tired, because how could you not be, dearest Grandmother, no, not even if you had steel in your veins, and I'm sure that you do—why, if anyone doubted it, this astounding journey of yours across Europe is proof enough!—yes, even though I know you're tired, I'm afraid I have to insist. And so before answering all the details of all the questions you've brought with you from so far away, some of which you've asked already and some of which you haven't yet, I must insist, dearest Grandmother, that you come with me right now, just as you are, in your marvelous traveling outfit and your boots. Don't think I wasn't thrilled to see them the minute you stepped off the plane, your hiking boots from the Schistan Forest! How clever of you it was to wear them. There's the wife of a military man for you! O most wonderful Grandmother, what a big hug I'd give you if only everyone weren't looking, because we don't want to do anything improper. Please, then, let me insist, before we do anything else, on taking you just as you are, in the same high spirits with which we started off this fabulous, this most incredible, this absolutely fateful meeting between us, here in this place and at this time, yes, fateful is the word, to the top of that hill right above us . . .

—No, no, it's not a mountain, Grandmother. You were born on the plains of Holstein, and so you think that every hill is a mountain. It's really just a little hill, believe me. Mountains don't look like that, and here, on this island, there are some real ones . . .

—Step by pleasurable step we'll do our best to reach that round summit that you can see so clearly from here.

—Exactly.

—Exactly.

—Yes, the visibility is magnificent today, Grandmother. I don't know if you can begin to appreciate the extent of the view that you'll have. It's as if the windows of the world have been especially scrubbed for you, and the island rinsed with clear wine, and even the clouds washed down with the finest suds! Because up in our moldy north you never see more than half of the visible world, and here you'll see the other half, and maybe more. We couldn't get over this glorious weather all morning. Just see how clear the sky is, everyone kept telling me, it's in honor of your grandmother Sauchon . . .

—Everyone knows. Everyone is thrilled by your visit. Our commanding officer, Bruno Schmelling, is even thinking of giving a little banquet tonight in your honor . . . in honor of the good old, little old Germany . . .

—Of course he's expecting you. But meanwhile, Grandmother, please, we mustn't miss a minute of this most magnificent, this best time of day. Our leisurely climb will take us to five stations, five observation points from which I'll tell you my story in the order and way it should be told, because nothing can be safe or sensible without order, isn't that what you always used to say? Well, I subscribe to that wholeheartedly, which means we don't have much time, only a few hours, of which we mustn't waste a minute in small talk or childhood reminiscences. We've got to get straight to the point and to all of the difficult questions, because it's perfectly true, Grandmother, that I've hardly been in touch for three years, hardly written to you, never taken a single leave, even though I knew how I was hurting you and Mother, because I was afraid that if I left this island I'd never come back. Who knows, perhaps deep down I did it just to lure you here, Grandmother, to this place that soon, yes, indeed, we will all have to leave without ever having bothered to understand it despite our great enthusiasm for it in the beginning. And you can see that I succeeded, because here you are! In fact, Grandmother, believe it or not, from the unforgettable moment that the most delicious news of your arrival first reached me over the wireless, I've done nothing but plan this visit! I've even written and learned all my lines by heart, ha ha . . . why, I couldn't fall asleep all night long . . .

—That's quite all right. No one's short of sleep here. We hibernated the whole first winter, and I'm still withdrawing sleep from that account.

—I've put on weight? Perhaps . . . it's certainly true that . . . after all, until recently things couldn't have been more peaceful here. The local inhabitants were friendly, the British pulled back to their great North African desert and dug in there, the Russians were falling apart—there was no one to make any trouble. And the air here gives you an appetite . . .

—Yes, Grandmother. First it was Stalingrad that gave us a bit of a jolt. Then came the invasion of Italy, and now it's the landing on that beach in France . . . what's it called?

—Exactly, that's it. So you see, as remote and peaceful as it is here, we're waking up little by little. Shall we start out?

—No, it's absolutely necessary. Please, Grandmother, I'm sure it is. I'm not trying to get away with anything. I'm ready to answer all your questions, and with that dreadful old honesty of ours. You know your grandson: would he insist on this hike if he thought it was possible to get to the bottom of things without a view of them from on top? Because it's not just a view, Grandmother, it's a character in my story. And we'd better hurry before it starts getting dark. Not that we're frightened of the dark, you and I—it's just that lately there are all kinds of hostile elements around and we have orders

not to go out after dark in groups smaller than five . . . and a
quintet, Grandmother, no matter how you count us, is more than
the two of us will ever be . . .

—Yes, it gets dark quickly here. Don't forget how far south
you've come, Grandmother. In fact, this is the southernmost point
of the Reich, and here, at thirty-five latitude, the twilight is quick
and insubstantial. None of your soulful, copper-colored, everlasting
sunsets in the bogs and woods of Schlesing that at first I was so
desperately homesick for. How I missed our merry little hunter's
lodge!

—Burned?

—And the little bridge? No, don't tell me . . . I don't want to
know . . .

—But why did they have to bomb them? Well, what does it
matter . . . we'll rebuild them . . .

—Of course I do. How could I not believe it? But enough!
Come, Grandmother, let's start out. Everything is ready. It's a good,
gentle path, a little winding, to be sure, but with an easy grade. I
checked it again this morning, trying to see it through your eyes and
judge it by your capacity. I even took a shovel to fill in the rough
parts, and pulled out some weeds, and made three special steps, and
chose our rest stops. An hour's walk, Grandmother, and we'll be at
the top, and there's a bench up there in an old Turkish outpost that
you can sit on pretty comfortably—it's protected from the winds if
there are any, but there won't be—and look out at the sunset . . .
See, I've even got a binoculars for you in this knapsack. You yourself said how clear the air is, the view on a day like this is too good
to miss. Just imagine, Grandmother, if it wasn't you but old Opapa
Sauchon who had the good fortune to be here—don't you think
he'd jump to his feet, all eighty-three years of him, and be up that
hill in no time? Do you think he'd miss a chance for a panoramic
and strategic view of the place where our Europe was born? Think
of it that way, Grandmother. Tell yourself it's for Grandfather and
try being his eyes . . .

—Thank you. Thank you, most wonderful Grandmother . . .

—Yes, Europa. The young maiden. Together with Zeus . . .

—Easy does it. Yes, I know. I've even tied a rope around my
waist and made a loop you can easily hold onto to make sure you

don't slip. Oh, someone will yet write about you—if, that is, anyone will want to write about us at all—and tell how, at the age of seventy-four, Frau Andrea Sauchon, the widow of the hero of the Battle of the Baltic, reached the southernmost point of the Thousand-Year Reich—which won't last a thousand years but may hold out a thousand days, although I'm afraid that each day will be worse than the one before it—and skipped right up a hill by the airport to look down on the Gulf of Heraklion . . .

—Sunglasses? Of course.

—I have a canteen.

—Yes. It's loaded.

—You won't be needing it.

—All right, we'll take this coat. But let me carry it.

—No, there's nothing crazy about it, you'll see . . .

—Things have gotten much worse this past month. Everyone listens to the BBC. It's reached the point that you sometimes think that the very earth is broadcasting in English under your feet. Not that the British are in any hurry to get here. Why should they be? If they wait long enough, we'll leave by ourselves . . .

—Just to shed more blood, Grandmother? What for? There's been enough bloodshed here already. Three years ago seven thousand German soldiers lost their lives on this island, and now you want more? No . . .

—But defend it how, Grandmother? A man sitting naked on his front porch couldn't be more of a sitting duck than we are. Every little fishing boat that you see down there in the harbor is spying for the enemy. Every little boy playing ball near our headquarters is a secret agent . . .

—Exactly.

—Every boat . . . never mind . . .

—That little one down there too. Why not? Anything is possible . . .

—It could be. The local inhabitants are trying to give themselves a clean bill of health to make up for their three years of cozying up to us. Before we've made a move, the English already know about it on Cyprus. Which is why, Grandmother, as you can see down there, no, over there . . .

—Exactly. They're trundling your little plane off the runway and covering it with branches. Not that it will do any good, because the fishing boats are already signaling each other, and in an hour from now all of Cyprus will know that someone important has arrived in Crete, although the description of her will cause great confusion, ha ha . . . What can be the military purpose of such a grandmother? They'll have to call a staff meeting of all their brigadiers to decide what countersteps to take . . .

—No, I'm not exaggerating. I still can't get over their bringing you here. A whole lot of people risked their lives to fly you over the flaming Reich. It's one more proof of the legend of Opapa, which burns more brightly than ever as night falls. Who knows, Grandmother, maybe someone on the general staff thought that if you were flown over the front you might remember some old battle plan of Opapa Sauchon's, some secret stratagem he worked out thirty years ago that might stem the tide of the rout we're beginning to see all around us . . .

—No, it's not a name that rings a bell with people my age. But as soon as Schmelling heard you were coming, why, he was so tickled pink that he couldn't stop screaming at me for never telling him . . .

—Not a word.

—I didn't want to. Since landing on this island I've even stopped dropping hints about the grand estate that may be mine one day . . .

—I'm not complaining, Grandmother. You know perfectly well . . .

—I simply didn't want to arouse any military expectations that could only end in disappointment or embarrassment since the day I left the storm troopers and was posted to this garrison . . . and anyway . . . but look over there, no, more to the right, that's it, Grandmother, look! That's the sea over there on the horizon.

—Come stand where I am.

—You can lean on me.

—That's it . . . over there . . . that bit of horizon down there, which will soon light up like a red, glowing heart. Well, then, it was out of that very heart, Grandmother, that we came swooping down three years ago behind the sun, pushing its rays in front of us to blind the British, who were just sitting down to high tea. Yes, through that pinkish aperture slipped fifty airplanes all at once that have since become a legend, making the Australian lookout who was sitting here waiting for the sunset wipe the lenses of his binoculars and wonder why they weren't getting any cleaner, because suddenly he saw a whole lot of bright little dots. Who but a dedicated suicide pilot could have thought that such a fantastic operation was possible?

—No, Grandmother, we didn't think so either—that is, the handful of us who could or wanted to think at all. I'm not talking about that pack of young wolves that has been convinced since '36 that the whole universe is a playground in which it can kick the globe around like a football. If you had parachuted them into Calcutta to take the English high command there, they would have done it as blithely as they charged into Poland and Holland. But we, I mean the handful of us who still could and wanted to think a bit, sat huddled under our helmets, looking down in horror at the smooth water racing beneath us while asking ourselves what demonic power could be taking us to this strange, distant island if not the wish to see the best of us slaughtered on a self-propelled altar of grandeur and thus scare the wits not only out of the world but out of Germany too. Suddenly, Grandmother, I began to shake with sheer sorrow for my life that was about to be shot right out of the sky. I thought, yes, Grandmother, I thought of Uncle Egon and even envied him for having managed to be dead already . . .

—Yes, I did think of him, Grandmother, and it so upset me to imagine the fresh sorrow awaiting you that the stretcher strapped to my body began to twitch, and our battalion commander, Oberst Thomas Stanzler, a most wonderful and much looked-up-to man who was sitting across from me with his helmet in his hand, a ray of sunlight from a porthole falling on his bald head, smiled a bit because he must have seen the vibrations, laid a pitying hand on me, and said, "You, Private Bruner," he said, "look like some strange kind of bird, like Icarus who tried flying over Crete. But don't forget, Bruner, that your wings are made of steel and won't melt in the sun like his . . ." And then, Grandmother, I thought of that story, and my eyes filled with tears of gratitude to our knowledgeable battalion commander, who was soon to be mortally wounded, for having taken the trouble to remind me of the myth of Daedalus and his son, which made me think of that old tutor you once brought me . . .

—Koch . . . right you are, Grandmother, Gustav Koch . . . that old classicist with his stories of Greece and Rome . . .

—Exactly. Exactly.

—Of course I remember him.

—No, I was not too young to understand. He was the first to call for casting the rusty anchor of German history back into that sea you see down there, because there, he used to say, was the warm, true, blue womb of the German genius. Be more careful, Egon, he would shout at me when I mixed up all those mythical characters, those are your own ancestors, our poor Europe was born from them, if only the Teutonic tribes had pressed on to Greece fifteen hundred years ago instead of stopping in Rome, damn its soul! . . .

—Don't you remember how he sometimes used to swear?

—You mean he taught Uncle Egon too? How fantastic . . .

—True. And so all at once, Grandmother, in that growling, pitching airplane that was losing altitude now, all bundled up with my parachute and my knapsack and my stretcher and my rifle, with my helmet down over my ears, and my glasses, which I was too stupid to stick deep in some pocket, tied to a shoelace around my neck, I suddenly lost all fear and had an actual attack of ecstasy, as if savoring the real taste of war for the first time, Grandmother, and I actually became a physical link in old Koch's rusty anchor chain that had been flung over the Alps with such marvelous force onto the heads of our mythical ancestors, stirring the moss of black forests and the fumes of Hunnish swamps into those warm waves until the Teutonic dreams haunting us found their meaning in the sculptured white marble of Hellas . . . And so, when the red light went on, and the bell rang, and the dispatching sergeant began to bark, and the whole pack of wolves jumped to its feet with a great shout and put a bullet in the barrels of its schmeissers and disappeared one by one through the hatch with its legs out, I shouted as loud as I could too, Grandmother, I shouted for old Gustav Koch, that grade school classicist, and I went whooshing out into the space that you're looking at right now . . .

—Exactly.

—Right. From up there to down there . . .

—In a second. Just be careful, because this step is a little high for you. Here, give me your hand . . .

—By that olive tree, because that's our first station. Now look carefully at what you see and think of me, jumping with a great shout from the churning belly of that plane and carried off by my own private wind, which was waiting as though just for me, first to wildly snatch away my glasses and then to pull a white chute out of me while tugging at the stretcher that was now sticking straight out like the big, single wing of a strange bird. In no time I was whisked over that very coastline that you see there, floating among my comrades' cries of pain and surprise, the howls of the wolf pack pinned down by enemy fire between the sky and the earth, and flung sideways over that hill, toward those white houses scattered on the hillsides, those over there, Grandmother, which look like the sugar cubes that Opapa liked to suck in bed at night, and right smack into the branches of an olive tree surrounded by goats that greeted me with an indifferent silence . . .

—There . . . over there, Grandmother . . . those black dots out there . . .

—Exactly. That same flock of goats, so help me, has been standing there for the last three years. Day and night, summer and winter, it keeps reduplicating itself from the bushes . . .

—Yes, Grandmother, many men were shot dead in the air, thus saving their souls the return trip to heaven . . . most of my company, Grandmother, was wiped out in less than two minutes . . .

—You'd be surprised, Grandmother, what two beastly Australians with one machine gun can do. And where do you think they were, Grandmother? Come on, guess!

—Nevertheless, take a look around you and guess . . . after all, you're the widow of a famous fighting man . . .

—Nevertheless, try to guess . . .

—Wrong, Grandmother. The answer is: right where you're standing this minute! Here, their position was right by this rock. If we were to dig a little in the ground, we'd still find three-year-old cartridges. And now you see why I insisted on taking you up here, so that you could understand the whole story, right from the beginning.

—But why should they have told you about losses? It would only have spoiled your good mood and made the Austrian Genius look bad. Just remember, though, Grandmother, that a whole lot of men were killed in the operation. Months went by before we realized the full extent of it—gliders that crashed with all their occupants, dozens of men drowned at sea, parachutes that never opened, or that caught fire, or that got tangled up with each other. It was a miracle that I survived, and maybe I should thank the stretcher, Grandmother, which carried me far away from the rest of them, back behind that hill over there. In fact, if I hadn't wound up with my parachute straps caught in the branches of that olive tree, bruised all over, half-unconscious, and worst of all, without my glasses, I too, Grandmother, would probably have gone running off to look for some Englishman or Australian to put a bullet in me. But instead I stayed trapped in that thicket of branches, looking out at a soft, round world of bearded black goats whose shepherd had taken to his heels. They lifted their heads to look at me too, with a quiet tinkle of their bells—and I, Grandmother, who had never seen such black goats in my life, was more afraid of them than I was of an Englishman's bullet or some Greek's knife, because how did I know they weren't about to climb that tree and take a little bite out of me, eh, Grandmother?

—No, they weren't the least bit friendly. They were just stupid animals without the slightest curiosity. Even when I managed to free myself by cutting all the straps and strings with my medic's knife and climbed down among them, they didn't pay me any attention. They just went on grazing as if I were some kind of stone that had fallen from the sky—which is indeed how I lay there, Grandmother, like a stone, without moving. My hand was hurting me badly, and worse yet, my vision was as blurred as it was in the fifth grade, that year that you insisted I didn't need glasses . . .

—No, I didn't lose consciousness. I was just in such a state of shock from all that quiet around me that the only conclusion I could reach, Grandmother, as desperate as it was, was that the assault had failed and everyone was already dead or taken prisoner.

—Yes, that's what I thought, Grandmother. It was getting on toward dusk, and I felt an odd calm, quite resigned to the fact that the Führer had sent his best sons to bleed to death on this distant, rocky island simply to let Europe know that his long arm could reach the roots it grew from. And because I remembered the Ten Commandments we had been given before taking off from Athens, and especially, the sixth one, which Baron Friedrich von Heidte in person had drilled us in, *Thou shalt not surrender, thy badge of honor is victory or death,* I quickly bandaged my hand, spread my stretcher out between two rocks in a little fortified position I prepared, and, while waiting for someone I could challenge to a fight, an enemy who would be worthy of killing me, I lay down among the grazing goats and listened to the chirping of the crickets, which ever since then, Grandmother, for the last three years, has followed me around day and night without my being able to decide if it's a sound that I hate or am attracted to . . .

—Yes. Listen. It's as though this great cricketing were fanning out across the island, even though, oddly enough, it only makes the silence greater.

—They're everywhere, here too, among the leaves on the branches of the trees. You can't see them, but if you stick your head into these branches, you'll hear them sawing away . . .

—Exactly . . .

—It never changes. Just the same monotonous thrumming that saws the silence into dry little chips. And maybe that's what so hypnotized me, Grandmother, that I couldn't hear the shots and explosions coming from the airport in Heraklion, which was not exactly, as I later found out, blanketed by the deathly silence I thought it was . . .

—Later . . . in prison, when I sat going over and over what I had done that day . . .

—Yes, for a while . . . I'll get to it . . .

—I didn't want to distress you.

—Yes. That was one reason you didn't hear from me . . .

—But . . . just a minute . . . look here, Grandmother, this is *my* story, it's the only way I know of getting you to picture what I've been trying to tell you since starting up this trail—along which, Grandmother, if you're not too tired, I'll have to ask you to continue, so that you can see for yourself, not only the far end of the airport, which was finally captured after several days of bloody fighting by fresh forces that were landed from the sea, but the jump-off point for the private trek of Private Egon Bruner, who was temporarily cut off from history, Grandmother, in order to stumble into prehistory and into the great fan of cricket song that went on all night in deeper and deeper darkness—cut off from my olive tree too, beneath which I buried my white chute, and from the flock of goats, which I dispatched with my schmeisser to keep it from tinkling conspicuously after me . . . because I had made up my mind, Grandmother, I really had, to follow the sixth commandment and not be taken prisoner if only I could find someone worthy of killing me. And so I began to head south, Grandmother . . . there, take a good look at those two lovely hills over there, which the Australians, or so the Greeks told us, referred to as "Charlies," which is a term of endearment they have for a woman's breasts, although we Germans, having noticed at once that they were not the same size, changed their names to "Friedrich the Great" and "Friedrich the Small." And now just picture your Egon the Second, Grandmother, advancing nearsightedly between those two Charlies on the night of May 20, 1941, fully armed and toting a big knapsack with first-aid supplies, three days' battle rations, and his stretcher, on which no doubt he intended to carry himself once he was wounded or killed, heading south on a moonless night amid the smell of fires burning under a sky like none I had ever seen back home, all fantastically lit up with stars whose names I didn't know, moving warily through vineyards whose sour grapes I picked and ate, scrambling over stone fences, keeping away from the dark, shuttered huts and avoiding the roads, on which now and then I heard the sound of some speeding car, heading steadily south in my search for a hero from one of Koch's Greek myths whom I could challenge . . .

—Don't rush me, Grandmother. Please, I beg you, give me time, let me tell the story in my own way and at my own speed, and above all, trust me to guide you through it. Tomorrow we'll say good-bye, who knows for how long, who knows if not forever—and believe me, Grandmother, you're getting the shortest and quickest possible version I can give you, I even have it outlined here on my palm, station by station . . . so please, be patient with me, because now that we're starting up the trail again you'll see that the direction I took that night, which certain individuals insisted on interpreting as a cowardly flight from battle, or at the very least, as a panic-stricken error, was from my point of view a deep penetration, a nocturnal

sally into the bright womb that Koch lectured me so brilliantly
about. Because now I know that if someday we're called upon to
justify this horrible war that we started with the clearest premedita-
tion, to justify the blood, the suffering, the conflagration that we've
spread everywhere, we'll know what to answer and won't just have
to stand there mumbling sheepishly like after the last beastly war,
when we were accused of invading France to force our blood on the
French and English without anyone, not even us, realizing what we
were up to, which was to drive south as we've finally done, to ancient Hellas, to this island of Crete, this most wonderful place that
has been from the start, Grandmother, in my own humble opinion,
the true grail of our German soul, whose deepest desire, to put it
most simply, is *to exit from history* by hook or by crook, if not
forward then backward, so that if the French, back then, in the first
war, hadn't insisted on stopping us at the frontier, we would have
rushed through their country without damaging it in the least, just
like, yes, like tourists of sorts, because deep down we Germans are
nothing but the most passionate tourists who sometimes must conquer the countries we dream of in order to tour them unhindered,
with the thoroughness to which we're accustomed . . .

—No, I'm not joking . . . certainly not now . . .

—That could be. Perhaps it's just a fantasy of mine. And perhaps
it's not. At least let me finish explaining myself before you judge me
. . . Here, hold onto me tight while you take this step. The trail
gets narrower here . . .

—I am not stalling . . .

—I'm getting to that . . . just a few more steps, there's a chair
waiting for you up there . . . this is the second station, Grandmother . . .

—I brought it up here this morning, just for you.

—Why not? Don't you think you deserve it?

—Of course I'll return it. But now sit down, please, yes, right
over here, and take these binoculars and focus them as is best for
you on that broad valley down there . . . yes, there, on that little
woods and the hill behind it . . . exactly . . .

—To the right of that village, Grandmother, where the hill grows
slightly darker . . .

—Perfect.

—They're not rocks. It's an archaeological site.

—Exactly. Exactly. That's ancient Knossos you're looking at, Grandmother, Knossos in all its glory . . .

—How can you not remember? The legendary Labyrinth . . . the palace of King Minos . . . *Then did Zeus first father of Minos, protector of Crete . . .*

—Homer.

—From the books you sent me. And thanks again for going to the trouble.

—Of course I read them.

—I know, you can't see much from here, but I wanted you at least to get a glimpse of it. I can't tell you how much I'd love to take you on a tour of that wonderful place, which I've become a student and a patron of these past three years, but Schmelling strictly forbade it. He's afraid to risk you in a partisan attack, and I couldn't get him to relent. You have no idea how worried he is about your safety—he almost wouldn't allow me to take you up this hill. He didn't rest easy until he had posted those five half-prisoners down there, those ex-Italian soldiers whom you see sitting at the bottom of the hill and keeping an eye on our little excursion.

—Yes, just for us. Why not? What else do they have to do? When we were winning the war, they were too lazy to fight it with us, and now that we're losing it, they're too lazy to run away. But enough of them, Grandmother. From here you have a clear view of the route I took that night. South! But I wasn't, perish the thought, deserting the field of battle, I was simply taking a leave of absence from it until the dead wolves in their chutes were reinforced by some living ones. And in the meantime, Grandmother, having honestly sworn by Opapa's memory not to be taken prisoner, I decided to penetrate even further, just as I was, all bruised and scratched and aching, and above all, keep in mind, exceedingly nearsighted, into the mountains, to look for some private battlefield of my own that might do until I obtained new glasses. I walked blindly on in the darkness, guided perhaps by the spirit of old Koch, which may have heard itself invoked when I jumped from the plane, making my way over fences and through orchards with the crickets sawing all around me. I must have walked a good five kilometers, although it seemed like thirty to me. And then all at once, without any warning, I found myself in the ruins of that wonderful palace of the Labyrinth, whose immense significance, Grandmother, I sensed immediately even though it was built three thousand five hundred years ago and I couldn't see it very well, so that I plunged into it faint with excitement, climbing up and down the chipped marble stairs from hall to hall and passing through the reddish columns that divided the rooms, in whose corners, by the dim, flitting starlight, I saw huge clay urns glazed with colors so magnificent that I could make them out even in the darkness. And painted on the walls, Grandmother, were slender-waisted youths and maidens in a long line that followed a beautiful, enormous red bull, whose huge V-shaped horns I already had seen on the roof of some ruin. And it was then, Grandmother, walking as though in a dream in that dark silence, that I suddenly felt very close, but unbelievably close, to the Führer, to our own Hitler, because although I still had no idea where I was, I already had guessed the secret purpose of the bloody expedition he had sent us on from afar. He was not looking to decimate the English in Crete, or for a jumping-off point to Suez—those were just excuses for his generals, so that they would order their army to this place. No, Grandmother, the Führer was obeying old Gustav Koch's imperative to look for that most ancient source at which, Grandmother, I, Private Egon Bruner, had arrived all by myself, the first German arrow to be shot from that great bow, a one-man conqueror in the night. Which was why, Grandmother, in the spirit of the sixth commandment, I decided right then and there that this was the place I was going to fight and die for . . .

—No, not to fight for those ruins, Grandmother, but for what might be resurrected from them, for the new man we talked and thought about so much on those long winter evenings back in '39 when I was studying for my German history exams. You already knew for sure then, Grandmother, that a world war was unavoidable, and you were worried about being blamed for it as we were for the last one and left without justification while the fruits of victory rotted in our hands . . . And so I thought that perhaps here, on this island of all places, the rationale that my grandmother was looking for might be found, which is a thought that I've been gnawing away at for the last three years . . .

—I swear.

—But what makes you say I vanished? I never did . . . how did I?

—But I was simply cut off . . . I had lost my glasses . . . and I misread the battle, because I confused south with north . . .

—How can you say such a thing, Grandmother? You, who pushed for the transfer of a nearsighted person like me to a unit of tigers and wolves . . .

—Not at all! If I really had deserted, I would have been court-martialed and shot at once . . . It's unimaginable that you should judge me more harshly than the general staff of the 7th Paratrooper Division. Why can't you see that I was saved by a miracle, and that it's a miracle that I'm standing before you right now? From a purely military point of view, it would have been far easier to die with the thirteen hundred other pack wolves who were killed in the first twenty-four hours on that triangular battlefield you see down below you . . .

—Yes. One thousand three hundred. It's a number I happen to know by heart, and you'll soon see why . . .

—Soon . . . if you let me tell my whole story. I'm beginning to think you'd be happier if I were one thousand three hundred and one . . .

—Because you'd finally think I had something in common with the real Egon . . .

—I meant . . .

—Never mind . . .

—I'm sorry, Grandmother . . . I really am . . .

—I'm sorry . . .

—Because I know that deep down you've never come to terms with the basic fact of my existence . . .

—Sometimes I can't help thinking that . . .

—Well, then, I was wrong, and I have to ask you once more for forgiveness, Grandmother. I'm sorry, I'm sorry, I'm sorry: I'll say it a thousand times before I let this day with you be spoiled . . .

—How? Why? On the contrary, on the contrary, Grandmother, I never dreamed of dishonoring Egon, far from it, I was acting for the glory of Germany. Who if not I, Grandmother, shared your anguish from the time I was a child over the unfair blame put on Germany for that pointlessly beastly first war, a blame so great that I even imagined it weighing on the soil of his grave in France, in that field full of crosses . . .

—Of course I remember that visit. I even remember how awful those French peasants were in that village of Méricur, when they saw Opapa standing in his white uniform and saluting his son's grave.

—But I do . . . why shouldn't I? How old was I?

—That's all? Really?

—You see? And I really *do* remember it, honor-bright as only a child can be when dreaming of the day when someone in white uniform will come to salute *his* grave . . . so that not only haven't I forgotten Egon's death, I've done everything to make it more meaningful . . .

—It wasn't the fatigue, Grandmother. It was the isolation that I wasn't used to. Why, from the day I was drafted until that night, I never had a moment to myself. I was surrounded all the time by the wolf pack, wherever I went I marched in line under some officer's watchful eye, if it wasn't one set of orders or superiors it was another, day in and day out, in the end I was even dreaming other people's dreams . . . and now, all of a sudden, without the slightest warning, I was totally alone, in a strange landscape, without a single German in sight, and worst of all, Grandmother, without an officer to tell me what to do. And so my first task was to find myself a CO, which I did, for lack of anyone better, by commissioning myself, a promotion that was so successful that I bowed to its authority immediately and ordered myself to prepare a strategic position behind those huge urns that could double as a hideout and a lookout. And since without my glasses my combat capabilities were inevitably restricted, I opened my stretcher, Grandmother, lay down on my back, and ate my first battle rations to the song of the crickets while staring in a trance at the sky, which was full of glorious new stars that you'll soon be seeing for yourself. And thus, at the end of the first day of battle, on the night between the twentieth and twenty-first of May, 1941, I fell into a deep, almost prehistoric sleep, from which I was awakened in the morning by the whinny of a mule that had been led into the palace by two Greek civilians—whom, on the spur of the moment, I took prisoner at once, jumping out of my hiding place.

—Yes, I had to take them prisoner, and in a minute you'll understand why. But first, if you're rested, why don't we go on to the next
station. I promise that from here on the trail is much easier going.
We'll swing around now to the western side of the hill and look
down on the city . . . here, let me help you up . . .

—No, it won't get dark for quite a while. We started out at four,
and we'll be back at seven sharp, untouched by darkness and in time
for Bruno Schmelling's dinner . . .

—Don't worry . . . I'll send one of the Italians tomorrow to
fetch it . . .

—It's all right . . . it really is . . .

—No, I won't forget. But really, Grandmother, instead of worrying about that wretched chair, why don't you look at the fabulous
view now coming into sight in the special light this place has whose
clarity is so great that it sometimes stretches my mind almost pain-
fully. And listen, Grandmother, to some poetry that I memorized:
*There is a land called Crete amid the wine-red sea,/ Beauteous, fertile
and girdled by water,/ Settled by peoples innumerable and boasting of
ninety cities./ Many are the tongues there spoken,/ And on it is Knossos, citadel of royal Minos,/ Friend of mighty Zeus. Nine years did he
rule there* . . . etcetera, etcetera . . . ha ha . . .

—Maybe . . .

—Maybe.

—Just like that . . . I felt like it. But hold on to my belt now and
listen to that Greek ship tooting away down there as it enters the
harbor. When I hear those ships' horns in my sleep at night, I
sometimes think that I've managed after all to board one of Father's
warships . . .

—I mean, Grandfather . . . I was thinking of Opapa . . .

—Perhaps you're right and I'm purposely dragging out the story.
And it may well be, Grandmother, that already then the first seed
was sown of what you call my "vanishing" and Schmelling calls my
"entanglement," although I simply call it my POWer play. Because
the minute I saw those two Greek civilians, the truth about whom I
couldn't have imagined then in my wildest dreams, coming into that
big room . . .

—I'll get to that . . . in a minute . . .

—No, that's a surprise . . . I have to keep you in suspense to make sure you'll stay with me to the end . . .

—Soon . . . soon. Anyway, these two men were leading a mule loaded with two or three saddlebags that they meant to hide up there for a rainy day, because they, Grandmother, hadn't the least doubt that we Germans would win the battle that was still going on. And knowing the place well, they realized immediately, by the way the urns had been moved, that someone was hiding there. They froze . . . and before they could run off to tell the English—who, because of the silence, *I* thought had won the battle—I decided to take them prisoner rather than be taken one myself, and so I jumped out of my hiding place with my schmeisser pointed straight at them, at least as far as my vision permitted, and yelled at them in English to surrender.

—*Hands up!* That's what they taught us in Athens to say to any Englishman trying to strike up a conversation . . .

—Kill them?

—But what for, Grandmother? They were civilians, and in May '41 killing civilians wasn't standard procedure yet. No one knew at the time that they were our worst enemies . . .

—Two, a father and son. And of the two of them it was the son, who was only a few years older than me and looked like one of us, well built and blond with a rather pleasant face, who panicked at the sight of my schmeisser, while the father remained cool and collected, perhaps because in any case he looked like a ghost who had just stepped out of a grave in the palace. He had on a dusty black suit and a thin, striped tie that was knotted around his neck like a rope, and he was bald and wore glasses . . . which, to tell you the truth, Grandmother, was reason enough in itself for my preemptive strike . . .

—Of course . . . although as soon as I snatched them off his nose and put them on my own I saw that I needn't have bothered, because the same world that had been all big and blurry now became as tiny and far-off as if I were looking through a telescope. Not that I returned them to him, because I confiscated them and stuck them in my pocket for further examination. I could tell from the glimmer of a smile on his face that he realized at once that the black scorpion that had fallen on him was a German paratrooper with the bad luck to get lost and lose his glasses, which seemed so perfectly natural to him that right away, without waiting to be asked any questions, he began chatting politely in simple but quite understandable German. He began by introducing himself as a tour guide to the old palace who had come up there that morning to see if the fighting hadn't ruined his ruins, to which he added that he would be glad to take me home with him to look for a better pair of glasses . . . and seeing that I looked doubtful, because I suspected a trap . . .

—Exactly.

—Exactly . . . and so right away, no less calmly than before, he suggested sending his son for the glasses and remaining with me as a hostage, which was far too logical and fair an offer for me to turn down, Grandmother . . . at which precise point my odd relationship with those two men began . . .

—In a minute . . . I'm getting to it . . .

—No, they're not around anymore . . . but wait . . . just wait . . .

—No, you're wrong. It wasn't a trap, and it was no fault of their own that the battle was over by the time I got back to the battlefield. You see, I still was convinced that the island was swarming with English, and although I was determined to put up a fight and not be taken prisoner, how could I fight without my glasses? And so, as I said, I gladly accepted that German-speaking ghost's offer to be my hostage, although I took every precaution and made him descend to an inner room of the palace, where I tied his hands and legs thoroughly with first-aid gauze and then, seeing as how he was very small and slender, helped him to climb into one of those giant urns, in which I could be sure he would stay put. As for his son, who was white as a sheet and too frightened to move at the spectacle of his father being trussed up so efficiently, I sent him off to fetch the promised glasses, although not before ordering him to bring his mule to a back room too and to leave it tethered there as an additional deposit . . .

—Yes, indeed, Grandmother, I was full of grand notions of honor . . . although for someone who had just met the enemy for the first time, you can see I behaved very sensibly. Since then I've arrested and tied many more people on this island, but I can remember my hands shaking as I wrapped gauze around that wrinkled ghost, who actually smiled at me most considerately, as if he couldn't have agreed more with what I was doing . . .

—But I really needed them. Because whatever you may think, Grandmother, I have definitely been nearsighted since the fifth grade. . . .

—I wish to reiterate, dear Grandmother Andrea, as patiently as I can, that I did not hear any sounds of battle. That's one reason I took you up this hill, so that you could see for yourself how far it was from the isolated valley I landed in to where the fighting was going on. The actual battle took place down there, along the coast and right outside Heraklion, which you can see directly beneath you . . .

—Perhaps I didn't believe it.

—Perhaps I couldn't believe it. Don't forget, in those first few days the whole brilliant operation was hanging by a hair . . .

—Perhaps I didn't want to believe it, either . . . I don't deny that you have a point there, Grandmother . . .

—That's so. I admit it. Sometimes I despair prematurely to avoid disappointment later. I admit it.

—But look here, the minute I try to be nice and take part of the blame on myself, you want to lay it all on me . . . just like you've always done . . .

—As usual? Automatically, Grandmother? Have I been to blame from the minute I was born? In that case, there's really no point in going on with my story . . .

—No, I've had enough! Let's stop this, then . . . let's go back down . . . what's the point of even trying to explain . . . let's stop this right here and now . . .

—Yes. Of course. I'm angry at you for not wanting to listen to me, Grandmother, because you've already passed judgment on me and decided that I ran away from the battle when I didn't at all and was simply trying to understand it. From the minute I was thrown out of the belly of that airplane, all by myself into the world, with all those bullets whizzing by me and the screams of dying men, I realized that getting killed was easy but that understanding was hard, and I made up my mind to do things the hard way. That's why, having disentangled myself from that tree, I headed south toward solitude, Grandmother, trusting in the power of the pure reason within me to issue the proper commands, or at least, commands as proper and responsible as any of the general staff's. And so great was the command for solitude, Grandmother, that I even about-faced and killed a flock of goats to keep from being followed, or from being distracted by the human expression on their dumb faces. And thus, Grandmother, as solitary as could be, I stumbled in the dead of night on the remains of an ancient civilization that stirred and enchanted my soul. But I still had no idea how to connect with it, which made it only natural, Grandmother, that, finding myself with a Greek tour guide in my clutches, I decided to make the most of him. And in fact, he was most generous with his time despite the humiliating position I had put him in and began talking to me not as my foe or captured prisoner, but as a potential intellectual compan-ion, trying his best to converse in the slow, simple German that, so he said, he had acquired leading tours. You have to realize that, although as soon as he saw the sky full of German parachutes he was convinced of our victory and even assumed that there would be among the invaders a few culture-loving humanists who would want a guided tour of the famous Labyrinth once the fighting was over, he had never dreamed that, already on the first morning, he would be facing his first humanist while bound hand and foot . . .

—Me, naturally.

—At first just to pass the time until his son came back with some glasses. Little by little, though, I began to be fascinated by the story that he was telling me so wonderfully well. His bald head was stick-ing out of that old urn like the head of some wise snake, and even though his German, Grandmother, was very basic, you could see he had a way with words the minute he began telling me about the men who dug and were dug up at Knossos, whom he described as though they were all one big family, Sir Arthur Evans and his En-glish archaeologists who came here at the turn of the century and King Minos and his royal court who lived here three and a half millennia ago. In fact, I was so impressed that it occurred to me at once that, if all went well, old Koch might get to see at least part of his dream come true, and that Germans would come to the ruins of the Labyrinth from all over the Reich to study their own history and be solaced by another, ancient civilization for the sorrow and disillusionment of our own, which we take so seriously, Grandmother, that it turns to a dragon in our hands. Just imagine, Grandmother, even then I began . . .

—Yes, while the battle was still raging all around me.

—I plead guilty to that too . . . Anyway, I jotted down some notes, and I was so carried away that in the end I couldn't restrain myself, and as evening began setting in and the young man still hadn't returned, I decided to let my hostage out of his urn before killing him for his son's absconding, although I was careful then too not to give him his glasses back, so that he couldn't run away. And so, as nearsighted as I was, he began leading me from room to room and wall painting to wall painting, pointing out all the things he had already told me about. I was determined to pump him for all he was worth, because the more he told me about that ancient world, the more it excited me . . .

—Because it bore no guilt, Grandmother, and therefore had no fear . . .

—That's how he explained it.

—For example, for example, Grandmother, even such details as no fortifications having been found around the palace, which itself is eloquent testimony not only to the inhabitants' basic peacefulness, but to their taking peace for granted. And the paintings on the walls really do radiate such happiness and calm . . . even the great bull was so loved by everyone that the young men held tournaments in which they leaped over its back . . . and except for one double-bladed ax, not a single weapon was found anywhere . . .

—No. That's the opinion of all the scholars, whom my guide was merely quoting . . .

—What?

—What did you say?

—You're astonishing, Grandmother!

—I'll get to that in a minute . . . aren't you a shrewd one, though!

—In a minute . . . in a minute . . . just wait . . .

—Jewish scholars . . . how odd . . .

—I'm getting to it . . . in a minute you'll understand everything . . . although permit me, wisest Grandmother, to congratulate you right now, even though, historically speaking, there were no Jews in the world at the time . . .

—Not a blessed one.

—They simply hadn't invented themselves yet.

—Well, then, Grandmother, it would seem that they're not quite as old as they think.

—I understand . . . I understand . . .

—He said the same thing to me that first night while describing the island and the people who lived on it . . . which was why . . .

—Of course he did.

—Mani.

—Yes. Perfectly simple.

—Mani nothing. Just plain Mani.

—I don't think it's a shortened form of anything . . . but . . .

—Maybe of mania . . .

—Josef.

—Killed him, Grandmother?

—Wait . . . wait a minute . . . why are you in such a rush . . .

—But he did keep his promise. His son was just waiting for it to get dark before slipping out of town unseen, because the Greeks were sure that the English were successfully repelling our attack and might have endangered his father in their rush to get at me, which was the reason he waited. As soon as the first stars came out, though, there was a rustle in the underbrush, and before I could reach for my schmeisser, Grandmother, a short, delicate girl of about my age was standing there, the son's wife and my ghost's daughter-in-law, who had come to get the lay of the land. She had brought a pot of hot food and a jug of coffee for the night, and also, as if I had an insatiable lust for glasses, five pairs of them wrapped in a towel. The only problem was that they were all old folks' reading glasses that must have belonged to the young Manis' grandparents. They looked just like your glasses, Grandmother, which only used to make me see worse when I tried them on as a child . . .

—Of course. It was the first thing I did. Don't think I had forgotten where I was. Mani Senior translated the news that the young lady and her husband had gathered, because meanwhile, Mani Junior, looking very confused and frightened, had stepped slowly out of hiding too and had joined us shivering all over, holding a child in one hand, a little boy of about three, and a small sack of barley for the mule in his other hand. He was wearing a faded old overcoat, which he took off and gave to his father.

—They indeed had brought me their whole family, perhaps because they thought it best to die together . . .

—I'll get to that in a minute . . . Because Mani Junior was quite beside himself. He began hugging and kissing his father and actually sobbing quite shamelessly in strange spasms, like some sort of mental defective, so that his wife and father had to grab him and hold him to protect him from his worry at seeing the old man stuck in an urn for safekeeping. I myself had no idea then, Grandmother, that this was but my first taste of the sweet-and-sour dish known as Fear-of-the-Conqueror that we've been eating ever since then until it's coming out of our ears. I'm talking about the terror that each of us creates even when he's just taking an innocent walk and thinking the most humane of thoughts—the stares that follow your every movement as a soldier, though you yourself may be sick of your own self. I could feel it beginning that summer evening, standing there without my glasses but with my cocked tommy gun aimed at that family of civilians that kept trying to calm me with all kinds of promises to ward off any sudden desperation that my finger might feel on the trigger, because I had already told them about my firm commitment to the sixth commandment. And so, even though, looking back on it now, the situation of the German forces in Heraklion that evening was far from good, Mani Senior, who stood glimmering like a ghost in the darkness, quite extravagantly promised me an imminent German victory even though his family had just seen English reinforcements moving up a nearby road, because he was confident that the English would never recover from the shock of the German attack. The English, he assured me with a wry touch of Anglophobia, were only in their element when fighting Asiatics or Africans, against whom their Englishness gave them strength, just as barbarism did the barbarians. He knew them well— and against real Europeans, and especially real Europeans with air superiority, they were on much shakier ground. And yet the fact was, Grandmother, that even though I was greatly cheered by what he said, which turned out to be perfectly correct, I was still in a hopeless situation. After all, I could hardly have asked that young lady to take me by the hand and bring me back without my glasses, like a fled child, to my platoon . . .

—Did I say that?

—I meant a led child.

—Perhaps . . .

—Well, even if it was more than just a slip of the tongue, Grandmother, and the truth of the matter is that I really did flee a little, there's no need to shed any tears over it, because the story has a happy end . . .

—First of all, that here I am, standing in front of you, happy and alive myself. And secondly, that I've put these three years to use preparing the summation of the defense for the terrible Judgment Day that our poor Germany is in for, compared to which, dear Grandmother, the judgment of Versailles will seem child's play.

—Soon . . . that's a surprise . . . there'll be a time to tell you everything . . .

—But even if you're right again, Grandmother, and I really did overinvolve myself with that family by capturing it a bit too personally, it was collaborating with me for reasons that I didn't understand yet, though at the time I attributed it either to its fear of an armed enemy soldier falling myopically out of the sky, or else to its pity for the same soldier, who was really quite lonely and frightened and in need of some family warmth after many long months without leave, to say nothing of being all scratched and bitten by the wolf pack . . .

—I don't follow you, Grandmother.

—But how?

—Killed them? There you go again . . .

—And the little boy?

—But how could I?

—Maybe . . .

—Maybe . . .

—Maybe. Maybe. And again, Grandmother, and only tentatively, for the sake of the argument, I'm prepared to admit that my inexperience with occupied civilians may have made me act irresponsibly, and that I should have stopped such sentimental conduct immediately, nipped it in the bud. I should have accepted a cup of coffee from the jug young Mani's wife brought and ridden away on my commandeered mule, putting that ruined Labyrinth behind me and galloping blindly off into the night until its silence was broken by a fatal Australian bullet, or better yet, by the longed-for shout of a German officer. But it seemed that Mr. Mani, and perhaps not unjustifiedly, was worried that I might lose my head and come back to kill him as I had killed the flock of goats—and so, believe it or not, O most clever and astute Grandmother, even though he was falling off his feet, the ghost offered his services as a hostage once again, and after eating a bit of his daughter-in-law's food, embracing his son and grandchild, and even handing me a little tourist's brochure in German about the antiquities of Knossos, he went back and lay down by his urn, thus taking himself prisoner again, and roundaboutly, Grandmother, according to your logic, me too. Before I could even think, he had signaled his son and daughter-in-law to cover him with that warm old winter coat and beat a hasty retreat —and in no time, Grandmother, they had vanished into one of the anterooms of that ruined palace, which the darkness had turned back into an ancient maze.

—Supposedly, Grandmother, for the same purpose as before, that is, to find me some suitable glasses. And thus began Round 2, which commenced with the man's taking a candle from his pocket and lighting it without so much as a by-your-leave so that I might have a better view of his jail cell and not, God forbid, do anything rash in the dark . . .

—Yes, Grandmother, a glum, inscrutable type, but so decisive and efficient that I began to suspect him of having German blood. Right away, with that quiet, submissive cunning that becomes the second nature of all conquered civilians, he tried maneuvering me into spending a peaceful night with him—which he did, Grandmother, just imagine, by suggesting that I wrap him in gauze again so that the two of us could get a good night's sleep, all in a spirit of mutual trust. It was then that it first dawned on me, although by now I've had three years to consider it, that the whole episode of my lost glasses was simply a pretext for him to satisfy a suddenly surfaced whim to be a prisoner or hostage, bound hand and foot, before he died. Perhaps he needed to atone for some old feeling of guilt, or perhaps to pass it on to me, so that I would have pity on his family . . .

—Yes, Grandmother. Are you ready for the surprise?

—Hang on, I've gotten there. He died without any help from me, entirely under his own steam—and to the best of my knowledge, without even a single groan! His heart just mercifully stopped beating, as sometimes happens in books or in the theater but never in real life. First, however, he turned to me in the corner of that ancient room, with the crickets sawing away at the spring night and the flame of the candle flickering over the wrinkled parchment of his face, and asked me if I had any more questions before he went to sleep. To this day, Grandmother, I remember how startled I was by such obsequiousness coming from a man old enough to be my father, and how, in all innocence, I thought he was overdoing it, because I didn't realize that it was his way of taking his final leave of me and giving death the green light—the same death that was already casting its first beams inside him like the blinking headlight of a locomotive rounding a distant bend. In fact, his submissiveness only made me feel suddenly callous, and without even answering I went off to eat my battle rations in a corner while he turned away and snuggled up in his coat, preparing for his descent to Hades, which before long was well underway. He lay there in a perfect fetal position, all trussed and bundled up, while I went out for a walk about the site and discovered all kinds of little niches I hadn't noticed before, even getting lost for a while before finding my way back to my prisoner, who, rather oddly, I thought, was as serenely asleep as if he hadn't a fear in the world. And so I went over and woke him, Grandmother, with a light prod of my schmeisser and asked him who the gods of that ancient civilization had been. He awoke with great difficulty, as if climbing out of some deep well, opened his eyes that flickered like two fireflies, and told me quite firmly that this particular prehistoric culture had had no gods at all, which was why he was so fond of it. I asked him how he knew that, "Didn't you yourself," I said to him, "tell me there were no decipherable written remains?" But he wasn't fazed by that at all, "That's just it," he said. "If the people who lived here had had gods, they would have learned to write about them . . ."

—Exactly . . .

—Grandmother, I liked that answer so much that I still remember it three years later. It even made me warm up to him a bit and ask him if he was born here in Knossos. For the first time he hesitated and seemed uncertain. He had come to Crete years ago, he told me, because of the English, who had banished him from some small, desert city in Asia whose name would not mean a thing to me . . . and that, in fact, was the last thing he ever said, because as soon as I stopped questioning him he bundled up again beneath the coat, and sometime during the night, while I was sleeping in my corner, he died . . .

—In a minute . . . I'll get to that too . . .

—I'll get to it, just let me do it in my own time . . .

—But I do insist, Grandmother . . . because from here you can already see clear into Heraklion, and ahead of us is a chair that was brought up here this morning, waiting for you at the third station— which is where, Grandmother, we're going to take an English break and pour ourselves high tea from my canteen to wash down our dry English cake with . . .

—Lately I've discovered that there's something comforting about those English pound cakes. Each crumb that you eat is more phlegmatic than the one before . . .

—You'll see in a minute . . . Anyway, Grandmother, it wasn't yet light out and I was feeling terribly lonely again. At first, when I noticed how perfectly still he was, I thought that perhaps he had slipped away and left the coat behind as a dummy. When I went over for a closer look, though, I saw that he had breathed his last and that all that was left there on the floor was his lifeless body, which proceeded to pass every test of death taught me in medic's school. Right away I untied his hands and feet and tried getting him to look a bit less fetal, not wanting there to be the slightest suspicion of any untoward act, because back then in '41, Grandmother, war atrocities were still something you swept under the rug, not a flag you raised on high . . .

—You know what I mean.

—You know.

—You know perfectly well what I'm referring to.

—Never mind, let's not argue about it now. Don't forget, though, Grandmother, that I had never before been so intimately alone with

a dead person, because even though I begged to kiss him, you covered Opapa's face before letting me say farewell to him when I was
thirteen. You thought, Grandmother, and maybe you were right,
that I was too young for death. Well, by May 1941 I was if anything,
like everyone my age, a little too old for death—but still, there in
that dawn light, I was facing my first real corpse, which looked
natural and intact despite its strangeness, and was mine to do with
as I pleased. Since that morning, Grandmother, three years have
gone by, and I have seen—and seen to—plenty of dead people, but
for some reason that ghost of a Mani has stayed with me, even
summoning the other dead around him and making them a part of
himself, as he now, lying there among those big urns, summoned an
old, familiar sorrow that made me decide that it was time for me to
leave. I didn't want to have to deal with the grief and horror of the
young Manis, even if that meant forfeiting the right glasses they had
found for me, and so I folded the stretcher, hitched myself up to my
medic's pack, and covered the dead man with that yellowish overcoat, although first I went through his things and took a few candles,
plus what looked like a passbook in Greek with an old photo of him
that I stuck in my pocket in case I ever had to explain his death.
Which just goes to show again, Grandmother, how naive I was then
to think that a German soldier in Europe in 1941 might have to
explain to anyone what he did to an occupied civilian, much less to
one who had died of natural causes! Next I went to the mule's room
and rummaged through the bundles there, which contained some
canned food and lots of bags of rice and flour and all kinds of
strange spices. The mule itself was standing quietly in its place with
its barley bag still tied to it, surrounded by a circle of turds. At first I
thought of shooting it like the goats, but I changed my mind and
began pulling it by the halter with its feedbag still around its neck,
half-blindly dragging it with me in the hope that its instincts might
guide me as a farmer guides you through his fields. And that's exactly what happened. The first cricket was already chirping when I
left Knossos, bent beneath my load and all but hidden behind the
big hairy belly of the mule. I left the ruins as nearsightedly as I had
entered them and headed back north, groping my way through
morning mist as thick as breakfast porridge . . . and thus, Grandmother, most roundaboutly, following the mule's nose rather than

my own, I crossed the English lines not far from the first Greek houses of the city and found myself between the two Charlies again as though in the bosom of an old love. And indeed, just then I heard German being spoken in a juicy Weimar accent, which turned out to belong to two loudmouthed guards from the 4th Brigade, which had jumped the day after we did, who were sitting under a tree so engrossed in philosophic conversation à la Goethe and Eckermann that I was able to creep right up on them without being challenged. They were amazed to hear that there were still survivors from the 3rd Brigade, which had been almost totally wiped out, and suggested attaching me to them at once, although just for the record they advised me to report to what was left of my old unit—which I found in a vineyard, Grandmother, billeted flat on its back. It was only then, carefully picking my way between the wounded and the dead, that I first realized what had happened in history during my twenty-four hours in prehistory, and how lucky I had been. Not that I was indiscreet enough to tell anyone who noticed me about the ancient civilization over the hills. I didn't even bother checking in. I just put down my stretcher, laid a real wounded soldier on it for a change, opened my medic's kit, and went to work with my hands up to my elbows in blood, administering first aid and cauterizing and bandaging and snipping and comforting the wounded and putting the dead in body sacks. I didn't say a word to anyone and no one asked me where I had turned up from, so that I could have easily, Grandmother, rejoined my old brigade as just another soldier if I hadn't noticed in the twilight, as I was carrying a wounded officer to a hut we were laying the dying in, a stretcher on top of some stones, and on it, in a heap of blood-soaked rags that had once been a uniform, my dying brigade commander, Oberst Thomas Stanzler, who had jokingly called me Icarus before we jumped from the plane. And then, Grandmother, I couldn't resist—and in fact, if I hadn't gone over to that stretcher just then you need never have come looking for me here, because by now I would be a bleached-out pile of bones near Stalingrad and you would have gotten a lovely death certificate to put on the wall beside the first one, where it would have hung perfectly quietly, not talking a blue streak like me. But not only did I go over to my revered commander, I actually knelt by his side, and despite the fog of death he already was in he recognized me at once, although he couldn't talk and could only listen with his eyes closed, the blood tracing a smile on his face. And since I knew that he was going to die and would never see the Labyrinth of Knossos, or the V-sign of the Minotaur's horns, or the urns or the double-bladed ax, and would never know about the paintings of the youths and maidens following the bull in a line, I began feverishly describing it all, so that, crushed in the jaws of history, he might at least be gladdened by the comforting nearness of prehistory. And he really did listen to me, Grandmother, with his eyes shut—and the more silently he lay there, the more carried away I became, until finally he opened his eyes, fixed them on his adjutant standing quietly next to him, made a sweeping sign like a crooked swastika, and began to wheeze out his soul. Well, just as I was getting to my feet to pay my respects to death, the adjutant hurried to a tent and came back with two orderlies whose hands were soaked with blood, and as Oberst Stanzler gave up the ghost, the adjutant ordered them to disarm me and tear off my brigade insignia and place me under arrest on the insane grounds that Stanzler's hand movement before dying had been a verdict of guilty for my having premeditatedly fled the field of battle . . .

—Exactly. That's how it started.

—Yes. No one but the adjutant.

—Not a word . . . just that movement of his hand. The next day, after Heraklion had been taken, I was marched, dazed and humiliated, without a chance to say a word in my defense, with the English and Greek POWs to the municipal museum, which the barbarians of the staff company had turned into a prison. You can see it right down there, Grandmother, that building with the columns that's covered with green tiles. I've set the chair up at just the right angle for you to sit here and look at it . . .

—No, Grandmother. Try to make out the third window from the right on the second floor. That's what I looked out on the world from while stewing in my thoughts during the long summer and short autumn of 1941.

—So I guessed right . . .

—But when did you find out?

—I knew it! I knew it!

—I knew you'd find some way of finding out I was in jail.

—Because I was sure that as soon as you discovered that I wasn't in the East, you'd wonder why.

—No, I wasn't trying to hide anything. I just didn't want to write you about it, because I knew my letters would be read, and I didn't want to stain the family honor you held sacred. And yet why pretend, Grandmother . . . I was longing all along for a word of comfort from you . . .

—I said comfort, not agreement . . .

—Because no one wanted to get involved . . . they all washed their hands of it . . . if the great commander had passed sentence on his death stretcher, there was no possible court of appeal. And that beastly adjutant, who had made it all up in his sick imagination, flew off to Berlin with a planeload of coffins a few days later to represent our brigade at all the funerals, after which he disappeared in the Adjutant General's office there, leaving me with a sentence that was not only irrevocable and unappealable, but unspecifiable as well. Every week I petitioned the commander of the prison to be told how much time I had to serve, but no one wanted to take responsibility even for that . . .

—As a matter of fact, I was quite simply forgotten about, Grandmother.

—Precisely. But . . .

—That's so, that's so. You couldn't have put it any better. You know the mentality of staff officers. But before we go on, here's the English tea that I promised you, still piping hot and with milk in it, made to perfection by a Scottish prisoner.

—As sweet as could be . . . and with just the cake to go with it . . .

—Lately we've been training on bland English food to prepare for our rematch with them . . .

—Who knows, Grandmother, where we'll meet up with their food again . . . perhaps in one of their prisoner-of-war camps . . .

—It's not a matter of fear. It's just facing facts.

—Absolutely not, Grandmother. No one intends to shed any blood for this island a second time. Enough of it already flowed like water once. Don't you want your cake?

—But it's really a very light and soothing sort of cake . . .

—Never mind . . . here, give it back to me, maybe you'll change your mind later. But do please look carefully at that window, and try picturing me, Grandmother, standing there for hours on end, looking out at the hillside that we're on now . . .

—That very room and window. From the twenty-third of May to the ninth of December. Twenty-eight weeks. Look at it. I paced back and forth in front of it for whole nights at a time, totally devastated in the beginning. That's the very window I sometimes wanted to throw myself out of, especially—when he wasn't busy saluting and pinning medals on my brigade—each time I saw General Student appear with his staff to raise and lower the flag . . . the window from which I saw all the adjutants swimming and frolicking in the sea, the same sea I hadn't even put my foot in yet, though I would have given anything to do it. One day I heard some English prisoners singing before being shipped off to a POW camp in Germany, and I was green with envy and longing . . . And there was a night in June when, after the 7th Paratrooper Division had received its orders to fly out of the island and I saw that everyone was determined to forget me, I lost control and began screaming into the darkness at a group of soldiers standing below me in battle gear . . .

—Yes. I really screamed.

—Because I kept telling myself, it simply can't be that I don't mean anything to anyone. No one paid me the slightest attention, because no one knew who I was anymore. My fellow wolf-packers were long dead, the adjutants were all off attending funerals, and the command of the island kept changing too. German units pulled out and Italians began to arrive. The prison guards called me "the paradeserter," and it all became too much for me. I was even thinking, Grandmother, of telling them who I was . . .

—I mean, who *you* are . . . I thought that maybe the name of Admiral Sauchon would at least get me a hearing. But then, on June 22nd, the stunning news arrived of Operation Barbarossa, and all at once, most ardent Grandmother, I had a change of heart and quieted down completely . . .

—Not at all. On the contrary, I understood at once, Grandmother, what a dreadful mistake had been made.

—No, Grandmother, no . . .

—No, Grandmother, no. Old Redbeard doomed the Reich that Saturday once and for all. Because instead of pushing on southward to bathe and cleanse our age-old barbarism in a civilization more ancient than our own, folding ourselves back into the blue womb of the Mediterranean and slowly letting our history slough away from us, we were stupid enough to turn east. What for? What for, Grandmother? Supposedly, to look for living space. In point of fact, however, the only purpose of it all was to encounter other barbarians like ourselves. What were we trying to prove? How superior we were? As if we didn't know that already . . . That's when I realized that Student and his fellow generals had succeeded in bamboozling our Führer, our poor Hitler, who had taken leave of his senses and quite forgotten what that thoroughest of teachers Gustav Koch had taught us all. And that, Grandmother, was when I understood my mission: to point out to the fast-approaching Judgment Day the existence of an escape clause. And all at once I felt at peace, because I knew that something bigger and more important than that beastly adjutant, bigger and more important than Thomas Stanzler's dying hand, had landed me in jail . . .

—Even if it's only in a whisper, Grandmother, and only between the two of us, I don't mind saying, and lord knows it's without the slightest arrogance, *that it was destiny, destiny in person.* Or perhaps I should say, a remnant of destiny, a shadow thrown by those famous myths that took place here. From that day on, until my release in early winter, I clung more and more fiercely, right through that window that you're looking at, Grandmother, to this wonderful island; I studied its sounds, its smells, its shades of light by day and by night, at first in that long, blue summer, whose unexcelled clarity kept getting deeper and deeper, and afterward on into autumn, when the authorities finally gave me the right glasses, which enabled me to refine my observations and take in little details that I hadn't noticed before, like the hills of the Chaios Range over there, or the outline of the more distant mountains. And all that time I fell back in my thoughts on those first forty-eight hours of freedom, which now seemed to have a mysterious magic . . . on the memory of that wonderful jump, and of landing in the olive tree, and of hiking like a sleepwalker that night to Knossos, and of the halls of the ancient Labyrinth with their reddish columns and giant urns, and of the mule led in at dawn by the two Greeks I took prisoner, and of my ghost of a hostage all trussed up in his urn while delivering a spirited lecture on that precivilizatory civilization. I thought of his family too, of that blond young man who broke into sobs while holding the little boy's hand, and of his young wife whose image kept haunting me, stepping silently out of the darkness to shyly hand me a soft towel in which five pairs of old granny glasses were wrapped . . . and the more I thought about them, Grandmother, day after day, putting two and two together, the more I was tormented by the odd suspicion that they weren't Greeks at all, but something else—which filled me, Grandmother, with the most terrible wonder . . .

—I mean, Grandmother . . . that they were Jews . . . some sort of Jews . . .

—Because it all added up.

—That's so. But still . . .

—That's so. I had never seen a Jew in my life . . . you had never even wanted to discuss them with me . . . but still, none of us can help thinking about them all the time . . .

—Well, part of the time, anyway.

—I don't know. The thought began to obsess me. I actually felt indignant . . .

—At the thought that I might have been tricked out of fighting by Jews . . .

—No, none of them wore hats.

—No, no, they didn't even have those little braids behind their ears. Don't you think I'm familiar with all those photographs from the encyclopedia too? Anything like that would have put me on guard . . . No, Grandmother, these were ordinary people, that was the whole point. They were perfectly ordinary. But if you've finished drinking your tea, let's head on for the next station . . . we don't want to get caught by the dark . . .

—No, Grandmother, I'm not skipping any of it, and neither are you. You'll never have another chance to be in such a wonderful place. In the darkness that is about to descend in Germany, on all of us, this sweet light flowing to the sea will always be a precious memory, and you'll at least be able to comfort yourself with the thought that for more than three whole years it was ours . . .

—No, it's not far, I promise . . . one or two hundred meters, that's all, and it's an easy, pleasant climb. It's crucial not to miss the view east.

—Yes, for the sake of my story, only for it. If you had come a few months ago, I wouldn't have bothered to bring you up here. I would have given you some goggles, put you in the sidecar of my motorcycle, and crisscrossed the island with you, making sure to show you every inlet and mountain, every monastery and temple. But you put off coming here too long, and now this island is slipping through our fingers. Soon we'll have only the flag flying from the military government building to call our own . . . and so please, Grandmother, hold onto the loop on my belt and let me pull you gently upward . . .

—Easy does it . . .

—In a minute . . . I promise you . . .

—Everything. I won't keep a thing from you.

—True.

—No. It's important. Listen. I began to put two and two together . . . all kinds of things that you felt too, or else why would my story have made you think of Jewish ideas and scholars . . .

—Exactly. It was the same with me. In the middle of one night I woke up from my sleep and said, but they must have been Jews . . . which depressed me terribly . . .

—Maybe depressed isn't the right word. Maybe upset or disappointed would be better. I couldn't believe it . . . here too? Even on a wonderful, special island like this, between the sun and the sea, among all the prehistoric antiquities? Did they have to get here before us too? And just how did they get here anyway?

—Because, Grandmother, it was elementary logic that if two Greeks rose early on the first day of the fighting to load a mule with bags of sugar and flour and spices and canned goods, they were doing it to prepare a hideout. And why would two Greeks prepare a hideout unless they were Jews who knew, not only that we would win the battle, but exactly what they could expect once it was won . . .

—What they could not expect, Grandmother, was tender loving care.

—Yes, rumors of the clean sweep that had begun in Eastern

Europe had reached us here too. And then I thought, Grandmother, of how terrified they were when they first saw me, and of how quickly they chose to collaborate, and of how oddly eager the father was to offer himself as a hostage, and of how he stood there in that urn enthusiastically lecturing me about his fearless, guiltless ancient culture, getting history and prehistory all mixed up with each other . . . to say nothing of his confession that he wasn't born in Crete but in some small, barbaric town in Asia whose name he didn't want to reveal . . . and maybe, Grandmother, it was that secret, which he insisted on keeping to himself, that killed him in the end . . .

—In a minute . . . I'll get to that too . . . there are still more surprises for you . . .

—Well, Grandmother, the thought kept tormenting me that it was Jews who had gotten me into trouble, and that if anyone ever found out about it, I'd be in even worse trouble. And so I made up my mind that I wouldn't leave this island without finding out the truth and doing something about it if necessary . . . and it was just then that Major Bruno Schmelling and his police force arrived in late November to bring our amateur army up to snuff—the first step toward which was moving the prison from that ridiculous museum to a larger, more private building that had lots of cellar space, such as that winery down there, no, there, more to your right, at the far end of that square . . .

—Yes . . . the building with the little windows . . .

—Exactly. Until a few years ago it was a large, active winery, but with Schmelling's arrival it became the central prison. Not, Grandmother, that it ever stopped pressing, fermenting, and distilling . . . it just doesn't use grapes any more. Anyway, as I was on my way from the museum to the winery in a long line of prisoners, totally alone and forsaken, I was suddenly discovered, a fighting paratrooper, by a true German soldier—who, as soon as he heard that I had never had a trial and was serving an unfathomable sentence, took me aside and began questioning me. It didn't take him long to realize whom he was dealing with and to free me at once for restoration to my element, that is, to the Sixth Army on the Eastern Front—which, now that the weather had turned cold, was using up soldiers as a hungry fire burns wood. At which point I—and once again I plead guilty, Grandmother—hastened to ask for special consideration as an orphan and to be allowed to stay where I was . . .

—No, as a war orphan. I explained to him that my platoon had been wiped out, that the 3rd Brigade was demolished, and that Oberst Thomas Stanzler was dead, and I implored him to have me transferred to a normal, living unit instead of sending me on a wild-ghost chase to the East—which could be most simply and least time-consumingly done, I suggested, if I were attached to his own police force. After all, on such a wonderful island the police must be wonderful too . . .

—Yes, Grandmother. Joining the police was my own idea.

—But why a betrayal? That's going a bit far, Grandmother!

—But how was I dishonoring our good name? How can you say such a thing? To say nothing of the fact that no one here even knew I was connected to that name . . .

—Don't the police fight too, in their fashion?

—To be honest, it's not quite the same . . . but still . . . in their fashion . . .

—But it *is* combat . . . in a minute you'll understand . . .

—Schmelling may not have had the authority to attach me to him, but he didn't hesitate to use the authority that he didn't have, with the full confidence of an officer in the secret service who has temporarily come in from the cold and will soon go back out to it . . .

—I really don't know. Maybe he took a liking to me, Grandmother, or maybe it was the very weirdness of my story. Perhaps he thought that my propensity for abstract thinking could be useful to the police, if only to raise their cultural level. But in fact, Grandmother, he was probably only doing what any sensible officer would have done, which was, spotting a certified medic with his equipment intact, to grab him immediately. My stretcher and knapsack were located in the warehouse of the museum with my name, serial number, and date and reason for imprisonment neatly written on them . . . and in that same knapsack, dearest Grandmother, which I had never thought to see again, I discovered, besides some rather moldy battle rations from the month of May, the forgotten passbook that I had filched from Father Mani's overcoat before he gave up his ghostly ghost. And believe me, Grandmother, although I have subsequently checked no end of passbooks and birth certificates on this island and become such a great expert on them that Schmelling jokingly calls me his "birth-and-identity sergeant," no document has ever given me the pleasure that I got from that one, because I saw at once, Grandmother, what a brilliant hunch I had had.

—No, his kind of passbook didn't say if you were or weren't a Jew, but it did state the date and place of birth, which is how I discovered the name of that barbaric little city in Asia that our Mr. Mani was born in . . .

—Guess.

—Oh, come on, Grandmother, it's not that hard . . .

—But it's a name you know well. In fact, before you joined the death-of-God crowd, you even used to sing it now and then . . .

—How stubborn you can be, Grandmother . . . suddenly you don't know or remember anything . . .

—Baghdad? Why on earth Baghdad? Since when did you ever sing hymns to Baghdad?

—No . . .

—It's so obvious, Grandmother . . . guess again!

—But what else could it be but Jerusalem, Grandmother! What else could it be?

—Of course I knew that. It didn't mean he had to be a Jew. He could have been an Arab or a Greek or a Turk or an Englishman or anyone else born in Jerusalem. But I also knew that these weren't our real enemies, that at most they were obstacles in our way, whereas the Jews were the underlying reason for the whole enterprise, the bull's-eye flickering behind every target in this war. And so, Grandmother, how could I have sat quietly a minute longer when I was already contaminated by my contact with them? If there were any Manis still left on the island, I had to find out who they were, because how could we possibly purify ourselves in the ancient womb of our ancestors, as old Gustav Koch desired, with a lot of beastly Jews running around and demanding with their typical insolence to be our partners here too, to share our most primeval myths . . .

—*I* am? I am, Grandmother?

—Maybe it's you who are . . .

—Yes, you back home in the fatherland. You're the really crazy ones, drunk on your army that went galloping off to Moscow . . .

No, there was nothing crazy about me . . . all I wanted, all I still want, is the salvation of Germany . . .

—I'll walk slower. Just hold on tight.

—No, Grandmother, there's no turning back now. That would be depressingly defeatist . . . and it's such a nice path . . . the air is so invigorating . . . we've already come most of the way, and best of all, we have some spectacular views still ahead of us . . .

—Jerusalem?

—From here?

—No . . . we can't see that far, ha ha . . . that's a good one . . .

—No. Even though between Crete and Palestine there's only a smooth stretch of sea that the ancients crossed without difficulty, it's still too far from here to see Jerusalem, not even with eyes as sharp as yours . . . No, my dear grandmother Andrea, my sights are more modest, and more faithful to my slowly unfolding tale—all I want to point out to you in this panorama of pinkening light is what was once the house of the Manis, which is the same house that I arrived at a few days after my release from prison, riding free and easy on an army motorcycle like the one you once refused to let me buy with my savings, despite all my tears and pleas to you . . .

—Too young? Still? Well, perhaps . . . but it's odd how my youth seems to have evaporated all at once. Most likely, without noticing, we stuffed it into our kitbags in boot camp along with our civilian shirts, and it simply faded away there. You won't find any youngsters here, only soldiers, whose helmets and battle gear make them all look the same age in life and in death. But here, take a look down there . . . farther east, Grandmother, farther east, down in those vineyards . . . even if you don't see it, take my word for it, their house is hidden in there, along the road from Knossos to Ios. It was the first house that I entered, Grandmother, as a conquering soldier in the Year of our Lord 1941. Since then, Grandmother, I've entered many houses uninvited, turned closets and beds upside down, broken into drawers, made sieves out of mattresses with my bayonet, and learned that if I want to keep my sanity, I mustn't be too polite, which means that as soon as I kick in the door I blame whoever is on its other side and march firmly, with no may-I's or apologies, into rooms that enrage me by the very presence of closets, drawers, pantries, and even walls, as if a conquered house were expected to be a single, undivided space that you could charge through at the drop of a hat. But that winter evening, which was caressed by a thin, fragrant rain, I was still a novice, Grandmother, and so I stepped gently up to the door, even wiping the mud off my boots, and murmured "Excuse me" to the young woman who let me in without even recognizing me, not just because it was dark in the house, or because I had exchanged my paratrooper's uniform for a police outfit, or because I was wearing glasses instead of a helmet, but because on that night back in May, apparently, she hadn't realized that I was a human being with a soul and mind of my own and had simply taken me for a military dragon that lunged at her from the depths of the Labyrinth and left her husband's father stone dead. But her husband, Mr. Mani Junior, who hurried into the room when he heard my voice, still dragging his little boy after him like a big kangaroo whose pouch was ripped, recognized me at once, Grandmother, and all that terrible anxiety flowed back into him, as if he saw the ghost of his father spread-eagled on my back with its passbook in its hand. And for a moment, Grandmother, I was on the verge of shooting him just like I shot the flock of goats, because I was still innocent enough to believe, back in 1941, that fear was a sure sign of guilt. But although I still didn't know then that there is a fear that is pure, guiltless, and utterly sin-free, I controlled myself and turned to him without anger or threats, I just looked him straight in the eye and said very slowly in the simplest, easiest German I could think of, "So you are a Jew, sir . . ."

—Yes, Grandmother, without any of those cat-and-mouse tricks from the detective stories. Because not only didn't we share a common language in which to beat around the bush, I had decided in any case that direct shock tactics were the best way of showing him and his wife that I knew everything, even if I didn't yet know what to do about it. And then, Grandmother, Citizen Mani squared his shoulders, threw a desperate glance at his wife to see if she understood what was happening, looked brightly back at me, and said (I'll never know, Grandmother, if he thought it up on the spur of the moment, or if it was something he had prepared well in advance, perhaps on the morning he came across his father lying dead by those big urns, and had now finally found the occasion for), these were his very words, Grandmother, which came out in a kind of stammer: "I was Jewish, but I am not anymore . . . I've canceled it . . ."

—I know, Grandmother . . . just a minute . . . I know . . .

—I know, Grandmother . . . hold on a minute . . . for God's sake . . . can't you listen for just once . . .

—Yes, Grandmother, yes. He even said it again in the same broken, embryonic German that he had learned during the six months of occupation, which were the equivalent of a few days of Berlitz lessons in Berlin. At first, Grandmother, I must admit that I was so stunned by his answer that I couldn't get a word out. I just stood there, like you, fuming and indignant. But then, Grandmother, I remembered what you taught me yourself whenever we listened to *his* speeches on the radio, that a fool is frightened by absurdity while a wise man finds something to learn from it, and so I just smiled at him, and took his dead father's passbook from my pocket, and opened it, and put my finger on the Greek word, and asked in the same easygoing German, "And have you canceled Jerusalem too, sir?" That was already too much for him. He stepped toward me clumsily with the little boy in his arms and grabbed the passbook away from me, as if now that his father had shrunk to the size of a small book he could finally free him from my clutches, looked desperately at his wife again, and then turned back to me, waved his arms in search of the German words, and said in much the same vein, "We have been in Jerusalem, but no more . . ." At which point, Grandmother, are you listening, I felt almost blissfully happy . . .

—Yes, yes . . . to the point that I actually bowed my head to Citizen Mani in grateful acknowledgment, made a little circuit of the room, a kind of pantomime house search, saluted the whole family, and left at once . . .

—An ordinary salute, like any well-mannered policeman would give a family of law-abiding citizens . . .

—I was happy for two reasons, Grandmother, the first being that my intellectual diagnosis had indeed been razor-sharp, and the second, that the infection had already cured itself, so that the blue womb that we had returned to was as pure and uncontaminated as ever . . .

—I assumed, Grandmother, that sooner or later I would hear that nasty word from you, and I've been bracing for it for the last half-hour . . .

—But you know perfectly well that I'm not that type.

—Because I'm not stupid, Grandmother, I simply am not and never was, neither in your opinion nor in anyone else's . . .

—If that's so, we should investigate how and when I became one, but it isn't . . .

—But for God's sake, Grandmother, will you listen to me . . .

—I hear you.

—Fine. I hear you.

—Fine, go ahead . . .

—I'm listening.

—Yes . . .

—Yes . . .

—Yes . . .

—Yes . . .

—Can I say something now?

—Hold on there . . .

—All right.

—I hear you.

—Now listen carefully, Grandmother. No, just a minute. I heard you out quietly, now you hear me out and tell me if it isn't ludicrous and in poor taste to talk like that, in such biological or zoological terms, about people and even whole nations. Why, it's humiliating even for us Germans . . . as if we were all different strains of dogs or monkeys. No, Grandmother, please, that was never the intention of our Daemon, because the word "race" was an allegorical refer-ence to another, more respectable word, namely, *nature,* which is what counts, and what is nature if not character, both human and national, which can be described and changed . . . Why, didn't Hitler himself speak of *the danger of the Jew in each one of us?*

—He did, I swear . . . he did too . . . in the youth movement, in Flansburg, there were those who knew his every word by heart . . .

—Of course . . . of course he did . . . which is why Citizen Mani Junior's answer made me so happy, because I understood that if that stubborn, beastly essence of Jewishness can cancel its own self, then there's hope for us too, Grandmother . . .

—Once more for two reasons, Grandmother. The first is that we won't have to hunt down every last Jew in order to destroy him, because each Jew will cancel himself. And the second is that, when the time comes, we'll be able to do the same thing . . .

—Because suppose there's another Judgment Day, Grandmother, and they'll want to make us pay like after the first war, when they caused you such aggravation. We too will be able to say then, "We were Germans but we are not anymore . . . we've canceled it . . ."

—But hold on there, Grandmother, hold on, you're losing your temper for no good reason. You're angry and you keep calling me names as if I were attacking you personally, but I'm not that stupid and I'm not that crazy . . . it's true that sometimes, I admit, I have strange ideas, but reality has always been kind enough to put them into practice for me . . .

—No, I'm not pulling your leg, heavens, no. Far from it, I'm simply telling you my story in proper sequence, and who knows, it may cause you pleasure in the end . . . perhaps even joy . . . because wait, I haven't come to the last surprise yet . . .

—In a minute . . . I'm getting to it . . . but first let's walk a few more meters to that big white box over there, in those trees up ahead of us . . . over there, do you see it?

—Yes, over there . . . that white box . . . which is . . . come on, Grandmother, guess . . .

—Never mind, just say the first thing that comes to mind . . .

—A mailbox? That's a good one, ha ha . . . No, Grandmother: who would come all the way up here to mail a letter? It's got to be something else . . .

—But here, Grandmother, take a look: it's simply a miniature little church, a pocket church, with a glass wall, and a tiny little altar behind it, and a teeny dish of oil for the dead, and a little doll of the Virgin holding her baby Savior who's no bigger than a needle. The Greeks put these sweet little churches everywhere, Grandmother, to prevent travelers and passersby who are in a state of ecstasy from the sun, or the sea, or the sky, from backsliding to the paganism of the ancients and going down on their knees, God forbid, before trees and stones. It keeps them honest and faithful to the religion of their forefathers . . . but don't look at me, Grandmother, look at the sky, because now begins its grand moment, just look at it blushing for you . . .

—If you're tired again, we can sit for a while on this bench. It's here for the faithful. Would you like to pray a little?

—But you're here all alone . . . no one will see you . . . and it's the same Virgin as the one in the Lutheran church near our estate, even if she is so tiny . . .

—If you don't want to, you don't have to, it doesn't matter. If you'd like, I even possess the vested authority to commandeer that little doll with her baby and make you a present of them, so that you can have them as a souvenir of this hike and this wonderful view, and even of me too perhaps, because who knows . . .

—What I'm saying, Grandmother, is who knows if I'll ever come home again . . .

—What?

—Go on!

—What makes you so sure?

—But how? Who?

—That's ridiculous. *I'm* being transferred to Germany? Who even knows that I'm on this godforsaken island?

—But what do you think? Tell me this minute . . .

—I want the truth, Grandmother. Was it your doing? The truth, Grandmother . . . have you been meddling again?

—But what can you know about it when you don't even understand what happened? I have to stay here . . . I have to find them . . . ach, damn you, why did you have to go rushing off again, Grandmother, without even asking me first . . .

—I'm sorry . . . I'm sorry . . .

—The two of them . . . the woman and the child . . .

—Playing games with Jews? Games? On the contrary, you'll see in a minute . . . just the opposite . . .

—But it's not for them, it's for us, Grandmother . . . for Germany . . . the Jews here, and everywhere, are simply guinea pigs on whom we can perform an experiment that we're still afraid to perform on ourselves. They even like being experimented on, they're so used to changing shapes and jumping from test tube to test tube. Just look at all I've learned these past three years, at what an expert I've become . . . even if you don't agree with my train of thought, you can't accuse me, Grandmother, of superficiality. Don't you remember how many exams I flunked in school because I refused to give superficial answers to superficial questions? Surely you don't think that just because the idea pleased me, I let myself be innocently carried away by it, or excused myself from the necessity of checking and double-checking it to see if young Mr. Mani's astonishing confession rang true, if it was at all plausible! I was so beside myself, Grandmother, so on fire with new questions, that that same night, when my shift at the prison was over, I climbed onto my motorcycle instead of into bed and went racing off at the crack of dawn to that house outside of Knossos, where I knocked loudly on the door. This time I didn't wait to be let in. I climbed through a window, went right to the back room, which happened to be their bedroom, shone my flashlight on the pile of blankets under which those canceled Jews were lying, and shook them out of the last of their sleep for another interrogation, shivering from cold, the woman all soft and wild-haired in a flannel nightgown embroidered in red, and the man in the same overcoat that had been worn by his father. I could see from his calm look that he wasn't surprised by my appearance, as if he had realized that one night was not enough to digest his confession but only to throw it back up at him . . .

—I thought I would search their house, Grandmother, for something Jewish that they took out at night, something that might refute his declaration, although in fact, I had no idea what anything Jewish might look like or how to go about finding it, because I was still so naive, Grandmother, that back then, in the winter of '41, I didn't know what was already clear to me by the spring of '42, that is, that there's nothing Jewish that a Jew can't do without . . .

—I mean that a Jew's identity, Grandmother, can exist purely in his own mind, which is why there is reason to believe it can be canceled there too . . .

—But that's precisely the point . . . that's the point, O wisest and most perspicacious Grandmother, that I keep trying to get across to you, so that you'll understand how difficult, how profound, how almost absurd is the war that the Führer has declared on them . . .

—No. I never said a word to Major Schmelling.

—Because I knew, Grandmother, that it was too subtle for him. Who is this Schmelling, after all? An elderly police officer of the old school who knows about Jews from the newspapers and hysterical speeches and slogans on the walls, which is why he takes them so literally, so that he thinks the world is like the Berlin Zoo, in which you can go from cage to cage comparing the animals until you find the Super-Ape . . . No, I wouldn't want to confuse him with an idea that I myself haven't finished working out yet . . .

—Have I gotten to the point? Not yet . . . not yet . . . especially since young Mani himself only sank to the bottom of the sea some eight weeks ago . . . although on the other hand . . .

—I'm getting there . . . in a minute . . . in a minute you'll understand . . .

—Of course, Grandmother. After all, I could simply have told myself, as you keep telling me, "He's just putting one over on you, this beastly Jew, he's just trying to dodge his fate." But I knew that was the easy way out, the answer you give when all you have patience for is blasting away with your schmeisser, and that, perhaps because I was helped to arrive on this island by a gentle push from above, I should first tune in to my surroundings, not for the sake of Mani Junior, but for our own sake, for the sake of Germany and the Germans, to see if one couldn't return to the starting point and become *simply human again,* a new man who can cancel the scab of history that sticks to us like ugly dandruff and put the dark, moldy rooms full of worm-eaten books, the faded oil paintings, the grotesque sculptures, behind him for the sunlit aperture, Grandmother, that you see spread out before you in all its glory, chorusing away in the crickets that won't, I'm afraid, let us hear ourselves think unless we get up and move on . . . Come, Grandmother, let's go . . .

—No, there's not much more . . . I promise . . . I beg you . . .

—No, we still have time before dark . . . and we're not far from the top now . . . Even if this story of mine only irritates you, the fantastic view that you're about to see, with its radiant expanse of air and water, will reward you for all your aggravation . . .

—Exactly . . . exactly . . . you see, you do understand me, Grandmother . . .

—Thank you, Grandmother, thank you . . .

—I know . . .

—Of course you'll have the right of reply . . .

—I promise you . . . for as long as you like . . . I'll listen to you all evening . . .

—Yes, exactly. That's what I told myself too, "Even if he's trying to put one over on you, you'll make him stick to his word," and so my first order of business was making sure he didn't take to the mountains, which meant that every day or two, Grandmother, I paid him a surprise visit just to check that he was still canceling away . . .

—At first just house visits, Grandmother, because we're still talking about the winter and spring of '42 when I was at the bottom of the ladder, an ordinary guard working the night shift in that big, dry winery that Schmelling turned into a prison. As soon as my shift was over, with the first light of dawn, while my brain was still on fire with the screams of tortured suspects, I would climb on my cycle and speed off from Heraklion to Knossos along roads still silenced by the curfew, which in those days was dutifully honored by the inhabitants, to pay a call on my own private, secret suspects, who began leaving the door open for me once they realized I wasn't going to leave them alone, so that I could step right into their bedroom without bothering them, two heaps of blankets that my flashlight played over as it looked for something Jewish whose name, shape, or nature I hadn't the foggiest notion of. In those days I still believed that, if only it existed, it was bound to emerge from the bedclothes at night *and cancel the cancellation* . . .

—No, Grandmother. Because by the early summer of '42 I had finally managed to persuade Schmelling to take the palace of Minos under our constabulary wing and even to maintain a small guard post there for whatever high police officials, aboveboard or undercover, wished to run their hands over the new map of Germany and delight in how big it had become by visiting us from the far ends of the Reich. Meanwhile, promoted by Schmelling to Feldwebel, I was appointed to be our guests' escort, and the first thing I did with them, Grandmother, was take them to the top of this hill to tell them the fabled story of our air drop and of the magnificent battles that followed. Then, when I had won their confidence and enthusiasm, I would convince them to come along with me to Knossos for a look at its ancient Labyrinth, which I tried getting them to see not just as an ancient ruin repainted to suit the whims of a fanatical British archaeologist but as a possible goal, a holy grail for all Europe, for the European of the future who will be free of fear and guilt . . . and there, by the entrance to the antiquities, not far from the statue of Sir Arthur Evans, I sometimes found my citizen, my canceled ex-Jew, standing in his little shop with his child next to him as usual, busy with his herbal jars and medicinal bottles and souvenirs for the tourists, little figurines of the Minotaur and miniature earthenware urns and tiny bull-horn V's, and since he still had his father's concession to the site, I went and bought half-price tickets from him for my party of guests, or sometimes from his delicate young wife if he himself was inside the ruins guiding some group of Greek tourists, who, back in '42 or '43, were still coming from Athens and Salonika to vacation on this island and even giving us Germans a friendly smile, as if we were tourists like them and the rifles slung over our shoulders were for hunting in the mountains. And so now I no longer had to keep a nightly eye on him, because I had him in my sights every day, my ex-Jew who had become, or so I tried convincing myself, an ordinary human being, pure unadulterated *homo sapiens,* at home in an ancient, blissful civilization that, free of the self-invented contamination of Jewry, had lived without guilt or fear, safely ensconced in its unfortified temple that had no protective walls, its marble steps cascading down to reddish halls in which youths and maidens walked happily behind the quiet bull. Sometimes, Grandmother, I would run into him by the huge urns where his father was bound and died, and the sight of him standing there and smiling peacefully back at me gave me no end of faith that a man could remake his own self by himself, and I must say, Grandmother, that if you're right and he was only playing a part, he played it to the hilt, he couldn't have looked more natural pulling that little boy after him, because he took him everywhere to keep him out of the way of my officers—who, in the gleaming leather boots they all wore, both those in black uniforms and those in civilian clothes, listened to me lecture on the ancient civilization that knew neither guilt nor fear while smiling mysteriously to themselves . . . ach, those gorillas with diplomas, those supermurderers, those geniuses of destruction—the scum, the scandal of Germandom! . . .

—Yes, yes . . .

—You know, you know very well, Grandmother . . .

—Yes . . . you know . . . you know . . . we all know, even those of us who think that we don't . . .

—Yes!

—Yes, yes, yes! Don't be so innocent!

—All right, I've calmed down.

—All right.

—I've calmed down.

—Fine, I beg your pardon . . .

—Soon . . . one more minute . . . here, we're already at our last station. We have finally arrived, Grandmother, at the old Turkish guard post that has been standing here since the last century. Come see why they put it here, the vista you have of the sea . . . of the sea and nothing but the sea. Yes, the Turks sat up here a hundred years ago, on the lookout for pirates . . . here, have a seat, Grandmother . . . please, sit down . . . I'm sorry I shouted at you . . .

—Who am I to be blaming anyone? After all, I'm part of it myself, even if, when I first arrived on this island, I was inspired by the belief in a new way, national and individual—because my canceled Mani was just an allegory, part of a much bigger philosophy, which, by the autumn of 1943, I knew would have to be put to the test . . .

—I'm getting there . . .

—Italy fell, and the same Italians who had been semi-allies now became semi-prisoners who had to be disarmed and guarded. We suddenly felt such isolation . . . and the more it grew, Grandmother, the more enemies we made, which meant we had to corral them and count them twice a day, morning and evening, to make sure we had caught them all . . . except that we didn't really believe that ourselves, which made us look for still more enemies, whom we found immediately, although since we didn't believe that they were all there were either, we tortured them to lead us to more enemies, and so on and so forth . . . And thus we were kept busy all day long, guarding and counting and hunting and searching and interrogating, which led to still more hunts and searches, so that by the time the midnight shift came on we discovered that our isolation had grown even greater and that by now we were the prisoners of our prisoners. It was at that point that we called for help. And so early last spring two experts came from Athens and at once scolded Schmelling for accumulating too many prisoners, which would never have happened if he had killed more of them and locked up less, which was why their first command was to round up all the Jews and ship them off to wherever Jews were shipped. You can imagine my shock, I who had naively thought that if the one Jew I found had been canceled all of Jewry had been canceled too, at being handed a list of still more Jews—who, it turned out, had been living all along in and around Heraklion, although some had already managed to escape . . .

—No, Grandmother, his name was not on the list, not because anyone higher up had accepted his cancellation, but because no one knew of his existence. His father was not a native, having been born in Jerusalem and banished to Crete by the British at the end of the last war, and since all those years he had kept his distance from other Jews, he was now beyond the pale of any non-Jewish inform-ers. Of course, had I wanted, I could have canceled that distance and returned the Manis to the fold in no more time than it takes to write a name on a list, but precisely this, I realized, was the great test, not only for him, but for me, Grandmother, because I had to decide on the spot, all by myself, if his cancellation was real or even conceivable, not only for himself but for anyone anywhere, or if we both had simply been playing with words for three years. And with-out thinking twice I decided . . . well, what do you think? What? Guess what I decided, Grandmother!

—Right you are! A most accurate guess, although I didn't do it for the reasons you think I did, that is, out of sheer innocent stupid-ity, but on the contrary, after profound meditation, and especially, in loyalty *to you,* Grandmother, and in the spirit of our conversa-tions on those winter evenings back in '39, when I was studying for my history and literature finals and you knew that the war was on its way. You asked me then to pray to the God you no longer believed in that the havoc and destruction wreaked by Germany should lead to a better future—which was why, accompanied by a soldier I took along to guard my clarity of mind, I went straight to Mani Junior, because I knew that many of the names on the list had already made themselves scarce. And it was a good thing that I got there when I did, because the mule was already tethered behind the house, loaded with sacks that no doubt contained flour and sugar and spices, which meant that he too had heard the rumors about the list in my possession and was preparing to take off. He was caught in the act, pale and bewildered, and so I said to him, "Mr. Citizen Mani, I've come to tell you that you needn't worry or run away, because you've canceled yourself and now you're null and void and nothing but a man, a pure *homo sapiens* living in the ruins of the ancient civilization of Knossos, which wouldn't have known a Jew if it saw one, because the Jews hadn't invented themselves yet. And now," I said to him, "is the ultimate test to find out if you believe in me as I have believed in you . . ."

—Aha . . . it's about time you paid me a compliment. So you do admit it, you admit that you see my point . . .

—Thank you, Grandmother, thank you.

—I'm listening, of course I am . . .

—Well, he listened to me very carefully, even though, after three years of occupation, his German was no better than before, a blood-less excuse for a language, and exchanged looks and whispers with his wife, who, three years after the night on which I saw her for the first time, still seemed the same age as me. She gave him a wise, thoughtful nod, and he went over and unloaded the mule, which I killed at once with a single bullet to relieve him of the need for any second thoughts. Then I said good-bye to them both and rode off to ferret out of their holes all the other Jews who either couldn't or didn't want to cancel themselves . . .

—By then there weren't many of them left . . . we had gotten off to a late start . . . by deportation day, the entire island had yielded only two hundred seventy of them . . .

—I'm almost done . . . in a minute, Grandmother, I'll be done . . . why, you're as eager to get to the end as a small child . . .

—Of course I had my doubts. Let me say once more that I've never been naive. In fact, the following night, which was the night of May 20, the third anniversary of my jump, I returned. I found a free moment amid the bedlam of registering all the prisoners, jumped on my trusty old cycle, which was old and scarred by now, and raced off to see him, even though this meant taking my life in my hands on the roads between the villages, because a special east wind had carried the smell of German blood from the steppes of Russia, and like a subtle spice it had put some backbone in the Cretans and a new impudence in their eyes. But that didn't stop me, because I had to know if he had stayed behind and trusted me as I had trusted him, if he really believed his own words about canceling his superfluous non-essence. When I got there I almost jumped for joy, because there was light behind the lowered curtains. And yet when I knocked on the door and entered the house, which I had gotten to know every detail of over the years, I could tell at once from the restless motion of his hands as he rose to greet me that something had happened, or was missing, and at once the thought crossed my mind that the woman and child had been spirited off to the mountains, which made me so mad that I pointed my schmeisser at his stomach, intending to kill him with a single long burst. But just then he let out a bitter cry in the shadows, and, grabbing hold of the barrel of the schmeisser to deflect it, he blurted out the plea, the explanation, the rebuke, that it was precisely the mutual trust and understanding between us that had made him send the child away with its mother, since he could not possibly demand of his son, who was too young to cancel himself, what he was able to demand of his own self, so that for the time being the boy had to remain an uncanceled Jewish child . . .

—I knew you would say that.

—I knew you would say that . . . I give up . . .

—But it was just the opposite . . . just the opposite, Grandmother . . . listen . . . if he himself had stayed behind, that could only mean that he had faith and confidence in what he had done . . . that much is undeniable . . . we had both passed the test, he had passed mine and I had passed his . . .

—I saluted him again and returned to Knossos, which was completely dark by then. I looked up at the sky full of stars and thought of that night three years ago, back in '41, after I had come floating down from the sky like Daedalus in Gustav Koch's myth, and then I stepped into the little guard post near Mani's store not far from the bust of Sir Arthur Evans and telephoned Schmelling, who was very upset about the disappointing number of Jews rounded up so far.

"It can't be," he kept telling me, "there must be more of them, there has to be, you simply haven't looked hard enough." and so I said, "I've found all the Jews I can, but is it all right with you if I arrest a citizen who helped a Jewish mother and her child escape to the mountains," and he said, "Of course, of course, bring him in," and so I went back to the house, wondering if Mani Junior still was there or had taken to his heels too, and there he was behind the curtains, which were drawn because of the blackout, faithful less to his promise to me, Grandmother, than to the insidious idea that had gripped him in a vise, which is why I startled him so by coming back to tell him that he was under arrest for helping Jews escape, for that and nothing else. He began protesting and putting up such a fight that I had to fire at the walls to calm him down, after which I handcuffed him, sat him in the sidecar of my cycle, and sped back along the empty roads to reunite him with his imprisoned brethren whom he thought he had renounced . . . But now look, Grandmother, look over there to the west, how quick and subtle the sunset is . . .

—Exactly. That's the surprise I promised you . . . you see, you needn't have worried . . .

—Well, then, don't. In the end he was thrown into that dry winery with all the other Jews who had been brought from all over the island—and since there weren't enough of them to suit the experts from Athens, our addlebrained Schmelling decided to add four hundred Greek prisoners, and since that still proved too little, he also threw in three hundred of our ex-Italian friends, who were now simply so many detained nuisances. On the sixth of June there were whispered rumors about a big enemy landing in France, and so we moved as quickly as we could and loaded all the deportees that same day on a small ship that was commandeered in Heraklion harbor. We clamped a curfew on the city to keep people away from the pier, but even then, when the deportees were marched from the prison, the rooftops and terraces were so lined with onlookers that we were ordered to fire in the air. And I, Grandmother, the birth-and-identity specialist, seeing how worried everyone was that the ship might be waylaid on its way to Greece, suggested to Schmelling and his officers that we change its name and give it a new identity. I even found an appropriate one in the books you sent me, *Danaë,* which was the name of the daughter of Acrisius, King of Argos. Old Koch would have been proud of me! And indeed, the sailors painted over the old name, and that evening the ship set sail for Santorini. It didn't get far, however, before a British bomber flying innocently overhead noticed an unfamiliar vessel and sank it not far from the point where our sun is about to disappear . . .

—Citizen Mani was on it too. Where else could he have been? He went down with the ship.

—Just once. Very briefly, as he was standing in line for his supper. I promised to have him freed if he told me where his wife and child were, but he wouldn't answer me, and I had no time to determine if this meant he had abandoned the logic that had spun the two of us around in its closed circle, or if, on the contrary, he had realized that this logic meant not only freeing him, but arresting his wife and child and sending them off with the other deportees . . .

—Of course.

—Of course. Why not? I was perfectly serious . . .

—Why not? It was only natural, wasn't it?

—If you, for instance, just for the sake of the argument, had been born a Jew . . .

—Now don't get angry . . .

—I'm sorry.

—All right . . . all right . . .

—Right, we'll start back down soon, Grandmother. As I told you when we started out, the twilight here is very short, not at all like in Germany . . .

—That was the end of it, Grandmother. This happened two months ago, and since then we've opened a new corral that's filled up amazingly quickly even though there's not a Jew left on the island—except, of course, for that woman and her child, whom I would gladly hunt down in the mountains if we weren't forbidden to leave the town limits of Heraklion, so that all I can do is come up here every evening before dark, to this old Turkish guard post, and look to see if they haven't snuck back home . . . if the lights aren't on in their house again . . .

—The woman?

—What makes you ask?

—But I already described her . . .

—I'd say average height . . . nice-looking . . . what more can one say?

—Why do you ask?

—No, no one in particular . . . maybe . . .

—Maybe . . . but why do you ask?

—At first I did think there was something . . . in the expression or the smile . . . maybe some old photograph we had at home . . . but little by little the resemblance seemed to fade . . .

—Not of Mother . . . not of her . . . of you, actually, Grandmother . . . a very old photograph . . .

—I'll go on lying in wait for her here. Perhaps I'll catch her and her little boy after all . . . because the thought that we'll soon have to leave this place for the swamps and the fog again, and that *they* will continue to look out at this brilliant bay through these ancient, enchanting olive trees—that thought so aggravates me, Grandmother, that I'm ready to go on sitting here forever until I lay my hands on them.

—Why?

—When?

—What are you talking about?

—Since when?

—But since when? Who told you?

—I'm fighting for Germany right here . . . that is, until the English come . . .

—How? Since when?

—Tomorrow?

—What are you talking about?

—No transfer order will ever get here . . .

—I don't get it . . . what order?

—But how can that be? Who gave it to you?

—But whose signature is on it? Who had the authority to sign it?

—Let me see it. I don't believe you . . .

—You went all the way to the top, didn't you? All the way . . . but why didn't you ask me first? Ach, what have I ever done to you, Grandmother, to make you keep meddling in my destiny?

—But I don't understand whom it's meant for. Whom do you intend to show it to?

—Let me see it, I don't believe you . . .

—Show it to me . . . it can't be . . .

—No, there's enough light . . .

—But let me see it. What are you afraid of?

—*His* own signature is on it? It's impossible . . . you're out of your mind, Grandmother . . . you went to *him?* I don't believe it . . .

—What does the name of Sauchon have to do with it?

—I don't wish to make a mockery of anything.

—But how? How, Grandmother? I give up . . . you didn't understand my story . . . you missed the whole point . . . why, it's just the opposite . . . all along what I've been talking about is *our* freedom. We can't go on hunting down every one of them until the end of history . . . we have to let them cancel themselves . . . my one worry is for our poor Germany . . . for our despairing Führer . . . for the future . . .

—You musn't say that . . . it isn't true . . .

—No, now I understand. You want me to be killed in a final, lost battle for Germany . . . just like you sent Egon to his death in the first war . . . I was right after all . . . you still don't accept my existence! I thought you had come to see me because you loved me, I thought you might even stay with me here, but now I see that you've come to take me away . . . it's out of the question . . . I don't agree to it . . . I won't go . . . no, Grandmother, don't show it to anyone . . . don't give anyone that order . . . I beg you, don't give it to anyone . . .

—But what honor? For the love of God, what honor? Whose honor?

—No, I will not give it back to you . . . not until you promise me to destroy it . . . it's a pointless, an unacceptable piece of paper . . .

—In that case I'll tear it myself . . . you can have his signature back, and I'll tear the rest and scatter it to the winds . . .

—I will *too* dare . . . I won't give it back . . . I won't . . . I swear to you by all that's holy, I've seen the dead and I don't want to join them . . . you can't decide that for me . . . you have no right to . . . you have no right . . . you didn't kill God to take His place . . . you're not Zeus's great-grandson Minos . . .

—Then I'll give up both the name and the honor. I was born as a compensation that didn't compensate anyone. As far as you're concerned, Creation itself was a mistake . . . the whole world is a mistake . . . deep down you're one of them . . . your despair comes from the same place . . .

—I don't want any part of the estate . . . I don't want a single speck of it . . . because I don't want any part of the insane suicide that the Führer is planning. I'm staying here, and I'm not leaving this island until the English come. No, Grandmother, you are not Minos, the great-grandson of Zeus . . . you can't judge me . . . you have no right to . . .

—No, listen . . . listen . . .

—Yes, listen, you must, it's from the Homer you yourself sent me . . .

—No, wait, here, listen . . . how beautiful *The Odyssey* is . . . *There I saw Minos, great-grandson of Zeus,/ In his hand a golden scepter, as he sat speaking to the dead,/ And they gathered round him, the destiny-decreeing governor of their fate,/ They who sat and stood in the dwellings of broad-gated Hades . . .*

BIOGRAPHICAL

Supplements

EGON BRUNER The news that his grandmother's plane had crashed into the sea took a few days to reach Corporal Egon Bruner, who grieved greatly for the old woman, both because he had been deeply attached to her in his fashion and because their farewell had been traumatic for them both. Nevertheless, Egon felt certain that he had been right to tear up the transfer order.

Despite the increase in Greek partisan attacks on the German army in Crete, Egon remained determined to discover the village or monastery in which Mrs. Mani and her child were hiding, but he searched in vain. In October, in response to a British breakthrough, he was transferred with his unit to northern Italy, and from there, via Austria, to the raging Eastern Front. In January 1945, in the midst of a particularly hard winter, he was stationed in an abandoned manor house not far from the Polish town of Oświęcim, where he served as a medic in a support unit for the garrison of a nearby concentration camp. In February 1945 he was taken prisoner by the Russians, who held him until January 1946. Upon his release, he returned to his grandparents' estate, which, in the postwar confusion, he took possession of as if it were his own. However, when the family attorney returned from a prolonged internment in a prisoner-of-war camp in Siberia and opened the Sauchons' will, it came to light that Egon was mentioned there as no more than a possible heir, nor was anything said about his being the admiral's son. Consequently, several nephews of his father laid claim to the property on the grounds that Egon had failed to prove his right to the title. Not wanting to reopen the episode of his "desertion" during the invasion of Crete, especially because he feared revealing the purpose of his grandmother's trip to the island, Egon agreed to an out-of-court settlement that deprived him of the estate's northeast quadrant.

Meanwhile, he had begun studying at the University of Hamburg. At first he thought of majoring in ancient Greek history, but classical Greek proved too hard for him and he switched to twentieth-century history. In the 1950s he taught history at a high school not far from his estate, and being a bachelor, he had plenty of time for his political activities in the Liberal Party. His relations with his mother and stepbrother were correct but little more than that.

In the 1960s, when the Social-Democrats came to power in Germany with Liberal backing, Egon was appointed to direct the Goethe Institute in Athens. It took a few months for him to gather the courage to visit Crete—where, concerned he might be recognized, he went about with a beard and dark sunglasses. But no one recognized him, not even the proprietress of the grocery store in Heraklion where he had bought tobacco during his three years on the island. He was able to establish that the Mani house in Knossos was lived in by an unfamiliar Greek family, but he did not dare approach and ask about its former inhabitants. Eventually, he rented a motorcycle and took to roaming the mountainous back roads of the island, knocking on the doors of little monasteries and asking about the Jewish woman and her son. He was unable to come up with any information, however, except for the standard assurance that there were no Jews left in Crete, because they all had gone down with the *Danaë*. It surprised Egon Bruner that no one sounded at all sorry about it.

Egon visited Crete several more times during his term at the Goethe Institute in Athens, and once, in 1963, he even continued on from there to Israel, where he spent an interesting week as a guest of the Goethe Institute in Tel Aviv. One day, while waiting there in the office, it occurred to him to ask his colleague's secretary to look up the name Mani in the telephone book. When asked by her how to spell it, he confessed to having no idea, and so she gave him a list with all the possible variations; yet seeing how long it was, and that it included families from all over the country and even one Arab, Egon Bruner gave up and did not pursue the matter further.

After the generals' coup in Greece, Egon Bruner returned to Germany, but in 1973 he went abroad again to direct the Goethe Institute in Istanbul. Subsequently, he left his work and retired to his small estate in northern Germany. Although occasionally he took part in the Jewish- and Israeli-German dialogues that were organized by the Liberal Party-sponsored Baumen Institute, he reacted with distaste to the Israeli invasion of Lebanon in 1982 and discontinued his participation in these meetings.

ANDREA SAUCHON   The old woman was so shocked and upset by Egon's tearing up of his transfer order on the hilltop in the Cretan twilight that for a moment she literally lost the power of speech. Even when she regained it, her indignation and sorrow were such that she resolved not to say another word to her grandson until she had thought the matter over. They descended the hill slowly. Although it was clear to her that she had failed miserably in Egon's education, she could not put her finger on what went wrong or what lapse in Egon's moral code could explain (if indeed there was any explanation) his behavior over the past three years in Crete. When they reached the army base after a slow hour's walk, dusk was already falling and an impatient Bruno Schmelling was waiting worriedly for them. At once he informed them of the banquet he was giving in honor of Admiral Sauchon's wife, but to his astonishment, Frau Sauchon begged off, pleading a headache and the need to rest up for her trip home. Schmelling turned red and was mortified. The meal, which he had prepared himself, meant a great deal to him, yet the old lady stubbornly stuck to her guns despite all his remonstrances.

Andrea Sauchon could not fall asleep that night. At first she was kept awake by her grandson's pacing outside her locked door, and later, by the premonition that she would never see her native land again and would die on her way back to it.

It was with this feeling that she ate the breakfast that Egon, who had spent a sleepless night too, brought to her room in the morning.

He managed to address her in a way that did not demand any answers, and although she was willing by now to talk to him, she could not think of a way to break her silence. And so at 7 A.M. Egon brought her, still not talking, to her light plane, which took off at once for Athens. Near the island of Phorus it was detected by two patrolling British Spitfires that sought at once to intercept such easy prey. Sighting them, the pilot called to Andrea Sauchon, who, unlike him, was not wearing a parachute, "I'm sorry to inform you, *meine Frau,* that you must prepare for the worst." "That's exactly what I have been doing for the last seventy-four years," was her answer. In another moment she was astonished to see the face of a young British pilot looking down at her. For a split second, before his machine gun opened fire, he reminded her of Egon.

THIRD CONVERSATION

Jerusalem, Palestine

7 A.M. Wednesday, April 10, 1918

T   H   E

Conversation

P   A   R   T   N   E   R   S

LIEUTENANT IVOR STEPHEN HOROWITZ Born in Manchester, England, in 1897. His father, Joseph Horowitz, immigrated with his family from Russia at the age of fourteen and went into the textile business. His mother Diana, née Elias, was born in Manchester to a Jewish family that came to England from Algeria in the early nineteenth century. At first Ivor attended a local grammar school, but he did so well in his studies that his parents transferred him to a prestigious public school in Derbyshire, not far from Manchester. Upon graduating in 1913, he was admitted to King's College, Cambridge, where he began to read law and English literature. After a year of debating between the two he decided, in consultation with his parents, to study law.

Ivor Horowitz was not immediately mobilized when war broke out in August 1914. During his second year in Cambridge, however, he was asked to report for his physical, and at the start of his third year, in October 1915, he was called up. After basic training in southern England, he shipped out with his regiment to France.

Ivor, a medium-height, chubby, bespectacled young man, tried unsuccessfully to obtain a position as a regimental clerk and in April 1916 was sent to the front—where, between the French villages of Dompierre and Méricur, he saw action in nine weeks of hard fighting and was nearly killed twice. In late June his request was granted to be sent to a hastily improvised officers' training camp in Normandy that turned out replacements for the depleted ranks. Meanwhile, having suffered heavy casualties, his regiment was pulled out of line for rest and regrouping.

In early September 1916 Ivor rejoined his regiment, which was then stationed at Compiègne, north of Paris. No position of command could be found for him, however, and so he was posted to the adjutant's office, where he served as a liaison officer with the French forces, especially in matters concerning order and discipline. Seeing that a knowledge of French would be most valuable for carrying out his duties, he set about learning the language with characteristic diligence, doing everything to make himself administratively indispensable so as to avoid being sent back to the trenches, the very thought of which made him quail. Nevertheless, despite all his efforts, a last-minute reshuffling of the regiment before its return to the front at Verdun compelled him to leave his new post and become a platoon commander.

However, on the twenty-fourth of November, 1916, Ivor Horowitz chanced to meet a former law don from Cambridge, Major Harwell Shapiro, now chief advocate of the 37th Division. Due to growing infringements of military discipline after two years of inconclusive fighting, the advocate-general's corps was rapidly expanding, and Ivor succeeded in convincing his ex-teacher that he could be of use. Major Shapiro managed to have the young officer transferred to the 37th's military police shortly before the division moved into line in December 1916. Divisional headquarters were near Lille, within range of the German artillery.

In the early spring of 1917 sweeping changes were made in the British high command, especially in the Middle East theater. After General Murray's abortive attack on Gaza in March, Sir Edmund Allenby, who was nicknamed "the Bull," was given command of the 52nd Division. Allenby sailed from Europe with a large complement of senior officers to restaff the division before renewing the campaign against the Turks in Palestine.

In May 1917 Ivor Horowitz, to his great delight, set out with Allenby for Egypt, a country he found most congenial and enjoyable. Henceforward he traveled with Allenby's general staff, on which he served as a military advocate. In late October 1917 he crossed the border into Palestine with Allenby's forces, and in January 1918, a month after the fall of Jerusalem, he was promoted from second to first lieutenant.

COLONEL MICHAEL WOODHOUSE Born in Wales in 1877. His father, Sir Ashley Woodhouse, was a Tory member of Commons and Assistant Minister of Justice under Gladstone. As a boy Michael was sent to a military school in Sussex, after which he joined the army in 1896. He served in the Far East, India, Malaya, and Ceylon, and gradually rose through the ranks. In 1912 he returned to Great Britain to take command of the 3rd Welsh Regiment. In 1914, now a major, he arrived with the first wave of the British Expeditionary Force in France, where his unit was among the first to see combat against the Germans. Major Woodhouse fought in holding actions on the Marne and the Somme in 1915 and was promoted to lieutenant colonel, in which capacity he served as chief operations officer of the 6th Battalion. He was taken prisoner, escaped, and rejoined his regiment, but in late June 1916 he was seriously wounded in the trenches of Verdun, losing his right arm and part of his vision. For three months he was hospitalized in Chenanceau Castle in the Loire Valley, which had been converted into a military hospital. In early 1917 he was released, promoted to colonel, and awarded the Distinguished Service Order, but he refused to return to England and insisted on remaining in active service. At first he served in a staff position, but after growing friction with his superiors, accompanied by excessive drinking and fits of depression, he asked one of Allenby's generals to arrange an overseas transfer. In September 1917 he arrived in Allenby's Cairo headquarters and was assigned to the military police. Soon he began to serve as a presiding judge at military trials, a role he relished despite his lack of legal education.

His half of the conversation is missing.

—Colonel, sir. Lieutenant Ivor Stephen Horowitz of the advocate-general's corps, attached to the adjutant's office of the 52nd

Division. I'm most grateful to you for finding time to discuss with me this matter of—

—Horowitz, Colonel, with two "o's."

—British, of course. Born in Manchester, sir.

—1897, sir.

—Yes, sir.

—My father, sir, did not have the good fortune to be born in the United Kingdom, although he arrived in it as a young lad. My mother, on the other hand—

—From Russia, sir. But as a very small child. What deucedly foul weather!

—It surprised us too, Colonel. We never thought we'd encounter such a stormy winter in Jerusalem, which our British imaginations had pictured, or at least mine had, as a sun-scorched sort of place. And yet it's done nothing but rain in the months since we've been here and the city elders swear that it's the wettest winter in memory. Still, sir, no matter how glumly a day like this begins, there are bound to be a few hours of clear skies. It's not your eternal Leeds or Glasgow drizzle . . .

—There's hope even on a day like this, Colonel.

—No, sir. We still haven't any dependable or even regular weather forecasts, sir, because the balloons sent up by the Royal Meteorological Service in Cairo do not cover Palestine. However, the barometer outside the house of the French consul does give reliable notice for up to a few hours. I took a look at it on my way over here, sir, and I'm happy to inform you that there's hope for better weather this afternoon.

—Horowitz, sir.

—That's correct, sir, with two "o's." I hope you had a good night's sleep, Colonel.

—Oh.

—Oh . . .

—Oh, I'm dreadfully sorry to hear that. It's considered, sir, the best establishment in Jerusalem. General Allenby himself stayed there after entering the city, and to the best of my knowledge, there were no particular complaints from his staff. I'm most distressed to hear you say that, sir.

—Quite so, sir. I daresay that their cook hasn't learned to make

proper British food yet. It's no secret that you can't find a decent
side of bacon in all of Jerusalem. Our governor's wife, Lady Hum-
phrey, was just saying as much to the brigadier. Although I've heard
say that the same cook has acquired the knack of a quite traditional
British porridge. You might want to try it, sir.

—I see, Colonel.

—The city itself, sir, is a small and shabby place, and after a few
months here I'm quite prepared to say that it's a frightfully dull one
as well. The population is extremely mixed, a hodgepodge of small,
unsociable communities that are as indigent and ignorant as they are
endowed with a messianic sense of superiority. As usual, there seems
to be no relation between the reputation of the place, which it owes
to the great books written in and about it, and the sordid reality, sir.

—What does it have to offer? Jolly little, Colonel. One renowned
and quite impressive mosque, the Dome of the Rock, which you no
doubt know about, sir. A few important churches, chiefly, the Holy
Sepulchre—which if you don't mind my saying so, sir, is rather a
disappointment. A few of the little churches outside the walled city
are far more charming and harmoniously proportioned. Any time
you would like a tour, sir, the advocate-general's office will be
pleased to put a first-rate guide at your disposal.

—As usual, sir, the Jews have little to offer except themselves. To
our great surprise it turns out that they are a majority here, even
though many of them were banished or fled during the war. Archi-
tecturally, they have only a few poor synagogues. And of course,
there's that big white wall they stand in front of, which is supposedly a remnant of their Temple.

—Yes, sir. They simply stand there and pray, as if they were
rooted to the spot.

—Half a day, sir, is more than enough to do the holy places at
your leisure. Everything is at frightfully close quarters, and the distances are so absurdly small as to be, I would say, almost tragic.

—Outside the walls, sir, are some new neighborhoods scattered
over the hills. A few of them, so I've discovered in the course of this
dismal winter, actually begin to grow on you. But it takes a while,
sir, I should think, before you can see their charm . . .

—The environs, sir, are poor indeed. If you're familiar at all with
Greece, you'll be reminded of the southern Peloponnese.

—I'm sorry to say, sir, that I've never been to Greece, but those who have speak of a resemblance, and I'm merely passing on their judgment. The olive groves and vineyards, for example, or the bare, round hills, primitive villages, and black-robed shepherds. And of course, one musn't forget Bethlehem, which is only a few miles away. It's a pleasant, gentle sort of place that nestles in the hills quite gracefully; there's the famous Church of the Nativity, and a most jovial Anglican priest who can tell you all about it in biblical English—he's really quite entertaining. I would also recommend, sir, an excursion to Jericho, and to the Dead Sea and the mouth of the Jordan, where the Australians are encamped. If Baedeker is right about its being the lowest spot in the world, then having come this far, sir, you wouldn't want to miss it. It's certainly a sight closer than the world's highest spot, what?

—I'm sorry, sir, but I didn't quite catch the name.

—I'll make a note of it at once, sir. Is it a new label?

—There's an Irish officer in our section who's quite a grog fancier, sir. He has excellent connections with the Armenian church, which has a most presentable cellar. I'll ask him to see to a bottle.

—Very well, sir, five . . .

—I've made a note of it, sir. Will any other label do as well?

—In that case, sir, we'll spare no effort. In any event, I'll report back to you during the day. Will there be anything else, sir? Cigarettes? Tobacco?

—Very well, sir. The trial begins tomorrow morning. There will be a car waiting for you in front of your hotel at eight o'clock sharp. It's about a five-minute drive. A small courtroom has been prepared in the Russian Compound, which is outside the walls, not far from the Eastern Orthodox Church. I believe it's fairly comfortable, sir, as local standards go.

—Sir?

—Ah, yes. I haven't looked into the matter, sir, but I'm quite sure we'll have no acoustical problems. The fact is, Colonel, that there won't be many of us, and the prosecution will ask the court to conduct part of the proceedings in camera so as to protect our sources of information behind enemy lines, which have done excellent work. Indeed, sir, barring the unexpected, the trial is unlikely to last more than a few days . . .

—No doubt you know their names already, Colonel. They're listed in the brief that the sergeant gave you yesterday, and I believe you'll meet them tonight at the governor's reception in your honor. On your right will be Lieutenant Colonel Keypore of the Australian Battalion, who drove up from the Jordan yesterday, and on your left Major Jahawala, an Indian from Intelligence. As for counsel, sir, the defendant has none, nor could he be persuaded to take any, neither Jew, Arab, nor Englishman. He's quite determined to defend himself, having studied law for a year or two in Beirut when he was young, and he seems confident he can do it. However, I've asked First Lieutenant Brian Oswald to be prepared to assist him, if necessary. I believe that's all, sir. Saving the witnesses, of course.

—Oh, dear, sir, of course. I beg your pardon. I myself will prosecute, with the help of First Lieutenant Harold Gray.

—Yes, sir.

—Quite so, sir.

—Yes, sir. Major Clark is our chief advocate.

—Oh. I thought, Colonel, that you already knew of Major Clark's absence. His personal correspondence to you should be in this brief.

—I see. Well, sir, in short, Major Clark sailed for England three weeks ago for his wedding in Blenheim Park. With the brigadier's permission, of course.

—There's not much I can tell you, sir. I only know that the young lady is the daughter of Lord Barton, and that the wedding was best held without delay to prevent any possible embarrassment. I believe that's enough said, sir.

—He made her acquaintance in Paris, sir. Did you never meet Major Clark? A most delightful chap.

—I'm afraid that's all I know, sir. But I can find out if you wish whether the young lady is Lord Barton's elder or younger daughter.

—As you wish, sir. In any event, that is the reason Major Clark could not prosecute the case and I shall be taking his place.

—Quite so, Colonel. I am not the ranking officer in his absence. But Major Clark preferred to entrust the task to me.

—I read law at Cambridge, sir, from 1913 until my call-up in October 1915.

—King's, sir.

—I was unable to take my degree, sir, because of the war.

—No, sir. I was first in France.

—No, sir. With the 38th Infantry Regiment, 42nd Division.

—From March through August of 1916, Colonel.

—No, sir. I was at the front. In eastern France.

—No, sir. I was a private at the time.

—Naturally, sir, in the trenches, sir, in combat and in frontal assaults, sir. What else could I have been doing at the front?

—In April and May of 1916.

—On the Somme, sir. Between Dompierre and Méricur.

—On the northern flank.

—Quite so, sir. The night of May seventeenth is a horror to remember. It was the ghastliest of them all.

—I'm speaking for myself, of course. We lost three hundred men in two hours, including two platoon commanders.

—So he was, sir. How astounding that you knew him!

—I was fortunate, sir. Just a bit of shrapnel.

—Thank you, sir, I'd be glad to. It's very kind of you. If you don't mind, Colonel, I'd prefer to sit by your side, so that I can show you a few documents.

—Thank you, sir. We can manage without the desk. I won't be long and you needn't trouble yourself. Now that the main features of the case are clear to you, there is something . . . something else that I wish to take up with you . . . I mean now, before the trial begins . . . since once it does, I shan't be free to raise the matter with the court, as you will have seen for yourself from the brief . . .

—I beg your pardon, sir.

—Indeed, sir, I was afraid you might not have time to read it all.

—Oh.

—Oh, dear . . .

—Oh, dear me, Colonel, we had no idea. I'm flabbergasted.

—Oh, dear, sir. I'm so dreadfully sorry. I'm quite devastated. We knew, of course, that you were wounded at Verdun. Your name, sir, has been a byword in our division ever since the Battle of the Marne.

—I'm so sorry, sir. No one breathed a word to us. Had anyone told me, I would have come to read the brief to you myself.

—Now? Well, why not! I'd be delighted to, Colonel. I'm entirely at your disposal, and I'm quite prepared to read you the brief and all its documents.

—I'd be delighted to, sir. A resumé, as the French say. It will be both jollier and quicker . . .

—Thank you, sir. With pleasure.

—Just a wee drop, sir . . . that will do for this hour of the morning . . . cheers, sir . . .

—So this is the whiskey, then, is it? It's superb . . . no wonder you insist on it, Colonel!

—Indeed, it is . . . that, sir . . . I mean . . . that's the very subject . . . you've hit the nail on the head, sir! The prosecution will ask for the death penalty in accord with wartime regulations, whereas . . . you see, that's just what I wished to talk to you about . . .

—Sir?

—Quite so. It's best to begin from the beginning. But just where is the beginning, sir, if you'll allow me to reflect for a moment? Suppose we say on the twenty-eighth of February, on a cold, foggy, rainy night, indeed, on a sleety night turning to real snow in the morning, the kind that falls here no more than once a year to the great consternation of the natives. That, sir, was the night the accused was apprehended. It happened some ten miles north of Jerusalem, just outside a small town called Ramallah, which means the hill of God, in a hamlet called el-Bireh, which is the biblical Bethel, I believe. It's a small village of olive groves and little vegetable gardens that marks the farthest point of Allenby's advance after taking Jerusalem in December. It's not at all clear why he stopped there— perhaps he wished to rest his forces after the excitement of Jerusalem. But since he didn't strike while the iron was hot, it grew cold and gray until its jagged lines hardened like fate. That's where the front runs now, with the Turks sitting on the other side of it, out of sight behind a ridge of hills. It cuts right through the village, several of the houses on the lower slope of which are in no-man's land. The Arabs living in them are poor shepherds who are allowed to come and go, and one of our more enterprising officers even issued them certificates of good conduct granting them freedom of movement among the hills and between the two armies. There's a bonny platoon of Ulstermen there with a brave bucko of a commander who's actually just a first sergeant. They've dug trenches and deployed their machine guns, and they sit there breathing the winter fog that rolls in from the sea to the desert and thinking of Ulster. Now and then they cluck to the goats, or call to some shepherd grazing his flock down the hill to come show them his certificate. Since they speak no Arabic and have no interpreters, they have no dealings with the natives, who pay them as much attention as you would to a lot of flitting shadows. Which is what makes it so extraordinary that he was even noticed that foggy dawn, let alone apprehended. And it's even more remarkable that, once he was apprehended, it was decided to detain him . . . so that, looking back on it now, I can't swear that he didn't do it deliberately . . . that he didn't do everything, in fact, for the sole purpose of being caught, so that he could have his day in court . . .

—Thirty-one, sir. A scraggly, dark-haired chap. On the short side. But though he's at most ten years older than me, he looks old enough to be my great-grandfather, with so many wrinkles you might think every one of his crooked thoughts had spilled out of his brain and over his face. Thirty-one, sir, but tough enough to be fifty, awfully earnest and not at all youthful. The morning he was caught he was wearing a peasant's cloak and had three black goats in tow, which were a rather symbolic representation of the flock he was supposed to have. He headed straight up the hill to Sergeant Mc-Clane's funk hole and woke him up from his sleep . . .

—Quite so, sir. And there, in those foggy wee hours, he was asked for his certificate; and when he didn't have it, he was taken aside until there was enough light to see what matter of man he was. But before a few minutes went by, sir, he tried escaping under cover of the last darkness; so that now he was taken, goats and all, and put in a little room; where he sat all day long as the rain turned to snow, refusing to eat and cursing darkly in Arabic while waiting for the Ulstermen to get so bloody sick of him that they would tell him to clear out. Which was not, I daresay, an unreasonable hope, especially since, huddled in his corner, he understood every word that they said, although he never opened his mouth to let on. And in fact, they would have packed him off soon enough, since the snowstorm kept them from bringing him to headquarters in Ramallah, if

Sergeant McClane hadn't laid down the law and insisted on waiting for the military police to look him over.

—I should think you would be, sir; so was I. A fortnight ago, when we ran through with him what had happened prior to recommending him for promotion and a medal, I asked him what had aroused his suspicion. Shall I tell you what he said, sir? "Sure now, the goats didn't like him. I know a thing or two about goats, and his didn't like him one bit." Tipped off that the man was a spy by three sulky goats, ha ha . . . that's what I call a keen eye! The next day a deputation came slogging through the snow from Jerusalem: two military policemen and an interpreter, Roger Evans, a Queen's man from Oxford—one of our university Orientalists who know the Koran inside out but lose their tongues when they have to ask for the time of day in Arabic, because their dons, who have never been east of the Thames in their lives, forgot to tell them there were Arabs in the world and thought they were teaching a dead language like Latin or Sanskrit. Well, there they were, the two of them, old Evans ruddy cross at having been dragged out in the cold for some daft shepherd, and the shepherd sitting in his corner, all huddled up in his cloak with his head bowed . . .

—Directly, sir. Picture him, if you can, huddled in a corner with that little Ulsterman sheepishly biting his nails; and old Evans jabbering away in his unspeakable Oxford Arabic; and the shepherd answering glumly; and the military policemen jotting it all down: a perfectly mad tale about some runaway goats whose tracks were washed out by the rain, and some village across the lines; and everyone ticked off at that obstinate Ulsterman who had raised the very devil for naught . . . and in fact, old Evans was already getting up to go when something about that shepherd rang a bell—by now he's told us about it a thousand times, because I had to put him up for a promotion and a medal too; so you see, sir, this episode has helped to advance more than one military career. Well, Evans asked for more light and told the Arab to stand; and then he removed his head cloth and looked him straight in the eye and told him to take off his cloak; and when the chap refused and began to protest, the soldiers stripped it from him; and dashed if he wasn't wearing a dark suit underneath with a little striped necktie; and there was a book in the pocket of the jacket with all sorts of papers falling out of it; so that old Evans burst out laughing and said, this time in proper Oxford English, "Why, Mr. Mani, is it you?"

—Mani, sir. That's his name.

—Joseph Mani. Sounds rather like money, but it doesn't mean that at all. Or like manic, but it doesn't mean that either.

—As far as I know, it doesn't mean anything, sir. It's just one of your oriental Jewish names. Because you see, sir, the shepherd wasn't a shepherd, and the Arab wasn't an Arab but a Jew, who suddenly changed his tune and began to speak the king's English in a Scots brogue so thick it could have been fished from a loch; and then, as if he had been simply playing a prank, threw his arms around Evans and began to walk out with him, because he too, sir, was an interpreter in His Majesty's service.

—Yes, sir, a genuine Scots brogue. You'll hear it yourself tomorrow when he enters his plea. He picked it up as a boy at St. Joseph's in Jerusalem, back at the end of the last century, from a Scottish priest who hammered it into him until there's no getting it out again. His father and mother were both British subjects, sir, which makes him one too, even though he's never been to England. That's why the prosecution will have to ask for the death penalty, since he's a national who has betrayed his country . . . which is why I've come to you, Colonel, to ask your advice before the trial begins.

—Of course, sir. Pardon me.

—Quite, sir, quite, it was my mistake to jump ahead. I simply didn't want to bore you with all kinds of details that I myself find endlessly fascinating.

—Utterly fascinating, sir. And I'll be delighted to. Well, there he was in that room, minus his cloak and in his frayed suit, with all sorts of papers sticking out of his pockets. Straightways he began telling some cock-and-bull story about a woman behind Turkish lines, a totally garbled, outrageous yarn; but our stubborn Ulsterman, now triumphantly vindicated, snatched the papers away from him and discovered a bundle of maps of Palestine, as well as some proclamations in Arabic, which he didn't need to read in order to know that they were not precisely what one brought one's ladylove; and so off he went to fetch a rope, tied up his prisoner, and—not trusting the policemen or the interpreter—set out with him for headquarters in Ramallah, from where Mr. Mani was taken to Jerusalem. I remember the night of his arrival. It was still quite parky, although the snow had begun melting in the narrow streets, and a few of us officers were sitting in the club and warming ourselves by the hearth when the police duty officer entered and informed us that a spy had been caught near Ramallah and was now under interrogation. Quite naturally there was a great to-do, and you know, sir, it strikes me that we British make rather a fuss over espionage, no doubt because we are taught from childhood on to be so trusting . . .

—Yes, sir, I do think so, sir. Who of us does not have his own private spy fantasy in which he singlehandedly brings some hidden bounder to justice? And so there was this police officer in the middle of the room with rain still trickling down his greatcoat, guardedly telling us what he could while we stood around him in a circle, until I stepped up to him—I remember it quite clearly—and asked, "But who is it? An Arab, I'll wager." It was obvious to me that no one else would spy on the British Empire. "Not at all," says he, his blue eyes twinkling, "it's one of our side." Well, there was general consternation at that—but he, sir, he just looked me straight in the eye and said, it was too much for him to resist: "I mean, not exactly one of *our* side; he's one of those Jews who've leeched onto us . . ." He knew very well who I was—he even threw me a cheeky, half-jesting smile—and I recall feeling, sir, if I may say so, thoroughly in a funk, not because of the anti-Semitic remark, which means nothing to me and is something I can shrug off quite coolly, but because of the quite maddening coincidence. Here was Major Clark about to leave the next day and finally give me a shot at trying a major case—and who should it involve but a Jewish spy in Jerusalem, a fact that an uncalled-for delicacy might regard as reason . . .

—Quite right, sir.

—Quite right, sir.

—To spare me the discomfort . . .

—Indeed, sir. You know what we military advocates generally have to deal with: desertions, brawls, petty thefts, drunkenness, insubordination—in a word, thirty- and sixty-day sentences and one-guinea fines. And here was a real investigation, something to get to the bottom of, where possibly lurked a man's death. I was so beside myself that I left the club directly and went straight to the divisional guardhouse by Jaffa Gate, under the assumption that that's where this Mani was being held. Of course, I had no idea at the time what his name was, but I was determined not to be elbowed aside, and soon I found myself standing out in the cold night across from the place called David's Tower, which is a sort of miniature version of the Tower of London, with my mind racing ahead. Just then I noticed a Jew dressed in black, hanging back by a little lane that ran into the empty square—and I knew directly that he was connected to the spy and had come to see what was being done with him; which meant that word had already reached the concerned parties in Jerusalem, who had sent a first scout to reconnoiter; and a most clandestine-looking, eternal-looking, metaphysical-looking scout he was . . . only later did I discover that he was not the least bit different from his scoutmasters . . .

—I'm sorry, sir, there I go again getting ahead of myself.

—The twenty-eighth of February, sir. The next day was a tense but quiet one at the advocate-general's office. Everyone knew about the investigation in the Tower of David, and the brigadier was beating the bushes for Major Clark, who had been absent from work for several days because he was busy packing and buying gifts—oriental baubles, silk scarves, and little rugs for the British gentry waiting for him impatiently, I daresay irately, at Blenheim Park. And now this spy had fallen on us out of the blue, and the major was terrified of having his leave canceled and being made to take up the investigation while his little bun was growing daily in its oven, which was something the whole British army couldn't have done anything about. He kept running from the tailor's and the jeweler's to the interrogation cell and the brigadier, and from there back to the advocates' office for a look at the lawbooks—and never a word to me, sir, not a hint that I might take the case upon myself, although he knew I would have given my right arm to do it. Wherever he went his hip flask went with him, and he had the squinty look of a beaten dog . . .

—I don't believe, sir, that he's partial to anything in particular; whatever's available will do . . . Well, that evening the first sergeant relayed an order for us four advocates to remain after work, and after a while Major Clark appeared, all bleary-eyed from drink and the day's intrigues; his little squint was gone, and he was wearing his dress uniform with the brass all polished and the decorations agleam. I could see at once that he had vanquished the brigadier and received leave to attend his own wedding, and I knew he would never be back in the Orient, since his future father-in-law had landed him a plum on the general staff to make sure he didn't fly the nest again now that it was properly feathered. And so he sat the four of us down with the Handbook of Wartime Jurisprudence and the secret file in front of him, speaking to all of us but looking only at me, because he knew his man and realized that for the past twenty-four hours I had been preparing myself for the case. First he told us about his adventures that day and about his tilt with the brigadier, and then he said to me: "And you, my dear Ikey, shall make this Jew your business, just don't forget whose side you're on; I want a proper investigation, and a proper indictment, and death, because that's what the law calls for and what divisional headquarters expects, seeing that this blighter is responsible for the loss of lives and artillery across the Jordan. You're the very man to do the job quickly and smoothly, since who could deny satisfaction to a Jew asking for another Jew's head? By Jove, it should be a special treat . . ."

—Yes, sir. Those were his words. A special treat.

—That's just his manner, sir. I've never taken it to heart, sir. I've served with Major Clark for over a year now, first in France and then here, and there isn't a more likable, decent chap anywhere, even if he has a sharp tongue. And his anti-Semitism is the most natural thing in the world; I mean, it's all a parcel with his views on women and horses, which are very solid indeed and have survived their encounter with the facts with hardly a scratch. But he wouldn't harm a fly and in fact there's no greater gentleman . . . Well, sir, we all drank to his health and went our ways, and I went mine firmly gripping the file as though it were a most wonderful book that I was about both to read and to write. I couldn't wait to talk to the prisoner, who was mine now, all mine! . . . I knew he was still putting up a brave front and admitting nothing, and no sooner had Major Clark left the room than I was out in the wet, lonely night, heading for the guardhouse. It was nearly midnight; the melting snow was trickling underfoot; a huge moon buzzed down above the city walls as if it were being hauled in on a kite string; and suddenly, as I was crossing the walled city in utter silence from the Nablus to the Jaffa Gate, I heard a snuffling and a tinkling of bells; and a shepherdless flock of black goats came charging out of a lane in such a dark frenzy that they might have been a pack of devils looking for the Archfiend himself, and vanished down another lane and were swallowed up by the cobblestones. The church bells were ringing away, and there was a smell of freshly baked bread, and I was actually trembling with desire to begin, already haunted by the momentous feeling that has gripped me, waking and sleeping, for the past five weeks . . . and which, Colonel, is the reason I'm here now, tiring you without getting to the point, because the story keeps coming between us, and I'm afraid I may already have tried your patience too far . . .

—That's very kind of you, sir. And so I climbed the stairs of the tower that the Jews call the Tower of David and the Arabs el-Kal'a; and I woke the sergeants and the duty officer and showed them the file and my authorization to conduct the investigation, which from now on I was to be in sole charge of; and I instructed them to let no one near the prisoner except by my express permission. Then I was taken to the cell block, past four hundred years of Turkish rule to a dungeon, a sort of round pit encircled by a walkway, in which our prisoner, the defendant, had been put like some sort of dangerous snake or panther, although in fact, in his black suit he looked more like a buzzard. He was seated on an army cot and reading a book by candlelight, a hard look on his gaunt, lined face; reading as though reluctantly, with the book half-pushed away from him. It was a Bible with both Testaments that an evangelical old officer of the guards, thinking him as good as hung already, had given him for his soul. He was so absorbed in his defiant, his recalcitrant reading that he didn't notice me looking down on him from above—not even when, like an actor on stage, he let the book drop, blew out the candle, cast himself down on the cot, curled up like a baby buzzard, and shut his eyes. My first thought was to let him be until morning while I studied the file and planned my attack; but the more I looked at him, the more something told me that unless I pressed ahead that very night, I would never get a confession out of him; no, the more time I let pass, the more tightly he would weave the tissue of lies he had cocooned himself in. And so I asked for a room and a pot of coffee and sat down to read the file and put my thoughts in order, and at 2 A.M. I returned to him. It was very cold down there. I removed his blanket and touched him; and he opened his eyes, which were so big and pure and young-looking that you could see they hadn't been made by whoever had made the rest of him; and I started speaking quickly and gently right into his dreams, casting a fine net to trap the fish of truth in its muddy swamp; while he, confused and tired though he was, in fact, thoroughly dejected, did his best in that clear Scots brogue you'll hear tomorrow to get a grip on himself and swim clear, carrying on once more about some woman of his behind Turkish lines, as if we were talking, not about villages of fanatically ignorant Mohammedans whose females go veiled and barefoot, but about some town along the Loire in a story by de Maupassant, with pretty young mademoiselles in embroidered aprons waiting for their lovers. And he too, he insisted, had "a ladylove," although you could tell at a glance that he wasn't a ladies' man but a man of words who couldn't picture the figment of his own imagination; so that had I asked him what the color of his lady's eyes was, he would have marveled that they had any color at all, let alone that he was expected to know it. It was a lie I wasn't having any part of. And yet the less I would hear of it, the more he clung to it, telling me about this woman he had been trysting with for a month, adding embellishments to his own ridiculous yarn that he clearly didn't believe a word of, as if it had taken hold of him and made him its master instead of the other way around; until at last he fell silent, shivering from the cold, and let his ladylove recede back into the mind that had concocted her. At that point, I took him up to the office; I let him warm himself there, made him a cup of hot tea, and introduced myself. "What will it take to make you trust me?" I asked him. He answered that he had a little son whom he hadn't seen for three days and missed terribly; and so I woke three soldiers of the guard, and at 3 A.M. we set out for one of those new quarters outside the walled city, Abraham's Vineyard was its name, and knocked on a door there. A middle-aged woman in a clean frock, with a rather nice, pleasant face, opened directly, as if she had been waiting for us. When she saw the soldiers she cried a bit; and the man touched her gently and murmured something in Hebrew and hurried up some stairs to a second story; and soon he came

back down with a four-year-old child in his arms, a handsome blond
boy who looked out of sorts, or perhaps a bit soft in the head. You'll
see him in court, sir, tomorrow; I've granted him permission to
attend the opening session, because I know that if the defendant
had counsel, he would use the child as grounds for clemency . . .

—Directly, sir.

—Yes, sir.

—No, sir.

—Quite so, sir.

—The point is, sir, that while he was kissing his son I ordered the
soldiers to search the house and make sure to go through every
drawer and collect every scrap of paper that they found. We sat
without a word in the kitchen, the two of us with the boy on his lap,
until they finished and came back with a large basket full of papers,
after which I told them to sit in the drawing room and had them
served tea. Meanwhile, there was already a first purple glow outside,
and a few lights came on in the neighborhood, because news had
spread of the police. And yet that was the only sign of life there was
in that utter, predawn silence. The woman put the boy back to sleep
and went to bed herself; and we sat there, the two of us; and I said,
"Look, why don't you tell me about it from the beginning, or if you
like, from even before that: just who are you?" By then we were
both so horribly fagged that only the truth could keep us awake, and
that's what he began to tell me while I sat there listening, that was
the opening through which I fished his confession. Afterward it was
merely a question of dotting the "i's" and crossing the "t's."

—Thank you, sir. Gladly.

—He is indeed. Born in Jerusalem, as was his father. His grandfather came here as a young man from Greece. Mind you, you don't
easily find such Jews, because Jews aren't naturally born in Palestine
as Englishmen are in England and Welshmen are in Wales. Most of
the Jews you see here are newcomers, and those who are born here
usually leave. Dashed few stay on, and those who do are rather
highly regarded, more by others, I daresay, than by themselves,
which is rather a boost to their self-esteem, although perhaps not as
much as all that . . .

—Right you are, sir. You would think, wouldn't you, that Jerusalem would be for a Jew what London is for an Englishman; but the

East End of London has more Jews in it than this entire country. I suppose that's because London is too substantial a place to carry about with you, whereas the Jews take Jerusalem wherever they go, and the more of them take it with them, the lighter it becomes . . .

—Up to a point, sir, up to a point. It's even true—why deny it?—of my own self. But my home is Manchester and the city of my dreams is London, and even if I have a warm place for this town in my heart, it's for the idea of it, not the reality. It's really quite extraordinary, sir, how, although I've been here for several months, the idea and the reality remain entirely separate.

—I appreciate that, sir . . . Well, then: why don't I sketch his biography on a thumbnail. His grandparents came here in the middle of the last century from Salonika, in the days when it was still part of Turkey, a childless couple who hoped that settling in Jerusalem might grant them their prayers for a child. And so it did, and our defendant's father, Moses Hayyim Mani, was conceived to his mother Tamara and his father Joseph Mani, who died before his son was born. Moses Hayyim was raised with no end of love by his mother, and grew up to be such a handsome, captivating lad that the British consul in Jerusalem, who was a neighbor of theirs, took him under his wing. He was a great Bible-reader, this consul, and perhaps it was because he saw in little Moses a metempsychosis of his biblical namesake that he decided to make him a British subject; in any case, for his thirteenth birthday he gave the boy a British passport as a present, which you'll find in this file here, Colonel. It's a rather unusual document, written in an ornate hand such as you never see anymore, with a lovely photograph of a child with the most candid, trusting eyes. It even has a number, and we've cabled London to run it down and see what series it belongs to, because it was not the common practice of British consuls to grant British nationality to children for being adorable . . . Be that as it may, however, the boy was pleased as punch to be a British subject and took his gift-wrapped passport with him everywhere, reciting Byron and Shelley and retelling *The Canterbury Tales* amid the pestilent poverty of this city, since his mother made a point of his studying English at a mission school. Then he was sent to Beirut, to study medicine at the American University. He was back within a year, homesick for both mother and Jerusalem; was persuaded to return;

somehow—although just barely, it would seem—persisted in his
studies while revisiting Jerusalem every few months; and finally took
his mother back to Beirut, where he pressed on doggedly out of
loyalty to his patron the consul until, at the age of twenty-seven, he
received his medical degree. By now it was time to marry him off
before he became a confirmed bachelor—at which point the consul
had the idea of finding him a British wife to make him more English
than ever. It took a while to locate one; but in the end he hit upon
another orphan, a woman slightly older than Mani, who was descended from an Anglo-Jewish family that had made a living as
camp followers of Napoleon's army until the Egyptian Campaign,
when it was taken prisoner by the Turks, from whom the French
forgot to ransom it. Eventually, it ransomed itself and stayed on in
the Orient; and so, in 1880, the two of them were wed. They had a
baby girl who died directly after childbirth, and then a second girl
who died, and then a boy, all because of incompatible blood; and
indeed, when our defendant came along in 1887, he seemed of a
mind to die too; but this time the Manis put their foot down; they
fought day and night to save him until he had no choice but to live;
and two years later a sister was born who survived too. By now the
doctor had been through so many postnatal crises that it occurred to
him to open a small lying-in hospital of his own—and so in the early
1890s, when Jews began building outside the walled city, he bought
the house in Abraham's Vineyard; found a tough old Swedish
woman, an old maid from Malmö who had come to the Holy Land
on a pilgrimage, failed to find God, and taken up free thought and
midwivery; installed some beds; and ordered the latest equipment
from France, including a large mirror in which the mothers could
watch themselves giving birth. Then he sat back and waited for the
fair sex of Jerusalem to knock at his gate. At first he got only the
fallen ones: women of ill repute, compromised young ladies, nuns in
the family way, pilgrimesses of dubious virtue. The Swedish midwife, who was quite cunning and resourceful, delivered each of
them with hardly a labor pain, as if she took it all upon herself, and
after a while Dr. Mani's surgery developed such a reputation that
mothers-to-be began flocking to it from all over. Our defendant's
father became rather the man-about-town: a debonair charmer, pop-
ular with the ladies and well liked by everyone; an excellent host,

much-sought-after guest, and honorable member of sundry deputations. At about this time he became an ardent Zionist and admirer of Dr. Herzl, appointed himself a delegate to all the Zionist congresses, and left the trusty Swede to mind the shop, arriving only at the last minute even if he was in Jerusalem, just in time to give the bawling baby a cheery slap on the back, joke with its mother, snip the umbilical cord, remove the afterbirth, and help decide on a name. His own mother, to whom he was unfailingly gallant, was always at his side, putting his wife in her shadow, while the little boy and his sister ran about among the beds. In the summer of 1899 the doctor went off to one of his congresses in Europe and came back with two Jewish youngsters from a small Polish town near Cracow, a sister and brother. Our defendant remembers them well, although he didn't understand their language. The brother was a doctor, the sister an attractive young woman; Dr. Mani sought to interest the former in his clinic and the latter in himself, since he had fallen madly in love with her as only an older man can with a young girl whom he has not time to court and seeks only to devour. The less devoured she wished to be, the more he dogged her footsteps, and before long all Jerusalem knew of his great passion, since Mani the Elder, unlike Mani the Younger, was not at all diffident about his feelings. It was indeed quite an infamous scandal . . . and when the two young Polish Jews made up their minds to return home despite the doctor's pleas that they remain in Jerusalem, he followed them to Jaffa, sailed from there to Beirut with them, and vanished. It took several weeks to discover that he had been killed in a ghastly accident in the railway station. He was fifty years old, and by the time the corpse was identified and brought to Jerusalem for burial, it was autumn.

—Yes, sir. I gathered all this information from the defendant himself, although I was able to corroborate it from other sources. I'm dreadfully sorry to be taking so much of your time, but I have my reasons . . . I assure you that I do . . .

—Thank you, sir. All this was nearly twenty years ago. But can there be any statute of limitations when we seek to trace, through the maze of their origins, the roots of treachery and espionage so as to keep them from spreading their rank weeds? The family was stunned by the disaster; their benefactor, the consul, was long dead;

the lying-in hospital was dealt a mortal blow. For a while the Swedish midwife tried keeping it up, at first openly and then
clandestinely, since the authorities revoked its license after Dr.
Mani's death; there were debts to be paid too, so that part of the
equipment had to be sold and some of the rooms rented out to
pilgrims; and gradually, the women of Jerusalem stopped coming to
give birth there. That Christmas the city was flooded by Christian
pilgrims who had come to mark the new century, and the faithful
midwife suddenly regained her faith and returned with them to her
native land. In December 1899 our defendant was twelve years old;
he had always been an independent lad, even when his father was
alive, and now he became even more so. If you try to picture him for
a moment, sir, as I can, you'll see a thin, black-haired boy with
glasses and a dark complexion like his mother's, a moody youngster
who daydreamed and even talked to himself. In late December of
that year the winter finally arrived; everywhere there were church
bells and parades of Russian pilgrims through the streets; the two
centuries, one coming and one going, were a source of universal
excitement. And then one afternoon, so he told me, young Mani
went down to the former hospital on the ground floor and was
startled to find a young woman in travail lying on a bed, one of those
Jewish adventuresses who had come to Palestine from Europe to
live in the new Jewish farming villages, partly out of ideological
conviction and partly to run away from home. She had reached
Jerusalem on her last legs, with the address of the lying-in hospital,
not knowing that it was defunct; had found no one there; and had
lain down on a bed. It was afternoon; the boy's mother, sister, and
grandmother had gone to see the processions and had not come
home yet; no one was there but him and the woman; and now she
began screaming and sobbing, throwing off her blanket and howling
for help while he stood there and stared at her, both straight-on and
in the mirror. At first he was too paralyzed to move; and when at last
he tried helping her undress, he couldn't get her clothes off, no
matter how she begged him, until he ran to fetch a knife and slashed
them. Then he stood watching the birth canal heave open and listening to her moans; saw the baby's head appear slowly in a pool of
blood; witnessed it all: the dreadful suffering, the screams; and was
made to swear while standing helplessly in that cold room that he

wouldn't leave her or lay down his knife before cutting the umbilical cord. And throughout all this he never shut his eyes. He looked now at the woman and now at the mirror, watching the birth on both sides of him . . . which is how, so he says, his intense political consciousness was born, gripping the knife in that cold room . . .

—Yes, sir, *political,* sir, those were his words and that's how he views it. Unbelievably intense; it's the only thing in his world that matters; it *is* his world. And thus, in a single cold, gloomy, *fin-de-siècle* hour, a skinny twelve-year-old with glasses became, as he puts it, a *homo politicus.* And here, perhaps, lies the first, subtle kernel of the bizarre, the hideous act of treachery that came eighteen years later, on account of which, sir, you were brought from Egypt to join your colleagues on the bench tomorrow while I hammer home his guilt . . . I say, though, look at how the sky has cleared! Didn't I remark two hours ago, sir, that Jerusalem wasn't Glasgow? Even the most torrential rains have their limit here . . . and so I ask myself, sir, and you too, Colonel, whether you haven't heard enough by now. To think of all the times my mother warned me not to forget myself, that is, not to forget my listeners, because my tongue has a way of getting carried away, especially when it has such excellent whiskey to carry it . . .

—Of course, sir. I have a most definite purpose in mind.

—I daresay, Colonel, that everything will fit together in the end.

—With all my heart and soul, sir.

—Thank you, sir, that's terribly kind of you. Well, then, where were we? Ah, yes, at the start of the century, which erupted right under our defendant's nose . . .

—Sir?

—What baby is that, sir?

—Oh yes, that one . . . but just what was the question, sir?

—Why, yes, sir.

—Yes, sir.

—Why, yes, sir. Quite thick of me, sir. Yes, of course. I reckon it was born in the end, but I'm afraid I didn't pursue the matter, because it seemed to me more of a metaphor . . . I do believe he cut the cord with his knife and gave the baby its freedom, but as to whether it lived or not . . . we must hope for the best . . .

—By all means, sir . . . Well, then, the new century dawned on

us all, each of us at his proper station, and on the Manis too, who
were still quite stunned by their tragedy. The old grandmother,
though pushing eighty by now, was as youthful as ever and still
adored by the young lad; the mother had put on weight and was
aging rapidly; the sister was only ten but already resigned to a fate of
being married off young; and the four of them barely eked out a
living from letting out rooms in the defunct hospital. Young Mani
was left pretty much to his own devices, and being a *homo politicus,*
as he puts it, he set himself goals and made himself friends accord-
ingly. His first decision was to study languages; it still rankled him to
have had to sit listening to his father converse with his young guests
from Europe without understanding a word. And having made up
his mind, he went about it as single-mindedly as an army crossing a
river—which meant secretly leaving the Jewish school in which his
father had placed him without bothering to inform his mother or
grandmother and roaming the streets of Jerusalem until he found
the Scottish Mission on Mount Zion and its School of Bible, a very
Christian institution, I needn't tell you. What interested young
Mani, of course, was not the Bible but English, which he quickly
mastered with an Inverness accent. But that was just the beginning.
Afternoons found him in the nearby village of Silwan, where a chum
of his father's, an old Arab sheikh, agreed to chat with him in Arabic
and put him through his conjugations. And that still left evenings,
when he sometimes frequented an Algerian family he knew to help
mind the children and pick up a bit of French. He was already, you
see, quite adept at moving among different elements before he had
even celebrated his bar-mitzvah, which is like a Catholic confirma-
tion or a Mohammedan *toohoor* and takes place in synagogue at the
age of thirteen, when you must chant parts of the Bible in a special
melody that is the very devil to master—believe me, Colonel, I can
vouch for that personally, and so can the Great Synagogue in Manchester . . . And so, as his bar-mitzvah approached, he betook
himself to one of your little Jerusalem sects, one of those black-
coated, fur-hatted, curly-eared lots whom you may have come across
in London, Colonel, if you even ventured east of Tuttenham
Road . . .

—Most assuredly, sir . . . that's where you see them, dressed
the same way. He presented himself to them as an orphan, which is

what he did everywhere, sir, as if he were motherless too; and they arranged for his bar-mitzvah, and taught him the proper chant notes, and even saw to the refreshments. That was the start of his odd ties with them, which have continued to this day. I've questioned them about it most thoroughly, trying to get to the bottom of it, because you see, sir, it's not as if he belonged to them or could have even if he wished to: first, because he's a Sephardi; second, because he's a freethinker; and third, because he's a Zionist, which is utterly foreign to them. And yet such ties existed; initially as a matter of mutual interest and eventually as one of subtle affection; because even the most hermetically sealed system needs a secret outlet, a man who is free to come and go on special assignments and is preferably an outsider, so that no control need be relinquished over one's own; and best of all, a queer bird like Mani, a none too reputable orphan who could easily be disowned. And so he rendered them various services, such as corresponding in English with wealthy Jews in America, negotiating the rental of flats from the Mohammedans, and preparing digests of the newspapers, which their religion forbids them to read, in return for financial remuneration or its equivalent. They made no religious demands of him, not even that he wear a hat—indeed, already as a boy he was in the habit of calling on their elder bareheaded and speaking to him respectfully but as an equal. Not that he considered himself antireligious. He sometimes even attended services, although never theirs but only those of his fellow Sephardim, whose hymns were familiar and didn't take all day—and then, of course, he clapped a red Turkish fez on his head before going off to pray. But he quite definitely did not wish to be considered religious either, because the one thing he could not have enough of was his freedom . . .

—In the Deity, sir? I believe he does, although he declines to profess it. In any case, he refused to answer the question, which I put to him with the greatest delicacy, on the grounds that it was too personal.

—No, sir, a Jew is not required to believe in Him. As a rule, however, he does, since he has little else to believe in.

—Are you quite certain, Colonel, that you wish me to expound on such questions of identity? It's a dreadful bog, you know; the Jews themselves start out across it with the greatest confidence and end up floundering madly. I can't tell you how sorry I am to be boring you like this.

—I would be most keen to, sir.

—With great pleasure, sir. I even have my own hypothesis. But for the moment, I suggest that we stick to our story. I daresay I should say a word about this sect, because from the day of his arrest they've gone tiptoeing after him and us, his handlers, like a flock of birds—crows, sir, if you will—all perched around the ringside; quite indistinguishable from each other, yet each of them with his clearly defined role and place. Already on that snowy night when I rushed off to the guardhouse and saw the first of them standing blackly by the edge of the square, I could tell by the way he stood there that he had been sent; not even his umbrella was his own, because since then I've seen it pass from hand to hand like a rifle at the changing of the guards. A night hasn't gone by without one of them trailing behind me—along the narrow streets, into the shops, up steps and down steps . . . but the moment I approach them, they vanish. What they're after, don't you see, is to try to read in my face whether the accused has said anything to incriminate them . . .

—Yes, sir. They were questioned quite stiffly with the help of an interpreter who speaks their language.

—Yiddish, sir. It would appear that they had no idea what he was up to and could not have been less involved in his schemes. England, Turkey—they don't give a fig for any of that. Their one concern is not to have his guilt rub off on them, although I do believe they feel a sort of solidarity with him, perhaps it even goes back to that bar-mitzvah chant . . . Anyway, we had better get back to our story. Well, sir, he grew up, the lad did, dark-haired, bespectacled, and homely, an independent and rather solitary *homo politicus* drifting among the identities of Jerusalem while working out his politics and acquiring languages as though they were a batch of keys to a house with many doors. He was still a bachelor, still stirred to the depths of his soul by that woman's womb and screams. In 1905, when he was eighteen, his grandmother died of old age, the one person in the world he really loved. Meanwhile, his younger sister was married off as she had known she would be, to the son of a wealthy Jew from North Africa who had come to purchase a grave in Jerusalem and was buried in it sooner than he had planned; once

the week of mourning was over, the young man departed with his
new bride and her mother for Marseilles, to which he also invited
her brother, who was employed as a court clerk at the time. Young
Mani, however, resolutely declined; he was awaiting political developments, which were not long in coming, since in 1908 the Young
Turks seized power and proclaimed a multinational, multiracial empire—a proclamation that so affected him that he resolved to study
law and serve in the Turkish parliament. And so, letting out his two
rooms in the defunct hospital that was now a pilgrims' hostel, he put
the family possessions into storage, gave his father's old clothes to
charity except for a large, warm overcoat, ordered a calling card
from a print shop that said "Journalist" even though he had no
journal to correspond for, and in the late summer of 1908 took the
train to Jaffa, departing Jerusalem for the first time in his life. He
did not once lift his head to look at the mountains sliding by outside
the window, but kept his eyes on the suitcase between his legs and
on his father's coat by his side, wanting only to put Palestine behind
him without a glimpse of the route whereby his father had deserted
him. From the railway station in Jaffa he took a black hansom
straight to the port, where he boarded a northbound ship for Constantinople. Three days later, toward evening, she cast anchor in
Beirut—which is, as you know, sir, a handsome and rapidly growing
city famed for its houses of amusement. All the passengers hurried
ashore, he told me, save himself; for he had decided not to budge
from the empty ship and there he remained, pacing the deck and
listening to the sounds of song and laughter from the shore while
regarding the brilliant lights of the city in which his father had
perished. Toward midnight the first passengers returned to their
cabins; yet still he strode the deck, watching the lights dim as the
song and laughter faded away. A late moon rose in the sky. And
then . . . then, sir, so he says, he heard a cry; as if a huge, powerful
infant were crying in the city, or so he says, sir; and with shaking
hands he packed his suitcase and went ashore, passing the watchmen and entering the little streets, through which the last revelers
were heading home and the last passengers returning to their ships.
And all along, sir, he kept hearing the cry. And so he struck out
through the winding lanes of the old city and came to the railway
station, where he quickly crossed the tracks and started up a steadily

climbing street until he came to a boardinghouse, a small establishment for travelers in need of a night's lodgings. There were voices
inside and a light swayed in the vestibule; and he asked if there was
a room available and was told that there was; and he climbed the
stairs and flung his suitcase on the bed and stepped out on the
terrace and gazed down at the station below, which was flooded
with moonlight, the tracks running north and south; and then, sir,
he opened the squeaking clothes closet and hung up his father's old
coat . . . and there it stayed for six years . . .

—I do, sir. He remained in that city for six full years, until the
outbreak of the war. And in the same boardinghouse and the same
room, where he would still no doubt be if not for the war, as if being
near the train station where his father had died held him in a vise.
And I ask myself, sir, whether his act of treachery, or espionage,
even if it surfaced many years later, was not conceived there in
Beirut, although all my efforts to determine whether he was already
planted then by the Turks have yielded nothing . . .

—Yes, Colonel. A most thorough investigation, carried out
around the clock, from every angle. There wasn't a stone left un-
turned. Were any Turks lurking in the background, I'm sure I
would have found them. But there isn't a Turk in sight, sir, or even a
German. The whole thing seems purely self-generated by his own
muddled, neurasthenic mind. That's the point I'm driving at, and if
anyone thinks there's a lesson to be learned here, anything applica-
ble to the apprehension of spies and traitors in the future, the only
lesson I can see is that every case is unique, Joseph Mani too, who
claims he spent his seven years in Beirut studying, sir. And he really
did attend the American University, which was easily done with his
British passport that opened all sorts of doors. His income from the
rent in Jerusalem paid for his bed and breakfast, and the rest of his
needs were financed by odd jobs that he found as a guide, an interpreter, and a hotel agent, because Beirut was full of visitors in those
years, tourists who came from all over. The town was booming; it
was the gateway to the Orient for Germans, Frenchmen, Englishmen; for Austrians, Russians, and even Americans; processions of
pilgrims passed through it; so did archaeological expeditions, Christian missions, journalists discovering the East. And Jews too, of
course, in every possible shape and form. A bureau of the Zionist

Organization was opened too, to help stranded pioneers on their way to Palestine, penniless Jewish youngsters without a visa for the Ottoman Empire, let alone Palestine, without money for a ship berth, so that they planned to continue their journey on foot and slip across the border. Mani picked them out at the train station, where he hung about every evening, as they stepped out of the coaches: pale young men and women from Russia, on the run from the law since the abortive 1905 uprising, unkempt and unwashed with their bundles roped together . . . and here was this dark, bespectacled Palestinian Jew come to meet them, wearing a little necktie and attempting to hit it off with them in Hebrew, then switching to French, then going over to his smattering of Russian. He directed them to the cheap doss houses on the hills above the city, which gave him a modest commission; explained where they might find an inexpensive café; told them about the Holy Land and pointed out the way to the Zionist bureau; but he never befriended them past that. From women, he kept away entirely; it was as if he had still not gotten over his twelve-year-old's memory of that winter day in the empty house with its womb that seemed less about to bear life than engorge it, and with a most ravenous appetite. And he had his studies to keep up too.

—Yes, sir, quite faithfully. Every morning he went to the university, where he continued to consider himself a student for six years, albeit a rather slow one and of a special status because of the king's English that he spoke. His examinations and term papers were postponed from year to year; his requirements were met at a snail's pace; most of his time was spent reading the daily and weekly papers in the library; since the age of twelve, after all, he had been his own headmaster; and now he had the run of the university, whose student body was a hodgepodge of different levels and backgrounds. And yet he had a sure notion of his curriculum; it was politico-jurisprudential; he studied the laws of the Turkish majlis, the American constitution, the philosophy of the Koran; but also English poetry, Sumerian archaeology, Byzantine iconography, choosing his lectures systematically and at his leisure; and if there were any he had failed to comprehend in their entirety, he waited a year or two for them to be repeated and sat through them again. Afternoons were devoted to field work, that is, to attending political meetings of

Druze, of Shiites, of Communists, of Christians, of Maronites, of Catholic priests, shuttling from identity to identity, although by now the identities were all jumbled up; a simple promenade down the main street of Beirut was an excursion to them all. And of course, he did not neglect the Sephardic synagogue, which he made a point of attending every Sabbath eve, although he was far from punctilious in his observance of the Law; he refused, for example, to kindle a fire on the Sabbath, but did not abstain from forbidden foods. Politics remained his goal; he regarded it reverentially, as a complete philosophy of life with an inner logic of its own and a reason and purpose for everything. Events in Europe and in the Balkans left their powerful mark on him, and his imagination was fired by the approaching world war. Each time his mother and sister urged him to join them in Marseilles, he refused. The Turkish authorities were growing harsher; the Germans were everywhere; foreigners were being asked to leave; he feared leaving Ottoman jurisdiction and not being allowed back. His British passport burned in his pocket like a hot coal . . . and to make matters worse, Colonel, in the early winter of 1914 he had a baby—and a motherless one to boot . . .

—A quite genuine baby, sir. Its mother died shortly after its birth, which took place in the room its father's gray overcoat had been hanging in for six years. And our Mr. Mani had to register it at the police ministry, where the German officers nosing about in the thick and hostile atmosphere of those prewar days could not help but wonder about this thin Palestinian student with the glasses, this journalist without a journal, who brought his infant to a Druze wet nurse every morning, a peddler in the souk of Beirut, and sat by her reading an old paper picked up out of the gutter while waiting for his child to drink its fill. Mind you, though, the paper was not too old for him to learn from it that Turkey would soon be in the thick of it too—and so, in late summer of 1914, as suddenly as he had arrived six years earlier, he took his father's coat down from its peg, wrapped up the baby, and made his way southward to his native city, which after Beirut seemed a poor and gloomy place, bathed in a hard, dry light. He arrived at the house in Kerem Avraham to find it full of boarders, since by now every boarder had a boarder of his own and there was no place for him, the owner, to lay his head; and so off he went to his sectaries—Hasidim, sir, is the name for them;

and he knocked on their door in his father's old overcoat with the baby in his arms and said to them, "Find me a wife." I rather doubt that surprised them one bit, sir; it's their habit, you see, to be surprised by nothing, so that they can concentrate on divine matters; and so all they asked him was, "Do you want a wife to mind your child or a wife to bear you more children?" "I'll think about that," says he, and so he does, and when he has thought he tells them, "I want a wife to mind my child *and* me." Well, sir, they have all sorts of women for a man like him: young widows and divorcées who will marry whomever they're told to; but that isn't whom they bring him; for although they never say so, they don't wish to have him too close to them; and in any case, they aren't at all keen on cross-marriages. In the end they find him a wife some thirteen years older than he is, a childless but attractive woman of nearly forty who came to Jerusalem from Mesopotamia at the end of the century and has already been through two husbands: one dead and one walked out on her; and has a bit of property and a souvenir shop for tourists in the walled city, between the Jewish and the Armenian quarters. Straightways she takes to the infant as if it were her own, with all the love and devotion you could ask for, and our Mr. Mani moves in with her, sinking into the piles of pillows and quilts left behind by her two husbands and hiding his British passport under the mattress. And thus, while great armies meet in battle along the blood-filled rivers of Europe, he sleeps his way through the winter of 1915. His new wife cooks her Babylonian dishes and serves them to him in bed as if he were convalescing from an illness, and the baby joins him there, crammed with goodies and smothered with gobs of love. And yet even there, sir, ensconced in his featherbed, he still considers himself a *homo politicus* and sends his wife out on urgent errands to bring him all the newspapers she can, which he peruses among the quilts and pillows, even those that arrive months late—boning up on the living and the dead and studying the maps and keeping track of the progress of the war and the lines of battle, some of which have long been erased; until finally, his Turkish fez on his head, he sallies forth from his lair into a Jerusalem made poorer than ever by the fighting overseas and resumes his identity shuttle. Mornings are spent in an Arab coffeehouse in the walled city, arbitrating petty tiffs and composing writs for the courts, because even though he has brought back no diploma from Beirut, he passes himself off as a solicitor; afternoons he comes back home for a sound snooze; then up and about once more without even a change of clothes, just a white hat in place of the fez, to call on a German-Jewish professor in the new city and teach him Arabic grammar; and from there to his Sephardic synagogue for the afternoon prayer; and then to his sectaries, to translate some English correspondence; and then back home for dinner with his wife and child; and then off again, this time with no hat at all, to the Zionist Club, where he sits in the back row with a drowsing Turkish secret policeman and listens to lectures and debates, sometimes rising to ask the Zionists a question of his own; and home at last late at night to hush the day's speakers in his head and tell them all what *he* thinks, which is still not at all anti-English, because it has not dawned on him yet that the English will soon arrive; so that if any thought of treachery crosses his mind, it is no more than a dim kernel, as lifeless as a pebble, as a pip that falls on dry earth and seems more the dross of the fruit than the source of a new tree. And so more long years go by, and 1917 arrives, and the expeditionary force lands in Egypt and crosses the desert until Great Britain is next door to Palestine, and on the ninth of January, as you know, sir, we took the border town of Rafah.

—Major General Philip Chatwood, sir, with his Australian and New Zealand cavalry. It was a short, easy battle, and by February news of it had reached Jerusalem and caused great excitement. Our Mani was jolly well shaken, so he told me, in a state of utter turmoil —and I asked myself, sir, what exactly was the meaning of it? Was this the jolt that turned under the dry pip that was playing dead, down into the warm, dark, blanketing earth?

—Yes, sir. What I mean, sir, if you'll forgive me for being rather literary, is, was this the beginning of the treachery that was soon to burst forth into the open? What could all that turmoil have meant in a man who called himself a *homo politicus* but sat through the war in Jerusalem with his face turned north toward Turkey, blind to what was happening in his backyard? What had he *thought* would happen? Was he still the boy waiting for his father to come home? Because all at once, here is Great Britain in the south, and he's as shaken as if his father had made a secret circuit of Palestine and come back at him from the opposite direction . . .

—His allegorical father, sir. I only meant it as a parable.

—I beg your pardon, sir. It was just an attempt at interpretation . . .

—As you wish, Colonel . . . why, of course . . .

—Yes, indeed, sir, that's what I'm aiming at. It will all fit together in the end. I'm dreadfully sorry, sir.

—I'll most assuredly be quick about it, sir; the events now become quicker themselves. The armies prepare to lock horns, and in March we suffer a stinging setback in Gaza, although it's clear to all that we haven't said our last word yet. All summer long there is a constant trickle of nebulous rumors; it's not that the Turks are deliberately spreading them, it's just that they themselves don't know where the English bull, our esteemed Sir Edmund, who in late summer moves his cavalry into the Holy Land, will strike from. By now it's autumn, sir, the season of the Jewish holidays, although quite frankly, autumn here is just more of summer with a bit of an evening breeze; but it's the time of the Jews' New Year, when they rise in the middle of the night to blow a ram's horn; and he felt the winds shift to southerly and rose one day himself and set out, taking his British passport from under the quilt and sowing it into the lining of his old coat. His first stop was Bethlehem, where nothing seemed to have changed: the Turks shuffled about as always and the Arabs were their usual sleepy selves; only in the eyes of the Jews did he notice a soft gleam that made him stretch his neck a bit, as if straining to hear foreign voices. A party of Jews was on its way to Hebron to pray in the Cave of the Patriarchs, and he traveled with them for a while until their way was blocked by a Turkish detachment bound for Gaza, at which point he left the main road and caught a ride on a cart heading down into the desert of Judea. It was late afternoon; the sun was setting; a mixed company of Turkish cavalry and infantry marched by, singing a jolly Turkish tune, as if homebound at last; their officer brusquely ordered the car aside and told its occupants to stay put; and our Mr. Mani had no way of knowing that as the last Turkish soldier marched by him, four hundred years of Turkish rule, the only rule he had known in his life, were peeled away as though they were a puff of wind . . . And so they remained there in that no-man's land, south of Hebron on the way to Beersheba, not far from the tents of some Bedouin, who extended them their hospitality. It was the thirty-first of October, and our Mani had no idea either that Sir Edmund had taken Beersheba that same night. They lit a fire to warm themselves and sat around it . . .

—I wouldn't say pleased, sir. Burning with anticipation was more like it. He was deucedly impatient to come in contact with us, even though he had no idea what that meant; but he did know that if he stayed where he was, there would no longer be any way back. And indeed, the next morning he found himself encircled by Chatwood's cavalry under the command of Captain William Daggett of the quartermaster's corps of the 67th Regiment. Captain Daggett's affidavit, sir, is here in this brief, and he'll be the first to take the witness stand tomorrow. An indomitable warrior, sir, a most esteemed member of Chatwood's staff; a vain old bloody-tempered Scotsman who refused to be questioned at first and had to be locked up for two days before we could get the story out of him.

—Quite so, sir. You see, sir, the captain, who is seventy years old, is an absolute fiend for horses, you'd almost think he were part horse himself. In Midlothian, sir, where he lives, a horse isn't raced without his say-so, and all he lives and breathes for is to breed a better, faster animal that will compete with his colors; his whole life, you might say, has been one long search for the ideal thoroughbred. When war broke out he joined up at once despite his age and was commissioned chief livery officer of the 67th Cavalry; his service in France was spent mostly poking about in stables, and I daresay he thinks the whole war is one colossal derby and can't understand why the jockeys keep shooting at each other. And when all the jockeys had their mounts shot out from under them in Europe and the tanks came to take their place, he was jolly well cheesed-off and 'eard the East a-callin', and so he signed on with Allenby and sailed across the sea to go on searching for his *equus idealis* among the fabled stallions of Arabia, hoping to find it and ship it back to Midlothian to the astonishment of all his racing mates. He's determined to track it down if it's the last thing he does, and this whole ruddy war, as far as he's concerned, from that duke shot at Sarajevo to the millions who died at Verdun, has been fought solely to transport him to the deserts of Arabia for that purpose. Wherever he goes, commandeering horses and camels for his regiment, he keeps an eye out; and so the minute Beersheba was taken, while the smoke was still rising from the burning houses and the dead and wounded were being gathered, he put on his plaid kilt and went galloping off into the wilderness with his cronies and two interpreters to look for the steed of his dreams . . .

—Thank you, sir, gladly. A wee dram. By George, it's raining again! I'm sorry to have to bore you like this, but I had a don at Cambridge who said that God was in the details, and that's so not only when God is an aesthete but when He's a jurist as well. And the details matter here especially, because now is when our defendant links up with His Majesty's forces, and had it not been for Captain Daggett's enthusiasm, he would never have penetrated so quickly to the privy chambers of regimental headquarters . . .

—Quite so, sir, and without the most cursory check on him. Captain Daggett, you see, had no time for anything but horses; he was charging about from one Bedouin camp to another, rousting out every quadruped with a mane and having them lined up in front of him so that he could look in their mouths and at their fetlocks, and whistle to them with his special Scottish whistle that works on every horse in the world, which answers with a special wiggle of its ears that only Daggett understands, after which he waits for old Dobbin to defecate and sniffs its droppings to know what's inside it.

—By George, sir, I've seen it myself. It's the sort of connoisseurship that borders on madness. And after that he summons the horse's owner to recite its family tree; and his two interpreters—who never recovered from the heatstroke they came down with in Cairo, to which they were whisked straight from Queens College in Oxford, where they studied with dons who had never been east of the Thames—are so terrified of him that they forget what little Arabic they know; so that each question he wants to ask the Bedouin calls for a lengthy confab on their part and much leafing through the dictionary, in which they don't even always understand the English; whereupon they stand there working out a final draft in whispers while the Bedouin wait patiently and the gray-haired captain grows flushed with rage; and when at last the magic words are carefully uttered in their atrocious accents, any resemblance between which and the speech of real Arabs is purely accidental, the Bedouin turn crimson and then white with anger; and spitting on the ground, they stalk off, fold their tents, take their horse, take everything, and vanish over the horizon, leaving nothing behind but a whirlpool of dust and two mortified interpreters with no idea what their mistake was . . .

—Perhaps, Colonel, I have availed myself of poetic license. But it's quite justified to explain our captain's enthusiasm when, on that morning of the first of November, he was approached by Mr. Mani, unshaven and wearing his black suit that was wrinkled from a sleepless night. Mani surveyed our captain, who had just finished circumambulating a horse and was now whistling to it in Scots while waiting for it to drop its turds; looked at the quaking interpreters making gargling noises with their tongues; observed the disheartened Bedouin, who were already resigned to the loss of their mounts; quietly took a few steps forward as his eyes bore into the uniforms, weapons, and bridles of the soldiers, who were the first Englishmen he had ever seen out of mufti; and then opened his mouth and in his best School-of-Bible Scots brogue translated for the captain with utter proficiency an entire discourse on equinology. Little wonder, then, that by late that afternoon Mr. Mani was already well tied to a commandeered horse with which he seemed to form a single creature, surrounded by British cavalry and in a place of honor beside the captain, who regarded him as his personal and heaven-sent savior. That evening in Beersheba he was brought to the house of the Turkish governor, above which the Union Jack was already flying; and there, sir, if I may be permitted a personal note, as I was going about my duty with the adjutants of the brigade, which included packing Turkish documents in boxes, identifying the dead, and covering the wounded so that they might finish dying quietly in the light of the desert sunset; there, among the shying-back horses, I caught my first glimpse of him, freshly untied from his mount: pale, exhausted, old-looking, treading on slivers of glass and empty Turkish cartridges that glowed in the waning sun as he climbed the steps to the governor's house; unlike any Englishman, unlike any Jew, unlike any Arab or Turk, unlike anyone at all, even though he was more of a native than any of them. Was he already thinking of treachery?

—It was the first of November, sir—1917, sir.

—Yes, Colonel.

—No, Colonel.

—Most certainly, Colonel.

—Not yet, sir. From that moment on he became the chief divisional interpreter, and since he could palaver a bit in Turkish too, he soon made himself indispensable. And yet, so he says, the thought of treachery had yet to sprout in him, for the cold, bare kernel that had worked its way into the dark, dry earth still lacked the stimulation of moisture.

—Yes, sir. That's how he put it during one of his interrogation sessions. And that was why he didn't reach for the British passport sewn into the lining of his coat, but rather sardonically told himself, "Aye, the foreigners have come to replace the foreigners." His mind, sir, was not yet made up. He was still watching silently from the sidelines, trying to puzzle out our intentions. Gaza was ours; the breakthrough was a success; our butting bull, Sir Edmund, spurred the army on northward along the coast, through the fields of Philistia, over sand dunes and swamps, urging it on to Jerusalem in time to make a Christmas gift of the city to Lloyd George and John Bull, because London was famished for a victory that might help it get over the endless slaughter at Verdun, the war being now in its fourth outcomeless winter. Was this the moisture that made the kernel sprout?

—No, sir. At first he was the personal prisoner of the old Scotsman, who hid him in his trailer and ranged back and forth with him between Beersheba and Gaza, looking for his dream horse. By now, though, all of army intelligence had heard of him; and so they commandeered him from old Daggett and put him to work as a translator while the interpreters tagged after him to learn and to marvel; for he was indeed most wonderfully adept at it: the words seemed to translate themselves without even passing through his brain, changing languages in midair, changing grammar, changing intonation, so that the speaker felt that quite miraculously, the unknown language was coming out of his own throat . . . Meanwhile, the army flowed like a mighty river up the coast, crumbling the Turkish positions, which were as weak as the sand surrounding them, one after another; one after another, the villages surrendered too; and wherever they went, the military governors took Mani with them to translate their proclamations. Picture him if you can, sir, in our midst, a thin, quiet civilian with glasses and burning eyes; wrapped in his father's already threadbare overcoat and still in shock from the sudden change; cut off from his son and household with no way of informing them of his whereabouts—and yet at the same time, getting to know his native land, even if he was tied to his horse, because he was still in the habit of falling off. There wasn't a village too small or out-of-the-way for him to be brought to, sometimes no more than a few mud huts and tents; and there he would stand, a ruddy little civilian surrounded by officers with their riding crops under their arms, translating their proclamations of occupation and their instructions for curfews to a band of ignorant Arab darkies in peasant cloaks and head cloths—and mind you, doing it so fast that the translation was done before the words were out of the officer's mouth, so that they seemed less a translation than a little speech cooked up on his own whose meaning no one could be sure of. In fact, sir, he might have been taken not so much for an interpreter as for a glum little commissar popping up out of the earth with a military escort to explain the war to the villagers. He would look out at all those Arab faces positively glowing with attention, straining to catch a whiff of the young Jew in his old overcoat surrounded by his train of Englishmen; if the village headsman had a question, he would answer quite firmly at once, adding "It doesn't matter" to any officer wishing to know what had been asked; and if the officer insisted, "But be sure to tell them such-and-such," he would reply, "I've told them all that's necessary" and give the sign to move on; and off they went to the next village . . .

—Oh, but he was, sir, he was every bit the martinet. You would have thought the officers were actually afraid of him . . . at which point, on the twentieth of November, as Allenby was pushing east toward Jerusalem, he stepped into staff headquarters one night and discovered on the table a telegram from London with news of Lord Balfour's declaration, which quite bowled him over . . .

—So I should think, sir. It was in the form of a short personal correspondence written by Lord Balfour himself. I've attached it to the brief, just for the record.

—Thrown for a loop by it, sir. He had never expected such a development, you see, and here he was, having been away from home for three weeks, and especially, from his son, whom he was

terribly attached to, rolling helplessly along with the British jugger-
naut thundering across the Holy Land—and all of a sudden, here
was this most wonderfully generous proclamation of intent that he
had not at all foreseen, although in all fairness, no one else had
either. He couldn't sleep at night; the thought of returning to Jerusalem made his blood race; he rose from his bed and roamed about
among the horses and the cannon; the rains had set in and cold
winds blew; Allenby's army crept slowly up into the mountains of
Judea; his father's old overcoat came apart and he was given an
army greatcoat and high boots; and before he knew it, he was in the
front lines, wearing a strange mishmash of mufti and field uniform,
peering through binoculars at forward positions and utterly amazed
by the thought that less than a month ago he had surreptitiously set
out southward from his native city—and now here he was, about to
reenter it from the west with the forces of the world's greatest empire! On the sixth of December, Colonel, he found himself with the
infantry in Nebi Samwil, where a fierce skirmish took place, gazing
down upon Jerusalem, which struck him as frightfully small, frightfully stubborn and hostile. On the ninth, as you know, the city was
taken, and two days later Sir Edmund entered it on foot with his
columns behind him. The church bells clanged away; the city elders
came out to greet him with bread and salt; our defendant marched
into the city with the conquerors, one of a kind among the bagpipes
and Aussie hats, peering feverishly at the onlookers; and then, near
the Jaffa Gate, he right-faced all on his own and slipped away home,
where he arrived as though after a hard day's work and took straight
to the quilts and the pillows with his son. For a week he didn't leave
the house; he had no friends to tell his adventures to, nor did he say
much to his wife; mostly he stared at the windowpane, down which
the rain ran in rivers, listening to the boom of the field artillery as
Colonel Chatwood beat back a Turkish counterattack and pushed
his front line to Ramallah.

—Yes, sir, a bloody fierce counterattack it was too. But I'm sure
the brigadier is looking forward to showing you the battleground
and explaining his military exploits, and I wouldn't want to steal his
thunder, especially since I'm a rank amateur at military strategy and
had better get back to our defendant and his story . . . And indeed, toward Christmas, sir, the skies cleared, and he went out into

the streets for a look at the brave new bedlam of a world. Several buildings had already been appropriated for the military government; barbed wire had been laid all around them; policemen and officials and statesmen and politicians were scurrying everywhere; the Jews were exultant; the Arabs in shock; the rain and fog set in again more strongly than ever, as if our army had brought its own English weather from London; and our Mr. Mani said once more to himself, "Aye, the foreigners have come to replace the foreigners . . ."

—Quite so, sir. I asked him that over and over. What did he think, a *homo politicus* like himself: that we would conquer Jerusalem, hand the keys of the city over to the natives, and retire with a modest bow?

—Jolly well put, Colonel! Here was the decisive, the fateful moment when the kernel of treachery, which had been slowly working its way down into the darkness, soaked up the sweet liquid trickling toward it through the earth and decomposed all at once, as if dowsed with corrosive acid, into thousands of thin little tendrils, frail, helpless gossamers that would seem to have no future in that heavy soil to all but the most discerning observer, who now notices two cotyledons, one the root's and one the stem's, each pushing greedily, unrestrainedly, off from the other . . . Well, sir, he walked into headquarters and was quite merrily hailed by everyone, because in the excitement of battle the trusty interpreter had been forgotten; and then he went straight, sir, to Major Stanford, the chief adjutant of the division, and showed him his British passport. The major inducted him on the spot. He issued him a uniform, a cap, and even an old pistol; added a mess kit and a dogtag; put him down for five pence ha'penny a week; and had our own Major Clark affix his signature on behalf of the advocate-general's corps. And that, sir, was the start of Interpreter Mani's career as a corporal in His Majesty's army . . .

—Indeed they are, sir. Every last document has been stamped and put in this file, which makes it a weighty one in more ways than one.

—I quite agree, sir. It was done a bit cavalierly and without a proper security check, because he had become known to everyone throughout the autumn months of the advance on Jerusalem. Which is why it shouldn't surprise you, Colonel, that not a few men would like to see both him and the documents thoroughly terminated. And indeed, from now on he was free to come and go in headquarters as he pleased. He even had his own desk in one of the rooms there, at which he translated the military governor's orders. But in his large bed at night, sir, where he lay with his quiet wife and his son, he shut his eyes and pictured himself orating to the Arab villagers in the fields of Philistia, and all at once, sir, his heart bled for the Arabs . . .

—Yes, for the Arabs, although not really for them, sir, that's little more than a pretext. In the darkness of the earth the root will suck any nourishment to aid the stem's growth.

—But I'm almost there now, sir, I've practically gotten to it. Because how does one explain his disappointment? Time passes, you see; he goes about in his British uniform and everyone shows him respect; but every day after work he exchanges it for his black suit and takes his son and crosses the walled city, passing the Wailing Wall and the great mosques and exiting via the Dung Gate, from where he ascends the Mount of Olives on which his father and grandfather are buried and reaches the Augusta Victoria Hospital and the monastery of Tur-Malka, which are all places, sir, that are marked on the map; and near there he enters a little Mohammedan coffeehouse and listens to the talk by the copper trays; and then he descends the mount and attends a Jewish meeting, where there are speeches and delegations of Jewish dignitaries who have come huffing and puffing from abroad to witness the redemption of Zion before taking the next mail packet back; and way up north he sometimes hears the thump of a cannon shot, a single round being lazily traded by the two armies; and still the spreading root of treachery knows not what fruit it will bear . . . until one day, sir, he walks into a room of the general staff to throw an old draft of something into the wastebasket; and the room is empty, sir, the only sounds are the distant laughter of some officers playing football with a tennis ball outside; and he spies a map rolled up in the basket; and takes it and sticks it under his jacket; and at home that night he sees that it is a plan for an assault by the 22nd Regiment east of the Jordan; and he folds it back up, and puts it in a little bag with his prayer shawl, and goes as he does every Saturday to the Sephardic synagogue on

Rabbi Isaac of Prague Lane; and when the service is over he brings
his son home and does not follow him into the house, but rather
keeps walking to the walled city, where he buys and dons an Arab
cloak; and then, heading north through the Nablus Gate, he walks
for three hours—here, sir, his route is marked on this map, if you
care to follow the trail of treachery yourself, with me as your faithful
guide. He reaches this little town here, Ramallah; passes straight
through it like a sleepwalker and continues on into the fields; sees
the British guard in its tents and shallow foxholes, which are not at
all like those at Verdun, sir, because here they're used only to rest
your feet in while having tea; walks up a hill, and down a hill, and
pretty soon runs into rain; smells tea himself and the smoke of a
Turkish campfire; and there they are, sir, in their tattered uniforms
with their faded ribbons, the same as ever, the same as they always
have been; aye, he's known them since first he saw the light of day in
the narrow streets of Jerusalem; the vanquished, warming themselves by the campfire, laughing in low voices, hungry as always,
chewing on their mustaches. And so he steps up to them and asks
for their sergeant and hands him the map with the plans and asks to
see an officer; and one comes and takes a look and doesn't understand; and so he asks to see a German, because there's always a
German with such troops; and while they go to fetch the German he
stands and waits, absorbed in the fire, the Turkish soldiers staring at
him wide-eyed, in the distance the houses of an unfamiliar Arab
village that according to the map must be el-Bireh; and he swallows
his spittle and waits some more, all but oblivious to the rain beating
down on his cloak, which might as well be someone else's for all he
notices it. After a while three men ride up on horseback, and the
German dismounts in a great hurry, one Werner von Karajan, a
cunning old fox, so we've heard. It doesn't take him but a minute to
see that the plans are real and inestimably important, and he can't
wait to rake in his prize; but our interpreter needs an interpreter,
who is found in the person of a dark-skinned, bespectacled Turk
with a fez, Mani's double from over the lines. There is a glitter of
gold coins; the defendant spurns them at once; in fact, sir, he never
took a farthing; all he asks is to have the two villages rousted out so
that he can deliver a speech to them. What sort of speech? the
Turks want to know. He doesn't answer them; doesn't even favor

them with a glance; simply says again that he wishes to deliver a speech. Well, sir, his audience is quite literally whipped together in a jiffy: farmers, shepherds, women, children, and old men; some still gripping their hoes and pitchforks; some with their sheep and donkeys. Here and there there's even someone with a little education, some village teacher in a dirty old red fez. It's late in the day by now, but the sky has cleared a bit and the rain has stopped; the burning red rays of the winter sun glint in the village square, glint on the mud and the dung. He asks for a table, but there is none in the entire village. A bed is fetched instead; a plank is laid over it; he strips off his cloak; now he is in a suit and tie, shriveled to a little black flame; and then, sir, he mounts the plank, and there is silence; and he sways a bit back and forth as if he were still saying his Sabbath prayers; and he begins to speak in Arabic; and what he says is: "Who are ye? Awake, before it is too late and the world is changed beyond recognition! Get ye an identity, and be quick!" And he takes Balfour's declaration from his pocket, translated into Arabic, and reads it without any explanation, and says: "This country is yours and it is ours; half for you and half for us." And he points toward Jerusalem, which they see shrouded in fog on the mountain, and he says, "The Englishman is there, the Turk is here; but all will depart and leave us; awake, sleep not!"

—Yes, sir . . .

—Just so, sir. "Awake, sleep not": that was the gist of it; the speech lasted but a few minutes. Whereupon he held out his arms to the Turkish officers standing about him with their shiny boots in the mud; and they lifted him and carried him on their shoulders to keep him from muddying himself. There wasn't a peep from his large audience. It hadn't understood a word; hadn't understood what this new thing was that was wanted of it; hadn't understood what was a country; barely knew where the borders of its village lay. He donned his cloak in the gathering dusk, much fussed over by the German; was escorted back to no-man's land; and promised to come again next Saturday with more documents . . .

—Yes, sir, that was his sole remuneration; we've verified it from sources behind the lines. But he returned every Saturday in January and February, eight times all in all; they even gave him a little flock of goats each time, so that he would look like a shepherd; not that he didn't manage to lose most of them on his way down the first hill and end up with only two or three. They had him vary his route each time, and the German organized a special task force to track him and pick him up. Straightways he would hand them the documents with a show of scorn, saying, "You don't deserve them," after which he would be taken deferentially to that week's village, where his audience had been waiting on its feet since dawn. By now every Arab between Ramallah and Nablus knew of him and was convinced he was a punishment inflicted by the Turks for their defeat—a most odd and ridiculous punishment, a sign of disarray and weakness. By now too he had his table, and a chair, and a blackboard, and even a glass of water; he stood with the Turkish officers about him and read Lord Balfour's declaration; and then he unfurled a colored map of Palestine that he had drawn himself, with the sea a bright blue, while the Arabs stared at it and failed to comprehend why, if this was their country, it was so small. He pointed to the blue sea, to the Jordan, to Jerusalem, and said, "Awake!" and they looked to see who had dared to doze off; "Get ye an identity," he went on, "before it is too late! All over the world people now have identities, and we Jews are on our way, and you had better have an identity or else!" And then he took a scissors from his pocket and said, "Half for you and half for us," and cut the map lengthwise, and gave them the half with the mountains and the Jordan, and kept the sea and the coast for himself. It rather distressed them to see it snipped up like that, and they pressed forward and some even tried to touch it, but the hungry, rickety-legged, rheumy-eyed Turkish soldiers pointed their bayonets and cocked their rifles, because the German had laid down the law that not a hair of the Jew's head should be harmed. Not that anyone would have harmed him, because the angrier he became and the more he swore at the villagers and provoked them, the sorrier for him they felt, even if they did blurt out to him like children, "But we want the sea too!" At first that stunned him, made him lose his temper; then, irately, he took another map from his bag and cut it horizontally . . .

—Some eight Saturdays, sir.

—In many villages, sir. He even got as far as Nablus and Jenin and visited prominent notables. He was much too stubborn and proud for them; he wouldn't even taste their coffee; hardly anyone

knew what he was talking about, and there were some who snick-
ered pityingly; but there were a handful of others who turned pale
and wiped the smiles from their faces, men with a smattering of
learning who had studied in Beirut or Haifa or Jerusalem and strode
about their villages with suits, ties, and white shoes as if they were
Virgil or Plato; they listened with trepidation when he talked about
the Jews who were coming; "Like locusts," he said; "one day they're
in the desert and the next they're upon you . . ." It's a mystery,
Colonel, how he was never spotted by one of our patrols. He
crossed the lines in broad daylight as though slicing butter, and
returned by night, walking quietly and quickly, a six-mile round-trip
all in all; arrived from the north, tired, wet, and dirty, slipped into
the old city through the Nablus Gate, and vanished down the
empty, rain-washed alleyways; and then, together with the moon
that rose from Jericho, pressed on to the stone steps of his house,
where his large wife opened the door even before he touched the
doorknob; never knowing where he had been or come back from
but helping him out of his clothes, and bathing him, and drying and
feeding him, and pulling back the quilt for him; and only then,
sinking into it, did he begin to tremble all over, while the moon sank
into bed beside him . . .

—I beg your pardon, sir, I truly do.

—Yes, sir, I beg your pardon, sir. I'm afraid I was a bit carried
away.

—Horowitz, sir. Oh, dear.

—Ivor Stephen, sir. Horowitz, sir. I'm afraid I was carried away.

—Yes, Colonel.

—Yes, sir.

—Quite, sir. I am rather fagged. I've been working on this case
day and night for the past five weeks, and my passion for the truth
has overwhelmed me. I've investigated every last detail; been in and
out of his home a hundred times; even walked the route of treachery
on foot—and if some fact could not be ascertained, I imagined it
back into existence, because I've been dreadfully anxious to get to
the bottom of it all.

—No, Colonel, absolutely not. A thousand times no. Had he been
an Arab, or an Indian, or a Ghurka, I would have done the same
thing. Wherever the Union Jack flies, it will be my passion to know

and understand. I rather fear, though, that the trial will flow by us too quickly; because Mr. Mani will plead guilty; and the prosecution —you musn't misjudge me, sir—will be razor-sharp; and Lieutenant Colonel Keypore and Major Jahawala have already made up their minds. And the fact is, Colonel, that when you see the quantity and nature of the documents he passed to the enemy, you'll be in high dudgeon yourself.

—Yes, of course we do, sir. It's all listed right here. He himself kept exact records and received a receipt for each document. It's all been verified, sir, because—and this is a little secret between us—we have an Englishman behind the lines who's passed for a German since the end of the last century, and from time to time he renders a small service.

—Right here, sir, although I'm not certain it's in chronological order. The 22nd Regiment's assault plan across the Jordan, the third of January, 1918. A roster of our brigade's sick and wounded from the thirtieth of December, 1917, to the sixth of January, 1918. A report on discipline in the 3rd Battalion from the third week of January, bearing the signature of Captain Smogg . . .

—There had been many complaints, sir. A divisional list of all officers on leave as of the thirteenth of January, 1918. A draft of a battle plan for the conquest of Damascus, signed by Major Sluce, from the twenty-sixth of January, 1918. The guest list for the gala evening given by the military governor of Jerusalem on the thirtieth of January, 1918. Two signed photographs of General Allenby, no date. A list of provisions sent to the 5th Australian Battalion. The deployment of our artillery in the Jericho theater as of the first of February, 1918. Some drafts of Lieutenant Colonel Keypore's personal correspondence with his wife.

—I'm afraid there's more, Colonel.

—A description of the firing mechanism of our F Howitzer, unsigned and dateless. A filled-out resupply form for artillery shells. A photograph of an unidentified young woman, apparently a tart, on the Via Dolorosa. A map of Jericho with the position of all artillery pieces from the third of February, 1918. Those, Colonel, were the cannon lost earlier this month in that unfortunate battle across the Jordan. The Germans counted each round that we fired, and when they knew we had run out of ammunition, they ordered an assault.

We lost one hundred and fifty men. Although I daresay the Australians were more upset about their cannon, because men are more easily replaceable.

—Just so, sir. He found it all in the wastebaskets or on his way to them.

—There already has been a jolly big scandal, sir. Officers were arrested and charges have been filed. New procedures have been instituted, and a special man was brought in from Cairo and has been on the job for a week. When you call on the general at headquarters tomorrow, you'll notice all the wastebaskets are empty. There's now a special sergeant with a detail of two soldiers whose assignment it is to burn the waste around the clock, which he does so industriously that I believe that some of it is already on fire before it's been thrown away. There's a permanent pillar of smoke outside military headquarters—if you look out the window you can see it right now. I say, sir, it's clearing again! And there's one of those black crows I've been telling you about. They already know that you, the presiding judge, have arrived and that I'm in here with you, although I'll be hanged if I know how they do.

—Yes, sir.

—Yes, sir.

—Over there, Colonel, if it's not too hard for you to make him out.

—A black spot it is, Colonel. And such black spots, Colonel, have been following me around for the past three weeks, because they know that the noose is tightening and that it won't be long now. Two emissaries of theirs have already been to see me, an old solicitor and a court clerk who can stammer a bit in English. They asked to look at the Handbook of Wartime Jurisprudence, and I gladly let them have it and gave them a place to sit in my room, where they spent the whole day reading and engaging in Talmudic disputations. I even had them served tea, which they wouldn't touch; at closing time, pale and exhausted, they handed the handbook back to me with the tips of their fingers, as if Mani's death were already inside it, and nodded sadly and looked at each other and asked if I knew the London Horowitzes. And when I confessed that I didn't, they began to ransack the rest of the world for some Horowitz whom I was prepared to be a distant relation of and could be given regards from, only to give up with a sigh in the end. "But this Mani is mad," said the court clerk to me in a whisper. "Is it not beneath the dignity of Great Britain to concern itself with a madman? Why, even his father took his own life; can you not show him mercy?" But I, Colonel, looked them straight in the eye and answered curtly, "You know as well as I do he's not mad."

—No, sir. Not even with that madness that masquerades as sanity until you sniff its sour smell in a warm room. No, there is absolutely nothing mad about him. He doesn't have even one iota of that first, slight, hardly visible wobble that eventually throws a man out of orbit. He has all his senses, Colonel; the man's soul may be a jungle, but neither his reason nor will are impaired, and he's in total command of himself; he says what he wishes to say, and holds back what he doesn't; and I happen to know that he is preparing a long political plea, not for the court's benefit, but for the public and the press. He's the sort of chap who likes his audience big and captive. He plans to let me say what I'm entitled to, and then to deliver a speech that will electrify Jerusalem, because it will be given by a man with a hangman's noose around his neck. I feel it; I *know* it; that's why he walked straight into that Ulsterman's funk hole when he could have easily gone around it. He was tired of playing to crowds of Mohammedans assembled by the whips of Turks; nothing would do for him but to perform for all Jerusalem.

—That's just it, sir. It's only a guess, but I reckon he's sharpening a poisoned dart for us. As much as I've tried drawing him out, I've gotten precious little out of him. He composed all the drafts of his speech in Hebrew, and when I sought to lay hands on them, he quite simply ate them. They're safely inside him now.

—You'll see him tomorrow, Colonel, in the dock. Don't be fooled into thinking he's following the proceedings, because the only thing on his mind will be his speech: about this eternal battlefield of a country that is spawning another catastrophe and about all the locusts waiting to arrive . . . although if you take a good look around you, Colonel, what you see here is one big wasteland with jolly few people anywhere. I told him as much, too. "Forget all that," I told him; "Find yourself a good barrister who will tell the court about your childhood, and your poor dead father; you're going to get yourself hung, and the more of your political balderdash, the more rope you'll wrap around your neck." But he just smiles at that, cool as a cucumber. A most political animal; and most politically calm! Quite certain that there's politics in everything he does . . . and yet I know, sir—and the knowledge turns in me like a knife—that there's another story here. There's someone else lurking in the background whom he's out to get back at, and all his politics are mere autosuggestion.

—A quite sensible thought, sir. In fact, I had it myself. I had a hook installed in the ceiling without his knowledge and a length of rope left in his cell one night, and I instructed the guards to look the other way in the hope that he would put an end to it. Well, sir, that night he pulled out the hook and coiled up the rope, and the next morning he handed them to me in a neat bundle without a word, which was his way of telling me that he meant to have his speech. And so he's been whittling away at it—and though I haven't a notion what's in it, I would be most delighted to be spared it, because it can only stir up feeling against us.

—No, sir. It's nothing that could affect the sentence. He's as good as dead already, sir, unless one of those crows can fly to Buckingham Palace and come back with a royal pardon. The case against him is open-and-shut, sir, and you musn't be misled by my qualms. Tomorrow morning I'll be there like an immovable body, and your two colleagues won't need to be convinced; Lieutenant Colonel Keypore would like nothing better than to see the man swing for those lost cannon across the Jordan, and I don't believe he'll relent . . . oh no, not *him* . . . but nonetheless, sir . . . and now, sir, I am . . . I am speaking not only as a soldier, but as a British subject too . . . if it were possible . . . you see, once the trial starts, it will proceed most speedily, with a rapidity we have no . . . control over . . . and so I thought that perhaps we should consider . . . since there is . . .

—Sir?

—Yes, sir, the interested parties have already made inquiries. It turns out there's a Turkish scaffold in the tower, with enough rope and tackle to hang us all. If the Turks had seen to their stock of artillery shells as they saw to their rope, we might not have taken this city so easily. And there's an Arab who served as the hangman's helper and claims he can manage things quite splendidly . . . so you see, sir, that's why I say . . . because . . . and I know I've been talking nonstop . . . but we have seen . . . we have seen . . .

—Sir?

—What boy is that, sir?

—Ah, yes, of course, the boy . . . but I have told you, haven't I, sir . . . I rather think . . . I mean . . . but in what way?

—Oh.

—Oh . . .

—Why, yes . . . directly, sir . . . why, of course, the boy . . .

—His name is Ephraim. Our Mani claims he's his, and there's no reason to doubt him, even though they don't look at all alike. The lad, you see, is blond and blue-eyed, and his dead mother, or so the story goes, was a tubercular young Jewess from Russia or thereabouts whom Mani picked out from all the bundles and luggage unloaded at the Beirut railway station, where he waited for his clientele. I can't say if she was a proper revolutionary—you'll find youngsters whose only terror has been directed against their parents, yet who are so certain they've committed crimes against the state that they feel compelled to flee. In any event, she attached herself to him; and accustomed though he was to the whims of such gypsies, whom he always managed to shake off, he could not get away from her. Perhaps she was as political as he was. Whatever the reason, something about her touched his stubborn, gloomy old bachelor heart. Perhaps she wanted a child from him, being afraid to push on to Palestine, or not believing she could get across the border, yet desiring something Palestinian of her own. Your guess is as good as mine. He didn't talk much about her, sir. In any case, they had no money, and they lived together for a year or two by the railway station in that boardinghouse I spoke of, which was in West Beirut, sir, in the Moslem quarter, an extremely poor part of town, so he says, by the old Sephardic synagogue, where he dropped in every Friday; with a bit of luck, sir, we'll be there soon and see it all for ourselves . . . When her time came they were afraid to go to hospital, lest they be asked for their papers and risk expulsion by the Turks as foreigners. And anyway, he believed that he could deliver the child by himself, because he had been through a birth once before and had even cut the umbilical cord. Still, he fetched a Moslem midwife for good measure; but the woman had a frail constitution; and she lost too much blood and died the day after giving birth. That left him with the infant, who grew up to be a bit slow and a stammerer, but an agreeable child who grew handsomer with each passing day and had his mother's good looks, which had already been ravaged by illness when Mani met her; only now, via her son who was unfolding like a flower, did he realize how beautiful she must have been. You'll see him tomorrow, Colonel, a four-year-old seated in the front row. I've allowed him to be present for the first session, so that he can enjoy the fine room and the officers in their uniforms and remember that his father was given a fair trial and not simply thrown to the dogs . . .

—Yes, sir. That's it in a nutshell. I do believe the weather's cleared for good now. The desert air will dry us out and bring us a sweetly golden Jerusalem afternoon. I feel in a dreadful dither, sir, for having bored you like—

—In a word, sir, my guidelines are clear and entirely in accordance with the Handbook of Wartime Jurisprudence, section 10, paragraph 3. In time of war, in occupied territory, when the defendant is a British subject who has engaged in espionage resulting in loss of life, the prosecution must demand the death penalty, which the court is authorized to inflict without right of appeal . . . However . . .

—Yes, sir, I understand that . . .

—Yes, sir.

—Those were my very words, sir!

—Quite.

—I see, sir . . . which would imply . . .

—I am surprised, sir.

—Colonel . . .

—Of course, sir . . . that would make it an entirely different matter . . .

—Exactly my feeling, sir . . . it's the only way . . .

—Excellent, sir . . . it will just take a bit of thought . . .

—Thank you.

—It did all come together, didn't it? Then I have succeeded.

—I'm most grateful . . .

—I'm greatly moved, sir, and most grateful for your patience in giving me a hearing. The fact is that when I was informed at head-quarters that you were coming from Egypt to preside at the trial, I had a most sinking feeling. And when I walked into this room two hours ago, sir, I was shaking, because I knew in whose presence I was. Your name, sir, has been on the lips of every officer for several days now: the hero of the Marne! And when I saw you sitting in this dim room with those dark sunglasses, with your empty sleeve on the arm of the chair and all your scars, I was alarmed and almost in tears. I had never imagined you were so badly wounded, and I thought, hang it all, the panther and the cobra have been joined on the bench tomorrow by the wounded lion! I could not know what lust for vengeance you might be harboring inside you; and here was a heinous case of wartime espionage resulting in loss of life; and the culprit was a ruddy Jew who refused all counsel and was quite prepared to be hung as long as he could give his ruddy speech that would cause the very devil of a row among the populace of this city; and once the trial began there would be no stopping it until it reached its bitter end, which it was my duty as prosecutor to pursue without quarter . . . Was this, sir, the way British history in the Holy Land was to begin, with the hanging of a Jew in Jerusalem? And yet I had to ask myself if I would be understood; and whether, if I talked candidly enough to make myself understood, I would be suspected of divided loyalties. You see, sir, I've never sought to hide my Jewishness as have certain other officers in this division, nor could I hope to do so given my name, my appearance, my eyeglasses, my low and protuberant rear end, and my presumptuous literary garrulousness that even an aristocratic Cambridge mumble has been unable to dispel. It's all quite distasteful, to say nothing of prejudi-cial, especially since I had to assume, sir, that you were anti-Semiti-cally disposed, if only in a sociological sense, as a member of your class and the circles in which you move. And so I was quite resigned to failure, perhaps even to a severe reprimand; but I remembered what my mother always told me; "Never give up, son," she said, "never be afraid as long as you know your intentions are pure"; which is how I put my case before you, sir; not merely as a soldier obeying orders, but as a subject of Great Britain, of the empire that rests assured of its approaching victory, of the war's end, and of the glorious era that awaits us and the entire Commonwealth . . .

—Sir.

—Sir.

—Sir.

—Sir.

—I'm quite ecstatic to have earned your trust.

—Do you really think so, sir?

—Why, of course, sir. Were he not a British subject, the prosecution need not ask for death, and he would then be a national of the territory under occupation.

—Most irregular, sir. I fail to see how such naturalization could be valid, the British passport notwithstanding.

—If we make a point of it, sir.

—His grandfather, sir, came from Salonika, which was in Turkey at the time and is presently in Greece.

—Why, of course, sir. We can definitely say Greece. But can we be sure they'll take him if we banish him?

—Then you think, do you, Colonel, that the islands would be best?

—Of course, sir. Every westward-bound ship from Jaffa calls on them . . . Rhodes, Crete . . . he can have his pick . . .

B I O G R A P H I C A L

Supplements

LIEUTENANT IVOR STEPHEN HOROWITZ served out the war with Allenby's forces, with which he entered Beirut, Aleppo, and Damascus, and was even present at the final assault on Mosul, before the armistice with Turkey in October 1918. After the surrender of Germany on the eleventh of November, he was released from the army to attend the spring term at Cambridge. He finished his legal studies with honors in 1920 and chose, after his acceptance to the bar in 1921, to do his apprenticeship with the district attorney of Manchester. He did not remain in public service long, however, but soon joined a well-known Jewish law firm and eventually married the senior partner's daughter. While continuing his practice he went on to get his doctorate, writing his dissertation on the judicial aspects of wartime espionage. This study was extremely well received and opened the way for an academic career. Dr. Horowitz joined the law faculty of Manchester University, and several years later, in 1930, moved with his wife and two small children to London, where he was appointed associate professor at the law school of the university. In London he was active in the Zionist Federation, serving as its volunteer legal adviser. His academic career was highly successful and he was considered a spellbinding lecturer. In 1957, on the occasion of his sixtieth birthday, he visited Israel; subsequently, he returned several times and met with various Israeli leaders, among them David Ben-Gurion. A grandson of his even settled in the country, on the kibbutz of Revivim. He died at the age of seventy-six in London, in October 1973, after a brief illness following a stroke.

COLONEL MICHAEL WOODHOUSE served through the remainder of the war and then continued to sit on military courts throughout the British Empire. Since his vision grew steadily worse until he became completely blind, the army assigned him a personal aide who accompanied him on his judicial missions to Malaya, Burma, India, and Ceylon. In the mid-1930s he was knighted by King George V. Sir Michael's reputation as a judge spread far and wide and was only heightened by his blindness. He presided at the trials of many British officers in the colonial service and was known for the originality and depth of his approach. Although when World War II broke out he was serving in Kenya, he insisted on returning to England at once to take part in the war effort. He was killed during an air raid on London in June 1941, at the age of sixty-four, and buried in his native village with full military honors.

FOURTH CONVERSATION

The country estate of Jelleny-Szad

near Cracow, in Galician Poland

Friday night and early Saturday morning,

October 20 and 21, 1899

T   H   E

Conversation

P   A   R   T   N   E   R   S

❪❪ DR. EFRAYIM SHAPIRO   a twenty-nine-year-old bachelor, born in 1870 on the estate of his parents, Sholom and Sarah (née
Pomerantz) Shapiro. Until the age of ten, Efrayim was taught Jewish
subjects and a bit of arithmetic by private tutors; subsequently, he
continued his education at a small Jewish school in a nearby town.
Despite his humanistic tendencies, his parents convinced him to
study medicine and helped arrange his enrollment at the famous
Jagellonica University in nearby Cracow, where—although he
showed little enthusiasm for his studies and was considered no more
than a mediocre student—he finished the seven years of medical
school. All of his vacations, no matter how brief, were spent on his
parents' estate.

In 1895 Efrayim Shapiro received his license to practice general
medicine. Since he wished to live with his family, he declined an
offer to acquire a specialization while interning in a Cracow hospital
and chose to open a pediatric practice in his native district.

Efrayim was a tall, slender young man with the perpetual hint of
an ironic smile on his face and a melancholic disposition. He was
not particularly attached to the local Jewish community and attended synagogue only on the High Holy Days. Much to the dis-
pleasure of his parents (who had put a wing of their house at his

disposal, in which he maintained his small clinic), he liked to spend his evenings in long conversations with the Polish servants, sometimes joined by his younger sister Linka.

In 1898 Efrayim's father, Sholom Shapiro, traveled to Basel to attend the Second Zionist Congress. He returned brimming with impressions and experiences and firmly committed to the new movement, for which he helped organize Zionist soirées that he went to with Linka, since his wife Sarah's health did not permit her to travel. In 1899 Sholom Shapiro planned to attend the Third Zionist Congress as the official delegate of his district; at the last minute, however, he had to cancel his participation as a result of his wife's poor health and to send Linka and Efrayim in his place. When the Congress was over, the two of them decided to forego a planned two-week vacation at a Jewish boardinghouse in Lugano and to visit Palestine instead. They returned home to Jelleny-Szad two months after leaving it.

SHOLOM SHAPIRO was born in Vilna, in Lithuania, in 1848 to an extremely poor family. He studied in a heder and a yeshiva and was an outstanding pupil, but his family's economic hardship forced him to stop his schooling without obtaining his rabbinical degree and to find work tutoring arithmetic and religious subjects in wealthy Jewish homes in the province of Pinsk. From there he wandered westward to Galicia, where in 1867 he was hired by Meir Pomerantz, the owner of a large flour mill in Jelleny-Szad, to tutor his daughter Sarah, who was three years older than Sholom. The two were married in 1869, when Sholom was twenty-one, and their eldest son Efrayim was born in 1870. The birth left Sarah confined for a long period and her recovery from it was slow. Meanwhile her father died, and Sholom Shapiro took over his father-in-law's mill. He proved to be a gifted and resourceful businessman who within a few years expanded the family's holdings, buying up more mills and acquiring the lumbering rights to several local forests while maintaining a reputation for fairness and reliability throughout the area. Although his son Efrayim was a joy to both parents, Sarah's ill health kept her from having more children. Nevertheless, the Shapiros persisted, and in 1879, when Efrayim was nine, their daughter Linka was born. Yet although the family's happiness was now complete, the birth damaged Sarah's frail constitution even more.

From its inception in 1897, Sholom Shapiro was greatly interested in the new movement of political Zionism. He attended the 1898 Zionist Congress in Basel and was highly excited by the debates and new ideas he heard there. He also had the experience of being introduced to the Zionist leader Dr. Herzl and of chatting with him briefly in German. Shapiro planned to attend the 1899 congress as well, but had to ask his son Efrayim to take his place. Besides wishing him to see for himself what Zionism was, Sholom Shapiro secretly hoped that Efrayim might meet a nice Jewish girl at the congress, since he was increasingly troubled both by his son's bachelorhood and by his avoidance of Jewish circles. Linka, who was twenty at the time and an ardent Zionist in her own right, pleaded to be allowed to go along. At first her parents had grave doubts about the matter, but at Efrayim's repeated urgings they agreed.

Sholom Shapiro's half of the conversation is missing.

—Over here, Father.

—Here . . . behind the commode, next to the sofa . . .

—No . . . just idling away the time . . . I was having myself a smoke . . .

—Hiding? What for?

—Ah . . . perhaps so . . . hiding, eh? I rather like that . . .

—No. I am not tired. It is agreeable here in the dark. The forest —the croaking of the frogs—how dear our native land is! And meanwhile winter has set in with a vengeance. I declare, you haven't left a leaf on the trees . . .

—I have had quite enough to eat.

—No, Father. I am absolutely sated—and besides, Stefa has brought me a samovar and some cakes. You should see how she cried and crossed herself and shook all over at the sight of me! And how she bent to kiss my hand . . . what on earth, my dears, were you so worried about?

—My word! Is it that, then?

—So that's it! It had not occurred to me.

—That is certainly so . . . I can't deny that they have a claim on it too . . .

—Well, Father, I simply had no idea what the great fuss was all about. Mrazhik actually went down on his knees, doffed his cap, carried Linka in his arms from the railway car to the carriage, and covered us with wraps like royalty . . .

—Church bells?

—So I do . . . what a simpleton I am, dearest Papa! And here I was convinced that it was a sign of how much they missed us . . . of how much they loved us . . .

—No doubt. But not enough to make them carry on in such a fashion.

—Lights in the village? Why, so there are . . .

—My word . . . I declare . . .

—Of course. It is their Holy Land too—there is no denying that —you don't know how right you are! Jerusalem and all the rest of it . . . I am quite willing to grant them their fair share of it . . . but still—such excitement—why, they even tried kissing the tails of my coat . . .

—No, Papa, I don't feel the slightest fatigue anymore. It has dissolved quite away in this damp clime of ours, this swamp air . . . How cozy it is by the fire! The trains are not heated, you know; the people on them are supposed to warm each other, but you have to expend a great deal of warmth before you get any back . . . which is why this undemanding fire is so wonderful—the whole last leg of our trip I kept myself going by imagining coming home to it—you are looking at a happy man . . .

—Yes, happy. When the train pulled out of Cracow, and I knew that we would soon be home, and the sun began to dip through the branches, and the fields stretched away to the horizon beyond the railroad tracks that converged from all directions, and I saw the wooden sign of our village pointing toward the black waters of the Vistula . . . upon my soul, I felt as if I had emerged from a dark tunnel into freedom, as if I had returned from a journey through the earth . . .

—*Through* the earth . . . I remember that when we were children, after Grandfather passed away, you once told us a story about the dead . . . about how, at the End of Days, at the Resurrection, the Christians would rise from their graves where they were, but we Jews would crawl through underground caverns and come out in the Land of Israel . . . which is just what I've been doing these past few days, but in the opposite direction—from there to here—cavern-crawling and turning over in many graves—as though traveling not upon the globe but deep beneath its surface—with the coaches groaning and the locomotive wailing and smoke and soot and great showers of sparks by night—from tunnel to tunnel and from one remote station to another—each time the same flicker of gas lamps, and the same onrush of blackness, and then the same total nothing—and wherever you looked in the foggy distance, our flour mills standing like titans—talk of resurrection! I am happy, Father; why, we nearly came to grief . . .

—To grief . . .

—I mean just that.

—No, you are exhausted, Father. You look drawn. Go to sleep now. Just fetch me another cigarette before you do, and here, in this corner of my childhood, beside the old sofa, I will wait for the dawn. I know myself well enough to know I can't sleep—I'll wait for you right here, and whenever you are ready, the trial can begin . . .

—I mean the accounting that I owe you.

—An accounting. Are you very angry?

—You have every right to be . . . every right . . .

—Undoubtedly . . . every right—until I make you understand —if you *can* understand—because I fail to understand myself . . .

—As you wish . . . are you quite sure? You can stop me whenever you want. Mother has already told me what you have been through these past few weeks, after our "oriental silence" set in . . . poor Mama! She does not look well. I bit my lips to keep from saying an unnecessary word—one that might betray the fear felt by the doctor in me. What happened, Father?

—When?

—Blood? Good lord . . .

—In the morning?

—Very well, then . . . very well . . . but not now . . . I will make it my business to look at all those vials and powders before he comes. If I am to help treat her, I shall have to have a good talk with Heshin. After all, you can't expect me simply to stay out of this;

there is no way I can be relegated to the position of a mere observer . . .

—. . . if I stick to my corner! Very well, then; but a corner with an unobstructed view. As you wish—we need not go into that now —it is just that I . . .

—Very well—you have laid down the law . . . My word, the water is still running up there! By now it is no longer her body that she is washing, it is her very soul, ha ha ha . . .

—No matter! Let her wash all she wants—it is no affair of mine. She has been dreaming of nothing but this bath for a solid week, as if she were encrusted with the filth of generations—perhaps the water will soothe her sorrow. Hydrotherapy: you can actually find it in the medical books . . . Just don't let her fall asleep in it, because she has not slept a wink for three whole days. She simply stewed in the compartment—for hours on end she stood with her head against the windowpane—she crossed the whole of Bulgaria like that . . .

—I already have sworn it to Mother . . .

—She is perfectly healthy.

—I suppose she has lost weight; what of it? She'll put it back on.

—I knew that would give you a fright—but surely you are not afraid that it won't grow back again . . .

—She did not do it in Jerusalem; it was in Stamboul, ten days ago. She woke up crying in the middle of the night and found her pillow crawling with them. The hotel had no soap—there was no water left, either—it was a cheap, filthy dive—and right away she began looking for a knife. I begged her not to—half of humanity, I told her, walks around with lice and is none the less human for it—don't be rash, I said—Father and Mother will still love you, lice and all . . . But you know how she is—underneath all her smiles, she is as stubborn as a mule—and perhaps she felt the need to do herself injury. I offered to pick them out myself, but she would not let me touch her. She rushed off to the doorman below, borrowed a curved Turkish dagger, stood in front of the rusty mirror, and cut away for dear life . . .

—I was beside myself too, Father. All that gorgeous red hair lying on the floor with those mortified Turkish lice—perhaps even a louse from Palestine—running about in it . . . for a moment I almost picked it up and saved it, but by then I was afraid of it myself—and that whole train ride back with her, with everyone staring at her cropped hair—I tell you, it made her more attractive than ever—they were walking up and down the aisles for a look at her! The devil knows why it made her so beautiful—perhaps the way it brought out those high cheekbones—or her eyes . . .

—Why, nothing, of course. What could I say? Nothing is all I have been able to say for many days now. She has become a different person: wild, bitter, heedless, morose . . . I have made up my mind—I have had enough—I want nothing more to do with her—I am leaving. I shall go live with Grandmother . . .

—I am leaving . . . oh, just wait until you hear about it all, dear Papa!

—Yes, but only there—in that hotel in Stamboul—while we were waiting for the train to Europe . . .

—We had no choice. My word, Father, we had no choice! Wait one minute—listen, Father—we were running low on money . . .

—I had no idea how we would ever get out of there . . . my word . . .

—Yes. That was my promise and I kept it. Everywhere—even in Venice—everywhere . . .

—In Palestine too. Naturally. There especially. The first night I slept a floor below her, surrounded by parturient women . . . and after that, in a hostel miles away . . .

—I will tell you about it soon enough.

—A clinic of sorts.

—Aboard ship too. Of course. We had private berths everywhere. And if none were available, we asked for a partition . . .

—Yes. But that was only toward the end of our journey. And we reached Stamboul in the dead of night. I did not want to leave the station, because I was afraid we would miss the train for Europe in the morning—we had had quite enough of the Turks—and there was only one room left there—not to mention the expense . . .

—What I am saying, Father, is—but listen to me, will you!—why must you be so damnably suspicious?—that we entered Turkey with exactly one hundred bishliks . . .

—About thirty thalers. I did not want to touch the gold coins—not until I knew where we stood. Look—they are still strapped to my waist—not a coin less than you gave me . . .

—I know exactly. Everything can be accounted for. You will have an account of every penny.

—Of course, Father, of course. It's not the money but the principle. I know that. But there were mishaps. There was a tragic accident in Beirut, where we had to stay an extra night—and our ship sailed for Stamboul without us, with all our luggage aboard—by the time we caught up with it, it was gone—even the gifts we bought in Jerusalem had been pilfered . . .

—Later . . . one thing at a time . . .

—A man was killed. A good friend.

—But for heaven's sake, Father, I am telling you. I was afraid we would run out of money, and we—

—No. I am not shouting. Forgive my asking, but what exactly is it that you want?

—In mourning? In mourning for what? For Linka's hair? That much at least is retrievable.

—Other things are not.

—For example . . . for example . . . no matter . . .

—No. I do not wish to frighten you.

—For example . . . suppose, Father, I were to say innocence . . . or happiness . . .

—Happiness. Yes.

—In no special sense. Happiness. Innocence. I do not wish to distress you, but we were close to losing her there—she wished to remain—I pulled her out of the vortex with my last strength . . .

—Of Palestine, dear Papa. Your Eretz-Yisro'el . . .

—I am skipping around, that is so—you will have to excuse me— but not now, because I see you have not the patience. You are falling off your feet. Go to sleep, Father . . . tomorrow . . . just fetch me a cigarette first, because the ones I have are no better than straw . . .

—From Palestine. They smoke like the blazes there too.

—Not at all. Here, take the whole pack—how stupid of me not to have brought more—I should have realized what a cigarette from there would mean to you . . .

—This? The devil knows. I suppose it's some sort of camel.

—Perhaps a Jewish camel.

—They are actually grayer, more sand-colored—rather patient beasts—perhaps because they have such small brains . . .

—Thank you.

—The Mohammedans, of course.

—Some wander and some do not.

—Most? Most live in cities and villages.

—Yes, real cities.

—Where? Nowhere . . .

—I did not count, but there are some.

—No, dearest Papa, I am not cross. The wheels of the train are simply still spinning in my head. For five whole days we have been on rails: Europe is quite overrun by them. A young German engineer who came aboard at Salonika and shared our compartment for two days told me that in ten or twenty years it will be possible to cross the entire Continent in a single coach without having to step out onto a platform . . .

—So he said. But through the window, Father, Europe looks ablaze with unrest, with the profoundest gloom. The wagons are packed—in the villages you see great bonfires—the peasants are leaving their plows and turning into itinerant pilgrims—you see fires in all the fields. Everyone is talking about the *fin de siècle,* the last days of this century. There is a sense of exultation, but also of great anxiety, and everywhere there are seers and prophets. It is one great carnival, I tell you! Most of all, the Russian muzhiks, whom you see singing and kneeling and lighting candles all over. And everywhere there are Greeks and Turks out to swindle you, and wherever you look, Father, in every railroad coach, our shifty-eyed Jews too. Some are heading west, some south—very *practical* pilgrims, you may be sure—not a God-seeker among them—no, *Him* they carry around on their backs, along with their bundles and their children, quite crushing them—you have no idea how many unwashed Jewish children are underfoot wherever you go . . .

—We left Palestine two weeks ago. By the Feast of Tabernacles we were already in Beirut . . .

—With that man.

—The same physician who lured us to Jerusalem . . . did not Linka write you about him before we sailed?

—Dr. Mani.

—A Jew, of course. What did you think? You wouldn't happen to have any brandy around, would you?

—I am suddenly shaking all over.

—Well, never mind . . . as long as we can get this fire going again . . . I can't tell you how I dreamed of it . . . the colder the nights, the more I pictured myself coming home and making straight for it . . .

—It's the Sabbath? So it is . . . I have totally lost track of time . . . well, then, let's call for Mrazhik and have him poke some life into the coals . . .

—Are you sure that you want to hear about it? That you feel up to it?

—I believe I do . . . but first let's see to the fire . . . where is Mrazhik? Don't tell me he's become an observant Jew too. How quiet it is up there! Do you think she has fallen asleep? Or is she telling Mama her story in a whisper? Perhaps, Father, you would rather go upstairs and hear it directly from her—don't let me keep you—my feelings won't be hurt . . .

—Very well, then . . .

—Very well. Let there be two stories, an upstairs and a downstairs one. As for the truth, it can run up and down between them . . .

—From the beginning? And where, I ask you, is that?

—Don't be angry. No, don't; I am not being coy. Incidentally, I met your Herzl, although I had no chance to give him regards from you . . . it was too hurried and confused an encounter . . .

—From the beginning? But you already know all that. Linka wrote you three letters.

—All right . . . all right . . . but where does the beginning begin? I fear distressing you.

—To Palestine? But what sort of question is that? I mean, for a Zionist like you . . . or have you forgotten that you sent us to a Zionist congress, ha ha?

—Well, then, we simply took the next logical step . . .

—But what do you mean, what has that to do with it? Does not Palestine have everything to do with it?

—My apologies. All right, then: from the beginning. The beginning—the journey there—was wonderful. Everything about it. Even the warm weather and clear skies. Already in Katowice you could see delegates gathering in the train from all over Galicia and Poland —a totally Zionist train, except for the invisible driver. Toward evening a second train arrived from Moscow and flooded our car with a large group of youngsters who made a great impression on me. They're another breed of Jew, Father: full of life—earnest—simply dressed—unashamedly Jewish yet freethinkers, every one of them. They are different from us—self-assertive—the children of pogroms and Pobedonostsev—the bearers of bright hopes. All had brought parcels of food with them to save the expense of eating in the dining car. I could see at once that Linka was drawn to them. Oh, she tried not to show it—but not enough to keep them from noticing her and striking up a conversation. At first of course in Yiddish—and yet it did not take long to find someone who spoke a little French—and someone else who could jabber in English—at long last Madame Zwitowska's language lessons were bearing fruit! And from then on, Father, everywhere we went—in Switzerland, in Palestine—every one of those languages went with us . . . although it was only in Palestine—and in English—that the real, the worst damage was done . . .

—I'll get to that. Let me tell it in order. From now on it will all be in order, the painful parts too. There will be no avoiding them— they will grow harsher and harsher as this story outgrows its cradle —this story, Father, which—

—Precisely. We are still in that railway car, which by now was all Jewish, the Christians having fled long ago—still in that night that was so full of promise that it made Zionists out of us all, even out of me, who, as you know, has my grave doubts about the matter. Yes, even I was all ears. There was a young couple there from the Ukraine, a big bearded fellow in an embroidered peasant blouse and a girl he had with him. They could not get close to Linka, because she was already surrounded, and so they threw themselves on me— it has always struck me how couples are attracted to me most extravagantly—I am irresistible to them—and began explaining their "political position," because they had a "program" of their own. Each kept finishing the other's sentences. And they were not, I soon realized, even delegates, but only "observers," although terribly revolutionary and conspiratorial ones, with a detailed plan of action. They considered your Dr. Herzl to be as big a tyrant as the Czar and not at all a mere spinner of fantasies . . .

—A spinner of fantasies.

—There is nothing wrong with fantasy.

—I never said that.

—Of course, Father.

—Nothing is impossible . . . In any event, dawn broke over the marvelous spires of Prague to find Linka laughing merrily—she laughed her way through the forests of Germany and past the red-dish houses of Munich—and there, toward evening, the train spewed us out to stretch our limbs while the locomotive was restoked with coal and the cars were de-jew-migated . . . And so we went for a walk through the streets and lanes of that most beautiful city, although by now Linka was less walking than floating on air with all those young Russians while I brought up the rear with my couple—which had taken possession of me entirely—thinking that her beauty was far greater than had ever occurred to us here, in our remote little Jelleny-Szad. Apparently, dearest Papa, we had misinterpreted the silence of the flour mills . . .

—I am saying that that extraordinary, redheaded concentrate of femininity that I had always thought could be understood only by me now had everyone eating out of her hand, which left me imbecilically wondering how I could ever have doubted her powers of communication . . .

—It does not matter.

—It does not matter.

—Yes, I suppose that I do have a way of saying it does not matter when it does . . .

—Let me tell it in my own good time.

—I do feel up to it, but let me take my time. You know me: in the end even I always manage to get to the point . . .

—I did not betray a trust, Father. But even if I did not stick to our plan, don't you want to know why? There has to be a reason, does there not? Because at first everything went according to schedule. The train left at midnight for your Basel, and we arrived at noon, and took a deep breath of your Swiss air, and went straight to your boardinghouse exactly as you told us that you did last year, where waiting for us were two clean and agreeable rooms . . .

—So they were. Three flights up.

—Yes, Frau Kuralnik remembered you, as did Herr Frisch.

—And the old man too, of course, the old man too. Everyone was most sorry you could not come, and when I told them about Mama, they were most sorry about her too. And they were all quite taken with Linka, who curtsied to them very prettily. They tried so hard to make the kitchen kosher that there were separate shelves for dairy and pork. Some delegates from England and Belgium had already arrived—everywhere you heard the hubbub of Jews—and suddenly I fell into such a black mood that I went up to my room and threw myself on the bed, quite unable to understand what I was doing there. I must have fallen asleep at once—in fact, I could have slept through that entire congress if Linka had not woken me toward evening, all flushed and excited, with two fancy-looking delegates' cards that she had gotten hold of in the front office . . . *Dr. Efrayim Shapiro and Linka Shapiro, Delegates to the Third Zionist Congress* . . . the devil only knows how she managed to talk them into it . . .

—So it would seem.

—They were expecting you—and when you did not show up, your only son was recognized as your heir apparent—and for good measure the inheritance was doubled to let your little daughter in too—in such a fashion does our Jewish democracy grow by leaps and bounds . . .

—I do believe that she was the youngest delegate at the congress.

—She charmed them into it. The minute we left Jelleny-Szad our Linka began to grow up so fast, quite from minute to minute, that no one was not swept off his feet by her. Mind you, Father, all along —inside that virginal shell of hers—in her childhood room with its pale blue curtains and its windows looking out on our gray fields—a woman, a real one, was secretly making herself. I could not get over it: no longer was I an elder brother with a little sister in tow, but a mournful and slightly balding gentleman doing his quiet best to keep up with a vivacious young lady. At first everyone mistook her for my wife—"*Madame,*" I was told, "is over there"—or, "But where is the charming Frau Shapiro? She promised us she would be here"—while I stood there stammering with a silly grin, "I'm afraid, gentlemen, that she's only my younger sister." Ah, what a twinge of sweet sorrow! . . .

—No matter. I'm talking rubbish.

—Yes, I suppose I have said it again. But you are hanging on my every word while I am talking as though in a dream, Father—you mustn't take me so literally—because the truth of the matter is that everything was upside down—here were you and Mama, sending your obstinate bachelor of a son off to a Jewish congress to find himself a wife—and what does he discover when he gets there but that he already has a wife, and a young and attractive one at that, whom he had better keep an eye on . . .

—You know as well as I do, my dearest Papa, that your passion for Zionism was not the real reason for sending me . . .

—Suppose we say the covert, the unspoken reason.

—Fine, call it the additional reason. We can compromise on that. You have your dander up, while I am simply trying to tell a story. Because there is a story here, Father—a little tale that I have brought you back from your Palestine—it is with me on this old sofa like a baby that will cry on and on until it is listened to . . . Well, the day went by and it was time for the opening of the congress. The two of us were real delegates and had to behave like ones, although it was far from clear whose delegates we were, what district we represented, and where exactly that was. Were we the spokesmen of your fields and forests? Of your flour mills? Or perhaps of all the tracks and train stations we had seen? Because certainly, of the families in our village, neither the Mendels nor the Hefners nor the Urbachs had authorized us to act in their behalf . . . Still, delegates we were: so it said and so we would be. It was a bright, a most intense evening, with the shining stars looking down on us from afar with a comforting glitter.

—The thought that there was something more eternal than our Jewish worries and Jewish commotions.

—Never mind. It does not matter. To get back to my story, there we were, striding along the streets of Basel with delegates who converged from all over the city—making for the Casino, where the congress was held—and indeed, we were gamblers of sorts, although most respectable ones. The bow ties and black tails blended quite nicely with the colorful outfits of the Swiss girls, the evening dresses, the bare arms of our Jewish delegatesses, the shopping baskets, the hansoms, the taverns—in a word, the local residents regarded us with such indifference—from such depths of normalcy—that it would hardly have made a difference had we been wearing Buddhist robes or Eskimo parkas. However you looked at it, we were Jews, here today and gone tomorrow . . . while as for our Linka . . .

—Theaterstrasse . . . so it was . . .

—Exactly as you described it a year ago . . . and Linka . . .

—Most assuredly it was, Father, that tavern with the golden rooster . . . exactly . . . but listen . . . our Linka . . .

—I was acutely aware of following in your footsteps all the time, Father . . . and of feeling most sorry for you . . . but our Linka, if I may be allowed to proceed . . .

—Sorry that you could not be there yourself.

—Yes, the pastry shop with the whipped cream too . . .

—You gorged yourself there also? Ha ha, I like that . . .

—Of course . . . the synagogue in the Eulerstrasse is still where you left it . . . but our Linka . . .

—No, we had no time to visit it. If you will listen, you will hear everything. Because even there in the street our Linka stood out in festive splendor—she had about her a most portentous look that she had been practicing since Katowice and was clutching her delegate's scroll in one hand like the Magna Carta—and a most bare-armed hand it was too, extending from a black dress that she secretly had made for herself without my knowledge. I do not know if you were privy to it, Father—a most flimsy, foolish, reckless, scandalous bit of sleeveless décolleté! And those arms, mind you, were still a child's—still plump from a mother's milk with their childhood freckles—those most discreet freckles, Father—now flaunted for all to see . . .

—No, no, I don't mean the freckles themselves. They were simply a metaphor—something aggravating to think about during that grand walk to the Casino—which itself was but a brash overture to what followed—to that feminine promise she gave off wherever she went—you see, I am simply trying to help you to understand what happened later . . . are you with me?

—Are you with me?

—Are you listening to me? There was a great crowd by the entrance, and lots of applause and hurrahs, and even my Russians—I
mean my revolutionary, conspiratorial observers—were wearing
clean shirts and began to clap the minute they thought they made
out Herzl's beard. And meanwhile, two other young men from the
train who were lying in wait fell upon Linka and began pulling her
toward them while I tried tugging her back the other way . . .
except that at that very moment what did I see but the shining bald
pate of Professor Steiner, from the pathology department of the
university . . .

—Yes, he was. And Migolinsky was there too, decked out in
black tie and looking quite splendid and earnest—and here I had
thought he had baptized himself long ago . . .

—There was a rumor to that effect, anyway.

—Perhaps he had himself unbaptized again, ha ha . . .

—Who could have sent him? He was a delegate representing
himself, as was everyone. But if a billiard-ball head like him could
turn up at a Jewish congress and hug me enthusiastically—why,
then, I tell you, there is hope—hope that infected even me—because
the fact of the matter is that I was gnawed by doubt whether we
were truly ready for this adventure—whether it was not premature
to expose ourselves thus to the world—not a mistake, that is, to
display the full extent of our weakness—because, after all, we could
have gone on nuzzling a while longer at the Christian teat before
deciding in all seriousness to rally round a flag and an anthem of our
own . . .

—I believe one was chosen.

—Yes . . . I'm almost positive . . . blue and white on a field of
gold stars . . .

—No. It is pointless to ask, because I do not remember. So much
has happened since then—and of an entirely different nature—and
all I recall is the crowd surging toward the entrance and Linka in
her ridiculous dress being swept away by an ardent band of "observers," with me trailing after her behind my bald professor, who was
ushered to a balcony overlooking the stage while I was seated beside
him directly in back of a column.

—No. Please, Father, don't ask me now about the congress . . .

—An address? Of course . . . isn't there always? It was actually more of a report . . .

—No, I don't remember.

—Yes. About his meeting with the German Kaiser in Palestine . . .

—As far as I could make out, nothing. It was all very vague. Rather evasive. Perhaps I did not really understand it . . .

—About the country itself he said hardly a word.

—Well, perhaps a word. Something or other about Jerusalem. Something poetic about the night there and the moonlight. Having been there myself, I can tell you how little he understood. He is living an idea, not a reality. He talks about the moon, not about the streets—about the ramparts, not about the houses—about the Germans and the Turks, not about the Jews—about the future, not about the present. He is in love with the recipe, Father, not with the ingredients . . .

—Just three nights in Jerusalem, two of which, it seems, were spent tossing and turning on a billiard table in an inn called the Hotel Kamenitz . . .

—Apparently there was no bed for him, and so they made one on top of a billiard table. Perfectly symbolic . . .

—Sad? I would not say so. Not even pessimistic. Rather delirious, however. I was able to observe him from up close, even though I was not concentrating on what he said, because I had trouble following his Viennese accent—and suddenly, dear Papa, I felt a great wave of pity for him. He has not long to live, Father . . .

—Consider it a medical intuition.

—It is only an intuition—but why scoff?

—The way he perspires—his pallor—the barely restrained tremor of his arms—the black bags under his sunken eyes . . . If a patient came to me looking like that, I would be alarmed. I would send him at once for a blood examination, for a lung auscultation . . . he won't last long—he is living on borrowed time—and who knows if the whole business will not simply go poof when he dies . . .

—Fine, call it a medical fantasy . . . Scoff . . .

—It was purely my own private diagnosis. I stole a glance at Steiner, to see if he was of the same opinion, but he did not seem to be thinking along medical lines. He was following the speech—he was quite carried away by it—there was something almost violent about the way he applauded . . .

—Wait, Father.

—Wait . . .

—It was just a thought . . . don't be angry . . . perhaps I'm wrong . . .

—Then I am wrong.

—I most certainly hope that it is not a one-man movement.

—But wait . . .

—You? Hah!

—You will outlive us all, don't you worry . . .

—Palestine did not affect my mind. Although if someone had told me that night at the congress that twelve days later I would be in Jerusalem, I would have thought him deranged . . .

—But wait . . . don't be angry . . . it was just a thought . . .

—You make it sound as if I have already killed him! On the contrary, Father, the session went on and on—there were more speeches, and greetings, and even a few challenges from the floor— and all this time I was wedged between my column and my professor—until finally, late at night, we dispersed and I rushed off to look for my Linka, whom I had lost sight of earlier in the evening, still with my pathologist at my side, now delivering an oration of his own that was replete with original if rather brutal ideas. And so slowly the crowd jostled us out to the street with its din of people and carriages that made me quite dizzy, since I was not accustomed to the proximity of so many Jews, let alone to wearing evening dress. I began to look for Linka and finally spied her in that mob scene surrounded by a swarm of Russians—of pogrom-and-Pobedonostsev survivors—with her ridiculous dress all wrinkled—the very clasps were falling off—and her feverish arms piled high with papers. And on her shoulder, Father, quite nonchalantly but firmly planted—I can still see it perfectly clearly—was a male hand . . . Well, before I could come to our budding young leader's rescue, up popped an angry little old man in a top hat, straight out of the sidewalk, and shouted in Yiddish right under my nose: "Is there a doctor here? We need a doctor! Who here is a doctor?" I stepped up automatically, and he gripped my hand fiercely and led me back into the hall that had still pulsed madly with people and lights when

I had left it a few moments before. It was already dim and deserted; only a few Swiss help were still there, sweeping up the waste paper with large brooms, snuffing out the last candles, and opening the windows to air out all those moldy speeches. The little old man flew between the chairs with great vigor, pulling me after him to the proscenium—where suddenly he stopped and asked quite forwardly: "Where are you from, young man?" Naturally, when I told him, he had no idea where it was, but when I added that it was near Cracow, his face lit up at once. "But what kind of a doctor are you?" he asked, still standing with me there on the stage. "What do you specialize in?" "Pediatrics," I replied with a smile. You should have seen his crestfallen look! "Pediatrics?" He mulled it over for a while and then mumbled: "Well, never mind. Come with me." "But what is the matter?" I asked. "Come quick, someone has fainted," he said rather mysteriously. He commenced dragging me after him again, opened a door that led backstage into a large, dark billiard parlor, and started up an ornate staircase, pulling me down several long corridors into a room full of cigarette smoke, in which two men were standing by an easy chair. And who do you think, Father, was sitting in it? Herzl.

—Herzl in person, very pale and small—without his tie—without his frock coat—his white shirt open at the neck—but perfectly calm. He was holding a glass of water and speaking French with some friends, although the old man who brought me addressed him most familiarly in German. "I've found a young physician from Cracow," he said. "For God's sake, Dr. Herzl, please allow him to examine you." Herzl simply waved an impatient, a dismissive hand; but at once everyone joined the old man in cajoling him to agree, until at last he gave in and dropped his beard on his chest in a most touching gesture of acquiescence. The vigorous old man pushed me toward the easy chair—so hard, in fact, that I almost stumbled, for he appeared to be afraid that if I did not make haste Herzl would change his mind—at which point, Father, listen—listen to me!—I forgot all about my diagnosis. In fact, the same man who had struck me as being little more than a mummy on the stage now seemed terribly vital and real—even the bags under his eyes now looked like an inspired form of makeup. I had no idea what to examine him for. I assumed he had had an attack of vertigo—perhaps a slight syncope

—the whites of his eyes were prominent and there was nystagmus. I looked to see if there were any signs of regurgitation—I am quite used to children vomiting in such cases—but there were none; nor was there any smell. I was at a loss. I had no idea what was expected of me. I leaned over until I was close to him, quite overwrought with anxiety—and as I did he looked up at me and threw me a rather merry glance. He spoke in German, and I in a Yiddish that I hoped would pass for German. In an unsteady voice, I asked him what was the matter. He laughed, made some jest to his friends about the doctor feeling faint himself, and held out his hand to me—whether to take my own or in an expression of surprise, I could not say—and so I seized it and quickly began to seek—what else could I do?—the pulse.

—Sometimes it enables you to detect irregularities in the heartbeat.

—That was just it. I could not find any pulse. Perhaps I was not gripping his wrist tightly enough, or perhaps his pulse was too weak. Meanwhile, the door opened and in came two more men with another doctor they had hunted down, a handsome, brown-skinned, stocky man wearing a white frock coat. He bowed to us all with a great show of feeling, and—blushing with emotion, although quite freely and winningly—went over to Herzl and introduced himself in English as Dr. Mani. He made some reference to Jerusalem, where it seemed that he had met Herzl before, but Herzl—who regarded him in the same slightly jocular manner—did not remember him. And mind you, all this time I was standing there holding his wrist and trying desperately—with my heart in my boots—to undo his gold cufflink and find his vanished pulse while more and more people filled the room with more and more doctors, all urgently summoned by Herzl's entourage—each of whom had gone out to find a physician and some of whom had found more than one. It was beginning to seem more of a medical convention than a Zionist congress. Of course, all the doctors stopped in their tracks the minute they saw me standing by the easy chair and stubbornly clinging to Herzl's wrist in search of his lost heartbeat—which, even if I had found it, could not possibly have been counted in all that commotion—especially since the patient, who seemed quite delighted at the sight of all those people come to treat him, would not sit still. By now he had his color back and everyone was beginning to relax since the great man was clearly alive and even laughing as if he had simply played a prank on all the doctors to assemble them in one room. But although I had no reason to keep groping for his pulse, I could not let go of his hand; it was as though glued to mine. The more doctors poured into the room, the more paralyzed I became. Everyone was waiting impatiently—although I must say, with collegial politeness—for the impertinent young physician—for I obviously felt nothing and was not counting anything—to finish his absurd examination. And yet I would not give up—not until I saw the shiny crown of my professor of pathology come floating into the room too and grew so genuinely terrified that I finally let the hand drop—whereupon Herzl, with the most magnificent gallantry, rose, took my hand once more in his own, and shook it most heartily in a grateful adieu, ha ha ha ha ha . . .

—Ha ha ha ha ha . . .

—Most thoroughly amusing, Father, was it not? Ha ha ha ha . . .

—Sometimes the artery is collapsed.

—Of course it has a name. Why should it not? Everything in our body has a name.

—Why do you ask?

—The radial artery, or something of the sort . . .

—Absurd . . . perfectly . . . and yet there you are . . .

—To think that I, of all people, who am so accustomed to weak pulses . . . in the case of children it is quite common . . .

—Well, don't take it to heart . . . in any case, no one will ever remember it was me . . .

—*Fiendish* luck? Come, now, that is putting it a bit strongly . . . why be so upset by it? I am not about to have my license revoked, ha ha ha . . .

—No, no one else tried to examine him. They all just wanted to meet him. They were some quite famous professors there who spoke a wicked German, and before long a group of them had formed around him while I retired to a corner—where, if you must know, I was thinking not of Herzl but of Linka, who was no doubt worrying what had happened to me—the lord only knew if she had not already returned to our hotel and lost her way in its dark corridors!

And in that same corner—to which he too had retreated from that
boisterous outbreak of German—was the doctor from Jerusalem,
feeling rejected and rather shamefaced that Herzl had not recognized him—so much so that, when we were given the hint to leave
the room and let our pulseless leader rest, he slipped out a back
door and disappeared, while I—no doubt attracted to his mortifica-
tion by my own—ran after him. I found myself in a long, dark
hallway, which I realized at once was not the way I had come; but
not wishing to retrace my steps, I groped my way onward in pursuit
of the shadow ahead of me. He sensed that he was being followed
and halted; took a little candle from his pocket and lit it; and held it
up to light my way while waiting for me politely . . . from which
moment, Father, you may if you like draw a straight and ghastly line
to his death ten days ago in the train station of Beirut, even though
in my heart I know well that the two of us, Linka and myself, were
only a pretext . . .
     —A pretext.
     —A pretext . . . a pretext for an entirely different reckoning.
That is, I was a pretext for Linka, and Linka was a pretext for
someone else, perhaps even another woman . . .
     —I ask myself the same question.
     —I cannot stop thinking about it; cannot stanch the grief of
it . . .
     —No.
     —No . . .
     —You aren't tired?
     —I? I have just begun to wake up. Beware of me, dear Papa,
because the story and I have become one—my soul has been
smelted to it by this fire, which has bewitched me since childhood—
so that—who knows—perhaps when I finish this story I will leap
into it and vanish in a heap of ashes . . . brrrr . . .
     —I do not know why, but I have had this chill in my bones since
crossing the Bosporus. I feel as though I were levitating.
     —That may be so. For a Palestinian like me, though, the autumn
here is like winter . . .
     —Fill my glass up, will you?
     —No, not with tea . . . with brandy . . .
     —More.

—Thank you. And that, Father, was how it began: with an encounter in a dark hallway near the service stairs, where a man from
Jerusalem was waiting for me with a little candle burning in his
hand. I still cannot get over his having that candle ready in his
pocket—you would have thought he had spent his whole life being
trapped in dark passages—indeed, he had two candles, one for me
too, which I lit at once with great joy. To this day I wonder whether
had Herzl not had that weak spell, we would have met. Or suppose
he had had it and I had not run after the man? But I *would* have run
after him—I was drawn to him—I would have found him—perhaps
because from the very first he seemed to me, that stocky man from
Jerusalem, the complete antithesis to everything around him . . .
most vital with a great shock of hair . . . a rather handsome oriental gynecologist . . .

—Antithesis.

—To all of us. To you, for instance—to the other delegates—to
all those German Jewish physicians . . .

—I do not know.

—A gynecologist. Actually, more of an obstetrician. Do you remember, dear Papa, how I too could not decide whether to specialize in gynecology or pediatrics? You were in favor of women; Linka
thought I would do better with children.

—Of course . . . I can still change my mind . . . it's not impossible. But this man was a gynecologist through and through—an
obstetrician with a maternity clinic in Jerusalem—and something of
a public figure there as well.

—About fifty. But though he could not have been much younger
than you, forgive me for saying that he was still unspoiled—even
childlike—yet cunning at the same time—although not in an ordinary sense . . .

—A real clinic. Be patient and I will tell you about it . . .

—Why should it be just for Jewesses? For Arabs too and Christian pilgrims—for everyone. But be patient . . .

—A good question! At first we spoke in broken German. Before
long, however, we realized that this would get us nowhere; at which
point he suggested English, which, I already had noticed, he spoke
as flamboyantly as a peacock, rounding his syllables like hard-boiled
eggs in his mouth. He swore that it was the language of the future—

which did not deter me from throwing up my hands and switching
to Yiddish, a language I saw he had some knowledge of, although it
came out a mangled Hebrew when he spoke it—so that I suddenly
thought: well, then, why not Hebrew itself—it is certainly good
enough for two Jews groping down a dark hallway! And that was
how we started talking in Hebrew, which slowly started coming
back to me in the darkness, so that I thought how proud you would
have felt after all your efforts to drum a bit of it into me . . .

—Real Hebrew, Father, as queer and rusty as it was, with the
verbs completely unconjugated, just as you would find them in the
dictionary. I must have confused my masculines and feminines too
—and yet I must say that it was not unpleasurable to be using the
language of our forefathers in that hallway, and even to joke in it a
bit—because at first we kept losing our way and ended up descending some narrow little stairs to a wine cellar, each step of which did
wonders for my command of the holy tongue—which he himself
spoke in a guttural version of the language that sounded as if his
throat were on fire. Eventually we realized that we had taken a
wrong turn and climbed back up with our candles to the door we
first had exited from . . . only to discover to our dismay that it was
locked. There was silence on the other side of it—perhaps Herzl
had already been put to bed or whisked away by his friends for
another session of Zionism. In any case, I was beginning to panic,
because I kept picturing Linka out in the night, in that low-cut
dress, looking for me high and low. Just then, though, we heard
heavy footsteps, which belonged to a sturdy Swiss servant girl, who
was on her way up to her room after a hard day's work. She directed
us through the labyrinth to a back street behind the Casino—and a
most narrow and deserted street it was; you could not possibly have
guessed from it what a mob of noisy Jews had just been there . . .

—I already told you, Father. About your age—but unjaded and
full of energy—a total antithesis . . .

—In what sense? In every sense!

—For example? For example . . . do you think that you, Father
—being the person that you are—a respected member of the community—the owner of an estate—the father of a not-so-young but
quite capable doctor and a decidedly attractive young daughter—

could one day fall madly—passionately—head over heels in love . . .

—Yes, tormentedly in love . . .

—You.

—With a young woman—someone like—well, like . . .

—Ah!

—A devastating love that would make you leave everything—the estate—all of us—to follow your beloved to the—

—No.

—Well, then . . .

—What?

—Ah . . .

—*You?*

—You are jok—

—Then why don't you, dearest Papa? Yes, why don't you fall in love a bit, ha ha . . .

—That is so. What really do I know about you?

—I can only tell you what I think.

—That may be . . .

—What does anyone know about anyone?

—Hardly a thing.

—Two children—little ones—at my age he was even more of a confirmed bachelor than I am . . .

—Of course he had a wife.

—I will get to her.

—I will get to her . . . don't be so impatient . . .

—Haven't I told you? Mani.

—Moshe.

—It is a common enough name in the Orient.

—Oh, he was Manic indeed . . . just wait until you hear it all . . .

—Yes, the whole story—and nothing but the whole story—but please let me tell it in my own good time—it is a balm for my weary soul. Please let . . . I feel suddenly gripped by such sorrow over his death!

—I am not shouting . . . forgive me. Anyhow, there we were in that empty, desolate street, circling round to the front of the Casino. By now he was telling me all about Jerusalem and his clinic, which he had come to Europe to raise funds for because he wished to expand and modernize it. Mind you, I was listening with half an ear, because Linka, I was alarmed to see, was not at all where I had left her. The nearby streets were silent except for a dimly lit tavern here and there in which—when I peered into them—I saw nothing but red-faced, drunken Swiss speaking sadly to themselves. I could have killed myself for leaving her! Where could all our Jews have disappeared to? And meanwhile this Mani kept tagging after me, so excited to have found out that I was a pediatrician that he could not stop talking for a second—about his Swedish nurse who was an expert in painless births and about some new idea of his for building up the blood of postnatal jaundice cases—three of his own infants, so he told me, had died of jaundice themselves—while I simply kept nodding at everything he said, listening as though in a dream. Talk of fright! I could not help thinking of all kinds of things that a person has no business imagining . . .

—That she had been carried off . . . that she had been misused . . .

—I don't know. Nor does it matter. I was very frightened. Linka and I had never been so far away from home, and by now I saw that there was no hope of finding her in those empty streets—and so I asked Mani to excuse me, because I was in a hurry to get to my boardinghouse, and I told him about my vanished sister, Well, at once he stopped his chatter and offered to drive me to my lodgings in his hansom—first the man had a candle in his pocket, now he had a hansom up his sleeve! He led me to a little back street—and there, Father, was parked a real carriage with a fancy black top and a coachman in red livery, a big-bearded fellow slumped sleeping on his seat. It was, it turned out, the gift of some Jewish banker in Zurich, who had refused to give Mani a donation for his clinic but had agreed to put a vehicle at his disposal to help him put the touch on other Jews. I can still see it, Father, standing in the dead of night on a street corner not far from the Casino with a black, thoroughbred, high-legged horse that looked straight out of the Alps—it had the glitter of the moon in its big eyes! And it was starting there— from the moment I climbed into that carriage—that a straight line— I see it as though in a vision—ran straight to his death . . . to that

hideous tragedy . . . although the truth, I tell you, is that we were
only a pretext . . .

—Because it is not conceivable that the seed of it was not already
there, if only as a dry kernel that lies in the earth without knowing
that it is a seed . . .

—No, Papa, no. I said I would tell everything in order.

—If I am being obstinate, it is only to keep you from leaving me
here by this stove in the middle of the night once you have heard the
end of my story. Because only the suspense can overcome your
tiredness—can bring you to our boardinghouse in that wonderful
hansom through the pleasantly cool Basel night—our horse clip-
clopping briskly over cobblestones—up and down streets whose
inhabitants were already enjoying a well-earned sleep. I still had no
idea where all our Jews had gone off to, especially the younger ones;
they could not have all gone to bed already. But soon we reached
the boardinghouse, which was entirely dark—*her* window too,
which made my heart sink, because that meant she had not come
back. I was so afraid of the carriage driving off and leaving me a
nervous wreck in the sleeping boardinghouse that I implored my
Dr. Mani—who had by now finished telling me that he was born in
Jerusalem to a mother who was born there too—to stay and keep me
company. Not that he needed much imploring. He was only too
happy to oblige. Perhaps he craved human contact after the indig-
nity inflicted on him by Herzl. I burst into the lobby; shook the old
grandfather of a concierge who was sleeping on a cot in the dining
room beneath some gleaming copper pans on the wall—like red
little suns they were, glinting in the night light; snatched the keys
from his hand; and flew off to her room. It was exactly as she had
left it—exactly as she leaves her room at home—her dresses everywhere—her underwear all over the floor. I felt knifed by anxiety. All
evening I had gone about with the knowledge that it was her first
day—not the best time for her to be gallivanting around . . .

—No. Of her menses.

—I knew. I always know. It does not matter. I—

—I have always known since she was a girl. Since her first
time . . .

—Don't ask me how. I know it—I feel it—I—I don't know how
but I do . . .

—No. Never mind that, though. This is not her story but rather—

—No, she is not. *He* is—that wandering obstetric fund-raiser—
that Dr. Mani—who sat there with me in the dining room, facing a
little oil lamp that old gramps had lit for us, already preparing for
his doom—cozying up to his pretext—because that—although why
us? *why us?*—is all we ever were for him. The more anxious for
Linka I became, the more he sympathized. He was falling in love
with her before he had even seen her—he did not have to see her.
And I was beginning to detect a certain oriental softness in him—a
rather pariah-like patience—coupled with an ancient and obscure
grievance—together with a knack for latching onto you and quickly
putting himself in your shoes. He was still carrying on about his
clinic and his attempt to raise funds for it. I could see that he wished
to take my measure—perhaps as a financial or medical partner—
because the minute I told him about our estate, he grew quite ecstatic over his good fortune at having run into not only a Zionist
pediatrician, but a rich Zionist pediatrician in the bargain . . .

—As we were driving in the hansom. I believe I expressed my
pleasure at the horse's light gait and compared it to our own heavy
drays that Mrazhik can never get to shake a leg . . .

—From there it was but a step to the flour mills and the forest.
He listened openmouthed, as if trying to gulp it all down.

—No, I told him some medical tales too. About deliveries in the
villages. How the Jewesses scream and the Poles sob . . .

—But they do. Every last one of them.

—You never asked.

—They positively bawl, every one of them.

—The Jewesses? As loud as they can. It is to make sure the baby
hears them and remembers to be nice to its mother after all it has
put her through. But the Poles sob. The devil only knows why—
perhaps, ha ha, it's for shame at having brought another Polack into
the world . . .

—Idle chitchat, yes. But what was I to do? I was swamped by
anxiety, and Mani was the straw I clutched at to take my mind off it.
And he did seem a cordial and charming fellow, busily fusing himself to his pretext while the mountains turned purple outside . . .

—Yes, I am back to pretexts. You will have to put up with it, dearest Papa. That is the word and I had better stick to it if I ever mean to get any sleep . . .

—No, not yet. Because just then I heard her laughter in the quiet street, a laughter that had a new note in it. It sounded like some ticklish little carnivore's. A minute later she walked in with a new escort—no longer the children of pogroms and Pobedonostsev but three middle-aged *pans,* two from Lvov and one from Warsaw—a half anti-Semitic, pro-Zionist Pole who had been sent by the latest right-wing newspaper to find out if there was any truth to the rumors that the Jews were indeed thinking of packing their bags . . .

—*Narojd Ojcizna.*

—That is a tune we are going to hear more and more of. An insolent clown of a fellow he was, slightly tipsy. He bowed extravagantly to me and took the slyest liberties with all of us, and especially with Linka, draping his white cape over her bare shoulders—and not for modesty's sake, I assure you, but to hide the stains she had gotten on her dress in some tavern. She was quite flushed—her dress was creased—her hair was wild. She seemed flustered too by all that gross male gallantry—but believe me, Father, she was enjoying it. At once she began to throw on the table packs of cigarettes, resolutions, pamphlets, reports, manifestos—the whole cornucopia of documents we delegates had been crammed with—and then flung herself at me like a whirling dervish. How could I have gone and left her like that? Why, she had had to put these charming gentlemen to the inconvenience of searching all over for me! I clenched my fists, utterly humiliated. I almost hit her, Father. From the moment I heard that laughter of hers ring out in the night, I wanted to thrash her—*I,* for whom such a thought . . .

—You know I have never lifted a hand against anyone. But now I scarcely could control myself—I wanted to thrash her, plain and simple—I, who had never touched her in anger, not even when she was a little brat—not even when you went off to Vilna for Grandmother's funeral and left me with her for two weeks. In no time we were quarreling in front of everyone, right in the middle of that sleeping boardinghouse—even old gramps, who must have smelled the liquor on the breath of that Zionist goy, came tiptoeing over for a look . . .

—Everything. Don't ask. Everything! And most of all, that outlandish white shawl on her shoulders, draped over that most scandalous dress, which I destroyed the next day. All at once she had become the grand lady. You should have seen her holding her hand out for those Poles to kiss—that childish little hand stained with ink, which her admirer from Warsaw put his lips to with unconcealed desire—she was laughing, she was all in a whirl—a once neatly closed little pocket knife that had suddenly sprung open with all its blades . . .

—No, no, don't say anything. I was not looking to make a scene. And in any case, at that very moment Mani appeared from his dark corner, stepping out from beneath the burnished copper pans, and I presented him, embarrassed as he was—my pudgy jack-in-the-box—my antithesis—to everyone. "Straight from Jerusalem, gentlemen," I said furiously, "from Jerusalem itself!" You could actually feel that mysterious city blow through the room like a fresh breeze. The Polish *pans* grinned—*Jerusalem?*—you can't be serious!—while Linka turned to my antithesis with a warm glance. She held out her hand to him and he kissed it (it was then I first noticed that he had a special, an endearing way with women) most nobly and shyly. "He speaks English," I told her. "You can speak in English to him." And so she did, without the slightest hesitation—a soft, musical English it was too, like a sweet oatmeal porridge—to which—amazed but appreciative—he replied in that peacock talk of his, the language of the future, as he called it. The Polish gentlemen stood by grinning like idiots, and old gramps wanted to know what it was about us Jews that made us speak four different languages in as many minutes. And it was then, dearest Papa—or at least so I remember it—that I was so seized by the desire to travel to Palestine with that man that I made up my mind to give our Linka a taste of the real thing—to chuck her into the dark bosom of Zionism itself. Jerusalem? Then let it be Jerusalem!

—Let it be Jerusalem!

—Yes, and the sooner the better. I could not wait to be off, if only to get all those *pans* and their ilk off her trail. And just then I thought of you, Papa, and I felt my gorge rise . . .

—Because I knew you would never understand and would say no.

—In plain language, that you would not allow us to go.

—Well, it did have to do with you . . . or so I thought . . .

—But if we had asked permission, you would not have given it . . .

—No objection? But just look at yourself now . . .

—It's a fact. You are furious. You are . . .

—What?

—You were not angry?

—I don't follow you.

—My imagination?

—What?

—No. Where—

—You were glad? But how come? For what reason?

—Proud? How odd . . . proud! You truly felt that?

—Truly? And to think that when we cabled you from the post office in Venice before boarding ship, I was shaking like a criminal . . .

—Then Linka was right. I misjudged you . . . Linka knew better than I did . . .

—"Papa will only go through the motions . . . in his heart he'll be on our side . . ." But how—

—Still . . .

—That was all.

—I was wrong—I never thought—I am quite bowled over. Dear, dearest Papa, forgive me! And here I had already decanted your anger into me—I have gone about all this time with your accusing glance boring into me from behind—I have asked myself, "How could you have done this to Papa and Mama and gone chasing camels and donkeys in the desert when you should have been finding yourself a wife in Frau Lippmann's boardinghouse . . . ?"

—The congress? It was the Third Zionist Congress, Father. There will undoubtedly be a fourth one too . . .

—I mean . . . but was it not fully written up in *Der Yid?* The fact is, Father, that my mind was not entirely on the congress.

—A great deal of talk. Of speech-making. Of debate. Even our Dr. Mani delivered a little oration to the "Medical Committee" in which he asked for help and invited all the doctors to be his guests in Jerusalem. Why don't you ask Linka? She can tell you what made the fur fly and what was decided when it settled, because she sat through it all faithfully and did not miss a single session. You should have seen her in her embroidered peasant's dress—I had already gotten rid of that outrageous black décolleté—taking everything terribly seriously and even keeping notes—a most loyal and responsible delegate from an imaginary constituency. But what constituency was not imaginary? Was Moscow polled on its delegates or Warsaw asked about its? The fact is that I was rarely at the sessions because I was already secretly planning our journey to Palestine. I acted quite clandestinely, Papa. I did not breathe a word to Linka or to Dr. Mani, who had let slip the name of his ship, which was sailing from Venice to Jaffa on the first of September. I believe he had a sixth sense of it, though. He took to following us around, sitting with Linka whenever he could and speaking to her in the language of the future. But my thoughts just then were not of them. They were only of you . . .

—Of you. Of your anger—your shock—no, Father, you cannot deprive me so easily of the conviction that you were furious . . .

—Delighted? But how can that be? No, I don't want to hear another word, you stubborn man, you, ha ha . . . Why, this most whimsical journey of ours would never have tasted so delicious if it had not been partly aimed against you . . .

—Against all your bourgeois Zionists. You don't know how disappointed I am, Papa dear, to hear you say that you were not in the least annoyed.

—True—it is an odd thing to be disappointed about—but there you are. And do you think it was so easy to get from Basel to Palestine? I had no notion where to begin. I went to the *Bahnhof* to ask for train schedules and information, but I soon realized that there was little of either and that the Swiss would only drive me to despair, first by not understanding my German and then by not understanding my question, since Palestine for them was not a place on the map but a location in the Bible. Ultimately, however, they saw who they were dealing with and sent me to a Jewish clerk, a soft-spoken young lady not much older than Linka, who had run away from a fanatical family of Hasidim in Vilna to attend the first congress two years ago and decided not to go back. And so she had stayed on in Basel, living from hand to mouth between congresses, during which she found temporary work at the *Bahnhof*—where the authorities had seen fit to open a "Jewish bureau" for the delegates, who—once the proceedings were over—wished to travel to various boardinghouses, hotels, and sanatoria in the green heights of Europe and recover there from their national responsibility while digesting it thoroughly . . .

—No, that's true. There were good people there too, conscientious and with a sense of the occasion. But—why deny it, Father—there were plenty of freeloaders also—people like myself, for example—who only came to divert themselves at the expense of Jewish destiny, which they regarded as they might a game of whist . . .

—Why, our whole trip had been intended as nothing more than a diversion—until it suddenly changed course . . .

—Hold on a minute, will you! Don't you want to hear about the Jewish clerk from Vilna?

—As a matter of fact, she was not especially pretty, Father. She was pale and rather sickly looking—a consumptive, I had already decided—but a sharp-witted and free-mannered young thing, with a most Talmudical mind. And she was an expert in the map of Europe, which she knew by heart and could slice in any manner in her head. She knew every train—the name of each station—the departure and arrival schedules—the points of connection. She could describe the compartments for you in every class—tell you where each number seat was—advise you which coaches were best—and needless to say, quote the price of everything. In a word, an incomparable young lady! She took a liking to me too, and when she heard that I wished to travel to Palestine she all but made the journey her own, as if she intended to go with me. Despite her doubts about Mani's Greek ship that was sailing from Venice, which she thought too light a craft, she dashed off a telegram to the agent reserving us two of his best cabins and began to plan our route. She was—how shall I put it?—most enthusiastic, and at once my flagging spirits revived. And so I roamed back and forth between the congress and the *Bahnhof,* hatching my secret plan, which still seemed to me little more than a fantasy. On the afternoon of the third and last day of the congress I went to see my little consumptive and was handed a handsome folder with our train tickets, our travel papers, and our entire itinerary written out in Yiddish—and a most ingenious itinerary it was too, with all the travel at night and the days kept free for touring. Nothing had been left to chance: where we would stop, and what we would eat, and the sites we would see, and what it would cost—and of course, how we would return from Palestine . . . she had planned every step of the way. All that was missing was the height and direction of the waves . . . which, alas, Father, turned out to be the most important thing of all, ha ha . . .

—Wait, I will get to that. That evening, in her little cubby in the crowded *Bahnhof,* I paid her for the trip, took her small hand in my own, and—her eyes were suddenly bright with tears, that's how hard it was for her to say good-bye—kissed it devoutly . . .

—Four thousand Swiss francs.

—The exchange rate, I believe, is—

—More or less . . .

—More or less . . .

—Perhaps a bit more . . . is that really so dear? The boarding-house in Lugano would have cost something too.

—Of course. Nothing but first class, as befits the son and daughter of gentry . . .

—I had not said a word so far to Linka, who was faithfully attending the congress and not missing a single speech in that whole deluge of speeches. Sometimes Dr. Mani sat on her right and sometimes I sat on her left, quietly smiling to myself. I knew she suspected something, but—no matter how piercing and questioning her glance grew—she had no way of guessing what that was. We still had not made up after that night of the *pans*—when we talked, it was in short, brusque sentences—and that evening in the boarding-house—it was a particularly warm one—she showed me without a word her dress for the closing ball. I must say, it was perfectly presentable . . .

—Yes, there was a closing ball, Father. Was there no such thing at your congress?

—Well, this time they must have decided on a modest one to cheer us all up after the German Kaiser's cold shoulder. That is, "our elected officers" closeted themselves in a small hall and elected themselves to various positions, while the hoi polloi put on its frock coats, evening dresses, and jewels, and danced up a storm. The Viennese waltzes were already gaily playing when we arrived, and outside the Casino—in the line of carriages parked on the main street—I was astonished to see Dr. Mani's black-topped hansom packed with bundles and valises and already prepared to set out. The big coachman stood by in a blazer with his whip in one hand, while his horse, which was supping on a sack of barley hung around its neck, looked up from its meal with a heavenward roll of its bloodshot eyes. What—I asked the coachman—did all this mean? It meant, he explained succinctly, that they had decided to leave for Arth-Goldau ahead of time on account of the heat, since the horse did better in the cool of night. By now I was afraid that Mani might vanish before knowing we were about to be his guests, and so I hurried into the dance hall and found him in a black frock coat, waltzing a ponderous, old, diamond-bedecked English Jewess. He was talking to her quite somberly—no doubt about his clinic, for which he must have been hoping to pluck from her a last-minute contribution. Linka, despite her modest dress, was already besieged by young men, and so I went off to a corner and smoked cigarettes in a chain, my travel plans safely inside my head. Despite the great heat, I was actually trembling from my secret.

—Dance? I am not, you know, much of a dancer—and the women, apart from Linka, did not seem especially light on their feet —but the truth is, Father—the truth is—that if my little consumptive from the *Bahnhof* had been there, I might not have been able to resist asking her for one waltz.

—So it would seem. I grew rather fond of her, but she does not have long . . . believe me . . . a dry cough like hers . . .

—But again, what do you want from me? You take me for the murderer when all I am is the witness . . .

—Yes, perhaps that explains my fondness for her . . . how astute of you, ha ha . . . ha ha ha ha ha . . .

—No, don't say that, Father, not now. You will live, don't you worry—you will live for a long, long time. I don't think you have realized yet that this story is not about me. It is about him, Mani, who finally gave up on his Anglo-Jewess—she had not made herself one diamond lighter for his benefit—and parted from her with a deep bow before sitting glumly down beside me with his eyes on our merrily waltzing Linka. And I ask myself: if he was already determined to take his own life—if the idea was even then in him like a living seed—why did he not do it right then and there, in that blue-toned dance hall, in front of all the delegates? It would have made

an immeasurably greater impression than waiting for the dusk of day
in that wretched train station in Beirut . . .

—The devil knows, Father . . .

—The devils . . . no, no . . .

—Because I saw how he was clinging to me, unable to say good-
bye. And I, Father, suddenly began to shake, stirred by the journey
that was pressing on my heart like a hot coal. I was beginning to get
cold feet—it was not, after all, too late to change my mind—to
cancel everything—to let the itinerary in my pocket take the place of
the trip itself . . .

—I was frightened . . . I don't know of what . . . frightened
of Palestine . . .

—No. Your anger only spurred me on . . .

—Of Palestine itself. I kept picturing it, like a little yellow viper at
the tip of the large map that hung in my clerk's cubby with P-a-l-e-s-
t-i-n-e spelled out on it in black . . .

—Perhaps the shape of the letters . . . But anyway, Papa dear,
that was what I sat there thinking. And next to me was my brown-
skinned gynecologist from Jerusalem, feeling low over having to part
and waiting to say good-bye to Linka, to whom he had become quite
attached. All at once I felt sorry for him—odd as it sounds, he
seemed to merge in my mind with the travel clerk from Vilna, who
had labored over my trip—so sorry that I broke my silence and
asked him in a low voice—since I might soon wish to take him up
on it—if his invitation to Jerusalem still stood. He crimsoned with
surprise, which made me wonder whether all his generous offers of
hospitality had not been extended on the basis of the fullest confidence that there was no one who could possibly accept them. Presently, however, he stammered with great feeling: "You wish to come
to Jerusalem?" "Yes," I answered gently, fingering the packet of
travel documents in my breast pocket, which yielded with a soft,
pleasant crackle. "Yes, I do," I repeated, speaking in the first person, because I had no idea what Linka would say. "I am sailing from
Venice on the first"—I took a piece of paper from my pocket and
read what was written on it—"on the *Kereiti Zurakis.*" When he
heard me utter the name of his ship, he sat up and grabbed my
wrist, as if seeking to ascertain from my pulse whether or not I was
pulling his leg. For a moment or two he was speechless—and when

he could speak again, he said: "In Jerusalem you are my guest." "I will be most honored," I said—we were still talking in terms of "I" and "you," as if I did not have a sister with me. He rose and circled me in his excitement. "And will mademoiselle be coming too?" he asked. It was strange to hear Linka called that—strange too to hear him ask with such emotion—because—although I knew that he had fallen in love with her before seeing her—I had no idea that he was still in love with her after seeing her, since she was only a—

—Bravo, Papa! Yes, a pretext. You need not smile. That is all we were for the passion that had been lurking in him for so long that perhaps he had even snatched it from his mother's womb . . . Yes, dear Papa, that is an indispensable part of my conception . . .

—Wait, don't say anything . . . just hold on, for God's sake . . .

—Linka has not been talking to me since Beirut. The most I could get out of her were yes-or-no answers when it came to planning our travels . . .

—I never forced her to do anything. On the contrary, I said to Mani: "Mademoiselle? Let us ask her to speak for herself." I rose, waited for the music and the waltz to stop, spirited her away from the outstretched arms of her would-be partners—do not think, Father, that there was any lack of them—and brought her all flushed in the face to Dr. Mani, who kissed her hand—he was aware that by now she expected no less—while she radiantly flashed him her wonderful, prodigal smile. "Linka," I said to her, "Linka—Dr. Mani is inviting us to Jerusalem and I am inclined to accept—what would you say to our setting out tomorrow morning for his Palestine?" All she had to answer was, "My dear brother, I don't know what has gotten into you, but you are quite mad," and I would have gone off at once to a corner, torn up every last travel document without a thought for what it had cost, and gone straight to Lake Lugano as you wished me to—straight to Frau Lippmann's boardinghouse, Father—to ogle the Jewish lovelies of Europe gathered there for matrimonial purposes and to ask myself—not for the first time, I assure you—exactly what about them turns my stomach. But Linka's smile just grew brighter and broader, as though glowing out of the darkness where her newly hatched soul was beating its wings—as long as I live, Father, I will never forget how she showered me with kisses, hugging me with a childlike trust, as if I had providentially granted her very wish—as if during the two days of my secret comings and goings from the *gare* her intuition had already told her everything— had made her guess our destination without comprehending that there had to be some means of getting there—that there was no magic wand to transport us straight from that dance hall to the center of Jerusalem. I tell you, I felt butterflies . . .

—My stomach?

—Yes—ha ha—that is where I feel things . . . I was in fact slightly nauseous—but it was only my lack of resolve—you need not worry about me—a most yidlike lack of resolve, which I shall over- come one day in order to find myself a yiddess and jump right into bed with her . . .

—No.

—No . . .

—Perhaps we should stop here, Father. What is the point of going on? Linka can tell you the rest of the story, and I will spread a blanket here by the stove and lie down. I must have caught some- thing from one of those damned pilgrims. Why, I'm shivering! The fire could not be any colder if it were just a painting of one. Is Stefa sleeping also? Here, let me stir up the coals a bit—by now God must be asleep too . . .

—Such virtue as I have displayed can be allowed at least one little sin . . .

—If you insist. By now it was midnight. Our elected leaders, led by Herzl and Nordau, filed out of the small hall to a burst of cheers and applause. There were some short, rosy speeches and some toasts, and all at once everyone was talking about the next century and about the next congress. *"Fin de siècle!"* somebody called out— a shiver ran through us all—*"fin de siècle!"* the cry was taken up— you could feel the hatred for this old century of ours, which every- one will be glad to say good-bye to, and the warmth for the new one on its way—the twentieth. The three of us stood excitedly off to one side, no longer a part of it all. Mani could not bear to leave us. Indeed, he might have lingered there forever had not the coachman entered the hall in his traveling blazer, swept in upon his black beard. He sullenly elbowed his way, whip in hand, through the crowd of cheering Jews—he had quite run out of patience and was

in a thoroughly vile mood—it made a splendid, a perfect antithesis
to all that Jewish dignity to see the three of us marched out of there
—all but whipped out—by Mani's coachman, who practically flung
him into the hansom. It was thus, rather dejectedly, that he bade us
farewell, unbelievingly asking over and over: "But will you truly
come?" Linka promised him we would. She hugged him as a child
hugs a father—all in English, of course, which by now was their own
private language—and suddenly gave him a kiss. You would think
that I, who found that sudden kiss most charming, would have
realized that it was only the first—but I did no such thing. I was too
busy gaping at all the bundles and valises tied to the black-topped
hansom—at that earnest black horse—at the passenger sitting inside
—who did not look—no, not then in the middle of the night—like a
man bound for a country that was our common goal, but rather, like
one being sent back to some starting line. That night—

—No. That night—

—Yes. That night Linka wrote you her first letter, which I confiscated in the morning, because I was so concerned for you and
Mama that I was still thinking of calling the whole thing off. Now,
however, it was she who would not hear of it; it was just like her to
feel obliged to honor her promise to our Eastward-ho-ing doctor;
and I grew so fearful that she might decide to make the voyage by
herself that I had no choice but to give in. The next morning we
went to buy traveling clothes more suitable for our trip than the lace
dresses on Linka's shopping list. We bought ourselves blazers like
the coachman's, and cork helmets for protection against the sun,
and fine silk scarves for protection against the dust—here, this rag
around my neck is what is left of one! At teatime we boarded a train
for Arth-Goldau, and the next morning, by the lakeside there, Linka
wrote you a second letter, which I expropriated too: I still had my
doubts, you see, about the entire business. But evening found us on
a train again, heading southeast, for Lugano, where we arrived on
Saturday morning. Since we had a long stopover there, we rented a
carriage to tour the town and even dropped by Frau Lippmann's
boardinghouse, entering incognito in our blazers and cork helmets
for a gander at the dressed-to-kill yeshiva students who had just
finished the morning prayer and were now assembled in the lobby
to bless the Sabbath wine while keeping an eye out for possible

wives. In the end, we introduced ourselves to Frau Lippmann. She was quite furious about the cancellation—she would not, she said, refund so much as a franc from the advance you had paid—she even refused to surrender a letter from you until Linka wheedled it out of her with gracious smiles. And so we sat down to read your lovely correspondence, passing it back and forth to make out what it said while thanking our lucky stars for sparing us the torments of such an establishment—after which we continued our tour of the town, which is quite beautiful. That evening we boarded a sleeping coach for Milan, from which I wrote you my first letter, although in my concern for you I pocketed that too. On Sunday morning we arrived in Milan. We found an overcast city drenched by a summer down-pour with lots of Italians buzzing all around us—with church bells ringing—with all the restaurants shut down. And so we joined a crowd of worshipers for mass in the *duomo,* taking refuge there from the rain and kneeling when everyone else did, although you may rest assured that we did not touch the Sacrament. And that was all we saw of that gray, busy city, because we were in a hurry to catch the train for Venice—in the compartment of which we struck up a conversation with a most helpful German. (This was not the first time I noticed that Germans on trains befriended us with great ease. There was something about us they took to—we must have seemed to them a charming couple—and finding out that we were brother and sister only made them grow fonder of us.) This particu-lar German was an educated man, a novelist, who traveled to Venice every year and was well acquainted with the city and its treasures; he gave us much useful information, such as the fact that there are epidemics in Venice at the end of every summer that the authorities try to hush up. We must not, he made us promise, drink any un-boiled water or eat any fruit—indeed, he so thoroughly alarmed us that I all but pulled the emergency brake and returned to Frau Lippmann's at once in the hope that she might take us in in her mercy.

—Yes. I had an attack of panic and wanted to turn around and head back—to pretend that it was all just a fantasy—a passing dream—that we had indeed never left Lugano. But when—ex-hausted and practically sleepwalking—we stepped out of the train station onto the Grand Canal and saw the marble palaces shimmer-

ing above the slimy water—saw that city—that jewel of culture—
tottering on the banks of its fetid, scummy waterways—we grasped
in a trice how magnificently tenacious the human spirit is—we felt
such a surge of love for humanity—for its suffering and—yes!—its
epidemics—that we walked—wide awake now—into that dream of
our own free will, because Venice is in fact a waking dream . . .

—Yes . . . yes . . .

—Yes . . . we remembered . . . we both remembered it simul-
taneously . . .

—Yes . . . yes . . . so you were . . .

—It was Grandfather who paid for that trip? What ever made
him so bold and original . . . ?

—Yes . . . we were following in your footsteps without having
planned it that way . . . how cunning the human soul is!

—Thirty years ago! Wait . . . that was in 1869! We kept imagining how the two of you must have looked then—you, Father, still
with your sidelocks—a Jew in black in a black gondola, ha ha . . .

—A young woman, of course . . . hardly more than a girl . . .
the same age as Linka . . .

—Thirty years, I kept telling myself. Perhaps I was even conceived there, eh, Father? The canals have rather a placental smell
. . . was it there?

—But we wrote you every day!

—In back of San Marco, in the Hotel Roma . . .

—Two rooms, of course—each of them palatial . . .

—A thousand lirettas per diem.

—You can figure it out according to the exchange rate.

—Quite sumptuously . . . and no one would believe that Linka
was Jewish . . . *ma no,* they simply all said . . .

—Terribly hot.

—There was not a sign of it—a pure figment of the literary imagination . . . One morning we crossed paths on one of the canals
and called out jokingly, "Where is your plague, signore?"

—We were careful, naturally. We drank wine instead of water
and asked for tea when we were thirsty and let it cool while looking
out at the sea that sent its long, lavishly bejeweled fingers into the
city—fingers, mind you, that could easily have seized and swallowed
us had the tide but risen a little . . . On our last evening we went

to the harbor to see if Mani's ship really existed. And indeed, it looked like a mirage, a small, flimsy thing equipped with an auxiliary sail. I shuddered at the sight of its frailty—but Linka just laughed as though drunk and insisted on going to a restaurant by the water to eat seafood.

—Shellfish. Clams—snails—all sorts of underwater grasshoppers that are fried in butter . . .

—I don't know what got into us . . . perhaps our excitement . . . or the sheer abandon of sucking away at all those pinkish mollusks . . .

—Perhaps we feared ending up at the bottom of the sea without ever having tasted any of those creeping-crawling-Christian delicacies . . .

—Most heathenishly . . . Linka could not eat enough of it . . .

—Boiled—fried—grilled . . . were you not there?

—No matter. We ate, and the next morning we rose early and went to the harbor to make sure of our cabins. We hung our clothing in their little closets and went ashore again—and only then, when I knew that you could no longer call us back, did I send my first telegram and let Linka post the letters to you. Then we reboarded the ship and waited on deck for Dr. Mani—who, however, did not appear. There was a steady flow of Arabs, Egyptians, Greeks, Turks, even an English couple, even some Russian monks— but our doctor had vanished into thin air, as if he indeed had been a fantasy of ours. A chill ran down my spine. What was I to do? Where, madman that I was, was I taking her? I was all for abandoning ship while there was time, but Linka refused to lose hope— no, not even when the ship began to rumble and a large sail was run up on the yard. And just then what did we see but the same carriage that had set out from Basel in the dead of night, crawling up the pier beneath its cargo—its coachman hatless, jacketless, in his shirt-sleeves—his beard unkempt—most agitated and besotted—cracking his whip at the pavement. Beside him was our portly Dr. Mani in his white suit; bareheaded too, with his hat tied to a lanyard on his shoulder; but fresh-looking and in fine fettle as he ordered the longshoremen to unload. We shouted to him from the deck—he saw us at once and waved his hat buoyantly—the porters and deckhands fell upon the carriage and—for time was short—quickly whisked all its baggage to the hold. Meanwhile, the coachman was tussling fiercely with Mani, who was wagging a little black notebook at him. We had no idea what the fellow was so upset about—he kept clinging to the bridle of the horse, which was pawing uneasily—until suddenly the Greek deckhands returned, hustled him away, freed the horse from its harness, pulled a large gray sack over its head, and —cheered by the onlookers—tugged it with much hilarity aboard the ship. Mani followed close behind them; the rope gangplank was raised; and the ship, which was straining at the leash, began to move from its berth, leaving the Zurich banker's hansom all alone on the pier with its traces drooping on the pavement. The big coachman stood in the space vacated by the horse, a despairing and incredulous figure, until he and his carriage shrank to a single small dot.

—Yes, dearest Papa. He made off with the horse. He would have appropriated the hansom too, had it been possible to get it aboard ship; he would have shanghaied the coachman, could he have gotten away with it; he would have ripped out the cobblestones beneath the carriage wheels had he been able to, so great were his despair and anger at the rich Jews who had turned him down. He was an infinitely hungry man; and had I but taken the trouble to scrutinize that desperate, that artful hunger of his instead of mooning at him and Linka bantering in English and bringing each other up to date on their adventures, I would have had the wits to realize that it could not be sated by a horse—no, not even if it were the noblest thoroughbred.

—The horse? I will get to it in a minute . . . You are just like a child, Papa dear . . .

—In a minute . . . For the moment I was still gripped by fear and anxiety, although I must say, by pleasure too. I thought of my telegram that was speeding, letter by letter, through the air to you— humming unchallenged over the wires and down through the tile roof of the old post office—handed there on a gray slip of paper to Wicek—who would jump on his bicycle and pedal off with it to your office, for you to read it between consignments of flour . . . Such were my thoughts as we brushed through the mists of Venice, which—golden and wondrous—vanished in a violet fog. I sought to fix my mind on the rocking motion of the black waves beneath me, leaning on the railing and breathing in the new salt air. At first it was pleasant, like being an infant laid in a cradle. Little by little, however, I began to grasp that not only was the motion not going to cease, it was going to grow even greater. We started to pitch more strongly, and with it came the first wave of nausea. My body felt cold. The very soles of my feet were covered with a chill sweat. I began to vomit, throwing back to the sea all its denizens of the night before—followed by my breakfast in the hotel—and then the steak from the night train to Venice—and on and on, wave after wave until I had puked out my guts, which I would have heaved into the great ocean too if only they had been detachable—after which I buckled to the ground, collapsed on the wooden deck, and passed out . . .

—Yes, seasickness, of the malign nature of which I could have had no idea. To think that a man can live his whole life and never know that the sea is not just a compendium of rivers! Most of the voyage I spent drugged with sleeping powders that our friend from Jerusalem prepared for me, limply sprawled on my cot in my little cabin. Linka and Mani ministered to me with English tea, dry biscuits, and soft gruel, all conveniently easy to regurgitate. They did their best to cheer me up with funny stories about the black horse imprisoned below in the hold; it too was seasick and quite wild-tempered, kicking out to protest its destination—it was not, after all, a Zionist—and if fate had decreed that it be one, it did not wish to be of the pioneer variety—no, it would have vastly preferred to wait for Dr. Herzl to obtain his international charter from the Turks so that it could make the voyage first-class with the accompaniment of a German naval escort, ha ha . . .

—Ha ha ha . . .

—Well, we are landlubbers, solid citizens of Central Europe—is it not inhuman to toss us up and down on the waves?

—Unremittingly, for seven whole days. All the way to Crete, which is the island that ship is named for, because that is its port of call on its route to Europe and back. Indeed, legend has it that Europe was born there . . .

—Only one night. It is a night that the sailors spend with their wives in their shanties. I demanded to be brought ashore—where, on the sand amid some rocks, I curled up beneath a blanket and clung with all my might to terra firma, trying to put my shattered self back together while watching Mani and Linka lead the black horse in its headsack out of the hold, because the captain refused to put up with its tantrums any longer and demanded that it disembark.

—Yes, Linka too. What with my sickness and the horse they had grown quite close to each other—although now I know that it was not until that bright night—that night strewn with stars on that strange and desolate isle—that it started . . .

—Their romance—their love—their bond—their passion—their dependence—their pity . . . will that do? The minute I saw him insist on taking that horse aboard ship, I knew that there was nothing simple about him, that he was most exceedingly Mani-fold . . .

—They sold it that night. Some Jewish trader took them far inland to find a buyer in one of the villages.

—Where are there not Jews, Father? Tell me that. Tell me!

—He asked her to help negotiate the sale. He must have sensed that a canny merchant's daughter would know how to drive a hard bargain.

—Did I not already tell you? A wife and two children.

—Of course we did. A rather bleached-out woman, a bit older than him. A stay-at-home, vitiated by three infants who died soon after birth . . .

—That same night.

—I was stretched out on the sand, swaddled in my blanket, gazing up at the stars. I could feel the whole island rocking up and down in the water. When I saw them come back late at night, I understood that something had happened. They seemed suddenly timid with each other—careful—even wary—and there was something too about the way Linka flung herself on me, about her worry for me . . .

—They had sold the horse. I envied its being able to remain behind in the mountains.

—How extraordinary that you should want to know a pointless detail like that . . .

—Don't ask me. Ask Linka. She was a party to the sale.

—Three more days to Alexandria. And then to Jaffa, where we docked on the first day of Rosh Hashanah.

—I had nothing left to throw up. My seasickness had turned into sleeping sickness, I simply could not keep awake. It was of course from those powders that Mani used to calm the nerves of his parturients. The morning we reached Jaffa, I was brought out on deck to revive before the Turks decided that I must be ill with the plague and could not be admitted to the Holy Land . . .

—No. It does not exactly have a harbor. The ships cast anchor at a distance from shore, and the stevedores come aboard and throw you down into dinghies.

—Mohammedans, of course.

—Local residents.

—Are you back to that again? Why should they be nomads? Where do you want them to wander to?

—In a word, they are not nomadic.

—Most in houses. Only a few in tents.

—I did not count.

—Don't be in such a hurry to dismiss them . . .

—The Turks? They are adorably lazy and corrupt . . . We were not asked many questions. Mani's British passport worked wonders.

—The immensity of the light.

—Because there is nothing to deflect it. No forests. No woods . . .

—Here and there you see a tree.

—Soft white sand. Golden dunes. They are pleasant to look at, but wearisome to walk in. Your legs grow enervated.

—It is a sunny country. There will be enough sunshine for all of us there, that much I could see at once.

—We went straight from the port to the train.

—Yes, a real train. It runs from Jaffa to Jerusalem. It is smaller and slower than our own trains, a bit childlike. But since we arrived on a Jewish holiday, and the passenger trains in Palestine are religious also, we had to—

—Does that please you? I knew it would.

—They grumble and put up with it. It is the price paid for the privilege of living in the Holy Land.

—To a fault. But loathe to be stuck in the sands of Jaffa—Mani had promised his household that he would arrive in time for the holiday—we hurried off to a freight train, which was transporting — guess what, Papa!—what do you think?

—Guess.

—Guess again . . .

—Barrels of water!

—Ordinary drinking water. It had been a dry, thirsty summer in Jerusalem, and—since the Danube has yet to be diverted there—they needed a resupply of water . . .

—A single pipe that cuts across the mountains.

—It is not a desert—not yet—but the countryside is neglected—you see nothing but boulders and rocks . . .

—A few olive trees—bushes—all sorts of brambles. There is a tindery smell of straw and sometimes a sharp whiff of mint . . .

—There are no mountains, Father. There are grayish hills, which look like . . . like . . . I don't know what. Like hills . . .

—I was glad to be getting away from the sea, even though it was odd to be entering Palestine in such a fashion, in a sealed boxcar among big quiet barrels of water. And at the same time, I was delighted to be done with the diabolic motion of the waves.

—Linka had grown profoundly silent. She lay in a corner, in a light Egyptian smock she had bought in Port Said, red from the sun and frightened by the thought of soon meeting the family of her strange new love.

—How you keep coming back to the landscape! A person might think that nature meant more to you than people . . .

—I have told you that the car was sealed. There was but a small transom, through which I could not see very much. Near Jaffa, I believe, we passed an agricultural school—its name was . . .

—That's correct. After it came an Arab town whose name I do not recall . . .

—Perhaps.

—No, it was not large. Nothing is large there.

—Back to your tents again? But why should there be tents? There were shanties—mud huts—stone houses set like boulders in the landscape . . .

—Perhaps there were a few tents. We did not see much, because dusk falls quickly there. One minute the sun is scorching hot and the next it is gone. The train was still laboring uphill to Jerusalem as the last glow of twilight faded away in the car . . .

—At seven in the evening, after traveling for five hours and stopping for two more.

—Jerusalem? A small, poor, harsh city. And yet oddly enough, it does not seem remote. There is nothing provincial about it. Nor will there ever be . . .

—Spirituality? I suppose. But what might that consist of? Perhaps of the name "Jerusalem." That is all the place has to vouch for it. Its name is greater than anything in it—than any mosque—than any church—than all its ramparts . . .

—How greedy you are for details, Father—you simply cannot get enough of them! It is all I can do to stick to my story and keep from blurting out its bloody end, whereas you want a pilgrim's travelogue . . . It was nighttime when we arrived, and we saw neither ramparts, towers, spires, nor even men. It was a little country station, smaller even than Chozow's, more rudimentary even than Wylicka's. The only souls there were a few Arabs with wagons to load the water barrels on, and while Mani went looking for someone to take our luggage, Linka and I walked along the tracks to stretch our limbs—two travelers from faraway Galicia who had reached the end of the line, which was marked by a small barrier consisting of a wooden board. Beyond it was nothing, only a few brambles. We had arrived at the last stop. There were no switches, no sidings. It was a single, narrow, very finite line.

—Amen, Father.

—And all the way to Transjordan too. Why not? With northern and southern trunk lines, God willing . . .

—If the Jews make it their business to help Him a little . . . In any case, Linka, who had been immobilized throughout the ride, began imploring me all of a sudden to tell our Mani that we would not impose on him but would find lodgings elsewhere; she evidently was unprepared to face the fact that he had a home and a family. I refused. There were nothing but fields all around—Jerusalem seemed at that moment to be no more than a parable—the night was coming on fast—and if we had missed the first dinner of the holiday, there was still the second one, to which I had been invited in Basel. "Absolutely not," I said—and before Linka could think of an answer, the porters arrived and loaded our baggage on two flat wagons with swinging oil lamps. And so off we drove through the fields into the evening, giving the city a wide berth to avoid irritating any worshipers who might be wending their way home from synagogue.

We climbed a high hill on which stood a German orphanage named
for a man called Schneller; lurched across a field along a goat track;
and arrived at a large, isolated, two-story stone house.

—Of course, Father. All this was outside the walls of the old city.
There are several small but attractive neighborhoods there, among
them one of Jews from Bukhara that is not far from Mani's house.
There is even some greenery—upon my word, had I not known we
had left Switzerland, I would have thought we were back there
again . . .

—No, not only Jews, Father. The Arabs are venturing out of the
old city too. The place is simply not big enough for everyone . . .

—Yes, it stood all by itself, in a solitude serendipitous at so holy a
time, at the juncture between the two days of the holiday. It enabled
the porters to unload in a hurry in an inner, flagstone-paved yard far
from sacrilege-espying eyes—far from any eyes at all except those of
an old Mohammedan peasant, who was crouched by a cistern with a
cigarette cupped in his hand. Our Mani was beaming with excitement. "Come," he whispered to us without climbing the stairs to the
second story where his family was awaiting him, because he yearned
to see his clinic—and we stealthily followed him into a large room
full of white partitions that separated some beds, most of which
were empty, although from several of them pregnant women regarded us with curiosity. We nodded hello to them; noted with
surprise some large, white, well-scrubbed chamber pots all standing
in a neat row; and saw a hefty matron approach us from the room's
far end, a blond woman dressed in white. Upon seeing that it was
her doctor home from abroad, she let out a cry of joy and curtsied
low to us—she could not shake our hands, you see, because her own
were smeared with blood. Although I did not understand the
Judaeo-Spanish that Mani spoke to her, I could tell that he was
introducing me as a medical specialist who had come from afar to
see his experimental clinic and its equipment. Repeatedly I heard
him mention our estate as if it were a famous medical center—it was
a name he could never get right and that Linka had long despaired
of correcting his pronunciation of.

—Each time it was something else. If he did not say Jelleny-Czad,
he said Jelleny-Szak. In any event, before we knew it, the blond
matron—who came to Jerusalem several years ago on a pilgrimage

and proceeded to lose her faith there—was conducting us to the delivery room. At first I was astonished to see such a huge hall in a house that size—but soon enough I realized that I was looking at an illusion, for the walls were covered with mirrors cut and swiveled to face each other, while more mirrors surrounded the beds, so that the room—which was lit only by candles—resembled some resplendent grotto. As I stood wondering how we had ever fallen into the clutches of this most mysterious man, who had enticed us from so far away, the midwife brought us a basin of water to wash the dust from our hands and dressed us in hospital smocks. Wherever we looked we saw reflections—ghostly apparitions—images within images . . .

—Linka was invited to join us. Although she was glowing with wonderment and quite delighted that I had not taken her to some inn, she kept looking anxiously at a woman in childbirth who lay covered by a sheet, a swarthy female who called to mind a lithe wildcat. Her abdomen was soft. Her long, bare legs protruded from the sheet . . .

—You see, she was remarkably relaxed, Father, and at once I asked myself, what was the cause of her atonicity? I smelled no hypnogenetic agent; her face was alert; yet she lay there utterly tranquil, following us with her coal-black eyes, which seemed unperturbed at the sight of visitors. I could see at once that she had perfect faith in the Swedish midwife, who presided without losing her composure for a moment. Mani did nothing but smile at her quickly through his little beard and signal the midwife with a nod of his head to proceed with the delivery. And yet—are you listening, Father?—he managed to give the impression that had he not come back from Europe in the nick of time, everything would have come to a halt . . .

—Yes. I can still picture every detail of that screamless birth, which took place on the night of our arrival in a Jerusalem that we had not even seen yet. For the moment we could only scent the city through an open window that let in a most wonderful breeze, on which was wafted a precise compound of cool, dry air and an almost imperceptibly sweet, herbiferous essence—a most carefully concocted extract whereof consists, I submit, the true grandeur of the place. Linka clutched my hand, all but digging her fingernails into it.

She was actually shaking. For the first time in her life she was seeing a womb in action—in all those mirrors surrounding her she had more than a glimpse of what would one day be her own fate. The amazing Swede, having felt the next contraction coming even before the woman in labor, whose concentration was broken by our appearance, now leaned low over the bed and forced apart the long, brown legs, lowering her own body between them and thrusting her head toward the womb as if to lap up the blood that was dripping from it. She did not, however, do so; rather, she began to pant with short breaths like a faithful dog that has just run a course; whereupon the woman, slightly lifting her head to look in the mirror in front of her, which reflected the mirror behind her, began to pant too; and kept it up until the Swede stopped, at which exact second she stopped also. The Swede threw her a big, happy smile, which turned at once into a suffering grimace; she brought her clenched hands up to her shoulders as if fending off an evil spirit; and at once the woman arched herself like a bow and mimicked her, grimacing and expelling what was in her. The cervix opened a bit more; a thin trickle of blood ran off into the white sheet; you could not have said whose ordeal was greater, the midwife's or the woman in childbirth's, for before the woman could groan the midwife had done it before her, panting again like a thirsty yellow dog that was joined at once by its faithful black mate. And mind you, Papa dear, this was doubled and redoubled all around us—behind us, before us, overhead, and underneath—yes, even the tears that glittered in the eyes of Linka, who was enraptured by the mystery of birth, were increased exponentially—if only you and Mama had been there to see how ravishing she looked in her white smock, by the flicker of the candles! She was never more beautiful—she never will be. She held my hand and leaned on Mani, who put an arm around each of us. "There, do you see?" he whispered to us in Hebrew. "It is without pain. Without pain." We nodded. At that moment we both could have sworn that that Swedish Brunhild took all the pain upon herself . . .

—So far he had done nothing—nothing, that is, but glance in the mirrors, in which multiple births were taking place, one more curious than the next—and in which you now could see a curly lock of coal-black hair that belonged to a little man-cub—a somber, wizened little thing that had chosen to be born at the very tail end of this old century—that had not wanted to wait for the next one, the unknown twentieth. It slid quickly out of the vagina, which made me think of a mouth that could not stop yawning, silently cheered on by us all. Mani went to a corner; deftly seized a curved, dripping knife from a boiling pot with his forceps; gripped the newborn infant with one hand; held it up; slapped its back to get it to cry; and then—with the most amazing dexterity—cut the umbilical cord, stanched the bleeding, bandaged the wound with a large pad, and plunked the infant sweepingly down into the arms of Linka, who stood there in a daze. You would have thought her the mother and him the father—and I, dearest Papa, felt a shudder go through me, for he had, as it were, by that act, taken her captive . . .

—No, they were Mohammedans, Father. A tiny, yellowish little Muslim, one of those premature babies you don't expect to last a week—yet by some miracle it hung on, and on Yom Kippur it was still alive, measuring me with a friendly glance of its little, coal-black eyes . . .

—No, why? He has Jewesses too. Did you think they are childless there? The very next day a Jewess gave birth to twins—a boy and a girl—and screamed so hard that even the Swede could not calm her.

—But why? You have nothing to worry about. We Jews have our fair share of babies in the Land of Israel too . . .

—It is an open clinic. That was his way, Father. A multiethnic, syncretistic, ecumenical clinic, which it has to be to survive . . .

—A human laboratory, ha ha . . .

—That is one way of looking at it. As for our Linka—

—Now, now, that is putting it a bit strongly. As for our Linka— just imagine her standing there in a penitential-looking white gown, reverently holding the little baby, which meanwhile had stopped crying, and rocking him ecstatically—it just had been born and here she was already trying to put it to sleep! Mani was bent over the afterbirth, rummaging about in it as if searching for another infant, while the mother lay quietly, apparently feeling no need for words. For my own part, I was still groggy from the journey and delighted to be on solid ground, away from tossing waves, clattering trains, and lurching carriages. Our voyage was over; we were in Jerusalem, which could be breathed, if not seen, from the dark window! Dr.

Mani called me over to have a look at the afterbirth and explained something in a Hebrew that was no more equal to the task than my own. I nodded somnambulistically, staring at that portly, energetic man who must indeed have been a pied piper to bring us to such a place. The line leading from Jelleny-Szad to Jerusalem was mysterious—inspiring—perhaps impossible—but oddly delicious all the same . . .

—Perfectly delicious.

—So I felt.

—Delicious.

—Pardon me . . .

—His children? How strange that you should ask about them, because suddenly there they were: they had stolen unnoticed into the unguarded delivery room, because news had reached them in the synagogue of their father's return and they had run all the way home. For a moment it seemed that the room was full of children. And yet there were but two of them, a brother and sister, multiplied many times over by the phantasmagorical mirrors. The girl was about ten, a squat, graceless child with two short, sad-looking braids and lazy, cowlike eyes; her brother was slightly older, every bit a little Mani, although not at all like his father—a thin, somber boy in a black suit and little fez with the face of an old man. He studied us strangers carefully, impatient to be alone with his father, who was deftly stitching up the patient while joking with Linka, in whose arms the baby was already fast asleep. The midwife made a move to drive the children out; only the girl, however, let herself be driven; at once the boy slipped back in like a little snake, a hurt, querulous look on his face. Soon his mother appeared too. It was easy to see whom the children had gotten their cheerlessness from and why the doctor was given to travel and having guests in his house. She was a docile woman with a chronic eye condition who spoke only Spanish —and at once I was alert to the danger, because this was not a strong family that could override an outside love but quite the opposite, one that could only inflame it. No matter how suspiciously the boy stood guard, he was too young to be an obstacle, while I—I was powerless—I was still sleepwalking from the journey and balmy with the air of Jerusalem, which I sipped like fine wine—let alone scared to death of sailing back over the waves. Yes, there was a danger,

Papa dear, of being engulfed in that city, which—rather than cure us once and for all of our romantic notions—threatened to suck us down into it until you and Mama would be forced to come after us —to sell the mill, lease the forests, find someone for the house, and let go all the help . . .

—You do?

—Papa, you are wonderful! You honestly would sell everything? You are a man of ideals—a true Zionist—and a most innocent soul . . .

—Because you are, Papa. Half shrewd businessman and half dreamer. Here, let me give you a kiss . . .

—No, please! I have not given you a real kiss since coming home . . .

—Wait—I'm sorry—I did not mean to be rough . . .

—I will not break your glasses . . . here . . . one minute, old man . . .

—But I did not mean to hurt you. All of a sudden you began to pull away . . .

—I'm sorry, I truly am. It's all right . . .

—It was not insanely. It was lovingly!

—I am sorry . . .

—You are right, I have changed . . . What time is it?

—No—wait—do not leave me—look, the birth is already over. The bloody pads have been collected and the Swedish midwife has weighed the baby, handed it to its mother, and ushered in the father to see the new soul he has brought into the world—which, if it takes good care of itself, may live to see the tail end of the next century . . . This Arab was a man of few words. He looked at his wife, patted her cheek, went back out to untie his donkey, and rode off in the night to his village to get more wives with child.

—Four, I am told.

—No more than four.

—That is the maximum.

—The devil knows. I suppose they fine him—or confiscate the fifth—how should I know? A man who has not even one wife is not the right person to ask.

—No, he lived upstairs. And unlike the clinic, which was quite elaborate and spotlessly clean, the apartment was small and dingy, with an air of poverty about it. The place was poorly lit and full of shadows, and had a central dining room surrounded by little bedrooms piled high with odds and ends and linens. In it was a dinner getting cold because of the prolonged birth—indeed, I could tell by the number of settings on the table that Mani was unexpected too, to say nothing of his guests. By now I regretted not having listened to Linka and gone off to some inn. "I was wrong," I confessed in a whisper, "terribly wrong—why don't we leave right this minute?" But she hushed me at once, still burning with excitement over the birth that had possessed her whole being. "We mustn't embarrass him," she said. "He's a sensitive man." And so we stayed, hesitantly but hungrily led to the table to partake of a meal that was never intended for us. At the table's far end a personage was waiting to meet us. She was Mani's mother, a stately but almost blind woman dressed in black like the Greek peasants I had seen on Crete, who are already in mourning even before anyone has died. Mani hugged her with great fervor, kissed her hand, and introduced her to Linka and me in a Spanish mixed with Arabic. Once more I could see that I was being made out to be a specialist of worldwide repute—and once more he did not neglect to mispronounce Jelleny-Szad. The candles threw flickering shapes on the walls of the dark apartment, and once more I modestly inclined my head to acknowledge the honor accorded me in Jerusalem, taking the stately señora's shriveled hand in my own while she lavishly welcomed me with a radiance that shone through her blindness. This made Linka so jealous that she stepped forward and seized the soft hand too, kissing it devoutly and presenting herself. Sensing the passionateness of the soul that was seeking to take her by storm, the old woman rose and laid a hand on Linka's head to bless her. Nor, so it seemed, would she have released her had not little Mani, having removed his fez and jacket and become a small boy again, elbowed his way between them . . .

—Only a mother. Dr. Mani never knew his father. He did not even possess a photograph of him. The man died before his son was born, killed in a brawl in an alleyway in the old city. It was Mani's grandfather, his father's father, who—having come especially from Salonika to be with the young couple for the birth—took care of the widow in the first months. And yet instead of taking his grandson and daughter-in-law back to Greece with him, Grandfather Mani chose to leave them in Jerusalem and to return home by himself. Mani never knew him, nor anyone else in his family. He was raised entirely by his mother, a pampered and much-loved only son. These were all things I had already heard at sea, when he and Linka had sat up nights by my bed, ministering to my seasick soul while telling each other stories of their childhoods.

—Ones I had never heard before. Maybe she got them from Mama, or from Grandmother . . . or else she simply made them up . . .

—For example . . . for example . . . no, Father, this is not the time for it. You still do not grasp that this story is not about us; it is about him—that Sephardic gynecologist—that soft, cunningly naive man who for years was possessed by a passion for self-murder that he concealed so as to scare no one away—whose consummation he put off to heighten the pleasure of choosing the pretext he would use . . .

—Wait . . . First comes the dinner that we crashed, which was by no means a large one but rather an assortment of side dishes— apples, cooked vegetables, pomegranates, bits of fried brain—each little more than a symbol—each a wish—a buffer against fear—a warning to enemies—a desire—a fantasy. None were capable of satisfying—all only made you hungrier. And thus we sat, hardly speaking, Linka and I, listening to the unfamiliar holiday melodies that warbled on and on while saying an occasional "amen" and swallowing symbols—and all this, of course, in five different languages, which the darkness and our own weariness seemed to combine into one.

—Linka and I spoke in Yiddish; the Manis spoke Spanish; Linka and Mani used English; with Mani's wife we tried French; and everything came in a wrapping of Hebrew.

—Mani's wife knows some French. Linka tried talking with her to gauge the extent of her defeat.

—She had been sapped by her husband's fantasies—and being somewhat older than he was, she did not sense the threat that had arrived from abroad, neither then nor in the days that followed. She made no effort to follow our talk. She sat there listening as though to an inner drone in her own soul—and indeed, Linka and I must have seemed mere children to her, slightly older than her own, no doubt—why, we had even finished our schooling!—but children nonetheless, perhaps orphans of some sort who had been entrusted to her husband in Basel as his wards—the proof being that, when it was time to find us a place to sleep, she proposed putting us both in her children's beds, which were in an alcove next to her bedroom. Mani whispered in her ear—Linka and I murmured something or other—and a better solution was found: the girl was moved to the grandmother's bed, Linka was put in the children's room, and young Mani was sent to sleep with me in the clinic. The Swedish midwife was instructed to surround us with partitions and to screen us off from each other.

—Of course. It was a great mistake, Father. We should have gone to a hotel, especially since I had invaded the privacy of that dark, crowded house with its unattractive furnishings quite enough. But now it was Linka who wanted to live on the inside; she was ecstatic with the knowledge that she could go below when she pleased to watch a new birth; and without giving it another thought, she went straight to the children's room, changed into her nightclothes, and climbed into one of the two beds. Shortly after, the rest of the household drifted off to its rooms too, leaving me alone at the dinner table to cut furtive slices of the remaining hallah, since I was as hungry at the end of that symbolic meal as I had been when it started. I heard Mani climbing the stairs, no doubt thrilled by the thought that his latest love had become a little girl who slept on the other side of the wall from him. I did not wait for him but went in to see her and found her in bed, glowing, her eyes wide open, a large, colorful Turkish doll—a sort of belly dancer in silk pants—above her head, on which she wore a Turkish fez in place of a bonnet. "Forgive me, Linka," I said to her. "I was wrong—tomorrow we will find other lodgings and move out of here." She sat bolt upright. She was already burned by the Palestinian sun. "But there's no need," she murmured. "It's not that at all. There is lots of room here —we must not hurt his feelings—he cares for us dearly. I'm telling you, I know—let him play the host." I said nothing. I could feel her inner tumult, her new hope that had sprung from seeing his wife and children for herself. I sat down on her bed and tried to say something solemn—something about our journey having come to an end—but could not think of the words. "Well, then," I said, "here we are in Jerusalem at last." "Yes," she replied at once. "Here we are. How happy I am!" It was the most simple, the most touching declaration—all the more so for having been made in that down-at-the-heels little room, surrounded by a confusion of children's things —for having been so perfectly forthright. "How happy I am!" I smiled at her indulgently. I knew that her happiness had nothing to do with Jerusalem—of which she had so far seen nothing—and everything to do with something else; it was no more than an amusing illusion, I thought, that would soon come to naught. "And you, Efrayim?" she asked earnestly, too big for that child's bed that was gazed down on by the Turkish doll. "Are you happy?" I laughed. "Happy? As if happiness were possible for me—as if there ever has been a time when I was happy. Happy for what? For that premature baby? For being here? We have nine days to see this place and then we had better get ourselves safely home, because I promised Mama and Papa to return you in no worse condition than I took you in." She frowned at that. "Of course, of course," she murmured short-temperedly, "we shall see." I had the feeling that she was listening to something outside the door—to our host, Dr. Mani, who was standing there eavesdropping—portlier than ever in an open shirt, minus his jacket and tie—waiting bleary-eyed to take me down to my quarters, where the indefatigable midwife had made my bed. She had washed and changed clothes too, and she greeted me affably in bare feet and showed me to my bed, which was set apart from the women's beds but not by much, as if some obscure formula had determined its position vis-à-vis them. Next to it, behind a partition, was little Mani, who had not yet settled down for the night; he was standing on his bed in a black shift, the sort of tunic that Arab children run about in, and now he ran to his father unrestrainedly, pulling him away from me and behind his partition, where he clung to him with both arms. I could hear him scolding him in that Spanish of theirs, which is rather like a watered-down Latin. Here he had been waiting long months for him, pining away—and what does the man do when he finally comes home but show up with two monopolizing strangers! I could sense the doctor's impatience; his answers were brusque, for he wished only to be upstairs again, in the little room where his new daughter was lying. It was then, without warning, that the boy broke out crying bitterly, in a dry, harsh sob that rattled the silence in the clinic. It was an inconsolable sound. I rose and went over to him—he stopped crying and hung his head angrily —and so I turned to Mani and chided him for forgetting the most important thing of all. The black horse! "You see," I said to the boy, "your father wished to bring you a horse." At first he would not listen but merely pressed his nose against the wall and waited for me to go away, only half-understanding my Polish Hebrew. Little by little, however, the story enchanted him; he began peeking over his shoulder to watch me describe with my hands how the gray sack was tied around the horse's head, and how it was eased into the hold of the ship, and how it behaved so wildly there that it had to be disembarked in Crete and galloped off to the freedom of the mountains. The boy's tears dried; he was listening intently now, asking his father the meaning of words that eluded him; at last, his sorrow once more got the best of him. "But where is that island?" he asked, quite desolate to think that the horse was in Crete when it might have been in Jerusalem. "Can't we go there and bring it back?" he begged. Mani translated for me, and I promised that on our way home we would ransom the horse from the island and send it to Palestine. That gradually calmed the boy down enough to go to bed. A prematurely old little child!

—Yosef was his name. Since Beirut a day has not passed without my thinking of him. Even here, in this dark corner—in the middle of the night, thousands of miles away from Jerusalem—I feel a physical pain when I mention him, as if I had been shot. Does he know yet that his father is dead? And what else does he know? I picture him roaming past the mirrors and partitions of the clinic, which must be slowly going to pot, hating and blaming Linka, but also me. Is he capable of making a distinction between us? Will he ever understand that we were only an instrument in his father's hands, a wretched pretext for a profound passion that I must fumblingly grope to comprehend for the rest of my life—that we too were the victims of . . .

—Go back where?

—When? How?

—What, all over again?

—No, no. I have already been there—I have had enough—it is someone else's turn . . .

—But what? In what language? What could I write? What could I say that would not make his anguish only worse?

—No, Father, no. It is a bad idea.

—Money? What kind of money?

—For what? It would be an implicit admission of guilt . . . why should I make it?

—But what guilt? What are you talking about, Father? I ask you: what? You have taken leave of your senses! What guilt?

—No, wait—wait—don't leave me, Father. Father . . . wait—wait—I beg you—don't leave me to toss and turn in bed all night as I did that first night in Jerusalem—a Jerusalem I already was in and had not even entered yet. All I had seen of it was that lone, amazing clinic and the stars in its sky—which nevertheless were enough to make me realize that I too—but why should I not be?—was almost happy, even if I would never have admitted it to Linka—happy that the earth was not rocking beneath me and that I could turn my thoughts away from my heaving insides and back to the world again —to the voices I now heard—to the quiet steps and whispers above me—to the soft, barefoot movements of the Swedish midwife—who, it seemed, never slept—as she made the rounds of her sleeping prepartums to see which of them would be next. I lay there for a while like a doctor on night duty; rose to ask the Swede for a stetho-scope to listen to the newborn baby's heart; returned to my bed; gazed out the window at the fading stars while watching the dark-ness slowly lift; and listened to the unexpected sounds of the dawn —at first the sweet ring of a church bell, as if the little church of St. Jodwiga of Oświęcim had followed us to Jerusalem, and then, close on its heels, the clear voices of the muezzins . . .

—Those are the Mohammedan cantors who call the faithful to prayer. And although I was no Mohammedan, I jumped at once from my bed with the realization that—even if it was more heard than seen—dawn was breaking. I washed my face, feeling very hun-gry, and made up my mind to discover Jerusalem on my own and get to know it for myself rather than as a hostage of my doctor, whose intentions had begun to seem even more nefarious since crossing the threshold of his house. I stepped outside into broad daylight, pointed myself in the direction of some sounds that I heard, and struck out across the fields, passing some little house now and then until I arrived at the gray ramparts of the city and disappeared through a gate into its narrow streets. From that morning on, I walked the old city's streets every day, my feet skipped along by its cobblestones. It was a city that from the very first I understood perfectly—which is more than I can say of any of your other Jews, Zionists or not. *I* was there.

—I was. And I got to know that stone womb that is the mother of us all.

—No, not so much the inhabitants. Jews are the same everywhere. The only difference is that there the Mohammedans take the place of the Poles; the Turks—of the Austrians; the donkeys—of the horses; and the nimble black goats—of the hogs. Sometimes, with their little beards, they made me think that they were ancient Jews who had disguised and shrunk themselves after the destruction of the Temple in order to stay on in Jerusalem . . .

—I wandered from place to place, footloose and missing nothing, thoroughly learning the city, in which the distances are astonishingly small. From our Wailing Wall to the great mosque with its two domes is no more than a few steps; from there a short walk will bring you to the Church of the Holy Sepulchre; and not far from that are the synagogues and the holy places of the Armenians, the Eastern Orthodox, and the Protestants. Everything is jumbled together—it is a bit like entering a large shop for religious artifacts whose shelves are piled high—the believer can choose whatever catches his fancy . . .

—It is quite simple. You walk down a street that is no more than a few feet wide and there it is—a large wall—or buttress—however you wish to call it—grayish and covered with mosses. It is quite amazingly like the photograph you have hung on the wall of your office, Father. Perhaps the same Jews even pray there. I found it most appealing, Papa dear.

—Its formal simplicity—its improvised originality—its refusal to make any false promises or foster any illusions. It is a last stop of history, no less than that board in the train station—a blank wall with no open-sesames or hidden crypts. What more can I tell you, Father? What else? It is perhaps the ultimate dam, built to hold back the Jews in their restless proclivity to return to their past. "Halt!" it says. "No Passage Allowed Beyond This Point."

—Only at first. I won't deny that I stood there dismayed for a moment—even stunned—gawking in disappointment. But soon enough I got over it, stepped up to the large, cool stones, and—ha ha ha—even kissed them, would you believe it? A lazy atheist like myself ardently kissing not just one stone but two! The Jews and Jewesses praying there saw that my head was uncovered and sought to comment but did not; and so I tarried for a while, thinking of this and that, until I stopped an Arab boy carrying a tray of golden little loaves and bought them all for a thaler. I stood there eating one after another—they were wonderfully tasty—I shall never forget the taste of them. From that moment on—as if I had chewed the stones and they were made of dough—my memories of the Wailing Wall do not come without the fragrant taste of freshly baked bread . . .

—A narrow lane. The approach is dark and dank, very intimate. On one side of you is the ancient, holy relic with its huge stones, and on the other, a cluster of homes with flapping laundry and crying babies. It is an impossible but quite real combination. I would have lingered there longer had not the ram's horns begun wailing all around me, which made me think of you in the gray fields of Poland, waiting for some sign of life from us. I was directed to the *sarwiyya,* the Turkish governor's house in the Christian Quarter, and from there I sent you my second telegram—the one that Mama says only made you even more worried. But why?

—But what did it say, for goodness' sake?

—What was unclear about it? I was even given a Turkish telegraph operator who knew German, and we made up the message together. I remember it word for word: *We are well. Will start home after Yom Kippur.*

—*We are happy?*

—But I expressly wrote "well"! Who could have changed it to "happy"? Perhaps it was that Turk's own idea. But even if it said that, why be so alarmed by it?

—What do you mean, that was all?

—Let me see it. This is what you received?

—But the last words are left out. I paid good money for them— that postal clerk made off with them! Unless they fell out of the wires along the way—or else the Poles were too lazy to copy them . . .

—How do you know?

—I had no idea you could do that.

—And when you traced it back to its point of origin, what were you told?

—They confirmed it? But how could they have? What a scoundrel! Why, I paid for every word of it . . .

—Two piastres.

—Of course. I would never have kept you in the dark like that, without even letting you know . . .

—What a devilish business—he went and shortened it on his own! And he thought my visit in Jerusalem was *too* short—he could not stop telling me about the wonders of the city . . .

—But . . .

—My dears—you had every reason to worry—*We are happy*—an odd telegram indeed! A person might have thought . . . oh, my poor loves . . . and yet even then . . .

—The word "happy"?

—So it could have, Papa dear. Taken captive by our own happiness . . . a wonderfully subtle thought. Bravo!

—Indeed, he was our captor, that oriental gynecologist. There was a power in him—he could move you to do anything by his presence, as confusedly soft as it was—as full of surprises too, disappearing and appearing without warning. I had already noticed how he worked his will with his family—even the boy, who sought to fight back, was constantly squelched. The Swede was all but enslaved to him, and I had seen for myself how Linka trembled all over when he flung that gory infant into her arms, thrusting upon her—a stranger from afar—a most intimate partnership. How could I have known that his effusive—his soft, imaginative, and prankish nature—was unreal—unnatural—nothing but an illusory reflection, like those of the swiveled mirrors in his clinic—of the soon-to-surface destructiveness within him?

—Yes. There was even a danger of Linka's being ensnared to work for him as a nurse, to turn herself into a nurse-concubine . . .

—There is nothing insane about it . . .

—It is not a perverse thought. Nothing was impossible by then.

Why, I myself had begun to feel that morning a well-being as blissful as nirvana, a primitive, tidal oneness with that diaphanous light. I
wandered among the bright colors of the fruit stands, the rug dealers, the coppersmiths, accompanied by the savage wails—now rising, now choking—of the ram's horns, in seventh heaven to be on
solid ground, so brimful with happiness that the telegraph clerk who
saw it decided to rewrite my cable without a date of departure,
which made you here—holding the innocent gray telegram in your
hands thousands of miles from Jerusalem—instantly alert to the
threat that was implicit in the elimination of those words that never
reached you. Is that not wondrous?

—Yes, dearest Papa, a threat—the threat of happiness—that is a
threat too. And so I knew that if I wished to remain in Jerusalem as
a pilgrim and nothing more, albeit a most secular one, my first task
was to distance myself from Dr. Mani and his harem and to find
lodgings of my own, preferably in a pilgrims' hostel. It did not take
long to ascertain that there were indeed such places everywhere,
little hospices that offered bed-and-breakfast, and since I inquired
after one run by Englishmen, who Mani believed spoke the language
of the future, I was directed to a place near the Jaffa Gate called
Christ's Church, which combined a hostel with a biblical seminary.
Its director was a handsome, ruddy-cheeked Scotch priest who saw
at once that I was neither an Englishman, a pilgrim, nor anything
resembling either, but a plain ordinary Galician Jew in need of a
room, which made him regard me benevolently and usher me into
an inner courtyard off the chapel, where he showed me a dark
chamber that looked out on a green ravine and had a single bed. I
did not ask for a second bed or for a partition, because I knew that
one word about bringing a sister would suffice to get me thrown out
at once.

—So I thought. I was so thrilled by the room and the hostel that I
threw my hat on the bed to take possession of it and returned to the
Manis' via some dusty footpaths that ran by a few small Jewish
neighborhoods, plucking an aromatic leaf now and then from a bush
by the roadside and leaping over the rocks in the way . . .

—Here and there I passed a building—a street—the start of some
new neighborhood—a school—a hospital—a hostel—a sanatorium.
Outside the old walls, Jerusalem is still a collection of uncollated

ideas, of the private whims of individuals who have picked out some hillside and hatched their thoughts upon it. As of yet, however, no two thoughts have coalesced; there are not even any roads to connect them, just the trails beaten by persevering hikers. And thus, thirsty and dehydrated—for I had lost my way once or twice, there being no sounds to navigate by—there being nothing, in fact, but the profound silence of a holiday morning—I arrived back at the house I had left early in the day. It was deserted. The Swedish midwife suggested that I try the Bukharian synagogue, in which, she said, the service would soon be over—and indeed, as I approached it the worshipers came pouring out, among them Dr. Mani, who looked like a positive eminence with his large prayer shawl bag under his arm. He was slowly steering his little blind mother, surrounded by a crowd of people and assisted by Linka while his daughter walked alongside them; his son, dressed in black as usual, was trailing a few steps behind, alone by himself like the catchword at the bottom of a page that is waiting for a hand to turn it so that it can begin the new page.

—Yes, our Linka too. Just think of it—she, who cannot be gotten out of bed on a weekday before midmorning, let alone on a Sabbath or holiday, had risen at the crack of dawn to accompany the doctor to services, the long hours of which she had loyally sat through in the woman's section of the synagogue with Mani's mother and some other old women, a black kerchief covering her head, listening dubiously but not without pleasure to the Sephardic melodies, which do not whine up and down like ours but have a merry beat. Perhaps they derive from Turkish marches played during the Balkan campaigns.

—She sat patiently through it all, her prayer book in her lap. And now, in the courtyard of the synagogue, she was reaping her reward, because Mani was arranging her debut. He was making an odd fuss over her too, treating her like a *grande dame* and stopping to tip his hat to all his friends and neighbors while presenting her as the rarest of pearls. And of course, she played the part to the hilt, curtsying daintily and holding out a royal hand. People were drawn to her. He was more than twice her age—and yet—he behaved to her with great deference, so that—when I think of the two of them now, standing there in the noonday heat—I am shocked by my own blindness . . .

—Because—without a doubt—he had already then made up his mind to take his own life on account of her. That is why she was so precious to him, of such inestimable value. It was not for her own sake. It was for the sake of the horrible end that he had decided to make her the reason for. And the value thus conferred on her only spurred him on in his despair and passion for self-destruction, so that this end—the ruin he meant to bring upon himself—illuminated her also—coiled itself around her—insinuated its way into her —until her face became tragic too—a tragedy, Father—Father!— that was even greater—more terrible—than that which was to befall —that did befall!—Mani himself. And this made her more important than ever, although not so much in her own right, because the importance came from beyond her, so that she was no longer just our Linka—not just a plumpish, giggly twenty-year-old with flashing eyes from a place called Jelleny-Szad—but the deputy—the emissary —of innumerable women—some with child and some not—some mothers and some seeking to be—but all incomparably riper and more beautiful than she was—a long, long line of women ranged behind her—whom our tubby, good-hearted gynecologist was doing everything in his power to find room for in himself—was determined to redeem by means of those tragic, grotesque mirrors he had put in all the rooms of his clinic—was seeking to conjure through the medium of a red-haired young lady who happened to attend the Third Zionist Congress . . .

—I am, am I? You are perspicuous, Father. I was already raving then under those blue, torrid skies of a summer's end that was hotter than any summer. My shoes were caked with dust, and I was full of my morning's impressions from the walled city and wanted only to rest in perfect peace—which Dr. Mani would not let me do. "Why, it's Dr. Shapiro," he cried out, hastening to introduce me to the departing worshipers. "He is a children's physician from the Hapsburg Empire who has come from the congress to study the methods of my clinic." I bent to kiss the hand of his delicate mother —who, I had noticed, was partial to Polish kisses; patted the girl on the head; tipped my own hat too; and betook myself to Mani's house, from which came a sound of loud groans. Two Hasidic Jews were waiting for the doctor by the cistern in the courtyard. They greeted him and rushed him off to the clinic—and meanwhile, in a wicker basket in the courtyard, I came upon the previous night's baby, utterly naked and soaking up the sunshine, which—so Mani claimed—was just the thing to dissolve the hepatitic cells in its blood. Without bothering to look for a stethoscope, I crouched and put my ear to its chest—it was breathing quite energetically . . .

—No, Father, I did not participate in that day's birth, nor in any others. I had come to Jerusalem to be a tourist and an observer, not to deliver babies. I went to bed and had a long, sweet sleep, and that evening, when the Sabbath was over, I told Linka about my move to Christ's Church. I did not propose that she join me. "You were right," I said. "It is best that you stay here to avoid any injury to his feelings. Take a holiday from me and have many happy birth-days, so that—when your turn comes—you will know how to do it gladly and without pain." At first my moving out so resolutely gave her a fright. Yet I knew that only by distancing myself in such a way could I eventually muster the strength to break the chains of his captivity . . .

—He was holding us captive, Father, without our knowing it . . .

—No. That evening they all helped me move—Mani, his children, Linka of course, and even the Swede, who came along for "a breath of fresh air." Everyone carried some bundle of mine and we proceeded to the Jaffa Gate, where I took them all up to my room. We opened the window for a view of the Russian church with its onion domes and then went downstairs to that Anglican study house for a cup of tea with the men of the cloth, who were delighted with my escorts' English. After that, I took Linka to see the Wailing Wall. She faced it in aloof silence. "What," I asked, "will you not even give it one little kiss? This morning I gave it two." But she would not. And so we parted. I had given her her freedom.

—No. Of course we saw each other afterward. But I had given her her freedom—for the first time—and she knew it.

—I mean that you have always complained that I hound her— that I interfere—that I do not mind my own business—that I try to influence her. And so I gave her her freedom . . .

—The words speak for themselves.

—The entire ten days in that children's room next to the parents' bedroom, with the Turkish doll in the fez pirouetting over her.

—Who?

—Ah, the girl. She slept in the grandmother's big bed.

—In the clinic, behind a partition.

—I do not know.

—Perhaps . . .

—Occasionally.

—Perhaps . . . I have no way of knowing . . . I was a good several versts away.

—The room had to be paid for, of course. Apart from Englishmen and pilgrims, only Christ himself is allowed to stay there free of charge . . .

—Half a pound sterling per diem.

—Exactly a thaler.

—No, it was not cheap. But I was treated nobly; no effort was spared to make me comfortable. And their whiskey, Papa—it is unparalleled—a most mellow, a divinely inspired brew.

—The city, Papa. The city itself.

—No, not the inhabitants. The city is forever greater than its inhabitants. I plunged into it as deeply as I could—I roamed all about and around it, exploring it layer by layer—because I knew that I would never be back.

—Heavens, no, Father; I am not anti-Jerusalem; I am a-Jerusalem. After all, suppose there were no Jerusalem? I have freed myself— but with no illusions—from the dream that you will all continue to stumble about in, lost between imagination and reality—between accusation and guilt—between the fear to go on and the fear to stay put; angered by your hopeless entanglement. I have taken the honorable way out; I know what I am leaving behind . . .

—I wandered.

—In the narrow streets—the souks—the courtyards. Inside and outside the walls . . .

—I was not always alone. When Mani saw that the city interested me, he and Linka sometimes joined me. And being eager to present us and publicize his return home, he invited us all to high tea at the home of the British consul, whom he appeared to regard as his patron. Everyone there was quite taken with Linka's lilting English.

Another time, we startled the Turkish pasha one morning with a surprise visit, at which we were served coffee too bitter for words. At the Armenian patriarch's, on the other hand, we spent an evening sipping chilled wine. And one day Mani hired a private carriage in which he put his mother, his two children, Linka, and me, and took us to a Mohammedan village on a slope outside Jerusalem. We went to see a sheikh of sorts, a venerable old friend of the family, who apparently knew Mani's father and grandfather; Mani visited him every year during the autumn holidays. We were ushered into a large room where the old sheikh was seated on a cushion in front of a splendid wall carpet with a dagger thrust into it. He was surrounded by the members of his household, most of them rheumy-eyed with disease. Venerable though he was, he was thrilled by our visit and appeared to be a fervent admirer of Mani's mother; he bowed his head when she spoke to him and chose fruit for her from a tray set before him and laid it on her plate—figs, apples, and bunches of grapes that he pressed on her so attentively that I almost thought he was about to put them in her mouth with his own palsied hands. He was also delighted to be introduced to the two of us; he addressed Linka as "Madame Mani," being under the impression that Mani had taken a second wife, and immediately put a cluster of grapes on her plate too. His family took a great interest in me and wanted to know if I was a settler in Jerusalem or merely a tourist. Mani, who acted as our interpreter, began, I believe, to explain that I was touring with an eye to settling, but I cut him short at once with a wave of my hand and a word I had learned in the streets of the walled city: *hallass*—which means, "That will do." They were so greatly pleased with it that they all laughed and repeated it after me —*"hallass, hallass!"*—while Mani looked quite crestfallen. In the carriage on the way back I felt for the first time his anxiety over our coming departure. All of a sudden he said in low tones, "Perhaps, after all, you will stay on through the holidays to see a Palestinian autumn."

—Autumn.

—He was simply casting about for something. But I had made up my mind not to remain a day longer, even though the better I got to know the city, the more it grew on me. He noticed how it intrigued me and sometimes sent his son along with me as my guide. Perhaps too, he just wanted the boy out of the house. On the last days of our stay I would rise in late morning, descend to the quiet chapel below, and be met there by young Mani, who had a way of appearing all at once from behind the baptismal font or the altar. Sometimes I found him standing and preaching to himself, his old man's features passionate with anger.

—Hebrew, even though my pronunciation made him jeer, so that I constantly had to correct it to keep him from regarding my speech as a foreign and incomprehensible language. Still, he was a pleasant walking companion, with a quick, light stride and no end of ideas where to take me. In my last days there, we ventured increasingly beyond the walls; to the Mount of Olives, for example, which has no olives but large quantities of graves. We would stand there among the flocks of black goats, looking out for a long while at the city, and then head down past St. Elizaveta's, which he called the Church of Onions, and across the Hill of Evil Counsel to the Russian Compound. Everywhere, I noticed, he sought to befriend the Turkish soldiers; he invariably headed in the direction of their posts, waving to them when he saw them and calling out a few Turkish words. And everywhere too, I had the same feeling of cosmic space; "I am freeing myself of this city forever," I told myself, as I followed the boy back down amid the walls, through the narrow streets and courts of the souk, "without illusion or resentment." I was no longer an unknown stranger in Jerusalem; the same Jewish and Arab peddlers who had eyed me wordlessly a few days before now stopped me to greet me. It was then that I knew that our journey had come to its true end.

—Linka was still enthralled by the clinic. She spent her time helping Mani and the midwife. Sometimes, lying in bed at night in Christ's Church, she seemed as distant from me as if I were in Cracow and she in Jelleny-Szad.

—No. I did not spend Yom Kippur by myself. It began with their convincing me to join them for the meal before the fast. At the table, when we were done eating, Mani turned to me directly and demanded that we postpone our trip. At first I did not give a straight answer; finally, though, I said, "I must get back to my patients." I could not for the life of me, however, think of who they were, except for little Antony, whom I play checkers with after each examination.

—Why, yes, there is Szimek too. How could I have forgotten Szimek? How is he?

—Really? Oh, my! Szimek . . .

—Yes.

—Tomorrow . . .

—My goodness, Szimek . . . But where was I? Ah, yes: at the meal before the fast. He kept pressing me to stay while I pleaded my patients and Linka kept silent. That was when he let the cat out of the bag. Why, he suggested, did I not return home by myself and let Linka stay on through the autumn, or even until spring, when he would bring her back to Europe—to Venice, or perhaps even all the way to Jelleny-Szad? You could have heard a pin drop. Linka turned red. The boy bit his lips. Mani's old mother questioningly turned her blind, groping eyes toward us. I weighed my words carefully. "Linka," I said, "is indeed no longer a child and is free to lead her own life. But I am obliged to bring her back to her father and mother. Once that is done, she can of course go anywhere she wishes." I saw her start to protest and restrain herself. The old grandmother swiveled her head to divine the shadows at the table while Mani's wife rose to clear the dishes, shifting her glance from her shamefacedly love-stricken husband to Linka, the overgrown girl brought home from Europe who had managed to become a young woman within the space of several days . . . Just then we heard a strange, harsh scream from below, followed by the frightened cry of the midwife. Mani jumped to his feet with Linka and I right behind him, for it was clear that this was no labor pain but something far worse. Quite firmly, however, he told us not to follow him; he would see to the matter himself; we should finish our meal, he said, and go to synagogue. And so he went below and we continued eating in silence until Linka turned to me furiously and said—in Polish rather than Yiddish—"What do you mean, you are obliged to bring me back?" "But I am," I answered her quietly. "Not so much to Papa as to Mama, who is very ill. Now let us go pray for her." I rose, thanked Mani's wife for the meal, and asked the boy to take us to synagogue.

—Why did I do what?

—It was not to alarm her. It was to bring her to her senses.

—She would never have come back otherwise, Papa . . . never . . .

—Why alarm anyone? But the fact is . . . well, no matter . . .

—No.

—No matter.

—I said, no matter. We went to their synagogue. There were candles burning everywhere, and it looked like a mosque with all its carpets and cushioned benches along the walls. The boy led me to his father's seat and I was given a prayer shawl and wrapped in it, because the Sephardic men wear prayer shawls even before they are married. And so I abandoned myself to their merry hymns, which trot along at a cheerful clip without any whining arpeggios, only to look up halfway through the service and see Mani at my side, in his prayer shawl with bloodstains on his fingernails. "The baby died and I don't know why," he whispered to me morosely. I felt I should say something; but before I could, he added, "It wasn't the cord." After that he was silent except for joining his voice to the cantor's now and then in some hymn or tune. And so the prayer dragged on into the night.

—Nor can I.

—I could not get away. We returned together across the empty fields, walking slowly with the boy trailing as usual behind us like a catchword awaiting the next page. In front of the clinic two men in work clothes were waiting for us, Jewish farmhands from some-where outside Jerusalem. Within, in the big room, which was lit only by faint moonlight, we saw the woman lying with her face toward the wall; her husband leaned over her, trying to get her to look at him. Mani walked by them without stopping; he handed his prayer shawl bag to the midwife and led me by the hand to see the dead child in the delivery room. It was lying on a small table in the corner, wrapped in a folded bath towel—a little blue baby girl, perfectly formed, her eyes shut as though fast asleep. Mani picked her up and shook her, slapping her back as if still expecting a cry, and laid her so carefully down on a bed that you might have thought he hoped there was another baby inside her that might yet be born alive. He asked if I remembered my pathology. I nodded. Well, then, he said, why don't we do an autopsy to establish the cause of death? Although I tried to talk him out of it, he had already seized a scalpel—he was that frantic to find out—and begun looking for a place for the incision when a sound from behind a curtain made him stop. We went to have a look and found the boy hiding there—but before we could shoo him out the door, this was blocked by the father of the dead baby, who wanted the body, since his friends had come to take him and his wife back to their farm. Mani made an effort to dissuade him; thought better of it; wrapped the baby up again; and handed it, looking like a big, sleeping bird, reluctantly over . . . I hitched a ride with the farmhands on their wagon, grieving with them in silence; near the Lions' Gate they let me off and I slipped through the wall not far from the big mosque. There was not a sound. The streets were deserted. I had to cross the entire walled city to the Tower of David, and I tried to bolster my spirits by singing one of those Sephardic prayers that resembled an army march. I could not get the melody right, though—and all this time I was haunted by a vision of that dead baby lying in the bed. Besides which, I had a new worry now . . . are you listening, Father?

—Linka.

—I was so anxious that I awoke early the next morning, quite unable to spend Yom Kippur holed up in Christ's Church as I had planned. And so back I went to the Manis', hungry and thirsty, forced to partake in a fast that had imposed itself on me against my will. The house was empty. There was not a soul there, not even the midwife, who had gone to synagogue too. The kitchen was cold and the fire was out in the cookstove. I hurried off to the synagogue— and what did I meet on my way but a carriage, out of which climbed Mani with his doctor's bag, looking a wreck. He was returning, it seemed, from a vigil with a patient that had not gone well. We entered the synagogue together to find the congregation in the middle of the service, the military marches having yielded to heartbreakingly sad melodies. As we took our seats and joined the prayer, I made out Linka behind a white curtain in the woman's gallery; she was sitting perfectly still beneath her black kerchief with Mani's wife, his daughter, and the Swede, who was off in a corner beneath a large window ablaze with that Jerusalem light that had been an object of my contemplation since arriving in the city. It was only on that final day, however, during the Yom Kippur service, when there was nothing to do for long hours but look at it, that I began, I believe, to understand it . . .

—It is a light, Father, in which two different lights contend, a tawny, free-flowing one from the desert and a bluish one born from the sea that slowly ascends the mountains, gathering the light of the rocks and the olive trees on its way. They meet in Jerusalem—imbibe each other there—subsume each other there—and conjoin at evening into a clear, winy glow that settles through the treetops branch by branch and turns to a coppery red, which—reaching the tip of the window—inspires the worshipers to leap to their feet and bellow the closing prayer in a great wave of supplication that washes over the frozen world. Meanwhile, Mani was seeking to outdo the cantor—to outsing him—to outshout him—while little Mani and all the children joined in with loud cries, working themselves up to a fever pitch that abated only with the sounding of the ram's horn—which made me most happy, because I knew that as of that moment my homeward journey had begun. Are you listening?

—The prayer ended and large watermelons were carried into the synagogue and sliced and handed out to the worshipers to assuage their thirst. In the courtyard outside we met the womenfolk and wished one another a good year, after which we started slowly home, where we had a light dinner that filled us at once. People were already knocking on the door—women come to give birth after waiting for the holy day to end—and the Swede hurried below to admit them while Linka changed out of her white dress and went down to mop the floor and be of help. I went over the next morning's travel arrangements with Mani, who made some remark and added with a laugh, "But you will not go—I will have the Turkish army arrest you—I have come to like you too much." His making a joke of it made me feel better, as if he had already come to terms with our departure. Are you listening?

—In the morning a wagon came to pick me up at Jaffa Gate. Linka was sitting in it. I saw that her belongings had dwindled drastically. She had left most of her clothes with the Swede to give away to charity. She was pale and her eyes glistened redly as though after a big cry. Mani, on the other hand, seemed quite content with himself. He sat calmly by the driver, a heavy winter overcoat on his knees. If I had had my wits about me, I would have know what to make of that coat instead of simply staring at it blankly.

—Because since Beirut I have kept going over the clues, real and imaginary, that he gave us, until there is nothing that does not now seem a clue: the way he looked at the wheels of the train in the station—his asking the stoker how fast it could go—the seat he chose for himself . . .

—Yes, Papa dear, that was the first surprise. Instead of saying good-bye at the station, he boarded the train and informed us that he meant to see us off at the ship. In my innocence I assumed that he planned to take a carriage back that same night, which was the reason for the overcoat. I was actually glad that he was coming along, because I too found it hard to part from him and from Jerusalem, which vanished all at once behind the first downhill bend. Are you listening to me, Papa?

—No. But your head was nodding a bit—I thought that perhaps you had dozed off. I know that this has been wearisome for you, but I am nearing the end now—in fact, that is what I began with. Are you listening?

—We pulled into the station in Jaffa, where a crowd was rushing noisily about, and set out immediately for the port. Once again he began scolding our haste to depart. "But you have seen nothing yet," he said. "Do you think Jerusalem is Palestine?" We could spy our ship in the distance—I must say that this time my little consumptive from the *gare* had outdone herself and ordered us a big Austrian steamship. The three of us were rowed out to it in a lighter manned by singing Arabs who flung us on deck with heave-hos. We were received there graciously and shown to two most pleasant cabins, from which we proceeded to the dining room for a late lunch, elegantly served us by a galley crew that plied us with great quantities of wine. Linka was wan and silent—rather withdrawn—and Mani and I had to joke with each other by ourselves. "What will you do on the waves without me?" he asked. "Who will see to your tranquillity pills?" The overcoat lay on a chair beside us like a big, hairy, faithful pet. We went on deck to have a smoke and a look at the white houses of Jaffa with their great minaret. The waves lapped at the ship. More lighters kept coming all the time, and the boatmen sang and heave-hoed their frightened passengers onto the deck while Mani looked on with an ironic, slightly mocking expression that I had never noticed in him before—that made me think of a first Mani slowly bursting open and discharging a second one from its midst. We sat for a long while, enjoying the cool, moist breeze and letting the afternoon hours slip languidly by while the last of the passengers arrived. We discussed the recent days—the clinic—the big Swede—young Mani. All of a sudden I took some coins from my pocket and asked him to buy his children gifts from us, especially the boy. He listened with a preoccupied air as I told him about our excursions together—about how his son worshiped him and craved his presence—about how fortunate it was that he would now have some time for him. At last he said: *"He* at least will know what he is craving for; I crave a father I never had and of whose existence I know so little that each time I seek to catch a glimpse of him in my son, I see not the young man who was killed in a brawl before my birth in the walled city, but the wily old face of my grandfather, standing before me in his black rabbinical clothes." Linka sat there half-listening, as if she knew our talk was but a masquerade; she kept gazing out to sea, where the sun was now being punished with a fiery death. She was still very pale; she never touched the glass in front of her. She was waiting—without a word—for the farewells. Are you listening? Are you?

—But there were no farewells, that much you know. When the last call rang for the last lighter taking visitors back to shore, his movements grew suddenly lethargic; he cocked his head as if he had not heard, spread his coat out on the seat beside him, and said, "You have chosen a fine ship, but the waves are the same waves; I had better sail as far as Haifa with you to see how Efrayim makes out with them. This overcoat of mine will keep me warm on deck at night, but have no fear—I won't be going all the way to Europe with you." I saw Linka's eyes open wide with horror; Mani beckoned to one of the deckhands, gave him the coins I had handed him, and looked down just in time to see the last lighter slip away from the ship and head back for the shore, which now began to wobble slightly. The houses of Jaffa shook a bit as if struck by a mild earthquake, and the green orange groves on the hills staggered backward. You see, Father, that ship was so quiet—its motion was so imperceptible—that we appeared to be standing still while an invisible hand tugged Palestine to the south, so that the land—now cloaked in darkness—floated slowly away as we observed its extraordinary motion. "Well, then," said Mani, regarding me with a melancholy smile, "how is your stomach?" More to himself than to me, though, he whispered without waiting for an answer: "But what should be wrong with it? The fear, after all, has left you." Are you listening, Father? Are you?

—You are fading out, Father. I can't see your face. No, don't fall asleep on me; don't leave me all alone. Wait . . . wait . . . We sat silently on deck, wrapped in our blankets, watching the black land drift slowly by. The moon set. The stars flared up. Linka fell into a deep sleep and began slipping out of her chair, so that we had to take her down to her cabin. Mani helped me. Suddenly, feeling his hand against mine, I knew we were engaged in a wordless struggle for her . . .

—For Linka.

—Linka . . . are you listening?

—Give me some sign that you are . . . don't keep so vindictively silent. There is—there was—no sign of dawn yet; the only illumination came from the lighthouse in Haifa, whose beacon revolved on a treeless hill in the dark shadow of a Carmelite monastery. The ship cast anchor at a distance from the city, whose little white houses, all neatly arranged in rows, were still swaddled in morning mist. The two of us stood on deck. Mani made me promise not to wake up Linka, and I thought: at long last we are saying good-bye! We waited for a launch that brought out some German Templars, each of whom the captain welcomed aboard in Austrian. Mani stood near him in his large overcoat, which made his dark silhouette look bigger and stronger, as if there were a second Mani inside it, embracing the first. The last of the Templars came aboard, and the deckhands waited for Mani to lower himself into the launch before raising anchor. All at once, though, he said to me: "You know, I have an urge to see Beirut. Of course, I haven't been there for twenty-five years, but you still won't find a better guide to it than me." And that was when I felt my heart sink, Papa, because I realized that we were fated to have him follow us all the way to Europe—to Cracow—to Hasula—to Jelleny-Szad—to this corner—to the sofa by the fire— right into our beds. Are you listening? Give me some sign!

—In Beirut—it was noon now—all the passengers were invited to go ashore and enjoy the city until evening, when we would sail for Stamboul. Mani—his overcoat draped over one arm; the stubble of a beard on his cheeks; his hair looking grayer than ever—seemed—for the first time—to grow confused; his movements had become almost unrecognizably slow, as if he now were running on another—an infinite—time. We literally had to pull him ashore, where we stood by the wharves amid a crowd of passengers, many of them from other ships, looking for a cab. The hansoms kept trotting splendidly by, one after another, festooned with bright frills and bells; Mani, however, let all of them pass until at last he hailed one that was drawn by a coal-black horse. "Why, here is our lost steed," he said with a smile, putting Linka and me in the back seat, which was spread with a colorful Persian rug, and seating himself up front by the coachman, his broad back facing us like a threat, although one that was aimed at himself. For the first time since leaving Katowice and taking the night train to Prague, I felt Linka clinging to me for protection. She had turned back into a girl—the jackknife, Father, that had sprung all its blades was now neatly folded again. Are you listening?

—We began driving through the city, which Mani was less interested in showing to us than in sating his memories with. It was for him a nostalgic reunion with places he had not seen for a quarter of a century; he discussed them intensely with the driver, who stopped from time to time to point something out to him or to dismount and pilot him into some little street or entranceway, leaving the two of us forlornly sitting in the hansom, parked in the middle of some marketplace or courtyard and surrounded by a lively motley of Arabs. We could not have known that our Mani had finished writing his drama—had added the stage directions—had cast the lead—had even picked his audience—and was now only looking for a place to set up his theater and put on the play. You are not listening to me! Will you listen?!

—Because when the carriage wheels rattled at last over the rails of the railway line, he stopped the driver and got out wonderingly. You see, there had been no trains in Beirut when he had left it. At once he ordered the coachman to take us to the train station, as if it were there that the dispute between us would be settled. It was late after-

noon now, and the first frail wisps of dusk streaked the sweet, strong
Mediterranean light. When we reached the station, we saw that it
was not far from the sea, in which our Austrian steamship was
lolling regally. An unfamiliar flag was being run up on it. We entered the station house, which was as small as the one in Jerusalem
but dirtier; in the space in front of the tracks some white-gowned
Mohammedan pilgrims were hurrying to board a narrow-gauge train
that was only a few cars long and still had no locomotive. There was
no urgency, however; on the contrary, there was a sense of calm,
which was heightened by the slow pacing of two Turkish sentries
along the tracks. They had deep scabbards strapped to their sides
and were lazily chewing on their mustaches while looking scornfully
at the passengers. I could feel all eyes rest on us as soon as we
stepped inside. A railway official came over to see what we wanted
and Mani saluted him. *"Yahud,"* I heard whispers around us,
"yahud." Yes, we were *yahud,* Mani assured the crowd at once. You
could see that the place appealed to him, and when he heard that
the train outside was bound for Damascus, he ran his glance over
the soft clay hills as though someone important or beloved were
waiting for him there and began to walk along the tracks in the wake
of the Turkish soldiers. Only now, though, do I understand that—in
the yellow squall of time closing in on us—the one passion left him
was to set up the theater he had been traveling with for so long and
to augment the audience brought by him from Palestine with the
Turkish soldiers—the returning pilgrims—even the railway official,
who had begun following him, determined to ferret out the true
motives—were they really intending to take the train?—of the European tourists. But Mani was not about to tip his hand. "Well, well,"
he said, coming back up the rails with a look of perfect composure,
"so there is a railway line here now too. Who knows, perhaps in a
few years you will be able to take a train straight from Jerusalem to
that Oświęcim of yours without having to brave the sea!" All of a
sudden he stepped up to Linka and hugged her fiercely, then took
her hand and kissed it front and back—you might have thought that
the lust of that Polish *pan* from Basel had gotten into him. "Will you
not leave her with me?" he asked me a last time, an odd, un-
recognizable look on his face. I laughed nervously and said, "She is
not mine." "So you say," he accused me bitterly, "and yet you are

taking her from me. Let us say good-bye, then. The coachman will take you to your ship and I will take the train to Damascus. I never have been there. It is said to be a beautiful city." And with that he asked us for money. He—who had never even spoken to us about money before. It was not clear how much he wanted, or if he was referring to a loan or a gift, and I began to hem and haw . . . are you listening?

—I began to hem and haw. I promised to send him a contribution for his clinic as soon as we got home—I promised to take the matter up with you too, Father—but he would not take that for an answer. With a hopeless look he insisted that he needed some cash at once, for his trip to Damascus. He knew we had lots of money. Linka, who could only guess what all this was about, because we had spoken nothing but Hebrew since the morning, squeezed my arm hard, and out of my pockets I began to produce Turkish bishliks—Austrian thalers—spare change from Italy—all of which he took before heading with it to the ticket office. He was gloomy when he rejoined us. "We shall never meet again," he proclaimed, "and you are to blame. Do you not see that you are to blame?" I was still shaking my head when it flashed through my mind that I had made a terrible mistake—that the curtain had already risen—that before me no longer stood a doctor from Jerusalem but an actor forced to recite a script that he could not revise—one drummed into him immemorial ages ago—which—although he was the director and the theater owner too—he was not at liberty to leave unperformed and must stage to the bitter end. His expression had changed. He was staring at us with a thunderstruck, faraway look, through the telescope of his own contempt . . . and then he turned, slung the overcoat over his shoulders, and began to walk down the platform, alongside the crowded cars of Mohammedan pilgrims whose cigarette smoke spiraled out the windows like a first intimation of the locomotive that now could be heard whistling in the distance. Linka was overcome with horror. "Stop him!" she screamed in Yiddish. "Let's take him with us!" "But how?" I asked. "He is going to Damascus and we must return to the ship." She would not listen to me, though. She began to pull me after her, as if she wished us to board the train for Damascus too, just as we were. Mani had reached the last car by now. He let his overcoat drop to the platform—the thought struck me that he did not want to bloody it—and then—with a gentle movement—lowered himself onto the tracks. A Turkish soldier started to shout at him. But Mani just turned away his face, which—in the reddish light that drifted in from the sea—looked hard and vanquished, and resumed walking along the tracks, wagging a reproving finger at the black locomotive that appeared around the bend as if it were a child home late from school. The locomotive tore him apart instantly, like a sword stroke. Father, aren't you listening?

—What?

—Yes. I hung on with all my might to Linka, who began running toward him along with the Mohammedans jumping out of the cars —the news had reached every one of them in no time. As if I didn't know the common people's lust to stare at the dead and the maimed! The two Turkish soldiers began pushing the crowd back—striking out at it—striking at Linka—letting no one through but me —who was running with his overcoat, screaming and begging to cover the two halves of him before she could get to them . . . Papa dear—Papa—ah, look!—it is dawn already . . . I have been talking nonstop . . . Papa?

—You fell asleep, old man. Look at me . . . Papa, Papa, answer me . . . don't scare me . . . what is the matter?

—What is the matter? What did I say? Why are you crying?

—But I don't understand. Dearest Papa! You are crying. Why?

—But for whom?

—For him? *Him?* How can you? You . . . what are . . . oh, Papa . . .

—To blame? How? I told you we were just a pretext . . .

—How stayed with him? What are you talking about?

—By myself?

—Summoned you? From where? To where? You do not know what you are talking about . . .

—The master of what?

—But it *was* his own self. The demon inside him. You will drive me out of my senses . . . *stayed with him?* I like that, ha ha . . .

—What kind of cynicism?

—Nihilism? No, I have said quite enough . . . But what are you crying for? For whom? Can't you see that Mama is very ill? You are blind . . . she is going to die . . . if you must cry, cry for those you should cry for . . .

Although *EFRAYIM SHAPIRO* left his parents' estate as he promised to, it took him a year because of the sudden deterioration in the health of his mother, who died a month after her children's return from Palestine. It was not until the late autumn of 1900 that Efrayim moved to Cracow, where he took a job as a pediatric physician in a hospital. Linka, who could not bear the loneliness of life on the estate, followed him there and found work as a volunteer nurse in the same hospital. Before long she fell in love with a Catholic doctor and—after a bitter quarrel with her father and brother, who were opposed to the match—became his wife. She converted to Catholicism, moved with her husband to Warsaw, and had a son and a daughter there.

The dramatic estrangement was exceedingly painful, and soon the family was reconciled. Indeed, since Efrayim Shapiro remained a bachelor, he grew greatly attached to his niece and nephew, whom he visited often in Warsaw and saw during summer vacations on his father's estate, to which Linka usually came without her husband.

After the death of Sholom Shapiro in 1918, Linka sold her share of the estate to local farmers, while Efrayim returned to Jelleny-Szad and settled on his half of the land, which was run by a steward. Although his income from it was not as great as his father's had been, it was still a respectable amount, enough for him to cut down on his medical practice and limit it to occasional house calls in Oświęcim. In effect, he led a leisurely life of early retirement, the happiest moments of which were the visits of his beloved sister and her children—who, despite their having been baptized, took a lively interest in their mother and uncle's Jewishness.

With the outbreak of World War II and the German blitzkrieg that overran Poland, Efrayim Shapiro, who was sixty-nine at the time, went to Warsaw to be with his sister. It did not take him long to realize, however, that her home was not a safe hiding place for him and that she, her children, and her grandchildren were in no less danger than he was. Soon he returned to his estate, where—with the help of some loyal servants—he constructed the perfect hide-away and "disappeared." He remained there from 1939 to 1943, within sight of the nearby concentration camp, whose increasingly technologically advanced features the old doctor had more than an inkling of. When news reached him after the final liquidation of the Warsaw Ghetto that his niece had been sent to Auschwitz, he became so distraught that he gave himself up to the Germans for no good reason, thereby spelling the doom of his servants as well. He never reached the camp itself, however. Collapsing at the entrance to it, he was shot and killed on the spot at the age of seventy-three.

SHOLOM SHAPIRO   did not have an easy time of it after his wife's death. Having learned to live with the fact of her poor health, he had never dreamed that she would die so quickly. After his son and daughter left Jelleny-Szad, he tried to cope with his loneliness by intensifying his Zionist activity. He did not attend the Fourth Zionist Congress in London because it was held during the year of mourning for his wife, but he was present at the Fifth Congress, which took place in Basel again, and in 1909 he visited Palestine with a group organized by him from the Zionist Club in Cracow. It was a highly successful tour that strengthened the Zionist convictions of its members. While in Jerusalem, Sholom Shapiro went off one day to look for the Manis, but he did not find any of them. Although he was able to locate the clinic in Kerem Avraham, by then converted into a cheap tourists' hostel, and to identify it by the faded remains of some mirrors in one of its ground-floor rooms, none of the Mani family lived there anymore. Young Yosef Mani, he was told, had departed two years previously to study in Turkey, had stopped on his way in Beirut, and had vanished there. His sister had married a Moroccan Jew and gone with her mother to live with him in Marseilles. The neighbors who told Shapiro all this remembered well the brother and sister from Poland who had been in Jerusalem in 1899 with catastrophic results for their beloved doctor.

Despite his disappointment at being unable to locate the Manis and offer them financial compensation, Sholom Shapiro was highly satisfied with his trip to Palestine. Although no longer a young man, he formed in the course of it a romantic attachment to a young lady from Cracow, a member of the tour group, which continued after his return to Jelleny-Szad.

Like Efrayim, Sholom was greatly attached to his "Christian" grandchildren. Since his daughter's home in Warsaw was not ko-sher, he did not often visit them there, but each year he waited impatiently for their summer excursion to the countryside, during which he taught them some Hebrew and Judaism. He died after a brief illness in 1918, at the age of seventy, having lived long enough to rejoice at the news of the Balfour Declaration.

FIFTH CONVERSATION

An inn in Athens, on the corner of

Dioskoron and Lapolignoto Streets

Tuesday afternoon, December 12, 1848

THE

Conversation

PARTNERS

AVRAHAM MANI forty-nine years old, born in 1799 in Salonika, then part of Turkey, to his father Yosef Mani.

Avraham's grandfather, Eliyahu Mani, was a supplier of fodder to the horses of the Turkish Janissaries and followed behind the Turkish army with five large wagons that housed his large family, which included two wives and two young rabbis who tutored his sons. A shrewd merchant, he sensed immediately upon hearing of the outbreak of the French Revolution that Europe was in for a period of upheavals in which his services as a cavalry supplier would be in great demand. With this in mind, he began to move his activities westward. In 1793, as news reached him of the execution of Louis XVI, Eliyahu Mani crossed the Bosporus and proceeded as far as Salonika, where he found a flourishing Jewish community. And indeed, his gamble paid off and the political and military instability of the times proved a boon for his business. He was able to marry off his children to wealthy and prominent families, and these ties in turn enabled him to expand his affairs even more.

Eliyahu Mani dearly loved his eldest grandson Avraham, who was born at the very end of the eighteenth century. He did not, however, have many years of pleasure from the boy, because soon after the Treaty of Tilsit in 1807, he himself passed away. His concern was taken over by his son Yosef, who was born in 1776 in the Persian town of Ushniyya near Lake Shahi, then part of the Ottoman Empire too. Despite the many reversals suffered by the empire during the first decade of the nineteenth century, Yosef ran the business enterprisingly and did especially well during Napoleon's campaigns in Eastern Europe. At the same time, he did not neglect his children's education and sent his eldest son Avraham to study in Constantinople with one of the most profound and original rabbinical minds of the times, Shabbetai Hananiah Haddaya. Avraham Mani developed a great liking for this rabbi, who was wifeless and childless despite his over fifty years. Rabbi Haddaya, for his part, was fond of Avraham and decided to sponsor him for rabbinical ordination even though he was not a particularly keen student.

In 1815, however, Yosef Mani's business suddenly collapsed in the wake of both the Congress of Vienna peace agreements and the first signs of Greek war of independence against the Turks, which endangered transport and commercial shipments. In 1819 his son Avraham was summoned back to Salonika to help his father, who had lost everything and was reduced to eking out a living from a small spice shop in the port. Before long the brokenhearted man died, leaving the shop in Avraham's possession.

His forced separation from his rabbi weighed on Avraham greatly. Even though the war with the Greeks made travel perilous, whenever he was able to free himself of his business obligations he would take a week or two off and cross the Bosporus to visit Rabbi Haddaya. Although Avraham never received his ordination, the rabbi presented him with a certificate authorizing him to serve on a nonpaying basis as the spiritual leader of a small synagogue in the port that was frequented mainly by Jewish stevedores and sailors.

Despite his mother's urging him to marry, Avraham did not take a wife until 1825, when he wed the daughter of a petty merchant named Alfasi. The couple had a son and daughter: Yosef, born in 1826, and Tamar, born in 1829. In 1832 Avraham Mani's wife died of an unknown illness that was apparently transmitted by a sailor whom the Manis had put up in their home.

As Avraham's business began to prosper, he was able to travel to Constantinople more often. However, he did not always find his old teacher there, because Rabbi Haddaya, who had traveled widely as a

young man, was again smitten by wanderlust and was often away on
some journey. Generally, his trips took him south and east, and he
once even spent a few months in Jerusalem. There he met a woman
who several months later came to Salonika and became, to everyone's surprise, the wife of his old age.

After his son Yosef's bar-mitzvah, which took place in 1839,
Avraham, who was still a widower with two children, decided to
bring the boy to Rabbi Haddaya's school in Constantinople just as
his father had brought him. In doing so, he wished both to obtain
vicariously the ordination denied to himself and to strengthen his
ties with his old rabbi, for whom his admiration had only grown
with the years. Before setting out with Yosef, he even taught himself
a few words of French, the mother tongue of the rabbi's wife, in
order to help create a bond with her.

Rabbi Haddaya's wife, Flora Molkho, took a great liking to Yosef,
a vivacious and imaginative youngster who was more intellectually
gifted than his father. Having no children of her own, she treated
him as her own son and made him her closest companion, since her
husband was often away on his travels to the various Jewish communities that invited him to arbitrate legal disputes too knotty for others to unravel.

And so, even though young Yosef did not study with Rabbi Haddaya himself but rather in a school where his education was so laxly
supervised that he spent much of the time roaming the streets of
Constantinople, all were in favor of his remaining at the rabbi's
house: his father because of the connection this gave him with his
revered teacher; the rabbi's wife because the boy helped occupy her
solitude; and the rabbi himself because he regarded the youth
highly, even if the reason for this was none too clear to him.

Early in 1844 the news reached Doña Flora that her younger
sister's daughter, Tamara Valero, whom she had not seen since
Tamara was little, was planning to travel to Beirut with her stepmother Veducha in order to attend the wedding of Veducha's
brother, Tamara's step-uncle Meir Halfon. Doña Flora asked and
received her husband's permission to travel to Beirut and meet her
niece there—and since he himself was unable to accompany her, it
was decided that Yosef Mani, who was by now already a young man,
should go with her. Avraham Mani raised no objections, and Yosef

and Doña Flora sailed to Beirut. They remained there longer than expected and returned with the announcement that—subject of course to the consent of the two fathers and Rabbi Haddaya—Yosef and Tamara were betrothed.

And indeed, when Tamara returned to Jerusalem, her father gave his approval. But although it was agreed that she would come to Constantinople for the wedding, which was to be presided over by her renowned uncle, the revered Rabbi Haddaya, she failed to arrive —and in the end, unable to restrain himself, Yosef set out by himself for Jerusalem in the winter of 1846 with the intention of bringing his bride back with him. Instead, however, as the families in Constantinople and Salonika later found out, the two were married in a modest ceremony in Jerusalem, where Yosef Mani found work in the British consulate that had opened there in 1838.

Avraham Mani and Flora Haddaya were both greatly disappointed, since they had looked forward to a grand wedding in the rabbi's home in Constantinople and to the young couple's being close to them. Apparently, however, young Mani felt sufficiently drawn to Jerusalem to wish to remain there. In any event, since the mails between Jerusalem and Constantinople were highly irregular and a long while went by without any word from the newlyweds, Avraham Mani decided to travel to Jerusalem in the hope of persuading them to settle in Salonika, or at least, in Constantinople.

Avraham entrusted his shop to his son-in-law, took with him several bags of his favorite rare spices in the hope of finding a market for them in Jerusalem, and sailed for Palestine, arriving there in the late summer of 1847. Although he had expected to be back within a few months, he remained there for over a year, during which nearly all contact with him was lost. Meanwhile, a mysterious rumor that reached Constantinople in December 1847 told of Yosef Mani's being killed in a brawl. And indeed, in February 1848, a rabbi from Jerusalem who arrived in Constantinople on a fund-raising mission confirmed this story, to which he added that Avraham Mani had remained in Jerusalem with his son's wife Tamara in order to be present at the birth of the child she was expecting.

Throughout the first half of 1848, the elderly Rabbi Haddaya and his wife Flora were greatly upset at being out of touch with Jerusalem, especially since they did not even know when the birth was supposed to take place. The infrequent greetings or bits of news that arrived from Avraham Mani were vaguely worded and confused. And then, unexpectedly, on the first night of Hanukkah, Avraham Mani arrived at the inn in Athens where Rabbi Haddaya had been lying ill for several weeks.

FLORA MOLKHO-HADDAYA was born in Jerusalem in 1800 to her father Ya'akov Molkho, who had moved there several years previously from Egypt. In 1819 her younger and only sister married a man named Refa'el Valero, and soon after a son was born to them. Flora Molkho herself, however, remained unmarried, for there was a dearth of eligible young men in Jerusalem and her attachment to her sister and her little nephew made her spurn all suggestions to travel to her father's family in Egypt, or to her mother's family in Salonika, in the hope of finding a match. When Rabbi Shabbetai Haddaya visited Jerusalem in 1827, he stayed with the Valeros and met Flora Molkho, whose refusal to leave the city in search of a husband intrigued him. Indeed, Flora's adamance was now greater than ever, because her sister, having gone through two difficult miscarriages after the birth of her son, was well into another pregnancy.

Soon, however, all this changed, because shortly after Rabbi Haddaya's departure a devastating cholera epidemic broke out in Jerusalem that took the life of Flora's beloved nephew. Her sister, who meanwhile had given birth to a daughter, sank into a depression that led to her death in 1829. Flora Molkho, fearing that her widowed brother-in-law Refa'el Valero would feel obligated to propose marriage to her, hastened to leave Jerusalem for her mother's family in Salonika. Rabbi Haddaya followed her arrival there with interest and even sought, in 1833, to arrange a match between her and his protégé Avraham Mani, whose wife had recently died. Avraham Mani was keen on the idea, but Flora, although already a woman of thirty-three, refused. Her unmarried state troubled Rabbi Haddaya so greatly that he tried proposing other husbands for her, every one of whom she turned down, until he offered in his despair to marry her himself. Despite being forty years younger than he was, she did not reject his offer. The two were wed within a year and in 1835 Flora Molkho took up residence in Constantinople.

Although the rabbi and his wife had no children and he was away
on his travels for weeks on end, the two appeared to get along well.
As for Avraham Mani, he quickly recovered from his hurt at being
spurned by Flora in favor of his elderly teacher, resumed his ties
with the rabbi more intensely than ever, and in 1838 brought him
his son Yosef to be his pupil. The rabbi's wife received the youngster with open arms and—quite taken by his charms, his keen intelligence, and his many interests—chose to have him keep her company. Whenever Rabbi Haddaya went away, he asked his wife to
take young Yosef into their home because the latter was an independent and adventurous boy who took advantage of the rabbi's absence to enjoy the freedom of the city and needed to have an eye
kept on him. And indeed, Flora Molkho Haddaya watched Yosef
closely. He helped her around the house and sometimes, when the
rabbi was gone, even slept beside her in his bed.

In 1844 Doña Flora was informed that her niece Tamara was
planning to travel to Beirut with her stepmother Veducha for a
family wedding. At once she had the inspiration of arranging a
match between Tamara and Yosef in order to formally link her
young favorite with her family. She received permission for Yosef to
escort her to Beirut from both the rabbi and Avraham Mani, who
was thrilled by the prospect of a marriage bond with his revered
master. Although Tamara, for some reason, seemed doubtful about
the match, the firm inducements of Doña Flora, coupled with
Avraham Mani's encouragements from afar, resulted in a hasty betrothal in 1845. Tamara returned to Jerusalem to prepare for the
wedding, which was to be held in Constantinople. She did not,
however, set out, and the rather vague letters that arrived from
Jerusalem implied that the groom was expected to come there first
in order to meet the bride's family and make the acquaintance of her
native city. Finally, in 1846, Yosef Mani complied, and eventually
word reached Constantinople that he and Tamara had been married
in Jerusalem and that he was working for the British consul there.

In 1847, Flora Haddaya and Avraham Mani, doubly distressed by
the wedding's not having been held in Constantinople and by their
separation from the newlyweds, decided to travel to Jerusalem
themselves in order to visit their relatives there and persuade
Avraham and Tamara to move back to Constantinople. Since Rabbi

Haddaya, however, did not consent to his wife's making the trip alone with Avraham Mani, the latter had to go by himself. Once there, not only did he fail to bring his son and daughter-in-law back with him, he disappeared unaccountably for a long time himself until it became known that his son had been killed and that he was attending the birth of his daughter-in-law's child.

In 1848 Rabbi Haddaya, who was now over eighty, set out for Jerusalem and Avraham Mani, but on the way he suffered a stroke and lost the power of speech. He now had to be constantly cared for by his wife, who served as the link between him and an outside world that still looked to him for answers that it could no longer understand.

RABBI SHABBETAI HANANIAHA HADDAYA did not know the exact date of his birth. His rapid walk and young, energetic exterior often misled people as to his age. He himself did not take the question seriously, and since he had no family, there was no way of ascertaining the truth. In any event, he was in all likelihood born no later than 1766. His birth was known to have occurred aboard a ship that had set sail from the eastern Mediterranean, and it was jokingly said that he had been born straight from the sea, since both his parents died without reaching land from an outbreak of plague that swept through the vessel on its way from Syria to Marseilles. In France the little baby made the rounds of several charitable institutions until, inasmuch as it was circumcised, it was given for adoption to a Jewish family. Its foster parents were a childless old couple named Haddaya; according to one version, the infant was named Shabbetai for the false messiah Shabbetai Tsvi, who had lived in the previous century but whose remaining followers the Haddayas were connected with. The child did not remain with them for long, however. He was soon transferred to a Jewish orphanage, where he was raised and educated and given the additional name of Hananiah. Before long his intellectual capacities became apparent to his teachers, who arranged a special curriculum whereby he could advance in his studies.

Eventually, Shabbetai Hananiah was accepted into the talmudical academy of Rabbi Yosef Kardo, a descendant of a family of Marranos that had returned to Judaism in the early 1700s. So greatly did he excel in his studies that he was chosen headmaster after Rabbi Kardo's death, even though he was often away on his travels to various Jewish communities, which was something he had a passion for. He was thought highly of by his fellow French rabbis and in 1806 was even invited to Napoleon's famous convocation of Jewish leaders in the Tuilleries Palace in Paris, which met to debate the civil and national status of the Jewish people in the postrevolutionary era. His experience there, and in the discussions that took place in 1807 concerning the possible reconstitution of the Sanhedrin, was a deeply disturbing one for him. Unlike most of his colleagues, who basked in the honor accorded them and believed they were acting to ameliorate the Jewish condition, Rabbi Haddaya was seized by a strange pessimism. In 1808 he decided to leave the academy in Marseilles. After parting from his pupils, he sailed eastward to Sardinia and from there to southern Italy, from which he proceeded to Venice, where he resided for a considerable period. Subsequently, he moved on to Greece, wandered among its islands, reached as far as Crete, returned to Athens, and worked his way up along the Aegean coast until he arrived in Constantinople. Wherever he found himself, he offered his services as a preacher and a rabbinical judge. Although he kept up his legal erudition, theoretical studies did not greatly interest him and he preferred the active life of sermonizing and sitting on courts.

Not the least remarkable thing about Rabbi Haddaya was his bachelorhood, which seemed particularly inexplicable in light of his fondness for arranging matches and raising doweries for brides. Sometimes he even traveled great distances for the sole purpose of presiding at some wedding. And yet he himself declined to take a wife, a refusal that he justified by claiming that a childhood injury had left him unable to have children.

When Rabbi Haddaya first came to Salonika in 1812, he stayed at the home of Yosef Mani, Avraham Mani's father, and made a great impression on him and his family, especially by virtue of his observations about Napoleon, who was then in the midst of his Russian campaign. After spending several months in Salonika, the rabbi continued on to Constantinople, where he finally appeared to settle down. He ceased his wandering and opened a small school in the Haidar Pasha quarter along the Asiatic coast, and soon after

Avraham Mani arrived to study there. Although the boy was not a particularly good student, Rabbi Haddaya appreciated his good qualities, among which was a great capacity for loyalty.

Young Avraham Mani sought the closeness of the old rabbi and grew so dependent on him that Rabbi Shabbetai sometimes referred to him in private as "that little *pisgado.*" Nevertheless, he was sad to see the boy go when he had to return to Salonika after the failure of his father's business. Indeed, the emotion that he felt on that occasion quite surprised him. Soon after, his old wanderlust returned. Once again he began to travel all over the Ottoman Empire, particularly to Mesopotamia and Persia, although he also journeyed southward to Jerusalem, where he stayed at the home of Refa'el Valero and became acquainted with Refa'el's wife and his sister-in-law Flora, whose unmarried state was a cause of great wonderment to him.

Upon his return to Constantinople in the early 1830s, Rabbi Haddaya resumed his ties with ex-pupil Avraham Mani, who crossed the Bosporus from time to time to visit his former teacher. Rabbi Haddaya even tried to arrange a match between Avraham, whose wife died in 1832, and Flora Molkho, who had in the meantime moved from Jerusalem to Salonika after her sister's death. When Flora Molkho showed no interest in such a marriage, the rabbi invited her to Constantinople in the hope of changing her mind, and when this proved impossible, he suggested several other possibilities, all of which she rejected too. Finally, in a surprising and perhaps even despairing step, he proposed to her himself and was astonished when she accepted. The betrothal took place secretly in order to avoid hurting his dear disciple Avraham Mani; similarly, not wanting tongues to wag over his marriage to a woman forty years his junior, Rabbi Haddaya wed Flora in a ceremony conducted by himself in a remote town in Mesopotamia, for which he was barely able to round up the ten Jews needed for the occasion.

Despite the age difference between them, the couple's marriage worked out well. Rabbi Haddaya continued to travel widely, and his wife Flora was accustomed to being alone. When Avraham Mani sent him his son Yosef, the rabbi was pleased by the gesture of conciliation and took the boy in, even though he himself hardly taught anymore due to his frequent absences. Although Yosef proved to be a highly imaginative child who at times seemed out of touch with reality, he was able to charm whomever he met, and above all, the rabbi's wife, whose childlessness had left her increasingly isolated. Thus, he grew up in the Haddaya household, the excitable child of two elderly "parents."

Rabbi Haddaya did not play an active role in the betrothal of his wife's niece Tamara Valero to Avraham Mani in Beirut. For a while, he even seemed opposed to it. However, after the newlyweds settled in Jerusalem and Avraham Mani disappeared there too, and especially, after hearing of Yosef Mani's death from the rabbinical fundraiser Gavriel ben-Yehoshua, Rabbi Haddaya grew so distraught that his health was affected. He decided to set out for Jerusalem to find out what had happened, and since travel by land was unsafe, he resolved to sail from Salonika on a ship manned largely by Jews. In the late spring of 1848, more than thirty years after last having set foot in Europe, he crossed the Bosporus westward.

Rabbi Haddaya was received in Salonika with great pomp and ceremony and seen off at his ship by Rabbis Gaon, Arditi, and Luverani. Yet his own excitement must have been even greater than theirs, because the robust though slender old man had hardly been at sea for a day when he suffered a stroke, a thrombosis in the left hemisphere of his brain that caused him to lose the power of speech and all control over the right side of his body. Although able to understand everything said to him, he could no longer answer, and when he tried writing, the letters came out backward in an illegible scrawl. Since it was impossible to sail on in such circumstances, the captain changed course for the port of Piraeus, from which the paralyzed man was brought to a Jewish inn in Athens. There he lay, often smiling, nodding, and making sounds like "tu tu tu."

News of the revered rabbi's illness spread quickly and Jews gathered from near and far to help Doña Flora minister to him. In no time an entire support system sprang up that was most ably directed by her. The Greek governor of Athens stationed a permanent guard by the entrance to the inn, and Rabbi Haddaya, who sat covered by a silk blanket in a special wheelchair brought from Salonika, seemed almost to be enjoying his new situation, which spared him the need at last to express his opinions and left him free to listen to the Jews who came to see him while smiling at them and occasionally nodding or shaking his head. Nevertheless, his wife, who discerned a slow but gradual deterioration in his condition, did everything she could to avoid exciting him.

Thus, when the "vanished" Avraham Mani turned up unexpectedly one winter day at the inn in a state of great agitation, Doña Flora granted him permission to see his old rabbi "for a brief while and only for a single conversation."

Doña Flora's half of the conversation is missing.

—In truth, Doña Flora, for a brief while only, for one short conversation. I am compelled to, for the love of God! Please do not deny me that. Am I not, after all, besides a member of the family, also the eldest of his pupils?

—Yes. I will cry no more.

—There will be no raising of my voice or upsetting him.

—I will be most gentle.

—With much anxious supplication. Who of us does not pray for God's grace? "Though a sharpened sword lie athwart a man's throat, he must not . . ." But does the rabbi know I am here? Has he retained his active intelligence? The Jews outside say, "Rabbi Shabbetai has left his own self; he now ascends from dream to dream."

—The Lord be praised.

—The Lord be praised, madame.

—No, no more tears, Doña Flora. I swear to you by my departed son to choke back every one of them. As if I had any left! Since morning I have been saying psalms with them all—crying, saying psalms, and crying again.

—Yes, I promise not to cry in his presence. *Hallas,* as the Ishmaelites say . . .

—Directly from the ship. Before the first sail was folded I was already in a carriage speeding from Piraeus to Athens.

—No, madame. The bitter news reached us at sea, halfway through the voyage. We were boarded by a pirate boat out of a small port in the devil's own island of Crete, and after we were relieved of all our valuables, one of the pirates, who knew me from my shop in Salonika, said to me, "Your rabbi's lute has popped a string."

—Hush . . . hush . . . of course . . . but how shall I speak to him?

—With all simplicity? Ah . . . Your Grace . . . señor . . . my master . . . Rabbi Haddaya . . .

—More softly?

—But how will he hear me when he seems so lost in himself? His very soul is folded inward . . .

—My master, *maestro y señor mío* . . ." I create the fruit of the lips; Peace, peace to him that is far off and to him that is near, saith the Lord; and I will heal him."

—Praise be to God.

—Does he thus sign his awareness? Praise be to God . . .

—If he does not know me, madame, whom should he know? Ah! . . .

—In truth, a wondrous smile.

—Most nonpareil.

—Most true, Doña Flora. So winsome a smile never graced his lips in all these years—and six-and-thirty years, Doña Flora, have I been at his side, long, long before you were. 'Twas ages ago that first I was brought to him! "Yea, I was a lad and I have grown old . . ."

—Excessively burdened. All his life.

—Of course . . . as you say . . . señor, does Your Grace remember me? Truly, it is written, "All my life have I lived among sages and found no better course for a body than silence."

—Ah!

—Your Grace has consumed himself with his endless wandering and preaching, and now Your Grace deserves to rest. Only "bless me, even me too, my father"!

—Ah . . . forgive me . . . forgive me, Doña Flora . . . my feelings ran away with me . . .

—I did not know . . . I was not warned . . . I only wished to kiss his hand and ask his blessing as is my wont . . .

—I did not know . . . I was not warned . . . oh, madame . . .

—Ah! Have I hurt him? May I hope to die . . .

—I did not know . . . forgive me, Doña Flora, I was not warned . . .

—In truth, the hand seems stricken and withered.

—The length of his body? Master of the Universe . . . the entire length?

—How fearful and wondrous are the ways of the Lord! And I in my simplicity had thought it was widthwise—his lower half stilled as over against his upper . . . but how came it to pass?

—And in a twinkling shall come his salvation, madame. Believe me, in a twinkling! Let the rabbi be silent for a spell, let him smile—in the end we shall rouse him. We shall not let Your Grace leave us, shall we, Your Grace? We shall not!

—No, God forbid; in all quietude. I already have, Doña Flora, a notion for reviving the power of speech in him. I thought of it while still at sea . . .

—For example, I thought we might put before him a likeness of that French Emperor, the first Napoleon, to pique the rabbi's soul—for forty years ago Rabbi Shabbetai was summoned to him in Paris, he and some other sages, and since then he often spoke of him. I can remember sitting at his feet in our house in Salonika and listening all night as he dwelled on the ways of that Emperor, who was then sinking deeper and deeper into the snows of Russia . . .

—Of course not. Perish the thought . . . I did not mean this minute . . .

—Slowly but surely . . . we will bide our time . . . but did I truly hurt him, Doña Flora? He does appear to be looking at me with great wonder. Why, he cannot even cry out!

—How dreadful is the hand of the Lord! In a thrice it divides a man in two and creates an abyss between the two sides of him. But heaven forbid, señor, that Your Grace should feel diminished or divided, God save us! Your Grace should know that for us, his loving and reverent disciples, he will always be one and the same, his vegetative and animative souls joined together and worthy of our redoubled love. May I, Doña Flora, with your permission, and with the utmost care, take his saintly hand in my own . . . surely I may, may I not?

—And may I give it a little squeeze? Just a small one?

—And a kiss? May I?

—Bless me, even me too, my father and teacher! Bless your oldest pupil . . . bless a wretched, a much suffering man . . .

—No, Doña Flora . . . God forbid . . . I will not cry . . . no more tears . . . slowly but surely . . .

—No, madame . . . 'tis nothing . . . God forbid . . . I am already over it . . .

—Slowly but surely . . .

—But how did I vanish? And did I truly?

—How can you say that? Surely you know, Doña Flora, that I was awaiting a birth.

—Indeed it did. The infant was delivered on the night after the Day of Atonement.

—A boy child, señores, a boy child born in Jerusalem—and you, madame, will be his grandmother. Your poor sister of blessed memory did not live to be one, and you must be one for her.

—Yes, I too, it would seem . . . that is . . . well, yes . . . I too, with the help of God . . .

—Both mother and infant are well. I bring you greetings from them all: a greeting of peace from Jerusalem—from Refa'el Valero—from the rabbis of the city—from its streets and houses—from the Street of the Armenians and the Hurva Synagogue—from the cisterns and the marketplaces—even from your room, Doña Flora, your little alcove by the arched window—yes, even from your bed, the bed of your maidenhood, in which you slept so many a night. Wrapped in your quilt, I thought of your youth and of mine . . .

—In your very bed . . . and with great pleasure. Your brother-in-law Refa'el assigned the bed of your parents, may they rest in peace, to our young couple, and that was where the unfortunates slept, while I was put up in the little room nearby, between those two most wondrous looking-glasses that you hung on the walls, which played the very devil with my mind. It is not to be marveled at, Doña Flora, that you never looked for a husband in Jerusalem, because in such a room one feels sure that there is already someone with one, hee hee hee . . .

—I named him Moshe Hayyim in the hope of a fresh start.

—No, he was not named after his father. It is enough that I am accursedly boxed in by the same name before and after me. I am weary of the names of dead patriarchs commemorating downfalls and defeats; I had my fill of Genesis and went on to Exodus, from which I took the name of Moses in all simplicity. May his great merit

stand us in good stead . . . for there was a miracle here . . . before death could drain away the vital fluids, life saved a few precious
last drops . . . look, Doña, how wonderfully he smiles again. Does
he approve of the name Moshe?

—He is nodding. He understands! God be praised. I promise
you, Doña Flora, that the rabbi's salvation is nigh and that in a
twinkling of the eye he will preach again . . . 'tis but an interval . . .

—With   moderation . . . of   course . . . without   compulsion . . .

—With much travail, Doña Flora, although through clenched
teeth . . .

—Her father Refa'el so feared the birth that he ran off to the
synagogue to say psalms, leaving me standing there for ten hours in
my robe and shoes like one of the Sultan's honor guard, ministering
with hot water and compresses.

—No, madame. It was in your old bed, which had become my
bed and now became Tamara's. You may rejoice in the thought that
the infant was born in your bed.

—At the very last minute Tamara was stricken with fear and
refused to give birth in her bridal bed that had belonged to her
parents. She beseeched the help of heaven, and so we moved her to
the old bed of her beloved aunt, which conducted the efflux of her
uncle's great merit . . . and in truth, it was only his merit—does
Your Grace hear me?—that stood by us in that difficult birth.

—Ten hours, one labor pain after another . . .

—There were two midwives. One the wife of Zurnaga, and the
other a nunlike Englishwoman called Miss Stewart, a lady as tall and
thin as a plank, but most proficient. She was sent by the British
consul in Jerusalem, who has not yet ceased mourning our Yosef.

—'Twas at night, Doña Flora, before the first cockcrow, that we
heard the long-awaited cry. And if I may say so without fear of
misunderstanding, the two of us, the mother and I, so longed for
you, madame, at that moment that our very souls were faint with
desire for you in that great solitude . . .

—No, I will not cry . . .

—No, there will be no more tears . . . señor . . . *maestro mío*

. . . he is listening . . . I feel the lump of his silence in my throat . . .

—Your niece kept calling your name while racked by her pains. She was pining for you—she gave birth for you, madame—and in the times between one labor pain and the next, while I sat in the next room and watched her face dissolve toward me in the small mirror, I could not help but imagine you as a young woman in Jerusalem, lying in your bed in the year of Creation 5848 or '49 and giving birth too. We were too much surrounded by the shades of the dead, Doña Flora . . . we needed to think of the living to give us strength . . .

—Most truly.

—Again you say I "vanished." But where did I vanish to?

—In Jerusalem, only in Jerusalem. I walked back and forth between those stony walls with their four gates, thinking, "It was here that little madame toddled about forty years ago, among the stones and the churches, from the Jaffa Gate to the Lions' Gate, skipping over the piles of rubbish in the fields between the mosques, glared on by the red sun and in the shadow of sickness and plague."

—In truth, Doña Flora. I took upon myself all your longing for Jerusalem, and all the memories of His Grace too, my master and teacher, who honored our sacred city with a visit in the year 5587. There are men there who still recall sheltering in his presence. Who knows but that that poor city throbs on in his heart if not in his mind. Ah! . . .

—Is he listening?

—The Lord be praised.

—But how was I silent? And again, Doña Flora: why was the silent one me? All last winter I prayed for some word from you. The lad was already dead and buried, and our own lives were as dark as the grave, because at the time, madame, his seed alone knew that it had been sown in time. And since I knew that the news would travel via Beirut to Constantinople on the dusty black robe of that itinerant almsman, Rabbi Gavriel ben-Yehoshua. I hoped for a sign that it had reached you. I even entertained the thought that the two of you would hasten to Jerusalem with tidings of strength and good cheer, for I knew that the lad had been dear to you. You took him under

your wing . . . you indulged him and foresaw great things for him
. . . you lay him beside you, madame, in His Grace's big bed . . .

—No, there will be no tears . . .

—Perish the thought . . . God save us . . . I will not upset
him . . . I will speak as softly as I can . . .

—Not a whimper . . . God forbid . . .

—If there is a lump in my throat, I will swallow it at once.

—At once . . .

—Of my own free will . . . of course, Doña Flora . . . I do not
deny it . . .

—I would never pretend that the thought of bringing the boy to
you was not mine. He was a present that I made you to keep from
losing you, a wedding gift for your most surprising and wondrous
marriage that shone in heaven as resplendently as the saints . . .

—I was afraid that you would rebuff me once more, madame, as
you already had done . . . and so I hurried to bring the lad to you
as a whole-offering . . . just as my poor father did with me in his
day . . .

—To be sure. And now suddenly he was a young man . . . already a groom, with God's help . . . although that match made in
Beirut with your motherless niece from Jerusalem was entirely your
own doing, madame . . . fully your own conception . . .

—In truth, it had my blessing . . . of course it did . . . and
more than that . . . it had my love . . . what wouldn't I have
done not to lose you? I mean, not to lose His Grace, my only master
and teacher, who commands my loyalty "more than the love of
women" . . .

—He understands. He is listening and understands . . .

—No, I am not crying. No, madame, this time you are wrong. I
have not the tail-end of a tear left.

—Once more "vanished"? But even if I did, it was not for very
long. I was not, after all, the first to disappear, but the last. Before
me came your motherless fiancée, and after her, my only son Yosef.
Both were lost in Jerusalem and I went to look for them, not in
order to become lost myself but in order to bring them back, although in the end there was nothing to bring . . .

—The infant, Doña Flora? How could you think of it? Perish the
thought! For what purpose?

—Take him and his mother away from Jerusalem?

—But why? After all that went into giving Jerusalem a baby Moses, why take him away from there? And where to? Who would take responsibility for him?

—But how? You amaze me, madame. What would you do with an infant when you are in such perturbation?

—How? You already have an infant of your own, this holy and most venerable babe that needs to be fed and looked after, to be washed and changed and have its every thought guessed—why should you wish for another? Surely, you do not expect them to play together, hee hee . . .

—His Grace, hee hee . . .

—But look, Doña Flora, look, *mí amiga,* he is laughing without any sound . . . hee hee hee hee . . . he is listening . . . he understands everything . . . in a twinkling he will . . .

—Señor . . . my master and teacher . . . *caríssimo* Rabbi Shabbetai . . .

—I am not shouting . . . but look, *cara* doña, the rabbi is nodding his head . . . he is in high spirits . . . I know it . . . I feel it . . . I always knew how to make him merry. Why, back in the good old days, I would cross the Bosporus, go straight to his house, take a carving knife, wrap myself in a silk scarf, and dance the dance of the Janissaries, may they rot in hell . . .

—No, not one tear . . . there are none left . . .

—I am in full control.

—In truth, my dearest doña, I am in an agitated state. You are looking at a most distraught soul . . . do not judge me harshly . . . just see how you alarm me by speaking thus of the fatherless infant, whom you crave to have with you. As if it did not already have a faithful young mother at its side! And not only a mother, but a home, the home you yourself grew up in . . . and your brother-in-law Re'fael, who has little children of his own . . . and Jerusalem itself . . . why make light of Jerusalem, the city of your nativity, which is shaking off the dust of centuries now that Christendom has rediscovered it and given new hope to its Jews? Why make them pick up and leave all that? And for where? And how do it without a father? Because there is no one to take a father's place . . .

—No, no, madame. I myself will soon be gone. True, it is written,

"A man liveth will he, nill he," but still, yes, still, a man dieth sometimes when he willeth . . . You will yet hear of me, madame. "Rabbi Levitas of Yavneh used to say, 'The best hope of man is the maggot.' " Ah! Señor . . . let him be my judge . . . he will do me justice! Would he wish me to remove mother and child from Jerusalem?

—What say you?

—Ah! . . .

—Did he sign me?

—And what meant it?

—Ah! You see . . . thank you, señor! Did I not say? . . . did I not know? . . . was I not right? No one knows the rabbi's soul better than I do! I may not have studied much with him, for my poor head is a thick one—a pumpkinhead, that was what he called me—but I never stopped studying *him.* I know him better than you do, madame, and I say that with all due respect . . . because I have known him for ages . . . no, do not be cross with me, Doña Flora . . . when you frown like that and bite your lip, I am reminded of our faraway Tamara, our motherless, widowed young bride. I beseech you, Doña Flora, be good enough not to be angry, or else the tears will begin to flow again. Since losing my only son, I am quick to cry . . . grief comes easily to me . . . it takes but a word . . . the least breath is enough to shatter me . . .

—But . . .

—As long as I can be here, on this little footstool, sitting at his feet. "Better a tail to the lion than a head to the fox."

—She has recovered completely, Doña Flora. She bears herself well . . .

—Of course she is nursing, although not without some assistance. Her left teat went dry within a few days and left her without enough milk, and the consul made haste to send her an Armenian wet nurse who comes every evening with a supplement, for he heard say that the milk of the Armenians is the most fortified . . .

—In truth, he is a good angel, the consul. He has not withheld his kindness from us, and how could we have managed without him? We have been ever in his thoughts since that black and bitter day. He remains unconsoled for the loss of our Yosef, on whom he pinned great hopes. *Baby Moses* he calls the infant in English, and he has already issued him a writ of protectorship as if he were an English subject. Should he ever wish to leave Jerusalem for England, he may do so without emcumbrance . . .

—Little Moshe.

—In the Rabbi Yohanan ben-Zakkai Synagogue. Tamara dressed *baby Moses* in a handsome blue velvet jersey with a red *taquaiqua* on his head, and Rabbi Vidal Zurnaga said the blessings and performed the circumcision. The cantors sang, and we let the English consul hold and console the child for his pain, and Valero and his wife Veducha handed out candies and dough rings—here, I have brought you in this handkerchief a few dried chick-peas that I carried around with me for weeks so that you might bless them and eat them and feel that you were there . . . may it please you, madame . . . the consul and his wife blessed and ate them too . . .

—And here is one for him too, my master and teacher . . . a little pea . . . just for the blessing . . .

—No, he will not choke on it . . . 'tis a very little pea . . .

—Ah! He is eating . . . His Grace understands . . . he remembers how he used to bring me "blessings" from weddings, how he woke me from my sleep to teach me them . . . now I will say it for him! Blessed be Thou, O Lord our God, King of the Universe, Who createth all kinds of food.

—Amen.

—He cannot even say the amen for himself . . . ah, Master of the Universe, what a blow!

—No, I will cry no more. I have given my word.

—Of course, madame. God forbid that my tears should lead to his. But what can I do, Doña Flora, when I know that no matter how dry-eyed I stand before him, he—even as he is now—can read my soul! The great Rabbi Haddaya understands my sorrow. I have always, always been an open book to him . . . "like the clay in the hands of the potter" . . . ah, Your Grace . . .

—Slowly but surely . . . for I am not yet over my departure from your Jerusalem, madame, which is a most obdurate city—hard to swallow and hard to spew out. And hard too was my parting from the young bride, my son's widow and your most exquisite ward. But most impossible of all, Doña Flora, was parting from the infant Moshe, who is so sweet that he breaks every heart. If only madame could see him . . . if only His Grace, my teacher and master, could have seen *baby Moses* in his circumcision suit, his blue blouse and red *taquaiqua,* peacefully stretching his limbs without a sound, without a cry, sucking his thumb, meditating for hours on end . . . did I say hours? For whole days at a time, in a basket on the back of a horse . . .

—A most excellent consular horse, madame, which bore him and his mother from Jerusalem to Jaffa.

—I should bite my tongue!

—'Twere better left unsaid.

—In truth, on a horse. But not a hair of his was harmed, madame. He reached Jaffa in perfect condition.

—What winter? There was no sign even of autumn. I see you have forgotten your native land, Doña Flora, where "summer's end is harsher than summer" . . .

—Even if there was a touch of chill in the mountains, it did him no harm. He was wrapped in my robe, my fox fur that I brought from Salonika, and well padded in the basket, most comfortably and securely . . .

—Indeed, a tiny thing, but flawless. We miscalculated, she and I. Our parting was difficult, and so we longingly prolonged it until obstinacy led to folly . . .

—No, there was no guile in it; 'twas in all innocence. When we reached the Jaffa Gate and she saw me standing there, endlessly dejected, amid the camel and donkey train that was bound for Jaffa, she said to me, "Wait, it is not meet that you leave Jerusalem in sorrow, you will be loathe to return"—and she went to the consul's house and borrowed a horse to ride with me as far as Lifta. By the time she had tied the basket to the horse and wrapped the infant, the caravan had set out. We made haste to overtake it, and soon we were descending in the arroyo of Lifta—and the way, which at first seemed gloomy and desolate, quickly grew pleasant and attractive, because there were vineyards and olive groves, fig trees and apricots, on either side of it. When we reached the stone bridge of Colonia, there was a pleasant sweetness in the air. Jerusalem and its dejection were behind us, and perhaps we should have parted there—but then she insisted on continuing with me to Mount Castel. She thought she might catch a glimpse of the sea from there, for she remembered being taken as a child to a place from where she had glimpsed it. And so we began to climb the narrow path up that high hill. In the distance we spied my caravan, lithely snaking its way above us, and there was a great clarity of air, and the voice of the muezzin from the mosque at Nebi Samwil seemed to call to us, and we cried back to it. But we had no idea that the ascent would take so long or that the approach of darkness was so near, and by the time we reached the top of the hill there was not a ray of twilight left, so that whatever sea was on the horizon could not be seen but only thought. My caravan was slowly disappearing down the slope that led to Karyat-el-Anab, and all we could hear from afar were the hooves of the animals scuffing an occasional stone. What was I to do, Doña Flora? Say adieu there? I did not want to return with her to Jerusalem, because I knew that I then would have no choice but to become an Ashkenazi, and I had no wish to be one . . .

—Because I was down to my last centavo and all out of the spices I had brought from Salonika, and had I returned to Jerusalem as a pauper, I would have had to join the roster of Ashkenazim to qualify for the dole they give only to their own. And that, Your Grace, *señor y maestro mío,* I was not about to do—would His Grace have wanted me to Ashkenazify myself?

—He would not have, madame, even if he chooses to keep silent. I know him well enough to know he has his doubts about them.

—'Twas no effort, Doña Flora. We were riding now at a fair clip and were over the top of Mount Castel, I on my mule and she on her horse, with nothing but bare hills around us. Even Nebi Samwil was lost in the gloom, not to mention Jerusalem, which had been gobbled up by the mountains. I knew I had left the Holy City for good and would return to it only with the Messiah at the Resurrection, may it come soon! Meanwhile, we had to find lodgings for the night and a wet nurse for our Moshiko. And so we rode, no longer in any great hurry, down toward Karyat-el-Anab, and near Ein-Dilba we came across a shepherd and inquired about a wet nurse, and he gave a great shout into the silent night to a *compañero* of his in Abu-Ghosh, and a shout came back from afar. We headed on in its direction and soon found both midwife and caravan in a large stone house beneath the village of Saris.

—No, madame. Why should there have been rain? The earth was

still dry and the air was perfectly clement. It had a great clarity that lured one on—it made the vast countryside seem very near.

—A dream, madame? A dream?

—A sturdy, blond-haired village wet nurse, who gave *baby Moses* his dessert. We put him to sleep between us, protected from night crawlers, and in the morning, when I was sure that now she would bid me farewell and return with a caravan ascending to Jerusalem from Beit-Mahsir, she suddenly swore that she would do no such thing until she had seen the sea that I was about to embark on. And so we climbed to the top of the hill and saw the sea from afar, and I thought, "Now her mind has been set to rest," and I took my leave —yet it seemed that not only did the sight of the sea not assuage her, it increased her concern even more, because as I was hurrying down to join my caravan, madame, along a horribly winding and dizzying track in Wadi Ali, what did I hear like a far echo in that precipitous silence?

—A stone kicked loose by the thoroughbred hooves of the consular horse . . .

—In truth, *doña mía!*

—She was all by herself.

—With the infant, of course—with *baby Moses* in his basket, wrapped in my fox-fur robe and jouncing from bend to bend.

—Riding after me as boldly as you please.

—I took cover on a ledge of the hillside, among some large shrubs in that wild chaparral, from where I could watch her in the distance. She waited for the caravan to round a bend before carefully emerging from her concealment in the arroyo, small but perfectly erect on her black horse. Just then a ray of sunlight glinted off her head, illumining her hair a copper red.

—A saucy spirit, madame—but whom did she get it from? Must I venture a surmise?

—I too asked myself, madame, how far she was prepared to follow me. Well, toward evening, after many long hours of riding on that narrow trail without espying each other, we finally rode out of the verdant gloom into an open valley, which was the Plain of Sharon, and pressed on a ways, camels, donkeys, and mules, through fields of figs and olives, until we came to a high hedge of prickly pears that belonged to the village of Emmaus, where we

made camp and asked for water, basking in the setting sun. I turned
to Jerusalem to say the afternoon prayer—and there, from out of the
dark opening of the arroyo, from its very aperture, appeared the
consular horse, ridden by Obstinacy and bound for Folly.

—It went on like that all the way to Jaffa, all the way to the ship.

—We found a wet nurse in Emmaus too. And in Ramleh and
Azur also.

—No, Doña Flora. It was not lack of milk that made her go from
wet nurse to wet nurse, because I happened to know that the dried-
up left teat had begun to flow freely again since the Day of the
Rejoicing of the Law. The explanation I gave myself was that she
wished to give the infant a taste of all the ambrosias between Jerusalem and Jaffa so that he might retain some memory of his poor
father.

—How say you? Have you in truth, madame, forgotten him? Has
my only son already been forgotten?

—No, you see no tears, not a trace of them. I will ask His Grace.
Rabbi Shabbetai, has my master and teacher forgotten the only son I
offered up to him, my Yosef?

—Blessed be the Name of the Lord! Did he not sign clearly,
Doña Flora? He has not forgotten. Blessed be His Name! "Rabbi
Yannai says, 'We can account neither for the good fortune of the
wicked nor for the torments of the righteous.' "

—How making sport of you, madame? Why, had you not, Doña
Flora, insisted on bringing your motherless niece from Jerusalem for
a hasty betrothal, the three of us might still have the pleasure of
seeing him alive! Instead of huddling together in this shabby inn run
by Greek rebels against the Porte, we could have been sitting with
him on your big divan in Constantinople, by the large hearth facing
the Bosporus, enjoying the rosebushes in Abdul Mejid's royal gardens and pondering—but no more than that!—life in Paradise.

—What mean I? What mean you?

—In a word . . . in a word . . . with all due respect, you were
hasty, madame . . .

—No, Doña Flora, no, *rubissa*. How could I dare be angry with
you? And what would it avail me if I were? Tell me that! If it would
avail me, I would be angry at once. May I hope to die, madame, for
not having understood my son, my own flesh and blood! Accursed

am I for not realizing where he was leading us! I was an innocent, a *cabeza de calabaza;* too innocent for words . . .

—Because I did not know that behind every thought hides another thought.

—A thought born from the indulgence that you showed him in your home. Does His Grace know that when he was away on his travels, Doña Flora had my son sleep by her side, in His Grace's own bed?

—A boy! Of course . . . although not such a little one . . . and a most sensitive and astute one . . . I, in any case, never had the privilege of lying in His Grace's bed . . .

—Why not, madame? Who of us does not desire to lie with those greater and stronger than ourselves and be warmed by their superior heat? I, too, after all, was but a boy when sent to Rabbi Shabbetai . . . 'twas many ages ago . . . my father, may he rest in peace . . . after the defeat of Napoleon, the cannon would blast away over the Bosporus at night for fear of the Russ . . . and I was so greatly afraid that I ran to His Grace's bed from my little room at the end of the corridor. But I was too in awe of him to climb into it . . . Does His Grace remember me, a little lad standing there in my *blouson* and singing to him Tía Loja's *conacero:*

> All kiss the mezuzá,
> But I, I kiss your face,
> Istraiqua, apple of my eye . . . ?

He is smiling a bit, madame. He remembers the melody. He is smiling, God be praised! It would take but a word from Him to create him anew. His salvation will come in a twinkling . . . See, Your Grace, I am back! Your Grace's *pisgado* is back, and there yet will be song . . .

—Go? Where?

—No, madame, do not make me leave!

—No, do not send me away, madame. Nor are you able to . . .

—Most definitely not!

—I have a right . . . I am family . . . I have been for ages . . .

—I will not sing anymore.

—There will be no singing.

—To make a long story short . . . *betahsir,* as the Ishmaelites say in Jerusalem . . .

—That is just it, Doña Flora. Every thought has its pocket, and in every pocket is another thought. And from such a pocket our young lad took the thoughts discarded by the rabbi, those that fell out of his dreams at night and were left between his pillow and the wall, or lying under his bed . . . because why else would he have put his trust in so frightful a thought as that which led to his death?

—But all that already reached you with that irascible emissary, Rabbi Gavriel ben-Yehoshua . . .

—Once more?

—He had his throat cut, madame: like a tender lamb, or a black goat in the dead of night . . .

—Now it is you who shudder, madame—the tears are now yours . . .

—But what will it avail you?

—Why multiply your pain?

—If you must . . . Well, then, *rubissa,* he went out at night without a lantern, which is against the law in Jerusalem, with no light or badge, and in a black robe, to make matters worse . . .

—He turned into a lane in the Souk-el-Lammamin on his way to the Via Dolorosa. 'Twas the night of the nativity of the Christians' messiah, may his bones rot in hell. He was stopped by the watch— and rather than let himself be apprehended and brought to trial, he sought to flee. Nor did he run to the Stambouli Synagogue or the synagogue of Yohanan ben-Zakkai, where he could have hidden in the Holy Ark, but up the lane, through the Vidal house, and to the great mosque on the Haram-el-Sharif, perhaps because he wished to cast suspicion on the Muslims rather than on the Jews. And there, on the steps leading to the Dome of the Rock, he had his throat slit, madame. He was butchered like a black sheep.

—By our Ishmaelite cousins, those masters of the hidden knife.

—And thereabout did I wonder—did I grieve—did I sigh—did I question—did I beg to know—all during my stay with him, from the moment he pulled me to my feet in the sands of Jaffa, which I kissed with great love as soon as I was hurled ashore—yanked me to my feet and asked at once about you, madame—why were you not there —aghast to see me by myself . . .

—Because he was certain that I had you with me aboard ship, or that you had me with you.

—He knew nothing of Rabbi Shabbetai's last-minute ban on your coming, Doña Flora. He stood there on the shore, looking mournfully at the deckhands folding the sails, hoping that perhaps they would still produce you from the hold, hee hee hee . . .

—What was there to explain, Doña Flora? His Grace had explained nothing to me . . . did His Grace give any reason for it?

—He is looking at me, the poor man . . . he is thinking . . . "Heal him now, O God, I beseech Thee" . . .

—A kind of mother?

—Perhaps, madame. In truth, he never had enough of his own mother, who was in a hurry to depart to a better world. But were you only a mother to him, madame, or were you also a sister of sorts?

—I mean, a sort of elder sister, someone to share one's secrets with and tell one's strangest dreams to . . . There he stood, our Yosef, preoccupied with his own great grief and disappointment, yet at the same time, quite sure of himself and already gazing off into the distance, a high, black consular fez on his head, speaking to the villagers around him with much patience, as if they were his friends. I noticed that he could already chat blithely away in Ishmaelitic, and when I realized that my solo arrival was a far from joyous occasion for him, I sought in my despondency to cast myself reverently back down into the soft, sweet sands of Jaffa. But he seized my arm, and I could tell at once from how he did it that something had changed in him . . .

—From the firmness of it. He pulled me up out of the sand and commanded me, "That will do, *Papá,* the horses are waiting and we have a long way to go . . ."

—In truth, *mí amiga* in truth, Doña Flora: he had brought neither donkeys nor mules nor camels for us from Jerusalem, but horses, an entire horse for each of us—and most wondrous was the horse he had chosen for you, *rubissa* . . . I still can picture it, a most exquisite mare, with a brightly colored saddlecloth laid over her . . .

—Especially for you. He let no one mount her, and for three whole days she trotted by our side without a rider, all the way to Jerusalem, carrying only my bags of spices. Each time we looked at her, madame, we thought of you and of His Grace's prohibition. The more we sought to comprehend it, the more we simply sighed.

—With sorrow, but without resentment, for I still felt as if I were in a dream, as if I still were rocked by the motion of the waves. We left the noisy marketplace of Jaffa, which was bubbling with colors and smells, and made our way up streets of stairs that ended in orchards and fields of large flowers and fierce thorns . . . and suddenly, madame, there were only the two of us, father and son, with the broad land all around us and a harsh, inhuman sun overhead before which the very sky appeared to cringe.

—He pushed on that first day as far as the great khan of Kafr Azur, because he wished to catch the dawn caravan, in such a hurry was he to get back to his consul in Jerusalem. Does His Grace still remember the route?

—Truly, Doña Flora, truly I am confused! Indeed, the rabbi came from Damascus and entered the Promised Land by crossing the Jordan . . . and so it should be, by the front door and not by the rear one. Then my master and teacher never got to see Jaffa? A pity, for 'tis a saucy town . . .

—In truth, I clutch at my memories as one clutches at a lifeline, for I can picture nothing that happened without welling up with compassion. Thus it began—with a father riding behind his son in the Holy Land, rather chagrined and bewildered, regarding the wasteland around him, although 'twas not always waste.

—Well said, madame, that is so. Suddenly you see a fine grain field, or an orchard, or some date palms and fruit trees by a water course, or a peasant's hut, or a group of children playing by a well— and then there is wasteland again and the remnants of a most ancient devastation. At sunset we reached a large khan and found it deserted, because the caravan had already moved on to pass the night in Ramleh. Fresh straw was scattered for us in a corner of the hall, beside a blackened wall, and our pallets were made there. I stepped outside and looked at the vast and most exceedingly dark plain in which there shone not a single light. Smoke curled up from an oven where bread was being baked for our supper. Yosef went to see to our horses. I watched him, a handsome, erect young man, stride over to a hedgerow of prickly pears and hang the feedbags on the horse's necks while patting their heads and talking to them, his head nestled in the mane of your mare. Perhaps he was whispering some consolation to her for her mistress's failure to arrive! An Ishmaelite standing nearby made some remark to him and he listened with friendly attention—and once again I was struck by how the soft, pampered youth who went shopping with you in the bazaar of Kapele Carse, carrying your dresses and perfumes, had turned into a young man beneath whose newly grown mustache there was already something quite secretive. He resembled my father as a young man, before his bankruptcy, and I suddenly felt such a bitterness of spirit, señores, that I longed to return to the sea I had come from no more than a few hours before, which had played with me and tossed me on its waves. I thought of my parents of blessed memory, and all at once I felt a great desire to say the kaddish for them in the Holy Land and to pray for their souls. And so I asked my son if there might be a village nearby with enough Jews in it for a prayer group. At first he was as startled as if I had asked him to pluck a star from the sky. *"Jews? Here?"* "And is there anywhere without them?" I marveled. He cocked his head and stared at me, and then he smiled a bit—and I wonder, Your Grace, whether it was then that the frightful idea was born in him, or whether it had been there all along —and after mulling it over for a moment he said softly, "Right away, *Papá,* right away." He ducked through a gap in the prickly pear hedge and stepped into some mud huts, from which he pulled out one shadowy form after another and brought them to me. I looked about me and saw these dark-faced, bare-legged Ishmaelites, some with battered fezes on their heads and some with black keffiyehs, most silent and docile, as if they had just been torn out of their first sleep, madame. "Here, *Papá,*" says Yosef, "here is your *minyan.*" He frightened me. "But who are these men, son?" I asked him. And he, standing there in the still of evening, *señor y maestro mío,* he said, *mí amiga* Doña Flora, as if he were *loco* in the head, "But these are Jews, *Papá,* they just don't know it yet . . ."

—Yes, madame, those were his words. "These are Jews who will understand that they are Jews," he said. "These are Jews who will remember that they are Jews." Before I could even stammer an answer, he was chiding them in his friendly manner and making them face east toward Jerusalem, where there was nothing but a black sky full of stars, after which he began to chant the evening

prayer in a new melody I never had heard. From time to time he
went down on his knees and bowed like a Muslim so that the Ishmaelites would understand and bow too . . . and I, Your Grace—
señor—Rabbi Haddaya—my master and teacher—allowed myself to
go along with it . . . sinful man that I was, I could not resist saying
the kaddish and profaning the blessed Name of the Lord. I said it
from beginning to end in memory of my parents and of my poor
wife . . . madame, the blanket . . . it is falling off . . .

—Here, let me, Doña Flora, I'll do it. I . . . he is shaking . . .
something is bothering him . . . perhaps . . .

—I . . .

—But what means that, madame? "Tu-tu-tu"? What would he
say?

—But what wishes he to say, for the love of God?

—But the blanket is wet, Doña Flora. It is most wet. Perhaps we
should make a fire and dry it over the stove, and meanwhile I can
change His Grace . . .

—No. Why?

—Why a servant? Why a Greek? I am at your complete service,
madame, with all my heart . . . let the good deed be mine . . . he
was like a father to me, Doña Flora . . . I beg you . . .

—No. He is listening. His eyes are following me. Rabbi Shabbetai
knows my mind . . . he remembers what I said . . . that every
idea has a pocket and in that pocket is another idea . . . "There is
no man without his hour nor any thing without its use" . . . but
what means he by "tu-tu-tu"? What would he say? He seems most
agitated . . .

—Well, then, in a word, in a word, Doña Flora, so my visit began,
on that route leading from Jaffa to Jerusalem, seeking to catch up
with a caravan of pilgrims that kept a day ahead of us. For three
whole days we shadowed and smelled its trail, trampling the grasses
it had trampled, coming upon the embers of its campfires, treading
on the dung of its animals. The two of us rode, and your mare,
madame, which was now just an extra mouth to feed, trotted along
between us. Sometimes, in the twilight, it even seemed that we could
see your silhouette astride her . . . My son tried being a good
guide to his father. He pointed out to him the threshers in Emmaus,
and the winnowers in Dir Ayub, and had him dismount to smell the

wild sweet basil and the green geranium, and to chew the stems of shrubs and grasses from which perhaps some new spice might be concocted. The next evening too, by a stone fence belonging to Kafr Saris, he disappeared for a while among some rocks and olive trees and returned with a new group of wraiths, more *Jews who did not know that they were Jews*—which is to say, another band of drowsy peasants and shepherds who were rousted from their first sleep. This time he gave them all a quarter of a bishlik for their pains—and all this, señores, was entirely for my sake, to enable the touring father to satisfy his craving to chant the kaddish, not only for the souls of his parents, but also for those of his grand-, and great-grand-, and even greater grand-grandparents than that, until the first father of us all must have heard in heaven that Avraham Mani had arrived in the Land of Israel and was about to enter Jerusalem.

—Ah! That afternoon we finally caught up with the Russian pilgrims—who, now that Jerusalem was just around the corner, had taken off their fur hats and were walking on their knees from sheer devoutness, following the narrow road up and down in long, crawling columns from the Big Oak Tree to the Little Oak Tree and from there to the Monastery of the Cross, which was bathed by red flowers in its lovely valley. And then suddenly, there was Jerusalem: a wall with turrets and domes, a clear, austere verse written on the horizon. Soon I was walking through its narrow streets by myself, led by the consular mace-bearer.

—Because Yosef could not wait and went to return the horses to the consulate and tell the consul about his trip while I was packed off with my bundles behind the mace-bearer, who struck the cobblestones with his staff and led me along a street and up some steps to a door that did not need to be pushed open because it already was. I stood hesitantly in the entrance, staring in the looking-glass that faced me at the unkempt form of a sun-ravaged, sunken-eyed traveler. And just then, Rabbi Shabbetai, who should step out of the other room but Doña Flora herself, but thirty years younger! It was as if she had flown through the air above my ship and arrived there before me! A most wondrous apparition, señores—here, then, was the secret that explained Beirut and that had, so it seemed, quite swept Yosef off his feet! One passage through life had not been enough for so charming a visage, and so it had come back a second time . . . I was so exhausted from the trip and from the sun, and so excited to be in Jerusalem and its winding lanes—I already felt, *mí amiga,* that I had arrived in a city of bottomless recesses—that I whispered like a sleepwalker: "Madame Flora, is it truly you? Has the rabbi then relented?" Hee hee hee hee . . .

—That is how muddled I was.

—No, wait . . . I beg you . . .

—But wait, madame . . . You have no idea of the wondrous resemblance between you, which is perhaps what lured you to Beirut in the first place in order to meet your own double and give my poor departed son . . . I mean, tacitly . . . eh?

—We knew nothing. What did we know?

—The betrothal was carried out in haste . . . the rabbi too was notified after the fact . . .

—Yes. A tremendous resemblance.

—Yes. Even now—are you listening, *señor y maestro mío?*—when I look at the *rubissa,* I see as in a vision Tamara thirty years from now. The very spit and image . . . in charm as well as beauty . . .

—At first she was alarmed. She turned very red but kissed my hand and let me bless her, and then took my bundle and laid it gently and with great respect on your childhood bed beneath the large, arched window, madame, in which henceforward I slept, in hot weather and in cold. She set the table for me and warmed water for me to wash my hands and feet, and then stood over me to serve me as the sun was setting outside. I noticed that she seemed not at all surprised that Yosef was taking so long at the consul's instead of hurrying home, even though he had been away for a week; it was as if she were used to the consul's coming before her. When I was all washed and cleaned and full of food, she summoned her father Valero to make my acquaintance and take me with him to the synagogue for the evening prayer, after which we chatted a bit about Jerusalem and its plagues and then lit candles against the darkness of the night. It was only then that Yosef came home at last. He was carrying a lantern and was still disarrayed from his journey, which for him had only now ended. He greeted his wife and the rest of us with a polite nod, but he was so tired that he confused a bag of his clothes with a packet of some documents from the consulate and even began to speak to us in English until he realized his mistake. It was then that I first understood, *chère* madame and señor, that he was in the grips of a notion more important to him than his own marriage—of an *idée fixe,* as the French say, that mattered to him more than having seed.

—His own, madame.

—Of course . . .

—I will get to that shortly.

—As brief as I can make it.

—What will His Grace eat?

—But why should a little porridge disturb us?

—Of course . . .

—Perhaps, Your Grace, it was Doña Flora who first fired his imagination and put such mettle into him. The stories you told the lad about Jerusalem, madame, on those nights when he lay by your side in the bed of the *hacham,* were what filled his head with grand thoughts . . . what made him think you could roll the world around like an egg without cracking or spilling any of it . . . although all he had to roll it on were the *pensamientos pequeños* gathered from those that Rabbi Shabbetai had discarded. Because before many days had gone by, it was clear to me that he had not merely been humoring me by dragging sleepy peasants out of their huts for a quarter of a bishlik apiece. You see, ever since he had come to Jerusalem to fetch Tamara to her wedding and stayed on there because she would not leave, he had resolved that if stay he must, he would stay among Jews, even if they did not know yet that they were Jews or had completely forgotten it. That was why he treated them with such warm sympathy. Their forgetfulness pained him, and he feared the shock of remembrance that would befall them, so that, together with the British consul, he did all he could to soften it in advance.

—Yes, *muy estimada* madame. Is my master and teacher listening? Such was the thought that possessed my son's mind, the *idée fixe* rammed home as forcefully by the consul as if it were an iron rod driven into his brain.

—There was no knowing which of them was the bellwether and which prevailed upon which, because the consul, like all Englishmen, looked upon us Jews not as creatures of flesh and blood but as purely literary heroes who had stepped out of the pages of the Old

Testament and would step back into those of the New at the Last Judgment, and who meanwhile must be kept from entering another story by mistake—which made me realize at once that I must be on guard to protect my only son's marriage.

—Of course. The next morning the mace-bearer came to invite us to high tea with the consul and his wife. I bought myself a new fez by the Lions' Gate, Tamara cleaned and ironed my robe, and off the three of us went to present me to the consul at that time of day when Jerusalem is ruled by a cinnamon light.

—The consulate is near the Church of the Holy Sepulchre. You cut across to it from the Via Dolorosa.

—By way of the Street of the Mughrabites, via Bechar's courtyard and Navon's stairs. 'Tis behind Geneo's wine shop, on Halfon's side of it.

—No, the other Halfon. The little one who married Rabbi Arditi's daughter.

—The Ashkenazim are a bit further down.

—'Tis all built up there now, madame, all built up. There are no empty lots there any more.

—It is built up behind the Hurva Synagogue too. The Ashkenazim are spreading all over.

—For the moment, no. But they will build there too, never fear. There is nothing to be done about it, madame. You have greatly come up in the world since leaving the Holy City, but although Time remained behind there, it has not stood still either.

—As brief as I can make it. Nevertheless, Doña Flora, I must let the story unfold out of me in its entirety, with all its joys and its sorrows, its tangs and its tastes—and for the moment I was still in Jerusalem as an esteemed visitor, a *passer-through* and not a *stayer-on*. The consul and his wife received us most lovingly, and the consul even spoke a bit of Hebrew to me . . . Madame?

—Yes, madame, a rather Prophetic Hebrew. Yosef circulated about the house as if it were his own, and once again it struck me how adept the lad was at making himself liked and finding himself a father or a mother when he needed one. Meanwhile, more guests arrived: an old sheikh who had been fetched from the village of Silwan to provide me with company, and his son, an excellent young man who was a clerk at the consulate; some newly arrived French pilgrims; several English ladies who drank tea, puffed hookahs, and seemed quite startled by their own utterances; a German spy in a dark suit who had in tow a baptized Austrian Jew; and so on and so forth. But I, madame—I, my master and teacher—I, señores—did not forget the mission I had entrusted myself with, so that even as I listened to everyone with enthusiasm as a good guest should— "Who is honored? He who honors his fellow man"—I kept one eye, madame, on Tamara, who was sitting there silent but glowing among the Englishwomen, squeezed in between them like a baby lamb in a team of bony old nags and sipping her tea while nibbling a dry English scone in that clear, winy light. She was smiling absently to herself and considering the air, and I could see at once that her absence was due not to plenitude but vacuity. It was as if she were still not over her betrothal and had not yet been properly wed . . . and at that moment, I thanked God for having sent me to Jerusalem . . .

—I am referring to matters of the womb.

—No. Not even a miscarriage. Nothing.

—In a word, nothing, madame. And to make a long story short, it was from that nothing that I commenced my mission, that is to say, that I made it my business to see that that marriage bore seed and not only *idées fixes* that were bound to lead to some fiasco. By the time we guests of the consul returned home that night, each of us carrying his or her lantern *à la* Jerusalem and weaving through the narrow streets behind the mace-bearer, who kept rapping the cobblestones with his staff to warn the inhabitants of the underworld of our approach, I had made up my mind to become a *stayer-on*—that is, to settle as deeply as I could into the young couple's home, and into my bed in your little alcove, from which I could quietly carry out my designs. And that, señores, was the meaning of my *desaparición* that you were so worried about. Does Your Grace hear me? How charmingly he nods!

—No, I do not wish to weary him. But if I do not unfold my story to the end, how will he pass his silent verdict on it? Because that same night, Your Grace, I was already having my first second thoughts as I lay secretly plotting in bed not far from the two of them. Their door was slightly ajar; moonlight bathed the bottom of their blanket; a ray of it strayed back and forth between the looking-glasses; and as I listened to their breathing—to the sounds they made as they stirred or murmured in their dreams—to their laughter and their sighs—I tried reckoning how to tell the wheat from the chaff and how to read the signs, that is, to understand where the fault or impediment lay, and if it did not perhaps involve some flight or falling-off, some inversion or infirmity, that must needs be remedied if the seed was to be conjoined by the potency of its yearning with Constantinople and with what I held most dear there, namely, *señor y maestro mío,* with Your Grace. And so I was up the next day before dawn, with the crowing of the first cock, which I encountered strutting in our little street as I groped my way in the dim light to the Wailing Wall, brimming with the lusts and life of Jerusalem, to weep for the destruction of our Temple and say the morning prayer. I licked the dew from the stones of the wall and asked God to prosper my way, and then I turned and ascended the Harat Bab-el-Silsileh to the silent souk and bought some dough rings, hard-boiled eggs, and oregano from the Arabs there. I took these back to my young couple, who were still luxuriating in sleep, brewed them a big pot of strong coffee, brought it all to their bed, and woke them, saying: "I am not merely your father, I am also your two mothers who died in the prime of their lives, and so it is only meet that I pamper you a bit—but in return, as Rachel says to Jacob, "Give me sons or I shall die." The two of them blushed and smiled a bit, glanced anxiously at each other, pulled the blanket tight around themselves, and turned over in bed. Meanwhile, the muezzin had begun calling the faithful to prayer in the great mosque. Yosef listened carefully to the long wailing chant that was making my head spin and suddenly sat up and said, "That chant, *Papá,* is what we must work our way into until the truth that has been forgotten comes to light, because if we do not, what will become of us?" And with that he threw off his blanket, shook out of it the *idée fixe* that he had spent the night with, clapped it in his fez, and went off to wash and finish waking up.

—'Twas a jest, Doña Flora . . . a fantastical remark . . . a mere parable . . .

—I will not do it again. It was only to explain why I now changed from a passer-through to a stayer-on and began to establish myself in Jerusalem, which was rapidly exchanging the soft breezes of spring for a fierce summer heat that its inhabitants, Your Grace, call the *hamseen,* though so still is the air that I call it the *unseen.* Before a day or two had gone by I had a staff of my own to rap the cobblestones with and a lantern to make me visible in the dark, and within a week I was conferring the pleasure of my voice on the worshipers in the Stambouli Synagogue, who let me read from the Torah every Monday and Thursday. By now I was shopping in the market too, and helping Tamara peel vegetables and clean fish, and after another week or two I rented half a stand from an Ishmaelite in the Souk-el-Kattanin and set out on it the spices I had brought from overseas, to which I added some raisins, almonds, and nuts that I sold for a modest profit. I was becoming a true Jerusalemite, rushing up and down the narrow streets for no good reason, unless it were that God was about to speak somewhere and I was afraid to miss it.

—And sleeping all the while in your bed, madame, in the little alcove beneath the arched window, where I hung a new looking-glass of my own across from your old one to keep it company and to bring me news of the rest of the house, so that I might work my secret will. And though my big beard kept getting in all the mirrors, the youngsters seemed to be fond of me; not only did I not feel a burden to them, I felt I was breathing new life into a house that I had found dreamy, disorderly, and impecunious, because Yosef was paid more respect than money at the consulate, the consul being a dreamer himself who seemed to think he was not a consul but a government and who was already quite bankrupt from the prodigal sums he spent, partly on the pilgrims whose lord protector he sought to be even though most were not English, and partly on the Jews, whom he considered his wards and the keys to the future. No touring lady could visit Jerusalem from abroad without being royally put up in his home and having Yosef to guide her to the churches of Bethlehem and the mosques of Hebron, down to Absalom's Tomb and hence to the Spring of Shiloah and from there to the Mount of Olives, first putting everything in its proper perspective and then passionately, by the end of the day, scrambling it all up again, expertly stirring faiths, languages, peoples, and races together and pitilessly baking them in the desert sun until they turned into the special Jerusalem soufflé that was his favorite dish . . .

—A guide, madame, if you wish; also a dragoman for roadside

conversation; plus a courier for light documents; and a scribe for secret correspondence; and sometimes too, a brewer of little cups of coffee; and when the spirit moved him, the chairman of the disputatious literary soirées of the Jerusalem Bibliophile Society. In a word, a man for all times and seasons, particularly those after dark, for so accustomed was he to coming home at all hours that I had developed the habit of waking up in the middle of the night and going to see if he was in his bed yet, and of becoming frantically, heart-strickenly worried if he was not, as if the very life were being crushed out of him at that moment. And since I was afraid to step out into the silent street, I would ascend to the roof to peer through the moonlit darkness at the ramparts of the city, and then down into the bowels of the streets, hardly breathing while I waited to espy, bobbing as it approached from the Muslim or Christian Quarter, a small flame that I knew from its motion to be his. At once, madame, I slipped down from the roof and ran to the gate to admit him into his own house, as if it were he who was the honored guest from afar whose every wish must be indulged, even more than you indulged it when he was a boy, madame. I took off the fez that was stuck to his sweaty hair, helped him out of his shoes, opened his belt to let him out of his *idée fixe,* brought water to wash his face and feet, and warmed him something to eat, because whole days would go by without his taking anything but coffee. At last, relaxed and with his guard down, the color back in his cheeks, he would tell me about his day: whom he had met, and whose guide he had been, and where he had taken them, and what the consul had said about this or his wife about that, and what was written about them in the English press, and their latest protest to the Turkish governor—and I would listen most attentively and ask questions, and every question received its answer, until finally I teased him about his *idée fixe* that was lying unguardedly in the open and inquired, "Well, son, and what of your Jews who don't know that they are Jews yet?" At first my mockery made him angry. But after a while the anger would pass and he would say with a twinkle in his eyes, "Slowly but surely, *Papá.* They've only forgotten, and in the end they'll remember by themselves. And if they insist on being stubborn, I'll be stubborn too, and if they still don't want to remember . . ." Here his eyes would slowly shut, trapping the twinkle inside them until it grew almost cruel. "If they insist," he would say, weighing my own insistence, "we shall sorely chastise them until they see the error of their ways."

—Yes. He definitely said "chastise," although without explaining himself, as if all chastisement were one and the same and there was no need to spell it out chast by chast.

—Your Grace, *señor y maestro mío,* are you listening?

—Ah! And so, Your Grace, we joked a bit at the expense of his *idée fixe* until Yosef fell softly asleep and I helped him to his feet with the lantern still in his hand and led him off to bed—where, madame, his wife, silently opened the same beautiful, bright eyes with which you are staring at me right now . . .

—God forbid, Doña Flora! Not coerced but gently assisted.

—No further.

—My silent support, madame . . . my fondest encouragement . . .

—No further.

—I had to know.

—I was looking for a definite sign, madame.

—The looking-glass showed only shadows . . .

—Someone is knocking, madame . . . who can it be?

—Is it time for his dinner? Praise God . . .

—But how in the way? Not at all!

—God forbid! I am not going anywhere. I am most eager, *mía amiga* Doña Flora, to see how the rabbi is fed . . .

—I will sit quietly in this corner.

—So this is what Rabbi Shabbetai eats! It is, madame, a dish as pure as snow.

—So it is . . .

—Soft porridge . . . so it is . . .

—So it is. The poor man! Your Grace always hated mushy food . . .

—Of course. There is no choice. It is the wise thing to do, madame. Nothing else would go down as easily, filling the belly while soothing the soul. And who, may I ask, was the servant who brought it?

—A fine-looking young man. Would it not be best, though, for the holy rabbi to be waited on by one of our own?

—Well, a fine-looking young man.

—God forbid! Nothing to excite him, madame. Nothing to spoil his appetite. Why don't you rest and let me feed Rabbi Shabbetai myself? It would be a great pleasure and a privilege.

—Well, then, perhaps later.

—His bib? Where is it?

—One minute . . . in truth, he seems most hungry . . .

—Master of the Universe! Lord have mercy! Why, 'tis a perfect infant . . . a perfect infant . . .

—What, Your Grace?

—In a word . . . in a word . . . in the briefest of words, Doña Flora, but with much fear and trembling, because despite the cloudless summer—that is, we were now in the midst of a fiery, cloudless summer—there had even been a mild outbreak of some sort of plague, the exact name of which no one was quite sure of—I already had, Doña Flora, from all those dreams, nighttime walks, and—whoever was the bellwether—fantasies of that Hebrew-speaking English consul, a sense of impending disaster. Sometimes, when I lost patience standing on the roof, I went back down and took the lantern and waited for my son Yosef on the corner, by Calderon's barred window. I stood beneath the moon and prayed to see that crookedly bobbing little flame, which sometimes appeared from the south, with a herd of black goats coming home late from their distant pasture in the Valley of the Cross, and sometimes from the west, with a band of pilgrims returning from midnight mass in the Holy Sepulchre, to whom my son had attached himself in the darkness as an unnoticed guide to penetrate a place that Jews were barred from . . .

—Of course, madame. A most flagrant provocation. The Christians themselves are divided into mutually suspicious sects that ambush each other in the naves of the church and brawl over every key and lock, and they certainly did not need an uninvited Jew peeking into God's tomb and reminding them of what they did not believe they had forgotten and had no intention of remembering. And as if that were not enough, he sometimes proceeded from there to the Gate of the Mughrabites, from where steps lead up to the great mosque, in order to bid a fond good night to its two Mohammedan watchmen before heading home for the one place that he feared most of all—namely, his own bed.

—That is only in a manner of speaking, of course, Doña Flora
. . . most hyperbolically. But see how Rabbi Shabbetai looks at me
as he eats! Perhaps my story will take my master's mind off his
mush, hee hee hee . . .

—No, no, madame. I did not mean the bed itself. Just the idea of
it . . .

—I mean—

—God forbid! 'Twas always with the most friendly respect and
affection . . .

—Of . . . why, in all simplicity, of the sleep awaiting him there
. . . that was what troubled him so, madame . . .

—That he might awake to discover that the world had changed
while he slept . . . that something had happened in it without his
knowing or being a party to it . . . that his *idée fixe,* whose sole
reliable consular representative he considered himself to be, had
burst like a bubble before he had time to bring it back to life . . .

—So he felt, madame. "The day is short and the labor is great."
And perhaps—who knows, *maestro y señor mío*—he already sensed
his approaching death in that much-provoked Jerusalem of his.

—Tamara, Doña Flora, said nothing.

—That is, she heard and saw everything. And waited . . .

—She was not unreceptive to his views, provided that something
came of them . . .

—At night she slept. I kept an eye on her in the looking-glass I
had hung on the wall, which was reflected in your old glass, madame, which in turn was reflected in the glass hanging over their
bed, and I saw that she slumbered peacefully . . . But look, Doña
Flora, he is getting food all over his mouth and chin . . .

—Here . . .

—Perhaps we need a fresh towel.

—As you wish, madame. I am at your service. Perhaps that handsome young Greek made the porridge a bit too mushy . . .

—God forbid, madame! I am not interfering in anything. It was
just a thought, and I have already taken it back.

—Of course, madame. Briefly and to the point. Which is that I
found your niece an admirable housewife who baked and cooked
quite unvaryingly excellent food. She simply forgot at times to make
enough of it, so that I had to—

—*Mahshi, kusa,* and *calabaza,* and certain days of the week a *shakshuka* . . .

—Fridays she put up a Sabbath stew with *haminados.*

—Sometimes it had meat in it, and sometimes it had the smell of meat . . .

—Of course. She did all her own cleaning and laundering. The house, Doña Flora, was as spic and span as the big looking-glass. And she also helped her father Valero and his young wife, and took her little stepsister and stepbrother to the Sultan's Pool every afternoon to enjoy the cool water and play with the Atias children among the Ishmaelite tombstones . . .

—The Atias who married Franco's youngest daughter.

—'Tis on the tip of my tongue, *rubissa,* and will soon come to me. Meanwhile, *maestro y señor mío,* permit me to sketch the picture for you. Is he still listening? I was, you see, in Jerusalem to shore up a marriage that needed consolidating, for it had yet to outgrow its hasty Beirut betrothal; and so I did my best to keep the young bride from sinking into too much housework, and from time to time I took her with me to my spice-and-sundries stand in the Souk-el-Kattanin, where she could sit and catch the notice of the passersby with her winning mien, so that—after walking on and stopping short and doubling back for a better look and possibly even a word with her—they might interest themselves in a spice or two. And meanwhile, the air around her began to shoot sparks—one of which, I hoped, would fly all the way to her young husband, who was busy escorting the consul's guests to Bethlehem and Hebron. It would do him no harm, I thought, to wonder why his wife was attracting such looks . . .

—God forbid! God forbid! 'Twas done most honorably. And each day when the sun began to glow redly in my jars of rosemary, cinnamon, and thyme, and to tint my raisins with gold, I put away my goods and folded my stand and brought her to the woman's gallery of the synagogue of Rabbi Yohanan ben-Zakkai to listen to the Mishnah lesson and be seen among the widows and old women by the men arriving from the souk for the afternoon prayer. Sometimes Yosef came too, all in a great dither, his *idée fixe* sticking out of his pocket; and while he said his prayers devoutly enough, he kept running his eyes over us ordinary Jews who *could not forget that we were Jews* and so had nothing to remember, nothing to do but say the same old prayers in the same old chants. Now and then he glanced up at the women's gallery, squinting as if into the distance at his petite wife—who, like himself, though a year had gone by since their Beirut betrothal, still was daubed with its honey-gold coat that had to be patiently, pleasurably, licked away. And I, Rabbi Shabbetai, began to lick . . . slowly but surely, madame . . .

—A parable, of course, madame, never fear . . . *à la fantastique,* as the French would say . . . 'twas merely to bring them together . . . to conclude the good deed started in Beirut, Your Grace. And thus the two of us, madame, the motherless bride and myself, wandered through a Jerusalem summer that burned with a clear, bright light I first caught a glimpse of in your own wondering eyes, Doña Flora, the first time we met in Salonika. I was determined to see this marriage through, and I began taking my daughter-in-law with me everywhere . . . to the courtyard of the consulate, for example, where we sat in the shade of a tree by the cistern and watched the builders lay the foundations for a new house of prayer that is to be called Christ's Church, for the greater glory of England. The air shot sparks; the builders put down their tools and turned to look, for nothing disarms more than beauty; men walking down the lane slackened stride, even backtracked a bit, as if the sight of her made them unsure whether they suddenly had lost or found something. A gentle commotion commenced all around us, until the consul's wife had to step outside and invite us in for a hookah and some English tea with milk while sending a servant to pry Yosef loose from one of the inner rooms. At first he was alarmed to see us there; yet as soon as he saw that all were smiling and in good spirits, he inclined his head with loving resignation and took us under his wing. In this manner I was occasionally able to get him to come home for lunch with us, to have a bite to eat and cool off in his bed with his wife, whom the eyes of Jerusalem were beginning to make him most appreciative of. I did not remain to peer into the looking-glass. I went outside and left them by themselves, locking the door behind me, because by now I had an *idée fixe* of my own, a much smaller and more modest one than his, to be sure, but every bit as powerful . . . and with it, señores, with my craving for seed, I kept after them for all I was worth. And in those hot afternoons, at that most still and torrid hour when the air is dry and without a hint of a breeze, which is the best time for olfaction, I strode through the Lions' Gate and down to the house of the sheikh of Silwan village, where I was shown little fagots of weeds and grasses, roots and flowers that the Ishmaelites had gathered at the old man's behest from the mountains of Judea and Samaria, from the shores of the Dead Sea to the coast of our Mediterranean, for me to sniff and perhaps find some new species or plant from which to concoct the spice of the century . . .

—In truth, madame, one sniff was all I needed. And thus, sniff by sniff and weed by weed, I smelled my way through our Promised Land . . .

—A spice more aromatic and tangy than any of those I had brought from Salonika, which I had begun to run out of by that summer's end that was harsher than summer itself . . .

—In truth, madame, they were running low, and even though this drove up my prices, it did not drive the buyers away. They snatched whatever I had, be it thyme or basil or saffron or rosemary or marjoram or nutmeg or oregano, because it was the month of the great Mohammedan fast, which they broke every night with spicy meals that kept them smacking their lips throughout the next day until the boom of the cannon at sunset announced they could eat once again . . . and that, *su merced,* Rabbi Shabbetai Hananiah, was the sound that sent a shiver through my son Yosef one evening, when I found him sitting by himself in the half-light by his bed, straight as a knife blade and wrapped in a sheet, striped by a sun that was in its last throes above the Jaffa Gate. He had finished the siesta I made him take every day and had already smuggled his wife out through the kitchen window into the Zurnagas' backyard, from where she could proceed to her father's to take the children to the pool, and was now waiting for me to return from my *olfateo* in Silwan to open the locked door for him . . .

—Yes, he was waiting, madame, wrapped with thoughtful patience in a sheet. I took some fragrant herbs and roots from my robe and scattered them on the bed to dispel the mournful ambience of struggle and sorrow in the odor of seed that hung over it and its pale homunculi, sad-faced gossamer ghosts who were none other than the less fortunate brothers and sisters of our future *baby Moses,*

demon children spilled like pollen in that room that still shook from
the blast of the cannon, which now fired again, Your Grace, into
our holy hills . . .

—Madame?

—God forbid, *muy distinguida rubissa!*

—God forbid, Doña Flora, with all due respect . . .

—God forbid! With all due respect, but also, madame, in all
truth . . .

—But how am I disgusting? Surely not to him!

—No, our Yosef would not be angry. He would not even be
upset. He would understand how justified my little *idée fixe* was
. . . Why, in my honor he even had his own *idée fixe* devour it, so
that now the two of them thrashed about together in his soul, which
yearned to join the throng of believers gathered before the great
mosque—forgetful Jews who soon, with God's help, would remember and bow, not southward to faraway Mecca, but inwardly to
themselves, happy to be where they were, beneath the sky above
them . . .

—In truth, madame . . .

—How was it possible, you ask? Oh, but it was!

—More than once. In the mosque and in the Dome of the Rock
too.

—In truth, *mí amiga,* a frightful provocation . . .

—Yes. To them too. Not just to the Christians.

—A double provocation, the entire justification of which lay in its
doubleness, and therefore, in its peaceful intentions, since according
to him, once all remembered their true nature, they would make
peace among themselves.

—He felt too much compassion to feel fear, Doña Flora. You see,
he had already racked his brain for all the chastisements he would
chastise them with for their obduracy, for all the pain and sorrow he
would inflict on them and their offspring, and he was now so full of
compassion that he never dreamed that before he would have time
to pity them all they would seize and massacre him . . .

—But how, madame, do you restrain a thought?

—The consul? But that was the very root of the evil—that bound-
lessly audacious English consular enthusiasm that made him think
that the entire British fleet was at anchor just over the hills, some-

where between Ramallah and el-Bireh, covering his every movement . . .

—How, Doña Flora? How? Time was already running out!

—Because I had begun to despair of his accursed *idée fixe,* which
devoured every other *idée* that it encountered as if it were simply
grist for the mill, like that which madame is now spooning into His
Grace. I was persuaded more than ever that the marriage must be
made to bring forth a child, which alone could do battle—yes, from
its cradle!—with the unnatural thoughts of a father by means of a
simple cry or laugh, or of the riddle of its own future; and thus,
Doña Flora, thus, Your Worship, began the race between my son's
death and the birth of his son. It was the month of Elul, whose
penitential prayers broke the silence of the night, that time of year
when—perhaps you remember, madame—wondrous breezes are
born that get their odors and tastes from all over, taking a pinch of
the warmth of the standing water in the Pool of Hezekiah, adding a
touch of dryness from the scorched thistles in the fields between the
houses of the Armenians, mixing in the bitterness of the cracked,
furrowed graves on the Mount of Olives, whipping up a flying in-
cense that whirls from street to street. Only now do I realize, *señor y
maestro mío,* that the true spice, the spice of the future, will not
come from any root, leaf, berry, or pollen, but from the shapeless,
formless wind, for which I shall uncork all my vials and bottles to let
it blend with their contents and infuse them with strength for the
Days of Awe, awful in every sense of the word . . .

—No, Doña Flora, no, *su merced,* I made sure he did not miss the
services. The consul and his wife had gone to 8135.5 Jaffa on consular business, and the air was tremulous in that subtle way it is in
Jerusalem on Yom Kippur, as if the Merciful One, the chief judge
Himself, had secretly returned to the city from His travels and was
hiding in one of its small dwellings, in which He planned to spend
the holy fast day with us, the signed list of men's fates—"Who by
fire and who by water, who in due time and who before his time"—
already in His pocket, although He was afraid to take it out and
read it. Yosef seemed more at peace with the world too, full of an
inner mirth that took the edge off even his *idée fixe,* while Tamara
had been busy cooking her delicious holiday dishes, her eyes, which
were inflamed with dust all summer, now clear and wide—indeed,

Rabbi Shabbetai, they were so like madame's that are looking at us right now that the growing resemblance between Constantinople and Jerusalem sent a shiver down my spine. And so I awoke him before dawn, and took him to the synagogue, and stood with him not far from the cantor, so that we could be quick to snatch the tidbits thrown to the worshipers from time to time—a verse from "God the King Who Sitteth on His Mercy Seat," a word from "O Answer Us," or even a whole section of "Lord of Forgiveness"—and raise our voices on high in token of our piety and in hope that the Master of the Universe would hear us and let us have our way for once . . .

—What say you, Doña Flora? I never knew!

—Old Tarabulus? Who does not remember him? Why, he would bring tears to our eyes every Sabbath eve in the Great Synagogue with his "Come, My Love"!

—Truly?

—O my son!

—Yes, that old prayer shawl that was black with age . . . of course I do . . . it was already that color when I was a child . . . I always felt drawn to it too, but I never dared touch it . . .

—Truly? Oh, the poor boy . . . my poor son . . .

—O my poor son . . . you speak of him with such love . . .

—No, I will not cry.

—Oh, madame, oh, Your Grace, what sweet sorrow I feel at the thought of my boy standing wrapped in that grimy prayer shawl by the hearth of your salon in Constantinople, pretending to be the great Tarabulus . . .

—Of course . . . "This Day Hath the World Conceived" . . . the Rosh Hashanah prayer . . . "Be We Thy Sons or Slaves" . . .

—No, I will not sing now . . . ah, the poor lad . . . my poor son . . . because you see, even though I knew that all things were decided in heaven, I knew too that "If I am not for myself, who will be for me?" . . . and so I kept after him . . . because to whom could I pass on what consumed me if I let go of it? Your most agreeable brother-in-law Refa'el Valero had little children of his own, and his Veducha was pregnant again, and they certainly did not need another child, not even if it was only a grandchild . . . and so, because if I was not for myself who would be for me, and if not now, when, I began to pursue him through courtyards and down alleyways on his visits to Jews and to Gentiles. I never let him out of my sight, until I acquired a most infernal knowledge of Jerusalem myself, of the city of your tender youth, Doña FLora.

—Why, I was able to pop up anywhere, like a wise old snake . . .

—Because—and this I learned from Yosef—it is a city in which all places are connected and there is a way around every obstacle. You can traverse the whole of it by going from house to house without once stepping out into the street . . .

—For example, for example, by climbing Arditi's stairs you can get to Bechar and Geneo's roof, and then through their kitchen to the courtyard of the Greek patriarch, from where, if you cut straight through the chapel, you need only open a little gate to find yourself in She'altiel's salon. If She'altiel is home, you may have a cup of coffee with him and ask his leave to proceed, but if he is not, or if he is sleeping, you need not turn back. Just tiptoe down his little hallway without peeking into the bedroom and you will come to five steps belonging to the staircase of an old building destroyed by the accursed Crusaders, which lead directly to the storeroom of Franco's greengrocery. Once there, you need only move some watermelons and sacks aside and stoop a bit to enter the little synagogue of the Ribliners, where you will find yourself behind the Holy Ark. If they happen to be praying, you can join them, even if they are Ashkenazim, and if they are in the middle of a Mishnah class, you can ask to go to their washroom, which is shared by the guard of the Muslim wakf—who, no matter how sleepy he seems, will be happy to take half a mejidi to lead you across the large hall of the Koran scholars and back out into the street, where you will look up in amazement to espy the house of your parents, may they rest in paradise, the very house of your childhood, madame . . .

—From the rear? Why from the rear?

—But it is all built up there, madame . . . the buildings are now conjoined . . . that empty space is no more . . .

—Never once, Doña Flora. I myself was amazed that I was not once lost . . . because in Constantinople—does Your Grace remember?—does he?—that happened to me all the time, not just as a boy but as a young man too, and without the slightest effort, hee hee

. . . For example, *rubissa,* if I was sent to fetch something for Rabbi Shabbetai, some tobacco, or coffee, or a sesame cake, or cheese, I would end up wandering from bazaar to bazaar, past the rug dealers, past the fabric stalls, past all the colorful, good-smelling dresses, across the Golden Horn without even noticing, passing from Asia to Europe—and there, madame, I would get so hopelessly confused that I could no longer find my way back, so that evening would come—does Your Grace remember?—and Rabbi Shabbetai would see that there was no tobacco, no coffee, no sesame cake, no cheese, and no Mani, and he would have to leave his books, go downstairs, find some horseman or soldier from the Sultan's Guard, and give him a bishlik to go to Galata and bring me back home to Asia, frightened and white as a sheet . . . hee hee hee . . . he remembers . . . by God, he is smiling! Even after so many years, that Constantinople of yours is a maze for me . . . your crooked Stamboul, which to this day I cannot get straight in my head . . . whereas Jerusalem, madame, could not only be gotten straight, it was getting too straight for comfort . . . night by night I felt it tighten around me . . .

—Because at night, Doña Flora—in those nights that grew longer and longer now that we had seen the last of the last holiday, and on which the sun set sooner and sooner—the *idée fixe* that I thought had faded with summer's end now raised its head again with winter's start and was soon raging out of control, like an illness that had gone to sleep not because it had run its course but in order to wake up stronger than ever. And by now I was mortally afraid for my own soul . . .

—Of his *idée fixe* infecting me too, Doña Flora, so that I would start seeing the world through his eyes. Because there was more strength in his silence, in the calm way he shut his eyes while quietly listening to me, than there was in all my warnings and rebukes, which he crossed out with a single thin-lipped smile before donning a large, odd cloak that he had found in the market in Hebron and setting out on his nighttime excursions. It did not even help to hide his lantern, because his pockets were full of little candles, which he stuffed them with in case he had to light one and declare himself to the Turkish watch. The spirit moved him with the fall of night, so that while the two of us, Tamara and I, were preparing for bed, he slipped out of the house without his lantern despite the danger of it and—in the same roundabout way he had of going from Jewish house to Jewish house—went to call on his *Jews who did not know yet they were Jews,* most boldly walking in and out of their homes, without once stepping into the street, in his eagerness to find some sign or testimony that would prove them wrong . . .

—For example, madame, a scrap of parchment, a piece of cloth, a potsherd, a stone, some old ritual object—and when he despaired of all these, he would strain to catch some word murmured in their dreams and to seize it as if it were the handle of a coal scoop burning in the fire of forgetfulness, which he must snatch from the embers to let its contents cool until they regained, like soft white gold, their elemental form. And thus, Rabbi Shabbetai, thus, Doña Flora, he entered the houses of his forgetful Jews as they were turning in for the night, which was young enough for their doors to be still open, passing through hallways, up and down stairways, and in and out of dwellings whose inhabitants, soft with sleep, were getting ready for bed and having a last cup of tea while their new cuckoo clocks—for German salesmen had been to Jerusalem too—cooed away in the corners. He conversed with them gently, with that slight inclination of his head, most amiably and politely; gave them regards from one another; asked them for news of themselves; and listened to what they had to say. Not that they had the least idea of who he was or what he wanted from them—but his good nature was infectious and they welcomed him so warmly that they hardly even noticed that he was already in their bedrooms, bending down to look at something, pulling back a blanket, reaching out to touch a baby or to turn over one of the many children who lay wrapped in their little bed smocks, sound asleep as only youngsters can be who are busy growing in their slumber and not merely resting in it, their eyes sealed by the thin yellow crust still left over from the summer's trachoma. And then, thinking of the chastisements he must bring upon them for their obduracy, my poor son felt his resolve weaken, swallowed the lump in his throat, and ran his hands over the walls as if looking for a dark opening that memory might burst forth from. And thus, madame, thus, Your Grace, the autumn came and went with the winter on its heels. Freezing rains lashed the walls of the holy city, to which the Russian pilgrims were still crawling on their knees, bundled in their heavy fur coats, their reddish beards and mustaches making them look like so many giant silkworms with their heads in the air. They packed the square of the Church of the Holy Sepulchre and the streets all around, waiting in puddles of rain and mud for the birth of their god, their hate for the Jew greater than ever, because not only he had killed their Christ he had done it in the remotest and most forsaken of places instead of in Mother Russia . . .

—Because they were already mourning their approaching departure from that lavish sepulcher, which they were growing fonder of by the minute, and were quite distraught at not being able to tear it out of the earth in one piece and carry it back to their native land with them. And so, madame, it was hardly surprising that they should have been looking in their most pious ardor for a substitute corpse, preferably a young Jew's . . . and in truth, it was given them . . .

—*He* was given them.

—He gave himself . . . he let himself be passed from hand to hand . . .

—In parable . . . *à la fantastique* . . . Your Grace understands . . .

—Again? But have I not made you shudder enough, madame? I have already brought tears to your eyes . . .

—Again? I cannot.

—I saw nothing . . . I only know what I was told . . .

—I have already told you all I know.

—They slit his throat.

—There, you are shaking again, madame. And Rabbi Haddaya has stopped eating . . .

—He was passed from hand to hand.

—In truth, he stole into that pilgrim crowd, and on the night of the holy fire . . .

—I suppose his *idée fixe* had swallowed all his fears and made a fine grist of them.

—'Tis no wonder, madame. Even the Mohammedans are afraid to approach on such a night . . .

—Perhaps he expected to convert them too . . . who knows?

—I am saying that I do not know what my son really thought, or what he thought that he should have thought. Insofar as he had decided that everyone in Jerusalem was connected, not even the wildest or strangest of pilgrims could fail to arouse his insatiable curiosity, which was forever looking for ways to link strangers together and do battle with what he deemed their self-immurement . . .

—At first, perhaps, the motherless bride you found for him, madame . . . and possibly, he considered me too to be such a case of self-inflicted isolation . . .

—No, God forbid—he loved her, madame! He loved and honored her greatly, and always spoke to her with much tact and circumspection, as if they were still in the midst of their betrothal and he must not encumber her—which is why he went off each evening and left her to her own devices. And once he realized that I would stay with her, he grew more unbridled than ever . . .

—Followed him at night too, madame?

—At first I tried. But the nights grew colder and colder, the pilgrims having managed to their great satisfaction to bring their Russian snow and hail with them, and his *idée fixe* could no longer hold in check my own dreadful fright. And so I begged his friend from the consulate, the son of the sheikh from Silwan, to do all he could to save him from himself while I sat home by the coal-burning stove and sang Tía Loja's *conacero* to that little drop of fluid, which I knew by the first candle of Hanukkah, madame, to be safely deposited where it belonged . . . Here, this is how I sang it, Doña Flora—

—Because I saw no sign of menstrual blood.

—I always noticed, although don't ask me how. And I was so happy that I sang like this—

—I have a pleasant voice. Come, listen, madame . . . 'tis but a short *conacero* . . .

—No, he is. He knows the song . . .

—No, I will not!

—It was his favorite of all Tía Loja's *conaceros*. I beg you . . . I desire to sing it for him!

—No, he is looking at me. He is pleased. I will not sing much . . . soon I will be gone, madame . . . the best hope of man is the maggot . . .

—No. 'Tis not I but you who needs rest, Doña Flora. Your face is so pale that the light passes right through it. And the worst times are still to come . . .

—I will stay here . . . I will watch over him . . . I will take it on myself . . .

—I will not be a burden to him . . . I will lullaby him to sleep . . .

—Most pleasantly . . . until he falls asleep. Does Your Grace remember? Go now, madame. Adieu, madame. I am only lullabying him . . . go, madame . . . adieu, madame . . .

> When all go to the kehillá,
> I go to your house,
> Istraiqua, apple of my eye.
> When all kiss the mezuzá,
> I kiss your own face,
> Istraiqua, apple of my eye.
>
> To the graveyard has your mother gone
> For my death to pray,
> That I may take you as my bride not.
> To the graveyard have your sisters gone
> For my death to pray,
> That I may take you as my bride not.

She is finally gone, then, the woman! And you and I, my master and teacher, are alone again as once when we were young. She is most wondrous, Doña Flora! "A woman of valor who can find? For her price is far above pearls; the heart of her husband doth safely trust in her, so that he shall have no need of spoil." But will she have the strength? In the port in Salonika we had a saying, "What good is gold when the husband is old?" And suppose he is sick too? Once it seemed to me, Rabbi Shabbetai, that I envied Your Grace for his marriage, but today I understand that my envy was of her, for taking Your Grace away from me. Will she prove equal to the task, though? 'Tis the hand of God that has brought me, Your Grace's oldest and most trusty disciple, back to him. Now that the two of us are alone, I would be most grateful if Your Grace would kindly whisper a word to me. I am all silent anticipation. What can be the meaning of this great silence of yours?

Is it in truth silence, then? Is señor's muteness decreed? Perhaps the lute has indeed popped a string. Is it that, then: that there is no longer a voice to give utterance? Even the "tu tu tu" that Your Grace sounded before would be most welcome. "Rabbi Elazar ben Hisma says, 'Cryptic portents are but the crumbs of wisdom.'" But I would make something whole even of Your Grace's crumbs, for I am well versed in Your Grace's manner and have been for ages. Your Grace need not fear me . . . Ai, will you cling to your silence forever, then, or is this but an interval? Can it be that you will leave us without breaking it? Who would have thought it, señor, who would have imagined it! Not that I did not know that the day would come when His Grace would grow weary of us, but I somehow had never foreseen it as silence, only as a vanishing, a *desaparición* like all your others: one day the rabbi would set out again to preach and hold court in some far place, and while we were still thinking that he was there, or elsewhere, he would be already nowhere, quite simply gone and no more. So I imagined your departure: your tobacco on the table, your little nargileh next to it, the quill and inkwell in their usual place, an open book lying beside them, your cloak flapping near the looking-glass by the doorway—and Your Grace *gone.* I would go look for him in a place that I knew he always had yearned for, in Mesopotamia, señor, or Babylonia, where your furthest, your first father is buried. And I already pictured myself, Rabbi Haddaya, following in Your Grace's tracks and entering a most ancient synagogue at the time of the afternoon prayer, a synagogue rosy with age, in which a sole Jew sat on a divan saying his vigils and asking him about Your Grace—and without ceasing to recite from his book, he would point to the open window with a gesture that meant, "You have a long, long way to go, for he was here and moved on; he has crossed the purple fields in the bounteous light of a tawny, dry Eden and is gone . . ." *He is gone:* eastward into the great interior, into the land of primeval ruins, into the last light of the shattered blocks of giant idols, headless, buttockless . . . eastward . . . so I imagined it . . . and now, this silence. Is that all, then? Silence? Not a word to clutch at—not even a tiny pearl of wisdom—just this dark little room in a Europe that Your Grace swore never to set foot in again, in an inn run by Greek rebels against the Porte, bound to a bed on wheels? And what is this that I see out the window? A chapel for their dead saints, may their bones rot! Your Grace breaks my heart with his little eyes that are so full of pain and sorrow. See, here I am, *maestro y señor mío,* come from the Land of Israel, in dire need of a word, of a verdict—ah, *su merced* Rabbi Shabbetai, I am in need of a judgment from you! I demand that you convene a rabbinical court, right here and now . . .

Or is this your way, *señor,* of outwitting death? When my father passed away, and I was called back posthaste to Salonika, and I wept before Your Grace in Constantinople because I did not want to leave you and return home, you said: "It is your duty to return to your mother and say the kaddish for your father." And I asked, "But who will say the kaddish for you, señor, my master and teacher?" And I offered to do it myself. Your Grace did not answer me. You just stroked my head and smiled to yourself, and I knew at once from your silence that Your Grace did not believe in dying but rather in something else. Is this it, then? And yet nonetheless . . .

I am in a hurry to seek judgment. And though it says, "Make not an only judge of yourself, for there is One alone who can judge by Himself," I always knew that you were not one but two, as has now been made so frightfully clear, for half of you is here and half of you is not. The truth is out. "Ben Ha Ha says, 'According to the sorrow shall be the reward,' " but I, *señor y maestro mío,* make bold to say: according to the reward shall be the sorrow. And while I regret neither sorrow nor reward, I demand to know if I will have a share in the World to Come . . .

I am whispering, because perhaps Doña Flora is listening in the next room. *Her* I wish to spare sorrow, because even though she is a most clever woman, it is inconceivable that she has already understood what Your Grace—I could tell by the gleam in his eyes— understood in silence. For in truth, there was no seed, nor could there have been any, so that the seed could not yet know that it was seed but could only hope to be the seed that it longed to be. That is, it was the seed of longing, the seed of yearning to be seed—seed on the doorknob, seed on the parched earth, seed of shroud and sepulcher, "seed of evil-doers, children of corruption . . ."

With your permission, I will lock the door, because perhaps madame will try to enter nonetheless. And the court must brook no interruption in its labors—is that not what Your Grace taught me when Jews came to seek redress in your home in Constantinople and you shut the door to keep me out? Yes, that's better now, isn't it? And we will stir some life into the fire, because Your Grace is wet and the blanket is damp too. How could they have bound and swaddled you so? With your permission, we will free you a bit. Can this be, ah, can it be the Strong Arm of the Law that presided over an entire age? If I am hurting Your Grace, let him move his strong arm . . .

In actual fact, the case is not at all difficult. The defendant has already brought in a verdict of guilty and given himself the maximum sentence. He simply does not know if this will atone for the crime or if it will only compound it. Or to put it differently: will I have a share in the World to Come—even the tiniest share—no more than a peephole through which to see the honor bestowed there on Your Grace and to say to whomever will listen, "I too knew the man"?

Is that better? Here, let me rub your back a bit too, to help the lazy blood circulate. Does Your Grace remember how he taught me as a boy to scratch his back? There, that's better. The *muy distinguida doña* swaddled you too much. Her worry made her overdo it, the poor thing. The ties need to be loosened some more. There was a time, señor, I won't deny it, when I thought of madame as a kind of trust that Your Grace was safekeeping for me, for she had held out against marriage and had no father to impose his will, and I thought that Your Grace was merely trying to tame her. And indeed, I added a son to tame her even more—until little by little it dawned on me that the trust was not meant for me. And yet even when Your Grace forbade her to join me on my journey to Jerusa-

lem, I still supposed that this was only because he wished us not to
jump to any hasty conclusions. It was not until I saw my son's
anguish in the port in Jaffa as I stepped out of the ship by myself,
and watched him producing Jews who did not know yet they were
Jews on our way to Jerusalem, that my understanding began to grow
by leaps and bounds—and each leap and each bound leaped and
bounded still more when I entered their little house and saw madame's motherless niece for the first time, the Jerusalem damsel who
had been betrothed in Beirut. Did Your Grace have any idea of the
fascinating, the frightening resemblance between them? Why, she is
the very image of Dona Flora, just thirty years younger and fresher,
a thing of beauty!

Perhaps, señor, we should massage the soles of your feet a bit too,
both the good foot and the bad one. What made your *cara rubissa*
wrap you in so many layers? As if it were not enough for her to feed
you with a spoon, she has to diaper Your Grace like a baby! Perhaps she really thinks she has given birth to you, hee hee. With your
permission, let me poke the fire a bit and untie you, and then I will
tell you a one and only story, a story of sweet perdition—because
even if Your Grace realized there was no seed there, you could not
have realized that *there could not have been* any seed there, that is,
that no answer was given because no question had ever been asked.
For by that same secret light that shone from the snow that now was
draping the walls and streets of Jerusalem like a newly grown beard
on an old man, the time had come to know that there was a truth
that came before the truth . . .

Here? Or does it feel better here? . . . Let us return from the
funeral on the Mount of Olives and sit the two mourners, the widow
and the father, next to each other on pillows, across from the coal-
burning stove, their feet unshod and their tunics slashed. Rabbis
Franco and Ben-Atar did their tactful best to ease us into the week
of mourning, so that it might enfold us and warm us and cushion
the bleeding wound. We were fed dough rings and raisins, and
given hard-boiled eggs that are round and have no beginning or
end, and gently taught the laws of mourning word by word. The
consul, his wife, and their attendants sat pityingly around us, quite

chagrined that they too could not slash their clothes, pull off their shoes, slump down on the floor, and eat the never-ending egg. They too grieved greatly for the lad and felt anguished by his death—and perhaps guilty, too, for having plied him with dreams that were too much for him. By the door of the crowded little dwelling, between old Carso and a Turkish gendarme, I was distressed to notice, *señor y maestro mío,* the young sheikh from Silwan, who had returned with us from the cemetery to continue weeping for his friend and join the circle of comforters. And perhaps he too, señor, was asking the unasked question that haunted everyone and made all eyes sear the young woman who sat dressed in black, shivering by the coal-burning stove. In the several hours that had gone by since the death she had as though grown older and even more alike our Doña Flora . . . ah! . . .

. . . Assuming, that is, that it were possible, that the resemblance were not already perfect, that it could have been even greater—because I have already told you, señor, that we both were innocents when we failed to look more deeply into that betrothal in Beirut and to take the necessary precautions . . . But be that as it may, the evening prayer was concluded, and I bitterly sobbed the kaddish one last time, and the comforters wept along with me, and I saw Refa'el Valero rise to go, and his wife Veducha put a towel over the tray of food she had brought, the *mahshi, kusa,* and *burekas,* and went to join him, leaving Tamara with me—for such is the custom in Jerusalem, that once a mourner has eaten of the never-ending egg, he or she does not leave the house they are in. It was getting dark, and one by one everyone left, *even that murderer,* who rose and said good night as sweetly as you please. No one stayed behind but old Carso, who was assigned to chaperone us; he sank down between us, warming himself by the stove, his mouth open as if to gulp its heat. And all along I felt Tamara's eyes on me, as if she wished to tell me what my soul was too frightened to ask. The night dropped slowly. The snowflakes drifted outside, red in the moonlight. Old Carso fell asleep by the stove, taking what heat it gave all for himself. Until, *señor y maestro mío,* I woke him and sent him respectfully home. And even though I knew it was a sin for a man and a woman to be left alone by themselves, I did not lose my presence of mind, for had I lost my presence of mind over a little sin like that, how could I ever have gone on to a much greater one . . .

The fact is, Shabbetai Hananiah, that your silence suits me and that I find it most profound. I only wish that I could be as mute as you—that I could declare: I have said all I have to say, señores, and now you can make what you like of it . . . although since no one ever particularly listened to me anyway, no one would notice my silence either. But still, my master and teacher, I pray you not to cast me yet out of your thoughts. All I am asking from you is a nod or a shake of your head, a yes or a no, in accordance with your sentence. I already know the verdict. 'Tis but the sentence I require.

Well, señor, the stove went out early, because the coals brought by the consul's men were damp and would not catch. It grew colder and colder. I watched her keep going to the closet and take out more and more clothes to put on, but although by now she looked like a big puffball, she could not stop shivering. She even would have put on her husband's Hebron cloak, knife holes and all, had I not made haste to offer her my fox-fur robe, which she took without hesitation and draped over herself. And still the cold grew worse. I too kept donning layer after layer, and finally I wrapped myself in the bloody cloak and looked like a big ball myself. We went from room to room and bed to bed, two dark balls reflected by the moonlight from the looking-glasses, in which you could not tell which of us was which. Jerusalem had shut its gates for the night: no one came, no one went. It was as silent outside as if we were the last two people on earth, alone in the last vestigial shelter, each in his or her room, each on his or her bed, each looking at the other in the looking-glass. The candle was burning down in my hand, and before it went out altogether I blurted, "My daughter, I wish to comfort myself with the child that you will bear, and so I will stay here until the birth, that I may know that I am not the world's last Mani." And she, in my fox robe, a furry ball on her big bed, answered as clear as a bell: "You are the last. Do not stay, because there is nothing, and will be nothing, and was nothing, and could have been nothing, since I differ in nothing from the woman I was, as you have guessed since you entered Jerusalem. We never were man and wife, for we could not get past the fear and pain. Not even my father knows. I am still a virgin." At that, Rabbi Shabbetai, my heart froze. I was so frightened by her words that I quickly blew out my candle lest I see even her shadow . . .

But, my master and teacher, although her shadow disappeared, she herself remained sitting there, and the shadow of the disgrace left behind by my dead son fell upon us both and yoked us together. In truth, I wept to myself, I have failed as I knew I must. The marriage could not be shored up, and the lamp slaughtered too soon now lay on the Mount of Olives, his disgrace unavoidable at the hands of whoever married his widow. I was full of a great sorrow and a terrible wrath, Rabbi Haddaya—sorrow for my son, who lay naked beneath earth and snow, and wrath at Doña Flora, at our beloved madame, who had brought this misfortune upon us. And it was then that I thought of the words of Ben Bag Bag, who said, "Turn it and turn it, for all is in it, and in it you shall find all."

Now you are gaping at me. At last I have been able to unsettle you—I, your *pisgado,* I, your faithful, your dull, your charmless little *pustema.* Do you think, *maestro mío,* that you might sound another one of your "tu tu tus" to let me know where I stand with you? I remember you, sitting as a boy by the hearth in Salonika with my father, may he rest in peace, an old seafarer from the islands grumbling about Napoleon. Out in the hallway I heard them whispering, "He is a great mind but a most wondrous bachelor; there is none like him." And when I lived with you in Constantinople and saw how winning, how blushing and guileless, your bachelorhood was, I lost my heart to you. And then my father passed away and we were forced to part. You resumed your journeys in the east, traveling as far as the Promised Land—and there, in Jerusalem, you met Doña Flora and were no more insensitive than others to her charms. And in the goodness of your heart you thought of me, for I had newly lost my wife, and when Doña Flora journeyed to Salonika, you thought of me again. Was it only of me, though? Or was I no more than a pretext? For why, when madame rejected me, did you wed her secretly in a faraway place to the astonishment of your disciples? You, who were so guileless, so blushing, so pure—what was the purpose of it? What end did it serve? There in Salonika, I tormented myself thinking about it. I grieved and was jealous until, able to stand it no longer, I made you a gift of my boy—who, I thought, might unriddle for me the secret of your most wondrous and resplendent marriage. And in truth, he seemed close to doing so, for so Doña Flora, that most wondrous and fearsome woman, wished him to be. For first she introduced him, half a boy and half already a young man, to your bed, my master and teacher, and then she betrothed him to her niece in Beirut, her look-alike motherless virgin of a widow from Jerusalem, whose shadow, *señor y maestro mío,* was slowly being beamed to me from the looking-glass in the moonlight that now broke through the clouds . . . does Your Grace remember?

So you see, this then was the meaning of the *idée fixe.* (I am whispering lest madame be listening impatiently on the other side of the door, for she has been most suspicious of me since the moment I arrived at this inn.) This then was its meaning—for why else would he insist on his surreptitious visits to those unwashed Ishmaelites just as they were dropping off to sleep—why would he think them forgetful Jews, or Jews who would remember that they were Jews— if he had not, *señor y maestro mío,* already upon arriving in the wasteland between Jaffa and Jerusalem, been quite simply over- whelmed by his loneliness—a loneliness that only grew greater when he first glimpsed the ramparts and cloistering gates of that obstinate desert city of stone, in which he was awaited by his motherless Beirut fiancée, the look-alike of his adored madame? That was what made him decide to see a former Jew in every Ishmaelite! And yet, señor, or so I often asked myself, this fit of loneliness—was it only because he had been so pampered by you in Constantinople? Every- one knew how shamelessly your madame spoiled him there—why, he would barely appear in the morning at your academy long enough to propose some unheard-of answer to some Talmudic ques- tion and already he was off and away to the bazaars, across the Golden Horn to the bright carpets, the burnished copper plates, the fragrant silk dresses fluttering above the charcoal grills and the roast lambs, adored and smiled at by everyone, so that it was perhaps this very coddling that later made him afraid of the solitude that pos- sessed him. Or could it be that he was only coddled in the first place because even then his manliness was in doubt, which was why he so amiably—so mildly—so casually—sought to enlist those drowsy Ishmaelites in the procreation that he himself could not affect from within himself? Are you listening to me, Shabbetai Hananiah? You must listen, for soon I will be gone. The best hope of man is the maggot, says Rabbi Levitas of Yavneh . . .

And yet why should he have doubted his manly powers already then, as he was wending his way through the savage wasteland between Jaffa and Jerusalem with the slow caravan, or as he glimpsed from the Little Oak Tree the ramparts and spires of the city written like a sentence in letters whose language was no longer known to men? Why did he not rejoice to see his bride, who had come in all innocence with her kinfolk to a family wedding in Beirut and been trapped there by her aunt's love, if not for his fear of hurting the look-alike of the one woman he ever loved, half a mother and half an older sister, to whose very scent he had been bound since the days he tumbled in your giant bed, Rabbi Haddaya, a thousand times forbidden though it was?

It was then, my master and teacher, it was only then, sitting wrapped like a ball on the bed in that freezing room while seeking in the little looking-glass to make contact again with her shadow, which was traced with exquisite delicacy by the moonlight in its own furry ball, that I felt how my sorrow and pity for my dead son, who was lying naked beneath snow and earth on the Mount of Olives, were deranging my mind, and I wished I were dead. Because, knowingly or not, we had gulled him with a paradox that compelled him to produce his *idée* as a consolation in his solitude. I could feel it, that solitude, clutching me in its deadly grip, and I wished to atone for it, even though I knew that to be worthy of such atonement I first would have to die with him, would have to lie naked beneath snow and earth too and let myself be slaughtered like he was. And so, Rabbi Haddaya, layer by layer I began to strip off my clothes, until I was standing naked in that frozen room, in that locked, vestigial house, facing a looking-glass that was facing a looking-glass, thinking back to the night I sent him forth out of myself and preparing to take him back again. He was turning among the old graves on the Mount of Olives, he was icy and shredding, his blood was ebbing from him, his flesh was ebbing and being eaten away, and as I drew him back into myself his seed flew through the darkness like a snowflake and was swallowed inside me until we were one again, I was he and he was me—and then, by solemn virtue of his betrothal in Beirut and of his holy matrimony in Jerusalem, he rose, and went into the next room, and unballed the ball, and possessed his bride to beget his grandson, and died once more.

And died once more, Rabbi Shabbetai, do you hear me?

And so I too roundaboutly, along an arc bridging the two ends of Asia Minor, entered your bed, señor, a bed I had never dared climb into even as a lonely boy running down your long hallway in my *blouson,* scared to death of the cannons firing over the Bosporus. Now, in Jerusalem, I slipped between your sheets and lay with your Doña Flora, thirty years younger, in her native city, in her childhood home, in her parents' bed, smelling your strong tobacco in the distance, giving and getting love that sweetened a great commandment carried out by a great transgression. At dawn, when old Carso knocked on the door to take me with him to the Middle Synagogue for the morning service and the mourner's prayer, he scarcely could have imagined that the bereaved father he had left the night before was now a sinful grandfather.

If we undo this knot and that button over there, *señor y maestro mío,* and loosen the ties, perhaps we can calm the growl in your sore tummy with a little massage, so that the rice gruel cooked for you by that fine-looking young Greek can arrive at its proper destination. I hear little steps behind the door. Perhaps the Jews gathered outside the inn are afraid I am absconding with Your Grace's last words and are so jealous of our ancient ties that soon they will demand to be admitted too. And yet I have not come to amuse myself with Your Grace but to ask for judgment. Because when I returned from the synagogue, I was certain that Tamara would already have fled back to her father Valero's home, so that I wondered greatly to find her not only still wrapped in her mourner's shawl and blowing on the wet coals to make me breakfast, but looking taller and lighter on her feet, with no sign of the infection in her eyes that had clouded them all summer. The beds were made like plain, respectable beds; the floor was sparkling clean; the looking-glasses were covered with sheets as they were supposed to be. I ate, took off my shoes, and sat down in my mourner's corner to study a chapter of Mishnah. She followed me in her slippers and sat down not far from me. And when she peered in my eyes, it was not as a sinner or a victim, but as a fearless judge who wished to determine whether I was made for love.

I said love, *señor y maestro mío,* and even though, Rabbi Shabbetai Hananiah, your eyes are shut and your breathing is inaudible, I can feel your flesh tautly listening beneath my massaging hands. I beg you in your lovingkindness, be with me now, for I still do not know what the judgment is on such love, which began to blossom that winter. Does it mitigate my sentence or compound it? For it was not something that I sought for myself, and had she risen that morning and gone back to her father's home, I would have said nothing. But she remained with me, and all of Jerusalem was so frightened of the great snow brought by the Russian pilgrims that we would have been totally forgotten had not old Carso come every morning to take me to the Middle Synagogue, or to the synagogue of Yohanan ben-Zakkai, and had not Valero and his wife Veducha, along with Alkali, and the Abayos, and a few other acquaintances, come late each afternoon with their pots and trays for the prayer and to talk about the marvels of the snow. And in the evening the consul and his wife would come too, and sometimes they brought the Ishmaelite murderer with them, and they talked about my dead son and his sufferings into the night, until all sighed and lit their lanterns and went home. And then I sent old Carso home too, and spent the night getting deeper into love. And when the week of mourning was over, on a clear, sparkling day, we climbed the Mount of Olives to say farewell to him for the last time, surrounded by a great crowd of family, rabbis, consular attendants, and my son's Ishmaelite friends, and I saw that a little piece of white ice had remained at the head of the grave like a stubborn casting of the dead man's seed upward through the earth, and my spirit rebelled and I cast her out of me, falling faint among the gravestones for all to see that I too craved such a death. What says Your Grace to that?

But even if you persist in your silence, my master and teacher, measuring me with narrowing eyes, you must know, Rabbi Shabbetai, that I could not die then, for first I fell ill and ran a high fever and was cared for by the motherless widow of a bride, who looked after me with wondrous composure, with great patience and aplomb. She refused to put me in the hospital of the Italian nuns and insisted on keeping me at home with the help of the consul, who came every day with all the produce of the market. He would look in on me in my room too, and ask how I was in the few Hebrew words that he knew, which were all quite sublime and Prophetic, and whose British accent so alarmed me that it made my fever worse each time. Tamara, though, had the good sense to keep him from me, and by the first month-day of the death, Rabbi Haddaya, I was able to hobble with a cane to the graveyard and consecrate the tombstone that had been erected. And when the "Lord, Full of Mercy" was sung opposite the yellow walls of that drear city while a raw winter wind cut to the bone, I felt most certain, Rabbi Haddaya, that I had succeeded in preventing any future disgrace. That is, if that month of mourning had been started by the two of us, it was now being ended by us three.

The world would have its Manis after all.

And thus, my master and teacher, the months of child-carrying began. The days flowed slowly in Jerusalem, which was battling the winter winds that fell on it from the coast and from the desert. By now the whole city was pining for summer, even if no one knew what plague the summer would bring first. And meanwhile, all of Jerusalem went about feeling sorry for my Yosef, who would never see his own son, and most appreciative of his foresight in taking care to have one. No one wondered that Tamara and I were constantly together, because everyone knew that we were linked by the approaching birth, which was outlined for all to see and approve of by the lovely little belly she paraded in front of us. The consul, especially, took a great interest in it and allotted it a modest consular stipend of one gold napoleon payable on the first of each month. And indeed, without it we might not have made ends meet, even though I did my best to keep up my business, mixing my spices from Salonika, which were strong enough to retain their special flavor, with local ingredients and selling them in the hours before the afternoon prayer in the Souk-el-Lammamin or the Souk-el-Mattarin while Tamara sat by my side. Against her black clothes, her large eyes shone so brightly that passers-by hurrying down the lane sometimes thought that two lanterns had been suddenly beamed at them and turned around to ascertain the reason. And though I did what I could, *señor y maestro mío,* to persuade her to stay home and spare the little embryo the noise and tumult of the street, she insisted on coming with me everywhere, most gracefully bearing herself and her belly in the afternoon breeze. She showed not the least sign of illness or fatigue, and even her eye infection was late in arriving that year, as if the child in her womb were shielding her from all harm. "Dr. Mani," I called him in jest, regretful that I could not carry him too as a cure for whatever ailed me. And when spring came, and even the ancient olive trees along the Bethlehem Road broke into bloom, I could not keep from thinking, *señor y maestro mío,* that if my motherless little widow of a bride, the look-alike of her renowned aunt, was following me around everywhere, this could only be because she had been brazen and thoughtless enough to fall ever so slightly in love with me, thus atoning, though no doubt unwittingly, for my unrequited love in Salonika in the year of Creation 5552.

But Your Grace must listen to me, he must listen and not sleep! Here, let me rub your weary bones a bit with some of this oil. Not that I have any reason to doubt the excellent intentions of Doña Flora and her attendants, Jewish or not, but I do believe, señor, that they are afraid that you will come apart in their hands, which is why they wrapped you like a mummy, swaddling band by swaddling band, until, God forbid, you were hardly able to breathe. Let us then, my master and teacher, remove the last of these ties without a qualm, because only a trusty old disciple like myself who has known your most unphlegmatic body for ages will not fear to hurt you in order to make you feel better. There . . . that does it . . . a bit more . . . and now, Rabbi Haddaya, lie back and listen to how the *passer-through* who became a *stayer-on* was now a *beloved-of* in a Jerusalem that was being built from day to day, not always by us, to be sure, but always, with God's help, for our benefit—and there were times, I must say, when the love of that motherless widow both astonished and frightened me, because what could possibly come of it? "Why, I am a dead man, my child," I would say to her every evening when we sat down to our dinner of radishes, tomatoes, and pita bread dipped in olive oil while the sun set outside the window and the muezzin sounded his mournful call. "I will go to Rabbi Haddaya in Constantinople and get leave to strangle myself like Saul son of Kish." She would listen and say nothing, her big, bright eyes wide with tears, her little hands trembling on her belly, as if above all she wished to assure young señorito Mani that he need not fear the grandfather who had skipped a generation to sow him and was now threatening to miss the harvest. Then she would rise, go to wash the bowls at the cistern, and come back to make the beds, trim the candles, and take up the red blouse and *taquaiqua* that she was knitting for little Mani, never taking her eyes off me, as if I were already preparing the rope to hang myself. Now and then she glanced in the mirror over her bed to see what I was up to in the mirror over my bed. And thus, *señor y maestro mío,* from mirror to mirror I was so encircled by anxiety and love that I lost all my strength and began to flicker out like a candle. I went up to the roof to say good night to the last breeze of the day, which was winging its way to the Dead Sea above the last lanterns bobbing in the narrow streets, and when I came down again, I found her still awake, sitting up in bed. Unable to hold it back any longer, she burst out all at once into a great, bitter cry that I had to make haste to calm, swearing to her that I would not abandon her before the birth. And although, my master and teacher, she was firm in her belief that the final truth bound us together, even she did not know that behind that truth too yet another truth was hiding . . .

There, they are starting to bang on the door, Rabbi Shabbetai, they want me out of here. But I am not leaving until I have been given a clear judgment, even though "His son Rabbi Yishmael used to say"—is not that what you taught me, rabbi?—" 'he who judges not has no enemies.' " And he used to say: "Whoever is born, is born to die, and whoever dies, dies to live again, and whoever lives again, lives to be judged, to know, to make known, and to be made known." Well, let us stir the fire a bit to warm this room, and raise the curtain for a look at the sky dropping low over their chapel of graven images, may they all rot in hell, and tell at last and in truth the final, the one and only story, the story of sweet perdition that recurs in every generation.

Quickly, quickly, though, because the banging on the door is growing louder, and soon, *señor y maestro mío,* Doña Flora and her men will come bursting in here. It is time, Rabbi Haddaya, *betahsir, vite-vite,* to come forth with the story that I have kept for last, the story of a murderer—because I have already told you, *señor y mae-stro mío,* that there was a bit of a murderer here—or, *si quiere, su merced,* a *man*slaughterer, a *shohet-uvodek*—to whom, ever since that first night, one felt drawn again and again in the crowded lanes of Jerusalem—in the souks, by the cisterns, gazing out from the gates of the city—by a lightning-like glitter of a glance—a wordless nod—an imperceptible bow—a casting-down of the eyes—a sudden shudder. Ah, how drawn—on the chalky hillside of Silwan, among the olives on the road to Bethlehem—so powerfully that sometimes one's feet stole of an evening to the consulate, to one of its literary soirées, to listen to some Englishwoman praise some British ro-mance that no one ever had read or ever would read, for the sole purpose of staring wordlessly at the silent shade standing in the doorway and bearing the memory of my poor son—oh, rotting! oh, beloved in his grave! Yosef, my only one—who on that accursed night of snow and blood . . . But who could restrain himself, Rabbi Shabbetai Hananiah, from running after him through the streets in an attempt to forestall an assault that was in truth a retreat, a provocation that was in truth a flight from the pain and punish-ment that he imagined twirling over his bed like an angry, patient carving knife? And it was thus that slaughterer joined slaughterer by the light of the torches of the Russian pilgrims, who were bellowing their piety on the stone floor of the Holy Sepulchre—thus that the two of them, the frantic father and the Ishmaelite friend, the aristo-cratic, mustachioed sheikh's son—linked forces to catch in time the *idée fixe* that in its passionate pride was about to turn on its own self and become the very prototype that it was searching for of the *Jew forgetful of being a Jew,* an example and provocation for all recalci-trants. For as he elbowed his way into the crowd of pilgrims that was excitedly tramping through the mud and snow, wary of being recognized by some excitable Christian who might inform on him to the Turkish soldiers surrounding the square, he was seeking, or so I felt, Rabbi Shabbetai, to forget us all—Salonika, Constantinople, myself, yourself—as if he had been conceived and born from the very floor of the church, rising up from the cisterns and the souk as *a new Ishmaelite* who had discovered that he was a forgetful Jew who might remember . . . only *what?*

In truth, Your Grace has good reason to hold his breath and shut his eyes, fearful in thought and spirit for the story's end . . . and no less fearfully, although ever so gently and clandestinely, did the two of us, the murderer and myself, plan to pluck my son from that crowd of celebrants and lead him back home to his bed. But when we stepped up and seized his lantern so as to make him follow us, he took fright and started to flee—and seeing us run after him, the celebrants at once joined in the pursuit. He ran down the long, deserted street of the Tarik Bab-el-Silseleh with his cloak flapping behind him like a big black bird—or so, from that moment, I began to think of him, an odd bird that must be pinioned before it flew away above our heads. He ran and ran through the cover of snow that made all of Jerusalem look like a single interconnected house, but instead of heading for home, for the quarter of the Jews, and then doubling back through the Middle Synagogue or the synagogue of Yohanan ben-Zakkai, he kept going straight ahead, turning neither left nor right until he came to the Bab, the Gate of the Chain leading up to the great mosque. He shook it a bit until he realized that it was locked, and then, without giving it any thought, as if trusting in the snow to protect him, turned left and proceeded in the same easy, flying, unconcerned lope to the second gate, the Bal-el-Matra, from which he entered the great, deserted square in front of the golden dome, which the snow had covered with a fresh head of white hair. The echoes of his footsteps were still ringing out when he was seized by two sleepy Mohammedan guards. Perhaps they too thought that he was some kind of black bird that had fallen from on high and soon would fly back there, because why else would they have hurried to bind him with long strips of cloth and lay him on the stairs amid the columns, where his squirming shape now made an imprint in the snow?

My master and teacher. Rabbi Shabbetai. My master and teacher. Your Grace. Rabbi Haddaya. *Señor y maestro mío.* Shabbetai Hananiah. Hananiah Shabbetai. *Su merced . . .* can it be?

In no time he was surrounded, because the news spread quickly from gate to gate across that huge deserted square, from the golden dome to the silver dome, so that soon more sleepy guards appeared, although this time there was no telling what time of sleep my son had roused them from. They crowded about him and bent over him to read in his eyes the mad chastisements that he planned for them and that he was begging them to inflict now on himself so that he might demonstrate how he was the first to awaken and recollect his true nature. And although the guards could see for themselves that the man in the cloak spread out in the snow on the steps was an infirm soul, they did not, simple beings that they were, give credence to this soul's suffering but rather suspected it of taking pleasure in itself and its delusions and sought to share that pleasure with it, so that they began to make sport of it and roll it in the snow, a glitter marking the passage of a half-concealed knife from hand to hand. And I, my master and teacher, was outside the gate, I was watching from afar while listening to the distant bell of a lost flock, silently, wretchedly waiting for the worst of the night to wear itself out and the morning star to appear in the east, faint and longed-for, so that I might go to him, to the far pole of his terror and sorrow, whether as his slaughterer or whether as the slaughterer's inspector, and release him from his earthly bonds, because I was certain that he had already deposited his seed . . .

You have become, *señor y maestro mío,* most silent. Can it be that you are already gone?

Wait! I want to come too, Rabbi Shabbetai Hananiah . . . Why don't you answer me? . . . For the love of God, answer me . . .

'Twould take but a nod . . .

'Tis not as if I need words to understand . . .

In truth . . .

Is it self-murder, then?

Yes? . . . No? . . .

BIOGRAPHICAL

Supplements

AVRAHAM MANI received no answer to his question, nor was there the least movement of the rabbi's head for him to interpret as a yes or a no; indeed, at this stage of the conversation, even he, as agitated and carried away as he was, had to admit that Rabbi Shabbetai Haddaya, whose judgment he had sought, was dead. There was no way of knowing exactly when the rabbi had breathed his last, and although often, in the years to come, he sought to go over those last minutes in his mind, even staging them there by playing both roles, his own and that of his teacher, he was unable to decide when the moment of death had occurred. In any event, he remembered well his desperate, bizarre, and persistent attempts to resuscitate the rabbi, which were accompanied by loud, angry bangs on the locked door that was finally broken in. Once a local doctor was fetched and the rabbi's death officially announced, a great wave of emotion swept over the Jews of Athens. While Rabbi Haddaya's death had been more or less expected, those ministering to him, and especially Doña Flora, felt no sense of relief, for during the forty days they had been tending him they somehow had come to believe that he might remain as he was for many years. Naturally, an accusing finger was pointed at Avraham Mani, who served as the target of angry words and hostile looks, it being felt that his stubborn insistence on remaining by the bedside, where he cried and behaved unrestrainedly, had brought on the old man's death. Avraham Mani himself, however, was too absorbed in his own private mourning to be perturbed by these accusations, and especially, in the dilemma that continued to haunt him of whether or not to take his life and of the effect such an action might have on his share in the World to Come.

Be that as it may, though, Avraham Mani made himself a central figure at the funeral and during the week of mourning that followed. Although he was not a blood relation of the departed, he slashed his clothing, said the mourner's prayer by the grave in a loud, ceremonious voice, and spent the week of mourning sitting on a cushion at Madame Flora's feet as though he were a member of the family. He seemed to enjoy the many condolence calls, which included visits by Greek and Turkish religious and political dignitaries who came all the way from Salonika and Constantinople, and—since he was the only one present to have known the deceased from as far back as the Napoleonic wars in Russia—he dominated the conversation with his stories and anecdotes about Rabbi Haddaya.

Following the first month-day of the death, when Doña Flora began to pack her things, Avraham Mani considered proposing marriage to her, both as a way of "doing what the old man had always wanted," as he thought of putting it to her, and of making up for his original rejection. In the end, however, Doña Flora was so chillingly aloof toward him that he dared not even hint at the matter. She, for her part, apprehensive that he would follow her to Constantinople, decided at the last minute to set out for Palestine and visit her niece and her niece's baby, whom Mani's stories had made her greatly desirous of seeing.

Fearful that the secret of his paternity might be revealed and place him in an impossible position in Jerusalem, Avraham Mani did not follow her there. Reluctantly, he returned to Salonika and to his daughter, son-in-law, and two grandsons, still preoccupied with the thought of suicide and with various possibilities of carrying it out. Meanwhile, he comported himself as a mourner and went from synagogue to synagogue to tell of the rabbi's death. He especially liked to mount the podium on the Sabbath when the Torah scrolls were being taken out of the Holy Ark, give the prayer book a loud clap that brought the congregation to its feet, and compel the cantor to sing the special requiem for distinguished souls, which begins with the verses: "Whence then cometh wisdom, and where is the place of understanding? Happy is the man that findeth wisdom, and the man that getteth understanding. Oh, how great is Thy goodness that Thou hast laid up for them that fear Thee; which Thou has wrought for them that trust in Thee before the sons of men."

Yet not even these dramatic ceremonies were able to soothe his soul or to give it respite from the question of whether to take his life for his sin. In the end, he decided to wander in the footsteps of his master, seeking, in his words, "to fulfil his unfulfilled disappearance." In 1853 he set out for Damascus, from where he sent a brief missive to his five-year-old son-grandson with a *conacero* he had written himself, which was full of obscure allusions. But he found no peace in Damascus either, and after the outbreak of the Crimean War in 1853, he journeyed onward to Mesopotamia until he reached the region where his grandfather had been born. The last known Jews he lived among, word from whom eventually got back to his daughter and son-in-law in Salonika, were those of a small town called Dahaman, near Midshakar, an ancient port that had been silted in over time and was now no longer near the sea. Avraham Mani served as a rabbi-cantor there and died—from natural causes, it would seem—in 1860, the year of Herzl's birth, or in 1861, the year of the start of the American Civil War. He was sixty-one or sixty-two at the time.

FLORA MOLKHO-HADDAYA was deeply shocked by the death of her husband Rabbi Haddaya. Despite his paralyzing stroke, his loss of speech, and the difficulties imposed by their extended stay in an inn in Athens, the childless Doña Flora derived a special pleasure from caring for her distinguished invalid of a husband, who had become, as Avraham Mani accurately put it, "a venerable babe." When she and the Greek servant broke down the locked door and found Mani cavorting around the rabbi's dead body, she burst into uncontrollable tears and screams and fell upon Mani in a fury. She quickly got a grip on herself, however, and retained her aristocratic bearing through the period of mourning, even behaving with restraint toward Mani himself out of respect for her late husband. As soon as the month-day ceremony was over, though, she resolved to have no more to do with him and set out for Palestine in order to visit her niece Tamara and Tamara's baby boy.

Doña Flora arrived in Jerusalem in the spring of 1849 after having been away from the city for eighteen years, and was received with great warmth and honor. She moved into her parents' old apartment, in which she was given back her childhood bed, and became little Moshe's "second grandmother," as he called her. The British consul and his wife, who had recently inaugurated the new Christ's Church in a lavish ceremony, were quick to see that the distinguished doña, "Yosef's aunt," had much to recommend her and grew to be very fond of her. They even invited her to a soirée of the Jerusalem Bibliophile Society for a discussion of the newly published novel *David Copperfield,* although her English was all but nonexistent.

Tamara, of course, did not reveal to her aunt the true identity of her son's father, and Doña Flora felt happy to be back in her native city and country. She even consulted several of her acquaintances about the possibility of transferring her late husband's remains from Athens to Jerusalem and publicly reburying them on the Mount of Olives. But in 1853, during the Crimean War, a letter written by Avraham Mani arrived from Damascus with a poem for his grandson that contained several oddly phrased hints that Mani might soon come to Jerusalem. Tamara was gripped by great anxiety and emotion, and after much soul-searching and many excruciating nights of insomnia, she broke down and confided her secret to her beloved aunt. Doña Flora was horrified. Although at first she seemed to make her peace with her niece's confession, she gradually developed a strange revulsion for her surroundings, including Jerusalem and Palestine themselves. In 1855, following an earthquake in the city and riots between Greeks and Armenians in the Church of the Holy Sepulchre, and after taking part in the dedication of a new trade school for Jews established by the British consul in an uninhabited area outside the walled city that would one day become the neighbor of Abraham's Vineyard, she left Jerusalem for Alexandria, where her late father Ya'akov Molkho had cousins. She settled down there, lapsed into a prolonged melancholia, and died in Egypt in 1863 at the age of sixty-three.

☙   There was no way of knowing exactly when *RABBI SHABBETAI HANANIAH HADDAYA* died or for how long Avraham Mani had been talking to a corpse. Nor was it clear how avoidable the death was. True, a local Greek physician, who had been brought for a consultation soon after Rabbi Haddaya's arrival at the inn in Athens in the autumn of 1848, told Doña Flora that he personally knew several aphasic victims of strokes in the Pallaka quarter near the Acropolis who had lived to a ripe old age, but this was in all likelihood an overly optimistic prognosis. At the same time, it was not inconceivable that the rabbi's death was hastened by the excitement of Avraham Mani's sudden appearance. Was he still alive when his old pupil, the "little *pisgado,*" asked his final question? Did he attempt to rack his failing brain for a rabbinical ruling on the permissibility of suicide in such a case? And again: was his death foreordained, or could it have been prevented? There can be no definite answer to any of these questions. Certainly, Rabbi Haddaya was greatly frightened when Doña Flora left the room and Avraham Mani locked the door behind her and launched into a long harangue, in the course of which he took off the rabbi's clothes and removed his diapers. It was hardly surprising, therefore, that the Jews who broke down the locked door and found Mr. Mani dancing and singing before a naked corpse that he was trying to revive were extremely angry at him, even though they never doubted he meant well.

T H E

M a n i s

ELIYAHU MANI *(1740–1807)*

YOSEF MANI *(1776–1820)*

AVRAHAM MANI *(1799–1861)*

YOSEF MANI *(1826–1847)*

MOSHE MANI *(1848–1899)*

YOSEF MANI *(1887–1941)*

EFRAYIM MANI *(1914–1944)*

GAVRIEL MANI *(1938–)*

EFRAYIM MANI *(1958–)*

RONI MANI *(1983–)*